The Johnny Taggett Series

JOHNNY TAGGETT
GOTCH'EM

William D. Hoy

Copyright © 2024 William D. Hoy
The Johnny Taggett Series

ISBN:
978-1-966235-02-6 (paperback)
978-1-966235-03-3 (hardback)

All rights reserved.
No part of this publication may be reproduced, stored in a retrieval system, or transmitted in any form or by any means – electronic, mechanical, photocopy, recording, scanning, or other – except for brief quotations in critical reviews or articles, without the prior written permission of the publisher.

Published by:

OMNIBOOK Co.
99 Wall Street, Suite 118
New York, NY 10005 USA
+1-866-216-9965
www.omnibook.org

For e-book purchase: Kindle on Amazon, Barnes and Noble
Book purchase: Amazon.com, Barnes & Noble, and www.omnibook.org

Omnibook titles may be purchased in bulk for educational, business, fundraising, or sales promotional use. For more information please e-mail admin@omnibook.org

CONTENTS

Chapter One 1
Chapter Two 7
Chapter Three 11
Chapter Four 15
Chapter Five 23
Chapter Six 27
Chapter Seven 33
Chapter Eight 39
Chapter Nine 45
Chapter Ten 51
Chapter Eleven 57
Chapter Twelve 65
Chapter Thirteen 71
Chapter Fourteen 77
Chapter Fifteen 81
Chapter Sixteen 87
Chapter Seventeen 93
Chapter Eighteen 99
Chapter Nineteen 105
Chapter Twenty 111
Chapter Twenty One 117
Chapter Twenty Two 125
Chapter Twenty Three 133

Chapter Twenty Four...............139
Chapter Twenty Five..............145
Chapter Twenty Six...............153
Chapter Twenty Seven.............159
Chapter Twenty Eight.............165
Chapter Twenty Nine..............171
Chapter Thirty...................177
Chapter Thirty One...............183
Chapter Thirty Two...............189
Chapter Thirty Three.............195
Chapter Thirty Four..............201
Chapter Thirty Five..............205
Chapter Thirty Six...............211
Chapter Thirty Seven.............217
Chapter Thirty Eight.............223
Chapter Thirty Nine..............229
Chapter Forty....................235
Chapter Forty One................243
Chapter Forty Two................249
Chapter Forty Three..............257
Chapter Forty Four...............263
Chapter Forty Five...............271
Chapter Forty Six................279
Chapter Forty Seven..............285
Chapter Forty Eight..............291
Chapter Forty Nine...............299
Chapter Fifty....................307

CHAPTER ONE

So here's Johnny Taggett on his last day as a sergeant in the New York Police Department, October 23, 1939, staring around the forty-eighth precinct station. He's got his meaty hands buried in a stack of old papers and photos, cigarette ash drifting down from his six-foot-two-inch height as he sorts what he wants to keep from what he can't care about anymore. Old forms and memos, trophies he won playing football with the squad, framed snapshots from Christmas blasts and New Year's get-togethers, one or two pictures of sexy dames: the powdery ash falls over all this stuff as he rummages through it. Somewhere under that pile is his beat-up wooden desk with its two long-necked telephones rising from the mess the way skyscrapers tower over slums. He stands there, tie loose around his thick neck, sleeves rolled up, and keeps digging through all the various crap he's built up over his years in the department—his whole official life in the form of junk he's better off leaving behind.

"Too much," he mutters. "I could never keep up with all this secretary work." Almost in a daze, he goes on shuffling through the remnants of the mess on his desk.

A scream from out by the front processing area, and a smashing of glass blast his eyes all the way open and his instinct has him jumping over a couple of chairs before he even knows he's moving. "Holy shit!" he yells. "What the hell is going on?" His big muscular body joins a crowd of other cops from all over the tough precinct house with their guns drawn as they hustle toward the writhing grunting clot of guys in suits and uniforms the center of the station's big front room. He recognizes a bunch of detectives in the crowd: they're wrestling down some creep who must have thrown a metal chair through one of the glass doors. Taggett looks around at the chair lying on the floor, the smashed palm that used to decorate the lobby, the doorframe all wrenched out of shape, and figures that this creep must be all coked up. All these flatfoots with their nightsticks swinging free, smashing into the creep's skull, must have put that together too: they're not stopping till they can hustle his limp form down the hall to holding. It leaves a trail of blood as they drag it. "Make sure he's still breathing," someone standing next to Johnny hollers. "It'd look like shit if we killed this low-life."

Johnny turns to the hollering guy and says, "Hey, Captain Murphy. I guess this'll be as good a time as any to say goodbye." There's a little catch in his growling voice, as if something in his throat was trying to get out. He stands there staring at the tough old precinct captain for a moment. A flood of memories has got Johnny nailed to the spot and speechless. He can't help remembering his father, working hard to support a wife and the children he couldn't send off to the War or into marriage. Even as he keeps gawking at Captain Murphy, he sees the vegetable wagon slipping on the cobblestones, sees his father dying, his mother working herself into the same grave. He sees a young Johnny Taggett, fresh out of the peacetime army he ran away to, getting hauled in to the forty-eighth precinct house more than too many times for fighting. So many times being brought in that he gets to know the cops there, especially Patrick Murphy, the old captain even back then, who brings him into the police family. He gives him odd jobs for a couple of bucks here and there, inspires him into the force, and becomes a second father. Captain Murphy's gazing right back into Johnny's narrow grey eyes, watching him remember.

"You were always one for standing up for what's yours and knowing what's right," says the older man. "In every football game, in every brawl, you always kept coming until you knew the job was done, till you got what was yours, what was right. I like to think I taught you that. You sure this is right, going all the way across the country on your own?"

Johnny squints and thinks for a second. "I knew it was right when I lied about my age to get into the army, even though I didn't see the war. You saw when I got back how they trained me to fight, probably why you let me be a flatfoot. Anyway, this is just the kind of thinking you taught me to do, how to see my chance in a brawl or on the field. I see my chance in life here. I know this is right. I know I'm on my own anyway. Not one of my sisters sent a card when Mom died, and I don't even know if Tommy my brother lived through the War. It doesn't matter. I gotta make my own way." He goes to put his cigarette back between his lips and notices that it's smoked out. He tosses the butt aside and lights a new one.

"That's quite a speech, lad," the captain chuckles.

"Yeah," mutters Johnny. "Anyway, I'll drop you a line when I get to Frisco, let you know how I'm doing."

"Even if you'r fucking fingers are broke." Murphy sticks out his mitt. Johnny shakes it, turns around, and goes back to the squad room, leaving the captain to run the precinct.

And there's that crap still all over his desk for him to deal with. His rucksack on one side of it, a rusty trash can on the other, hungry mouths he's gotta feed his history into, one way or the other. His square jaw tightens as he notices a sealed envelope, yellow with age, stamped NO SUCH ADDRESS in ink faded to the pale red of an old wound. "Flagely," he grunts under his breath.

He remembers that night eight years ago the way he remembers his own scars: Patrolman Taggett, just two years in, following his sergeant, Flagely, up the fire escape toward the sixth floor where some creep with a hand-cannon's holed up. The rain's got the steps all slick as Flagely and Taggett scale up the outside, sealing off the creep's exit while they leave the inside to some guys a little less tough. The two cops climb up into the black sky, Taggett shivering behind, one hand gripping the slippery railing, the other clutching the little thirty-eight he carried back then before he knew better. Then he sees Flagely jerk and go stiff a second before the *Bang* closer than the thunder, the blaze of light that outlines the sergeant's body for a second as it starts to fall. Blind with shock, Taggett shoots twice. His little gun doesn't seem to do anything as Flagely's dying body falls down the metal steps toward him, bleeding, wrecked by a bullet to the head, tumbling over the railing down into the darkness. The sounds of the screaming creep and the shots from inside that end them fade above him as he stares and stares down to the invisible street. And as he stares at the envelope on his desk he remembers the collection everyone in the station took up for Flagely's wife and daughter, the collection they mailed to her, that came back marked NO SUCH ADDRESS. Turns out she'd taken the kid out to Michigan, where they'd been living for the last month before Flagely's retirement—his death. The tough old sergeant must've been too embarrassed to let any of his boys know about the wreck of his life. Taggett stands there muttering about it, cigarette smoldered to a butt between his lips. "Eight years," he says to himself, "and that fucking thing's been on my desk the whole time." After a minute or two he picks up the envelope and drops it in the trash can's maw.

After way too much of that the job's done. The trash can's packed solid with ugly souvenirs like that envelope and the rucksack's got his first squad football trophy and a few pictures from around the stationhouse he just can't get rid of. The surface of the desk, black wood pitted and scarred with experience, stares back at him. He glares at it for a minute and then rolls down his sleeves, pulls his double-breasted suitcoat on over his shoulder holster, and bends to his rucksack. It's as light as a ghost when he picks it up, slaps his hat on his head, and goes out to give the reception room one last look.

Some guys are sweeping up the last of the mess from that big scuffle earlier with the cokey wackjob. Johnny watches them for a minute, then turns to notice a crowd of cops looking at him. Joe McElroy, the guy he shares his desk with, is lollygagging around there, and so's the rookie, Mike Shanahan, who they're already starting to call Shanny. "Guess the water cooler survived for all you bums to stand around," he grumbles at them, chuckling a little in the back of his throat.

An answering chuckle comes back from the crowd, and some voice he doesn't even recognize calls out, "Good luck in Frisco, Johnny! Watch your back while you're drinking those beers! We won't be there to protect you!"

Taggett curls his lips into a mocking smile as he walks past. "I won't need you goons; I got my forty-five to protect me." His heels crack a fragment of glass the sweepers missed. The gang around the water cooler keeps gawking at him as he strides to the rectangular space the doors used to occupy. Without turning his head he lets out a "So long, suckers." Shrugging on his overcoat, he steps out into the cool night.

Down the concrete steps to the sidewalk, nearly dancing with relief, he murmurs to himself, "Last time I'll be on these steps. Ten years. Long enough." As he walks away, oak trees shading the streetlights into bars that stripe the asphalt, he looks back over his shoulder to see the old building he's spent half his life in just once more keeps pushing forward into the night.

CHAPTER TWO

On his way to the train station, Johnny feels the skin on the back of his neck get that tingle, feels a familiar itch. "Shit, a tail," he gripes to himself. "That crazy Russian doesn't quit. Well, what the hell, he's probably as well-paid as I used to be." He snickers to himself, glances over his shoulder, squinting through the smoke from his cigarette, scanning the random walkers dragging along the sidewalk behind him. No sign of the shaven-headed hit man the gambling racket has gunning for him. "One more reason to get out of this city," mutters Taggett. He keeps walking.

He remembers patrolling these streets with his best friend on the force, Walt McBride, getting into scrapes with the local hoods, the two of them looking out for each other and drinking the night away after the shift's end. It's in those late hours of getting sauced together that Walt fills Johnny in on the details Captain Murphy couldn't: the way a cop has to scratch a little to get what he needs. He explains how most of the precinct makes it through by watching the night shift at some bootlegger's warehouse, defending one group of crooks from another. "An honest cop can get by in this world real nice just looking the other way," says Walt. "Everyone pays off everyone else, so why shouldn't we get our share?" Wide-eyed Johnny takes it all in. After not too long he's doing more than just looking the other way. A big guy like Johnny Taggett finds it easy to slip into enforcing debts for the racket, scaring some low-grade degenerate gambler or another into line for an extra buck or two.

The funny thing is that Johnny's also a degenerate gambler. The same hunger for a rush that drove him to the army helped push him into the police department, and that fevered wait for the turn of the right card help get it a little closer to being fed. He never thinks about the price, just can't, until he gets his face shoved so deep in his mess that he can't keep ignoring the stink. A few bad tips, a few horses that don't come in on time, and suddenly the bookie he's been doing little favors for starts making demands. Taggett quits scaring low-life's for the racket and starts breaking legs. The more he does it, the more he has to do it: his bookie's got his markers, knows the dirty little secrets about his off-duty life that even Captain Murphy couldn't protect him from. And through all this he's still gambling, looking for that one big score to get him off the hook, the big score that never comes.

So he's been squirreling away what he can, living like a bum on bar peanuts and hamburgers while he saves up for his chance. Somewhere in there he even gets married, stays with her long enough for her to find out what kind of man he is. He comes home at random hours, usually stinking of whiskey and bellowing the stories McBride's been filling him up with. He tells her all sorts of lies at first about his cop work and his other work and then just stops telling her anything. Some anonymous dame calls her up for a week straight looking for him and finally just leaves a number, telling his wife, "That sexy son of a bitch can call me anytime." Johnny tries to remember his ex-wife's name as he recalls how she made her escape, just a note and half the apartment cleaned out.

McBride gives him the idea for an escape of his own just a couple months later, after a bullet in the hip from a botched bank heist chains Johnny's friend to a desk: "Private dicks in San Francisco, buddy, that's the life. Your own business, your own hours, you pick the client and charge 'em what they can pay. Soon as I serve out my time in the stationhouse and get my pension I'm on the next train." Johnny's hand slips into his overcoat to feel the flimsy paper Walt's telegram's printed on and he recites it to himself: "Made Frisco. All set up. Waiting for you."

He's been holding onto that telegram for a year or two, putting away his little bit here and there for the right moment. That moment's now.

Twisting his neck, Taggett scans the crowd around him again: he can feel that Russian behind him ever since the boss who runs Taggett's bookie decided the cop was in too much debt to be useful. "I'm losing my grip on you, Taggett," says the little weasel from behind the cloud of poison gas that oozes out of the crappy cigar that never leaves his mouth. "You just keep playing and losing. It's like you don't know what you're doing or you don't care if you live or die. Either you're a dummy or you're a nut, and you're no good to me whatever your problem is." That's about the time Johnny starts hearing about this crazy Russian enforcer with his own little goon squad, a crew for high priced hit jobs, roaming around the city with blood in his eye for a certain NYPD sergeant. He hears stories about the fun this Russian has breaking bones. Cops like to imitate his mocking laugh to put an easy scare into the creeps on the street. Some high-level gangster gets found all bloody, sliced open in his sleep, and everybody knows that the Russian's the only one crazy enough to pull it off. Just like everybody knows the Russian's the only hit man crazy enough to kill a cop. Johnny's no dope: he can figure himself for the kind of expensive problem mobsters like to just erase. He realizes it's high time to get the hell out. "Just hope I'm getting out fast enough," he mutters to himself.

A thin scar down the left side of his face, from the salt-and-pepper at his temple to the jut of his jaw, usually too narrow to register, starts throbbing the way it always does when he knows he's in trouble. Every time he feels it itch like this he slips back in his mind to the night he got it. It's a crazy mob scene, a couple of street gangs fighting for turf with Taggett and his men caught in the middle. Too poor for guns, the punks are swinging baseball bats and chains and switch blades and there's Johnny holding his ground, knocking down one screaming creep after another. Shocks vibrate up his right arm as his nightstick smacks into skulls. Then in a flash there's this kid in front of him, weird little smirk vibrating around his baby face. He smells like rotgut sweat and reefer, just stands there glassy-eyed staring at Taggett. "What the fuck?" says the cop and before he can blink the kid's got a razor in his hand, must have been hiding it in his sleeve, and he's slashing Johnny's face. Taggett lets out a little grunt of pain.

The kid snickers. "I thought you were some kind of tough guy, flatfoot."

"Tough enough for you," snarls Johnny. As the blood drips down his neck into his uniform he's got his hand in his jacket pocket, fingers curled around the brass knuckles. His fist comes out of there as fast and hard as a cannonball and catches the weird kid across the jaw. The punk shrieks as his face goes all diagonal, jaw flapping loose, but he somehow keeps standing, so Johnny just puts his size fourteen in the grasshopper's balls. That puts him down.

But not before Johnny's marked. Later, sewing him up under the precinct interrogation room's flat light, the doc says, "You know, Sergeant Taggart, you were just an inch from losing an eye. You really ought to be more careful in the line of duty. As it is, you're going to have a little souvenir of your night downtown for the rest of your life."

Raising his finger to his face, wincing a little from the pain, Taggett just grins at the flabby civilian. "I got all sorts of souvenirs, doc. Now, thanks for stitching me up, but I got work to do." He lights up a cigarette as the old doc fiddles with his eyeglasses and slips out the door and back into the daytime.

"All sorts of souvenirs," the tough cop mutters as he keeps pushing on through the night crowd toward Union Station with nothing to his name but his suit, his forty-five, a half-empty rucksack, and a couple hundred he managed to sneak out of one of his stashes. Nothing but his memories of corruption and death and a faint promise of a new life in San Francisco. That throb on his face tells him that someone's getting closer.

CHAPTER THREE

Taggett makes it into giant, echoing Grand Central Station, crowded even at this time of night, and lights up a new cigarette. Yellow light from vast rows of light bulbs stains the station's enormous marble floor, reflecting the citizens walking on it as pale shadows upside down. The place is probably amazing, but Taggett's head is on a swivel for other reasons. He's walking around in circles, examining faces, trying to catch whatever creep's been following him from the precinct and making his scar throb. He keeps up a commentary under his breath while he searches.

"So I'm looking for someone who dodges my look . . .not that guy, he's too straight-looking . . .any creep working for that crazy Russian's gonna have that weird dark stare a stone killer gets . . .no, that guy's too well dressed . . .and that one's just a tourist, look at him gawking around, he's gonna run into someone if he's not—oh, I see, a lifter looking for a heavy pocket, I better stay out of his way . . .shit, only a few minutes for my train . . .well, hello there, you gorgeous pair of pins."

She doesn't see him as he makes a meal of her with his eyes: she's got legs that go all the way up to a soft curvy ass, plump cheeks under a skirt just a little too tight hypnotically swaying back and forth as she walks and he follows. He's trying to remember to keep his tongue in his mouth. Glancing around, he notices where they're both going and mumbles, "Lucky thing she's on the same train I am or I'd end up in Saint Louis or something. Come on, Taggett, get yourself together."

So there he stands on the platform. He flicks away the burned out butt and lights up a new cigarette as he watches the hot number get on. "Hope she's in a sleeper car," he mutters. "Wouldn't mind running into her some dark night." Looking around, he notices the porter, calls the boy over, tells him, "I'm in the sleeper." The kid gives him a slow once-over: Taggett sees him observing the state of his suit and his lack of anything for luggage but a half-empty rucksack. Dead-eyed, the boy jerks his chin in the general direction of the car the babe stepped into. "Thanks a heap for all your kind help," Johnny sneers to the boy, who just snickers, scanning the sparsely crowded platform for a customer who'll actually tip. Carrying his sack of apparently worthless memories, Taggett strides to the car that hot dish got into, steps up a few steps, and gets on the train.

Feeling like a giant in a dollhouse, he shuffles down the narrow corridor with doors to one side. "Nice, wish I could afford a private room, it'd be so much easier to keep a low profile until I can get clear of the city," he gripes to himself. After four or five doors the corridor widens to reveal the open section. Taggett checks his ticket: he's got an upper berth toward the end of the car. He hustles his big body and his rucksack down there and slips into his seat, hanging his coat and hat and shoving the rucksack under. Staring out the window at the passing tourists, he waits for the train to get going.

As he's idly ogling the ripe tomatoes all dressed up to ride the train he happens to notice a couple of guys who look like they're trying not to be spotted. He chuckles to himself and wonders how he didn't catch them all the way back at the precinct, considering he knows the type so well, these half-smart half tough eggs with their overcoat collars sticking up, one holding up a newspaper like he's pretending it's a wall, the other staring at the tip of his unlit cigarette for some reason. "Wait a minute," he mutters, "I know these jerks. Where have I seen those ugly faces before? Don't think I ever busted these goons on the job, but that guy with the tip missing from his ear looks so familiar he could be my damn roommate."

Just then the one with the cigarette and an ear and a half seems to catch Johnny watching. He bends over to the newspaper guy, who's not only shorter but rounder to boot, and whispers something and just then a voice from behind Taggett's head intones, "Drink, sir?"

He whips around to see the porter maintaining a neutral expression. "What? Huh?" is all he can come up with as he tries to keep an eye on the goons on the platform while he fishes his ticket out of his pocket and answer whatever question he's just been asked.

The porter's deep brown eyes are mildly piercing into Johnny's brain like friendly little ice picks. "I say, care for a drink, sir. Train leaven soon and lots of passengers like a drink as they pull out. Sir."

"Uh, yeah, okay, scotch and soda," Johnny tells him. The porter just stands there, giving him the kind of patient smile people use on their half-witted relatives to keep from laughing in their faces. After an awkward moment Johnny figures out that he's not in the kind of speakeasy he's used to. "Oh, right," he says. "Glass of club soda."

The porter's eyes twitch to Johnny's hand, which doesn't move toward his pocket. "Ah, that'll be fifteen cents, sir." Growling a little, Johnny gropes around in his other pocket for a nickel and a dime and hands them to the old man, all the time trying to keep the window the transaction's got him turned away from in his field of vision. The porter glances at the exact change in the palm of his white glove, lets out a polite sigh, and moves toward the dining car with all the enthusiasm of a barefoot boy on the first day of school.

Taggett whips his head back around to the window. The thugs are gone. Right then, he snaps his fingers: "Of course! That guy with the ear, I remember him from the riot where I got my scar, he was working muscle for my bookie. Shit. I can't believe I didn't see those guys on the way over. Wait a minute, maybe I couldn't have, maybe they were here waiting for me . . . or someone else." He blinks. "Try not to get all jumpy, Taggett. You're not the only lowlife gambler in New York City, I'm sure. Lots of mugs got trouble. I'm on my way the hell out of here and no two-bit hoods are gonna scare me into making a wrong move." He squirms a little in the softness of his seat and lights up a new cigarette, squinting away from the smoke as he gives the platform one more once-over.

"Club soda, sir," says the porter behind him, and his hand still twitches toward the holster under his suitcoat. The old man stands their mildly blinking at him, extending the short glass of club soda still fizzing. Little beads of condensation slide down the sides of the glass as they stare at each other for a lingering moment, then Johnny takes the glass and grunts what he hopes is enough of a thanks to get this guy out of his face. Slowly, the porter drawls, "Enjoy your trip, sir," and makes his easy way back along toward the private berths where the passengers are a little more likely to tip.

Johnny waits until the porter's out of view down the corridor, then reaches into his hanging overcoat for a little flask. Holding his glass under the window, he tips a little bootleg whiskey, a supply he skimmed from his bookie's private stock, into it. A little smile curls the corners of his lips as he takes a sip, tastes that kerosene his bookie's bootlegger uses for starter, feels the heat going down and spreading in his chest. He barely notices the conductor's fatherly boom calling all aboard, the clanging of the bell as the last few passengers hustle into the car. With a couple of tremendous coughs, the train jerks and starts to slide along its track, faster and faster, as Johnny feels himself finally start to relax after what seems like years of looking over his shoulder. His body getting heavier sinking back into the welcoming cushion. Just at the brink of sleep's warm black embrace a sudden thought stabs him like a needle in the back of the brain. His eyes jolt open and he can't help saying it: "What if those hard thugs followed me onto the train?"

CHAPTER FOUR

When he opens his eyes again the car's flooded with amber evening light. "Shit," he mumbles, "I must have slept the whole day through right here in my seat." He fumbles for a cigarette and a match and lights up, looking around. Somehow the car's empty except for him, all the berths folded back up into the walls. The gurgle coming out of his gut gives him the clue: "Dinner time," he tells himself. "Guess I better find my way to the dining car." He drags fingers through his hair, uses the flickering ghostly reflection in the window to straighten his tie, and crams his hat back onto his head. "Eh, presentable enough, I suppose."

Still blinking away the cobwebs, he takes a moment to observe the landscape rushing past him in a bright blur: no buildings, no black asphalt sky, just the greens and golds of the country regular types live in. The sleeping car rattles gently as the train clicks and clacks along its track. He can't help smiling. "Here I come, Walt. Taggett and McBride, private dicks, world by the tail, just like you said." He can feel the motion of the train carrying him away from the city's darkness, from all that baggage he left there, as he lets himself dream for a second or two. Then he snaps out of it and staggers a little from the swaying of the car on its wheels as he makes his way toward his first meal since he grabbed a snack at the precinct house a day and a lifetime ago.

The dining car's just choked with passengers, men in suits with their hats hanging on hooks above them, women dressed up in elegant gowns. The buzz of conversation joins the clattering of forks on plates and the smell of steak and broccoli and butter to fill the car's close atmosphere. Johnny stands at the doorway looking in: a single table on the right seems open, so he pushes his way over there, trying not to knock over a waiter. He takes a seat, hangs his hat, and gets his head on its regular swivel, checking out the exits, who looks tough enough to start something, who's watching him. No one looks tough in this crowd, a bunch of Daddy Warbucks types and their dates pitching woo at each other, whistling while they can before the money runs out. Taggett lets a little smirk curl his lips as the waiter arrives, takes his order, leaves again. Soon enough a plate shows up weighted down with a thick bloody steak and a small forest of broccoli, all glistening with real butter. Johnny grabs his knife and his fork and gets to work.

He's barely started cutting his meat when his scar starts itching. He stops moving. His eyes dart around the dining car. The men at the tables around him seem to be concentrating on their dates, acting impressive, none of them the kind of hard case that could set off his instincts like this. The girls are just as harmless, everyone a regal citizen . . . except for the figure in black, regarding him from the other end of the car. A featureless face seems to be staring at him, seated at a large table next to a withered old man nodding in a wheelchair. It takes Johnny a second to realize that whoever's creeping him out this way is wearing a thick black veil that's ebbing and flowing as the dark figure breathes. "Well, I guess it's human," mutters Taggett.

As he looks closer he starts to realize: "Shit, that's a woman!" Along with that veil she's wearing a black hat, a plain black dress, and long black gloves. He can't see her shoes under the table, but he's got a pretty good idea they're not orange. The only color on her comes from the gaudy rings she's wearing on her gloved fingers. Sparkling as the dining car's electric lights come on, the rings flash gold and ruby and emerald and a bunch of colors he can't even name into his eyes. He blinks and keeps staring, ignoring the dinner that's cooling in front of him.

After a long weird moment he realizes that she's saying something. Worse, she's saying something to him: a voice breathy and ghostly but somehow as mellow as a glass of good whiskey is calling across the room, "Young man, young man, come over here." It's been a while since anyone's called Johnny a young man, so he pushes himself away from the table, grunting what the hell to himself, and makes his way over to the strange lady's corner of the car. "Young man," she says, "my husband and I have observed that you're unaccompanied at your supper, and I just can't abide to see someone lonely if I can help it; I insist you dine with us and tell us the fascinating story of your life. I won't take no for an answer, young man."

That's when he notices the other person at the table. An elderly party with a tuxedo flapping around his bony frame sits propped up in a wheelchair to the right of the woman in black. His black eyes glisten deep in their sockets, blank as a porcelain doll's would abandoned in a moonlit alley at midnight. Taggett forces his eyes away from the wreck's dangling head and back to the void the woman's veil makes of her face. "Uh, sure," he mumbles. A gesture from a black-gloved hand brings a squad of waiters over with Taggett's dinner and his drink and a chair, so he shrugs and has a seat.

Hungry as he is, it's hard for him to get much eating done. The old man's got a big bowl of some kind of gruel in front of him, smells like someone in the kitchen just ground up the whole dinner, and she's feeding him from it, filling up a soup spoon and wiping it over his lips, pushing it into his mouth, almost snarling at him to eat it up like a good boy. Every so often she has to wipe the brown paste from his jaw on a napkin tucked into the gaping neck of his tux. Johnny tries to keep his eyes on his own plate and away from the spreading stain on the napkin and manages to get through the meal without puking on his plate. This goes on for a while, and then the squad of waiters reappears and takes everything away.

And then there's a long awkward moment of silence. The strange veiled woman fixes a cigarette to a long ivory holder and slides that through her veil, which Johnny can see is made of three or four layers of netting. He gets his matchbook from his pocket and lights her smoke. "Thank you, young man," she says. "I observing you've been looking at my rings all this time. Perhaps you're interested in their provenance."

Taggett lights up a smoke of his own and lets out a little cough of a laugh: "Yeah, I don't really know what that means, but I'll tell you, I'm a lot more interested in who you are. You people got names?"

A sound that must be a chuckle drifts from behind the veil. "Of course, how rude of me. I am Mrs. Vivian Foulsworth, and this is my husband Edgar." Edgar seems to twitch a little at the mention of his name as Mrs. Foulsworth extends a black gloved hand, rings glinting right into Johnny's eyes. He takes the hand, mumbles his name, finds himself staring into one of the rings: an evening-colored stone so clear somehow that looking into it makes him think he's staring deep into the depth of a perfectly smooth lake so vast he can't even imagine the shore. Faint voices scratch at the surface of his awareness, whispers in a bunch of languages he doesn't know. He can feel his jaw going slack, his cigarette falling into his drink. "Fascinating, isn't it," murmurs Mrs. Foulsworth. "A ring seven centuries old, found on the finger of Genghis Khan himself, a diamond even older. We've traced it through stories and legends back to the court of Rameses the Great. Imagine it, Mr. Taggett. Imagine the power such a gem must have had, passing through the hands of uncountable collectors, feeling their gaze through all those millennia. Think of the brave men who gave their lives mining it, just reaching it, how their devoted souls must have entered its perfection. The Violet Diamond." Her voice has lowered to the kind of hushed tone Taggett remembers from the last time he was in a church. He hasn't managed yet to let go of her hand. Mrs. Foulsworth lets a soft sigh flutter her veil. "Edgar brought this back from Ethiopia for me. He's a great gemologist, he and his brother Sal." The creepy figure in the wheelchair gives another twitch. "We're just coming from Sal's funeral, actually. Such a strange ceremony, such odd characters behaving with such bizarre precision, as if they were in some kind of cult. Something happened to my husband and his brother there in Ethiopia, or perhaps it started when Sal ran into that odd one-eyed Chinaman . . . or when he told us he'd found the Fountain of Youth and got Edgar so worked up he had to hire a boat for Africa right then. I suppose I'll never know. When I met my husband at the dock at his return he was like . . . like this." She shudders. "Please excuse me. I have to . . . to compose myself." She takes her hand back as Taggett blinks and barely remembers to rise with her as she leaves the table, thin black figure swaying back toward the sleeper.

With Mrs. Foulsworth gone, Johnny can't think of anything better to do than light up another cigarette and get a better look at Edgar. The old man might or might not be staring back: the glistening of his glassy eyes can barely escape their cavernous sockets. The nose between them is somehow curving down over lips the color of calfskin to nearly touch his chin. Fine wisps of hair drift across the spotted expanse of his scalp, and the skin the face is made of, reminds Johnny of pictures he's seen of Egyptian mummies. Flecks of white matter seem to be flaking from it. Johnny smokes and shudders and then notices that the creepy old guy seems to be twitching with a purpose. Those leathery lips are twisting and a kind of feeble grunt seems to pushing them apart. One of Edgar's bony claws is gesturing, index finger out and waving like a palsied baton.

Johnny blinks. "You're trying to say something." A nod from Edgar. "Trying to point to something?" The head shakes from side to side. Taggett takes a frustrated breath and asks the ancient, "You need something to write with?" Another nod, and Taggett reaches into his coat pocket for the pad and pencil he's been carrying ever since he started working for his bookie. He lays them down in front of Edgar's unsteady hand as it reaches forth from the old man's lap.

Grunting with effort, Edgar forces his bent fingers to grip the pencil, to lift it, to drop it onto the paper and carve out letters. Taggett squints at the paper as letters form, trying to read upside down. "Death?" he says. "Is that what you're—yeah, 'Death in the . . . in the what?" The old man's wheeze is getting louder and faster and he seems to be trying to speed up his writing. Taggett glances away from the paper, and there's Mrs. Foulsworth, coming at them down the length of the car. He looks back into Edgar's crumbling face to see what looks like some kind of panic. "You don't want her to see this, do you?" Edgar's leathery head shakes back and forth as his hand stutters over the page. Taggett snatches another glimpse at what Edgar's trying to write—"DEATH IN THE RI" or something like that and then just a crazy spider web of scribbling—and smoothly slides the pad and pencil back into his jacket just before Mrs. Foulsworth makes it to the table.

"I hope you've been having an amusing time with my Edgar. No doubt you've been sharing many fascinating anecdotes." Another one of those wooden noises that must have been a chuckle blows the veil out a little as she fits another cigarette into her holder, slides that through the netting, and waits for Johnny to supply a light. It doesn't take him more than half a second to catch on and light her smoke for her. "I suppose I must apologize," she tells him. "My little joke is in poor taste. As I was saying, Edgar doesn't communicate, really. I suspect only I can understand him at this point, isn't that right, my darling, and half the time I have no idea what he's gibbering on about. He's trapped in his body." Her featureless head turns toward the old man. "Aren't you, my precious?" A gloved hand reaches to cover one of Edgar's palsied claws, and the leathery old man gives a twitch and a grunt. Johnny shivers a little but keeps his face from twisting into a scowl of revulsion.

The veil turns back to face Johnny. It flutters as Mrs. Foulsworth announces, "I see that all this conversation has utterly exhausted my Edgar. Be a dear, Mr. Taggett, and help me take him to bed." She gets up, and so does Johnny, and then she doesn't make a move. After a moment, he figures out what she's expecting and takes the handles of Edgar's wheelchair, pulling it back from the table, making a kind of three-point turn, and pushing him back toward the sleeping cars. While he's pushing, Mrs. Foulsworth takes his arm: he can feel her fingers clutching his biceps the way a banker clutches his most recent dollar. She's so strangely tall that her veil comes almost to the level of Taggett's face, that weird breathy murmur worming its way through those layers of netting almost straight into his ear. "I'll tell you a strange tale, Mr. Taggett. You'll recall that I described our journey tonight as the return from my Edgar's brother's funeral. Well, I could swear that I saw him there: Sal, my deceased brother-in-law. He was standing right there at graveside, looking younger than he did when we first met. I tried to catch his eye, but he was deep in conversation with some strange Oriental type. I looked for him after the service, but he had disappeared completely. Could I be losing my mind, Mr. Taggett? Or did whatever transformed my Edgar into this . . . this . . ." —her voice catches and something behind the veil makes a faint clicking sound—"this *mockery* have something to do with Sal? I can't begin to understand."

As the wheelchair squeaks along the aisle in front of them Taggett can only make what he hopes is a reassuring sort of grunt, and then they're at the door to the strange couple's private berth. Mrs. Foulsworth pushes the door open, and Johnny pushes in her husband. The three of them take up about half the space; a wide platform a little higher than Taggett's chest takes about a quarter of the rest.

Mrs. Foulsworth turns to him and extends her hand. "It's been lovely to meet you, Mr. Taggett, and I insist that you dine with us for the rest of our voyage together. You strike me as a strong man, and I must learn all about you and why you're leaving the joys of New York for whatever awaits you in the West." Taggett nods and mumbles something he figures is polite, wondering as he glances at the hand she hasn't taken back what happened to the Violet Diamond. He almost misses her saying, "There is one more way in which you can help us. That platform is where my Edgar sleeps, and he appears much too tired tonight to cooperate in getting up to it. Do you think you can lift him?"

Taggett sizes up the old guy and says, "Sure, he doesn't look like much trouble." He bends to slide his big hands under Edgar's arms, then straightens up, taking Edgar with him. As he lifts the body, he can feel his own back straining, the sweat breaking out on his forehead. After about half a minute more than he should have taken for the job, he gets the slack body onto its platform, nods to Mrs. Foulsworth, and gets the hell out of there.

"Crazy," he mutters to himself as he makes his way back toward his own berth in the open section. "Nearly threw my back out, and that mummy shouldn't have weighed more than my right leg. What's he got in there, some kind of metal brace? Well, don't think I'll be doing that again." Dipping his hand into his pocket, he glances around to see if anyone's looking. No one is, so he takes a swig from his flask and slips it back before he opens his berth and climbs in for the night, pulling the curtain shut. He's only been awake for the couple of hours it took to meet the Foulsworth's, but somehow he's just completely wiped out. His eyes drift shut to the constant clatter of the train ferrying him into his new life.

CHAPTER FIVE

His eyes snap open into darkness. His scar's crawling on his face like a chorus line of ants, and he can feel his muscles tensing for a fight. "What the hell," he growls, then shoves his hand in front of his mouth to shut himself up. It's just now that he realizes what woke him up: murmurs, almost whispers, voices he almost recognizes, like a face you can't quite place but—"Oh, shit," he can't help saying into his hand. "It's those goons from New York, the ones I saw at Grand Central." He reaches under his pillow for his forty-five and slips into his pants as quietly as he can. He checks his safety and gets ready to leap out of his berth and see what these tough guys have got. But then he stops himself: "No need spraying lead all over these innocent civilians," he mutters. So he lies there with his hand on his heater, listening to a couple of familiar voices get closer. If he closes his eyes he can see them walking along the central aisle of the open section: the tall thin one they called Beethoven on account of his missing section of ear, and his short round partner, Brutus. He's never bothered to find out what names their mothers gave them. "Hard to imagine hard creeps like that even having mothers," he chuckles to himself.

As he lies there waiting for them to pass or attack or whatever they're here for, he remembers the first time his boss the bookie introduced them. "You'll be with these guys tonight," the bookie tells him. "Serious hard case over down around Foley Square needs a little extra persuading, so they're here to help." Beethoven, as tall as Taggett, leers right into his eyes and in a voice just a little too loud snickers, "We're good at persuasion." Brutus, at least a head and a half shorter and at least a weight class heavier than Taggett, just grunts and stares off in some random direction. Taggett can't really afford to laugh in anyone's face right then, so he keeps himself shut up. "All right, whatever," says the bookie, "you don't have to love each other, just get going." With another snicker, Beethoven follows Brutus out the door, and Taggett tags along behind.

The three of them end up busting through the cardboard door of this crappy little thrown-together two-room cottage in the shadow of the big construction project. The guy in there was sleeping, but he wakes up pretty quick when Brutus smashes all the furniture in the front room to firewood and they just walk into the loser's bedroom. The guy leaps right out of bed when he sees them, ready to fight, barking the way losers usually do when they're cornered. The three tough guys let him wind down. Beethoven's grinning from ear to stump as he purrs to the poor skell, "Hey, pal, we're not here to hurt you . . . much . . . we just need the money you owe. That's pretty simple, isn't it?" Brutus casually cracks his knuckles. Taggett stands silent between the guy and his bedroom door, eyes in the shadow of his hat, arms folded, just an immovable lump of muscle. The skell's eyes dart around the room, finally resting on Beethoven's friendly smile, and he just stands there by his own bed in his nightshirt, shivering and sniffling like an abused orphan. After a long heavy moment Brutus twitches a thick fist in his direction and he flinches toward a cigar box on the bedside table. Brutus takes the box, puts his fist through the table, and lets the poor fool see the blank joy in his eyes. It's enough to make the guy start moaning. Taggett glances away, trying to keep himself from saying out loud how over the top this whole thing is getting. "Too much," he can't help muttering.

The next thing he sees is Beethoven holding this guy by the hand, bending it back, murmuring something Taggett can't make out, bending the guy's pinky back until it snaps. Then he does the guy's ring finger. Then his middle finger. Then his index. Brutus is staring at the spectacle, his lips glossy and hanging open as the guy's face goes corpse-white, then grey, then almost green. Beethoven's sighing a little, the way a working man does at the end of a good long day. Taggett's trying not to puke. "What the hell, you already got the money," he blurts out to Beethoven.

Beethoven drops the guy's hand, lets him fall back onto the bed, whimpering and holding his useless right hand to his chest, and gives Taggett a cute smile and a wink. "And I bet this deadbeat won't be making us come back for another visit." He swats the guy across the back of the head. "Will you, punk." The poor sucker can't even form words at this point, but he's shaking his head back and forth like a champion, the greasy ends of his hair smacking him in his cheeks.

A rumble comes out of Brutus, words grinding themselves into powder as he speaks: "Heh. I thought this was supposed to be a tough guy."

Beethoven cracks up and says, "All right, come on, let's leave this poor sap to his troubles." Leaning over the bed he whispers something in the guy's ear. The guy just sobs no no no no until they're gone.

Lying there listening to their voices getting closer, Taggett can't help snarling deep in his throat. He stifles it to listen to what they're saying.

That's Beethoven's nasal whine going, "I saw him, I know he's on this train, keep looking," and Brutus's subterranean grunt replying, "Whatever, let's just kill this loser and get off. I don't like trains."

This gets a snort from Beethoven: "A big tough customer like you? Oh, come now."

Brutus grumbles back, "All that clickety-clackety does something in my head, I don't, know, I just don't like it. You sure you saw him get on?"

"Oh, I saw him. You don't forget a scarface like that. Must be on another car, though, I can't see that mug holding enough scratch for a real bed. Anyway, I need a drink. Let's get back. It's not like he's gonna get past us while we're all on the train."

Taggett waits as Beethoven's snicker gets softer, as their footsteps get farther away, swallowed by the sound of the train. "Shit," he says to himself. "They're definitely after me, and I thought I'd shook all my troubles. Well, better stay to this part of the train, as long as they think I'm not here."

Slowly, carefully, he parts the curtains of his berth with his forty-five, trying to get his body as far to the side of the berth as he can. The black curtains open, letting in a dim flicker as moonlight seeps in through the moving windows. The car seems deserted, all the berths sealed off, curtains drifting back and forth as the sleepers behind them dream on.

So he lets his head stick out from between his own curtains, looks along the aisle toward the rear of the train, the way his tails probably went: nothing but the dark rectangle leading to the cheaper seats. Scar still throbbing, he turns his face the other way, toward the private berths and the dining car. "What the hell," mumbles, "that door hanging open looks like Foulsworth's . . . I better go check this out. That couple's weird enough and rich enough . . . maybe those hard guys got in there. Those Foulsworth's are strange but they don't deserve what these creeps can do." He swings his legs out of the bed and lowers himself to the floor as quietly as he can. In his socks, shirtless, forty-five heavy in his hand, he moves up the train toward the pool of electric light at the foot of the door swung into the room. He stops before he can cast a shadow, listening for voices from inside, getting nothing but the rattling of the train. Holding his breath, he edges up to the door and cranes his neck to get a peek in there.

The berth that must be Mrs. Foulsworth's looks as sealed up as a tomb. The curtains are still, but she must be in there: he can hear her smooth whisper seeping out from behind them, and she snores a little. She doesn't seem to make much more sense asleep than she does awake. Against the other wall sits Edgar's wheelchair, next to the hammock Taggett had to hoist the old man into. The hammock's swaying a little from the motion of the train—and it's empty. Taggett can't keep himself from grunting in shock.

He twitches back out of view before he wakes Mrs. Foulsworth, and he's muttering as he makes his way back to his own bunk: "Can't be . . . he can't go anywhere out of that chair . . . or can he . . . I put him up in that hammock just tonight . . . and he was so heavy . . .how can he possibly . . . this whole thing is getting too fucking weird . . barely even know whose way I should stay out of . . ." Reaching his berth, he climbs up into it, pulls the curtain tight, and slips his forty-five back under his pillow.

CHAPTER SIX

A sliver of light sneaks in through a part in Johnny's curtains to wake him up. His body jerks as he reaches for his forty-five, ready to shoot down the beam of that flashlight, when he realizes that its sunlight. It's morning. He's lived through another night.

So he lights up a smoke and sticks his head out of his berth to greet the new day and gets an eyeful of some guy's hairy leg sticking out of the bunk across the aisle, white as Formica all the way up to his flabby ham. "Nice," Taggett mutters and hops down to the deck. The open section's packed with bodies dressed for sleeping: some silk robes, some of those with fur collars, some flannel pajamas, a whole bunch of undershirts and boxer shorts. "Wonder why I even bothered to slip on pants last night," he snorts. The sudden memory of last night makes him stop in his tracks. He mumbles apologies to the guy that seems to have thudded into him from behind and fallen down, reaching down and pulling the poor tourist back to his feet. Thrusting his big body through the tide of passengers on their way to the washrooms, he heads back toward Foulsworth's compartment. The door's still hanging open, and now Edgar's wheelchair is gone and Mrs. Foulsworth's curtains are hanging open. "Early breakfast?" Taggett wonders. "Were they even in there last night? But how—cut it out, Johnny, you'll just give yourself the creeps." He shakes his head like a dog drying off, turns around, and lets the crowd push him along toward the washrooms.

His eyes are darting all over the place, checking for too much interest in someone's face, that look of someone knowing too much about you for your own good. The corridor's full of people and Beethoven or Brutus or even some creep Taggett doesn't know could be in this same crowd with his head in their cross-hairs.

He happens to glance at a lower berth as a long stockinged leg emerges, then another just as sexy. He reaches his hand down, and a soft warm hand takes it, the girl in there pulling herself up. He grins down into her blue eyes: "Glad I could help," he murmurs. She's dressed in some sort of clinging satin thing and doesn't seem to mind who's noticing. They lock eyes for a moment, the crowd parting around them the way a river splits around a rock, then she blinks and turns away to grab a red flowered robe from her berth and join the parade on the way to the washrooms. He can't help standing there to gawk a little as she goes until someone shoves him a little and he starts moving forward again.

As the mob inches forward through the empty dining car, chairs stacked on the tables, waiters leaning against the rattling wall and smoking, he's muttering to himself. "Wow, what a peach . . . smells nice, too . . . just as sexy as that girl I got on the train behind . . . wonder what bunk that one's getting out of . . . she was really something . . . these hot dishes are all over the place . . . a little like New York, really . . . wonder if I'll get as much action in Frisco . . . I bet a private eye gets plenty . . ." He keeps up this monologue under his breath as the crowd around him freezes into two lines, men and women, each trailing away from a little door at either side of the end of the car they've finally made it to. Everyone's staring at the floor or the windows or anywhere but at anyone else: the men clutch their little leatherette shaving kits and their towels while the women nervously pat their curlers back into place, makeup kits tucked under their arms. Taggett follows along, except that he didn't bring a shaving kit. "Knew I forgot something," he mumbles. The guy in front of him half turns his head back to trace the sound, then sees the size of Taggett behind him, the hard look on Johnny's broad square face, and snaps his head back to front with an almost audible click of bone. Johnny can't help chuckling a little.

By the time he reaches the front of the line he's done chuckling and starting to shift from foot to foot. Finally the door opens and the nervous little dude he's been behind all this time comes out all slick and shiny. "All yours," the guy says just the way every guy before him in line has said it all morning. Taggett just nods and shoulders his way into the little washroom.

As he's sitting there in the little room doing his business, he notices a sign on the back of the door: "PLEASE DO NOT FLUSH WHILE TRAIN IN STATION." That gets a laugh out of him. "Yeah, I'd hate to be the poor citizen that gets blasted by a turd from out of nowhere. Better on the train than under it." He finishes, flushes, stoops to give himself a quick once-over in the little mirror over the little shinny metal sink he washes his hands in, and decides that the face he's got will have to do.

As he's opening the door back out into the car and breathing in to tell the next guy whose it is now he feels a little push, so he pushes back harder. The door slams open, banging into the side wall, and Taggett looks down to see a guy sprawled on the floor, robe gaping open to show off his sunshine-yellow boxers. There's fancy stuff scattered all around this character: a few rings, a gold chain, a crimping iron for his big-city Marcelled hairdo. Johnny's not the only one laughing, but he is the only one who leans down to lend the dude a hand. The guy's glare is shooting daggers into Johnny's eyes, and he hisses, "You need to watch who you're pushing around, palooka." He cracks open his shaving kit to show Johnny the twenty-two he's got hidden in there. "Good for close work," he whispers up to Johnny, "and I know how to get close."

"Uh, okay sorry for the inconvenience, I'm not here to get into a fight," Johnny replies. He takes his hands off this rough dude as fast as he can. Wobbling a little, the guy turns like a dancer and slams the washroom door behind him. Lucky for Johnny he was one of the last in this line, so that the whole train isn't staring at him and wondering what this big guy's problem is. "I'll take what I can get," he mutters as he makes his way back through the dining car to his berth to get dressed and figure out how the hell to live through another day.

He's still working on it as he's shoveling fried egg and toast and ham and coffee down his throat. "Can't just walk back and forth through the train," he tells himself. "If I run into those goons they'll just attack, they don't care who else gets hurt . . . but I sure would like to find out more about that blonde . . . don't see her in here, she must have brought her own chow . . . don't see the Foulsworth's either, and that doesn't make a damn bit of sense . . . Edgar somehow walking around last night . . . out of that crazy little sling anyhow . . . neither of them anywhere I can't see them this morning . . . like a couple of fucking ghosts. . . ." As he's finishing up his breakfast he lights up a smoke and gestures to one of the waiters hustling past: "I want to stay in this car for awhile. That all right?"

The waiter pauses a moment, looking Johnny right in the eye. He sounds like he's really trying to choose his words carefully: "I suppose you can do what you like, sir. Ain't no passenger ever asked me permission for nothing."

"Heh, Okay. I'll try to stay out of the way," says Taggett, putting on his friendliest face, but the waiter's gone, obviously too busy for a little moment of emotion with the big white passenger.

So Johnny grabs his chair and drags it over against a wall, has a seat. "Someone's gotta come through here," he mumbles, "either those thugs or those Foulsworths or that blonde. Everyone gets hungry." He tilts his fedora over his eyes, slouches in the chair and makes little snoring noises every once in a while, just some passenger dozed off in a random chair. His fingers curl into fists on their own. He's ready to shake some kind of answer out of someone.

The next thing he knows someone's shaking his shoulder. "Sir," says another waiter, an older guy with hair like snow on the roof of his head. "Sir. Come on, wake up, man. Can't be all nodding off while the people have their lunch. I'll fix you up a nice sandwich or something, just straighten up, will you? Sir?"

Johnny squints at the waiter for a moment: "Huh? Lunch? Jesus, I must be slipping. Uh, yeah, a sandwich and a cup of coffee."

The waiter looks back at him, gives a couple of slow blinks, and doesn't laugh at him. Slowly, a smile curls the man's lips. He leans a little closer, his voice dropping to a whisper. "You look like an all right guy, man, but you been acting weird. You hiding from someone? Trying to catch someone?"

"A little of both," says Johnny. He's studying the guy, sizing him up. "There's this blonde . . ."

"Say no more, man. I can find out her name for you, maybe even get in a good word for you. Just slip me a few dollars and I'll ask around." The friendly drawl has gone out of the waiter's voice, and his eyes have stopped their happy sparkle. This guy's talking business, not putting on an act for a tourist.

Taggett's hand slides into his coat pocket as his eyes stay on the waiter's. The older man flinches almost microscopically, but the hand comes out with a nice clean five dollar bill. "Here you go. You seem like a guy who knows what goes on. I need to know about some of the passengers, so there's more of this depending on what you can tell me."

The waiter's smile opens into a grin. "Sure thing, sir. I'll find out whatever you need to know." He sticks out his hand, slips the five into his uniform, and puts the hand back out to shake Taggett's. "Just so you know, they call me Ike."

"Johnny," says Johnny.

"It's good to meet you, sir," chuckles Ike. "I look forward to doing plenty of business with you. I'll go get you that sandwich and coffee now." As he moves back toward the kitchen, he turns around to shoot that grin straight into Johnny's eyes the way a stage magician sells the end of his trick. "Oh, by the way, Mr. Taggett. Sir. Mrs. Foulsworth says you're expected for dinner."

CHAPTER SEVEN

So dinner time finds Johnny sweating into a fresh shirt across from Mrs. Foulsworth at her table, the blank expanse of her veil pointed directly at him, almost filling his whole field of vision with its aggressive emptiness. Her full attention's tickling over his scar. "I apologize for depriving you of the pleasure of my Edgar's company," she tells him. "He's, shall we say, indisposed. A brilliant man, my Edgar, despite the wreck he's become. Most importantly, he's a man of substantial assets. He's as rich as one of the Egyptian mummies I plan to preserve him as for exhibition after he dies." That weird purring chuckle filters through the veil as Taggett flinches. "Oh, I see I've shocked you. I should think that a hardened policeman such as yourself would have become immune to such mundane reactions as shock. Yes, you see before you a woman who married for money, no doubt the only one in matrimonial history. Be assured that Edgar understands the arrangement he and I have made. He knows as well as you can imagine that I have desires which must be satisfied and that satisfaction of my desires costs money. I've made it well worth his while to provide for the satisfaction of my desires." The tip of the weird brown cigarette sticking out of her ivory holder glows. "Of course, you of all people must also know the importance of the almighty dollar. A degenerate gambler such as yourself must be an expert on the subject. You also have needs, don't you, pressing needs which only money can satisfy. Or perhaps the two unpleasant gentlemen prowling the train in search of you aren't debt collectors so much as they are old friends from the old days. Somehow, though, you don't strike me as a man with friends so close that they would work so hard to find you. Perhaps you need better friends, Mr. Taggett."

Johnny blinks, trying to stare down the faceless figure across the table from him. He taps his cigarette into the table's big glass ashtray, stalling while he figures out what to say.

"Don't bother to frame a reply," comes the voice, its bedroom tone freezing up a little the way Ike's friendly waiter routine did: Taggett's discovering that playtime has ended. "I'm fully aware of your situation," she tells him, "of the large sum of money you owe to your bookmaker and to the men who employ him, and of the plan your two old friends have made to surprise you before this train reaches Chicago. To be honest, Mr. Taggett, I don't think they mean you well. Depending on your response to the, ah, rather forceful proposal they're planning to set forth, they may hurt you fairly badly."

"They'll try," Taggett snarls.

She comes back with that damned chuckle, rattling in his ear like a machine gun. "Oh, good for you, Mr. Taggett. That's the spirit. They'll try. Of course, they'll probably succeed, considering their numerical advantage over you and their strong motivation. You understand, I presume, that their instructions are to come back either with you or not at all, and they don't particularly care how alive you are when they return. You serve no function for them now that you're no longer in uniform. You offer them no profit. Indeed, you represent a fairly substantial embarrassment. In short, Mr. Taggett, you're a man in need of a considerable amount of help."

Taggett's body is holding itself as still as a coiled spring. He tries to find some sort of contact with the strange figure across the table, but his gaze just slides off her flat black surface. He clears his throat and says, "So I guess you've got the whole file on me. Swell. I don't even care who you had to pay off to get it. I just want to know, what's it to you? You playing some kind of weird traveling game? You like picking up strangers and airing out their dirty laundry? Sister, if life's that boring for you, you can just—"

"Relax, Mr. Taggett. I assure you that this is no game, but rather a very serious matter requiring a man familiar with both sides of the law. I believe you to be that man. However, I have no use for you if you must continuously occupy half your attention in looking over your shoulder. I can remove that distraction. I have a man aboard this train keeping an eye on your two friends in the commuter section. They're not having a very good trip, and they seem inclined to take you back the hard way simply out of spite. I can have them taken care of, them and whoever may follow them. Indeed, I can offer you complete freedom from your debt in addition to a payment approximately fifty times your salary as a police officer. I can free you, Mr. Taggett. Does that sound like help you can use?"

Johnny leans back in his chair, squinting through the smoke of his cigarette and hers, trying to read the situation. The clatter of the plates in the dining car, the rattle of the speeding train, the chatter from all the other passengers, all the sounds fading out as he figures out his next move. Finally he comes out with, "Sounds like a sweet deal—if I'm not just trading one cage for another. I've got my own plans out West."

"With Mr. McBride, I know. I assume your intention is to pay off your debt with the profits you and your partner make in the private investigation trade. Do you realize how long that could take? How many years of wondering whether today is the day your, shall we say, creditors lose patience and decide merely to eliminate you? Can you afford that? Or would you prefer an independent position, perhaps overseeing a staff of your own, with very little interference from me or any of my partners. Though you seem to me a man of action, perhaps a safe lodging in an office far away from your troubles might be best for you." Her gloved hand, its rings flashing the car's light into Johnny's eyes, takes the ivory holder out of the emptiness she uses for a face. She detaches the shriveled brown cigarette that has started to look like a finger from a long-dead corpse, inserts a new one, and holds it up until Johnny manages to get it lit. "Your hand's just a bit shaky, Mr. Taggett," she laughs quietly.

Taggett just stares. His scar feels like a parade of ants on his face.

"I want to demonstrate to you that I mean what I say," says Mrs. Foulsworth, "I'd like to offer you a token of my sincerity, something for you to retain in your possession until I have need of it." The gloved hand comes back out, closed into a fist with its fingers down, and hovers over the table between them. "Consider this a provisional reward for your patience with the ramblings of a fellow passenger, or perhaps a reminder of the importance of what I offer to you and your future. Take it in good faith, Mr. Taggett."

Taggett looks at that small thin fist the way a mouse looks at a cobra. One of those black velvet fingers doesn't have a ring on it, but the other rings are doing tricks, the car around him vanishing into their fireworks display. His hand slides itself under hers as he stares, and she lets the Violet Diamond drop right into his palm. Those crazy whispers fill his head again for a moment. He shivers at the ring's touch, can't decide whether it's freezing or burning in his hand. His mouth gapes open, his cigarette drops onto his plate, into the pork chop he's been ignoring all this time, and he mumbles something like "I can't."

"Oh, but you can, Mr. Taggett, you must." Her whiskey purr has deepened into a steel growl, her words slipping into his mind the way a knife might slip between his ribs. "Your fortune and perhaps your very life depend upon the powers of this ring. Those it accepts become powerful and wealthy beyond their own imaginings. This ring descends to us from the rulers of the ancient world, and it recognizes you. I know you can feel it. I can see the effect it has on you. Keep it. Don't wear it, but keep it in a safe place. Hold it until we meet again. You'll see that I'm right, that what I offer you with this ring is what you truly must have."

"Uh," says Johnny. The sounds of the emptying dining car fade back in as Mrs. Foulsworth folds his fingers over the ring. He shudders a little at the touch of her velvet claws on his skin. He can feel the ring almost alive in his hand, so he slips the thing into his jacket pocket and gropes for a new cigarette. "That's quite a ring," he hears himself saying.

"Indeed," comes the reply. "Have a care, though. Just as the ring's acceptance of its host can make a world of success, its rejection can cast its host into a hell of failure. I've heard it said that those who betray the promise of the Violet Diamond simply vanish from history, their hopes and dreams no more than a sprinkling of dust in time's relentless gale. That shouldn't scare a rough tough customer like Johnny Taggett, though, I'm sure." Her voice is back to that playfully seductive lilt.

"Lady, I don't get scared. I get mad. Then whoever I'm mad at gets scared."

"Very impressive, Mr. Taggett. I certainly look forward to our next meeting." Taggett jumps to help her to her berth as she pushes her chair back and rises. "No need for your assistance this evening," she says. "I can make my own way back. Goodbye and thank you, Mr. Taggett. Do be careful. So much depends upon you."

As Taggett stands there watching her narrow black figure disappear into the darkness of the passageway between cars, he notices Ike smirking next to him. "That's some woman," says the waiter. "I guess," says Taggett.

CHAPTER EIGHT

He's still guessing as he lies in his bunk that night, staring up at the bottom of the bunk above him. "What kind of crazy story am I getting tangled up in," he mutters to himself. "I can understand being chased by a couple of goons, they've got a job, I even know those guys, but this Foulsworth dame talks like she's from another world. What could she possibly want from me? Some kind of bodyguard? Does she want me to knock off that weird mummy of a husband? And what the hell's with that guy anyway? What was he warning me about? What kind of master plan am I supposed to be fitting into here? And that ring." He can still feel it in his palm, even though he's got it stashed in the hat hanging on a hook behind his head, those foreign whispers still scratching around the edges of his consciousness. "What the hell is that thing doing to me, why is she trying to get me to hold on to it, how does she know so much about my plans, why doesn't any of this make any sense?" The questions chase each other around in his mind for a while until they turn into sheep jumping over a fence and then into just one big black ewe bleating in a language Taggett knows he could recognize if he just paid closer attention, and then he's not thinking anything at all.

Some time later he wakes up. His eyes are wide open, but they might as well be closed as the train rockets through the bare plain under a sky clotted with thick dark rain clouds. He slowly realizes that he's holding himself perfectly still, with his fingers around the grip of his forty-five: waiting. He may have been waiting for minutes or hours, he has no idea. He can't really figure out what woke him up. He's barely even sure he's awake in the total darkness. He can hear the harsh whisper of his own breathing over the ticking of his watch. It threatens to drown out the rattle of the train, so he holds it, lets it out slowly, breathes in as quietly as he can, and holds it. With his eyes bugging out and his body shaking, he waits.

After he doesn't know how long he hears a soft thud and then Beethoven hissing, "Shit!" The thug's trying to be sneaky, and now on top of holding his breath Taggett has to hold in a chuckle at the thought of the last time either of these animals worried about getting caught at something.

Brutus seems to agree with him. "What the hell are we pussyfooting around like this for, anyway," mutters the torpedo. "Let's just blast this sucker, collect his head, and get off this fucking train. She said this was his car, right?"

"Quiet, monkey, this Taggett's no joke. If he gets the drop on us he could—"

Taggett hears another thump, heavier than the first. His hand tightens on the grip of his forty-five. Nothing but the train makes a sound in the darkness. Someone lets out a breathy grunt, then there's another thud, then nothing again. Somebody moans with a sound like a metal can dragged along a gravel road. Soft footsteps, barely noticeable, get closer to Johnny's bunk. In the dark he can feel his berth's curtain shift just a little: someone's out there breathing. Seconds creep by while Johnny takes a new breath of his own and holds it. His scar's throbbing. The floor beyond that black curtain lets out a tiny creak. Slowly, quietly, letting out that breath, Taggett pulls his legs back a little, ready to spring, ready for a fight.

That's when a screaming of metal breaks into the night and the train jerks and stops, each car banging into the next, a clamor like a chain of giant firecrackers going off. Taggett's body drives his head into the wall behind him, but he keeps his grip on his forty-five and manages to control his fall out into the sleeper car. He swings his gun at some movement at the edge of his vision: a naked couple scurrying back into the bunk they must have been sharing. As the red emergency light clicks on overhead the still car fills with a babble of moans and curses, one or two sharp little shrieks rising from a couple of old ladies in an upper berth, shiny faces covered in some kind of green mud and gaping open when they see the size of the pistol Johnny's clutching.

But he's not listening to that now. He's whipping his head around to see where Beethoven and Brutus might have gotten to. They're nowhere. Blinking through the red mist in his eyes, he sees the fancy jerk from this morning still wearing those snappy yellow boxers under his robe and standing at the back end of the car, twenty-two in his fist pointing up at the ceiling, face pointed at Taggett. Their eyes meet for a moment, and the dude sneers and winks. Taggett growls and charges down the aisle at him. The guy steps backward into the dark space between the cars.

Taggett follows him through it to the next sleeper and hits something soft and warm, falling over a blonde body barely wrapped in a little silk robe. She smells just as pretty as she did this morning when he helped her out of that lower berth. Her breasts swell up against his chest with her breath as she pants, "What happened? Did we crash?" He doesn't say anything, trying to pull away, but she's got a grip on his arm. She's tangling him up. "Come on, you gotta know what's going on," she keeps yelling into his face, her voice getting as harsh as a parrot's, her big blue eyes getting all misty with tears. He finally manages to push her back down to the floor and get to his feet.

She's not the only one down there. The aisle's starting to fill up with passengers, some of them lying on their bellies, some of them on all fours, most of them lurching to their feet and staggering around like a bunch of drunks after last call on New Year's Eve. Johnny's peering into every blurry half-awake face, thinking the thugs might have shucked their suits to sneak up on him in this weird slumber party of a mob, but he doesn't get a hint of them, nor of that creep with the twenty-two. He lets the blonde crawl back toward her bunk and picks through the crowd. He's muttering deep in his throat as he pushes along: "That guy, what the hell, is he working with Beethoven and Brutus? Against them? Some other mob? Does he know me? Jesus, this is just too crazy, and why the hell didn't they attack me?" People are blinking at him, getting out of the way of the big guy and his gun, and he barely even notices. "Did someone crash this train to get at me? The Foulsworths? Jesus, I need somebody to punch some answers out of!" That really gets people out of his way and back into their bunks as fast as their shaky legs can manage. In no time Taggett's alone in front of the sleeper's back door.

He checks the thick glass window set into the steel sliding door: nothing but his reflection sketched in red. He cocks his gun and reaches for the door's handle. Licking his lips, he pulls it down, slams the door open, jumps out into the dark, and slams it shut.

The little space between the cars echoes flatly for a second as his bare feet hit the cold metal floor. Then silence and darkness, the smell of his sweat and a trace of the blonde's perfume clinging to his skin. He waits. He's pretty sure he's alone, but he needs to be certain, so he waits, detecting a rustle through the door behind him, a sound like sheets sliding over each other as the passengers filter back out into the aisle. Sneaking a new breath in between his lips, he reaches out for the handle to the dining car's door with his left hand. His right slips its finger over the trigger of his forty-five. He finds the handle, yanks down, slams the door open.

And there's Ike, framed by the doorway with his white shirt open around his neck, staring back at Taggett and his forty-five with that unflappable smile. Behind him the other waiters are putting themselves together and starting coffee under the emergency light. Ike finishes buttoning his shirt, starts to knot his tie, and says, "That's quite a hand-cannon you got there, Mr. Taggett. Something we can do for you?"

Breathing heavy, Taggett says, "Uh," and then, "Train. What the—"

"Oh, that was just some fool pulled the emergency cord. Seems like we get one of those every trip, there's always a joker who likes to stop the train as we're going over a ravine," chuckles Ike. "You just head on back to your compartment and the train'll get started up again just as soon as we find the damn fool and throw him off." The chuckle becomes a laugh. "I mean, we're gonna escort the fool from the train at the next station. Not like we're gonna toss him off the bridge. This here ain't no excitement, Mr. Taggett. Nothing you need a big old heater like that for."

Johnny blinks at the gun in his fist and points it down to the floor. "Yeah, sorry, there was this guy—"

"Ain't no guy been through here, Mr. Taggett." Ike's laying his accent on pretty thick here, talking slow and easy the way a stage hypnotist works his subject. "These boys and me would take care of anyone runnin through here, don't you worry. Sir." Taggett stands there in the doorway, sweating, staring at Ike. The older man smiles back as the waiters behind him go about their business. The clatter of cups against saucers tells Johnny how carefully they're not listening. "Anything else on your mind," says Ike, not really asking. "We got to get this train going."

Taggett eyes the old waiter, who blankly stares back. Shrugging, Johnny mumbles, "Okay, I guess you've all got it under control here," and makes the trip back to his berth. By this time the regular overhead light's back on, and the conductor's making an announcement to the scattered passengers about what happens when you pull the emergency cord and why you should never do it. Taggett snickers a little as he passes, still on the lookout for one or another of the thugs on his tail. He doesn't see them before he gets back to his bunk, and he's just too tired to scour the train for them. "Figure I'll get the jump on them later tonight or tomorrow or something," he tells himself. As he's getting ready to climb back in, he notices the door to the Foulsworths' compartment hanging open. "This fake emergency probably riled up those queer old birds. I better check to make sure they're in once piece, not too scared." He steps to the open door and into the empty room: none of their luggage is in there, and the hammock's off the wall. Taggett can't figure out anything to do but stand in the doorway as the train gives a heave and starts up again. The lights in the sleeper car go off as he stands there in the darkness trying to figure it all out. After a while he makes it back to his bunk and lights up a smoke, its burning cherry tip the only light in the car. In otherwise total darkness the train carries him forward, deeper into whatever he's mixed up in.

CHAPTER NINE

The Foulsworths are gone, Beethoven and Brutus are gone, that crazy little creep with the fancy shorts is gone, whatever happened that night doesn't make a speck of sense, and Johnny couldn't care less. As far as he can figure, all the crazies got off the train when it stopped in Chicago. "That's just fine," he tells his reflection in the washroom mirror, "Chicago can have 'em." For the last three days and nights he's been feeling more relaxed than he ever has, the empty scenery, plain then mountain then desert, flying past him through the windows of the train as he lets himself doze in his seat. He hasn't even bothered to chase after that blonde, the one who's been avoiding him since that sudden stop. He refuses to worry about any of it. "Guess every train ride's like this, a cute little babe to stare at, some rich freaks finding a patsy to play with, everyone looking for a sucker to pull into some kind of fairy tale game. I'm just no fun, I suppose." He finishes tying his tie, giving himself a little wink. "Good thing that's all over now."

Except that he's still got the ring. That Violet Diamond's been resting in a secret pocket in his suit coat ever since that weird night. He can feel the heat of it over his heart when he's dressed for dinner, and sometimes those whispers, those voices trying to warn him or guide him or whatever, sneak into his dreams. Even now, as he's getting himself ready for the end of this cracked odyssey and the beginning of whatever happens next, he can feel it vibrating in the back of his mind like a half-remembered but desperately important dream. With a shake of his head he shrugs it off and leaves the washroom with a hearty "All yours" for the next guy in line.

As he walks back to his seat the conductor's coming the other way along the aisle, calling out, "Ladies and gentlemen, San Francisco, end of the line, the Jewel of the Coast, the City by the Bay, the edge of the continent, ladies and gentlemen, make yourselves ready please, this is the end of the line, ladies and gentlemen, end of the line." He and Johnny manage to squeeze past each other, and the soon-to-be detective slips into his seat, watching his future come at him as the conductor keeps walking and starts to repeat himself. The trains on street level, in fact it's going right down the middle of the street: citizens drive their private cars alongside, and Johnny can glance down for a second and get a glimpse of what they're doing when they think no one's looking. He sees a guy picking his nose and another guy eating a big sandwich and wiping the grease on his sleeve. Another guy's got no pants on. Johnny chuckles as the train slows further, gliding down into an underpass, into the welcoming darkness of the depot, and coughing enormous bursts of steam as it stops.

Shouldering his half-empty knapsack, he steps off the train and onto the floor of the Ferry Building. It's crazy with people moving in all directions, the air as dense as the inside of a beehive. Lines are coming from and to Johnny's train and from and to another pointed the other direction across the vast area and even from three or four of those famous trolley cars criss-crossing the floor at weird angles. Various passengers on their various missions are starting to form into ranks as they approach the massive staircase far off to Johnny's left, looking up at the arches labeled "GROUND LEVEL—STREET EXIT" or down at their feet as they start to align themselves. Suddenly they're marching. Their footsteps have become rifle shots echoing in the giant station. They're all going somewhere, headed the same direction for a moment, just the way Taggett and his fellow soldiers did in training after he lied his way into the army. Some of those men are dead now, even in peacetime: a live grenade doesn't care about the armistice. Blinking away a sudden tear, the tough guy stands by himself and watches the citizens and hears his old drill instructor barking obscenities at them, getting them together, and getting them ready to fight in case the next war breaks out. "I'm ready," mutters Taggett.

The memories take over his mind for a long minute as he stands and watches until he notices a strange detail at the edge of the scene. Two figures are standing as still as fenceposts at either side of the giant staircase: a couple of Chinese guys in sharp black two-piece suits and skinny black ties, pork-pie hats over their long braids, are scanning all the faces that pass, and they're trying hard to be invisible. They're pretty good at it, too, not drawing attention even with the weird spectacle of how they're dressed, but Taggett recognizes a stakeout team when he sees one. "Wonder what they're looking for," he says to himself. Then he shrugs. "Doesn't matter. Not my problem. Not like I'm a cop around here." Tipping his fedora down over his eyes, he lights up a smoke and joins the march toward the blinding light streaming through the depot's pyramidal skylight. The habits he's picked up from his years on the wrong side of the law make him speed up a little as he passes the Chinese guys, pulling his head back between his shoulders, ducking a little, faking a limp. "Even if it's not me they're looking for," he mumbles to himself, "better safe than sorry."

The crowd breaks like a wave around Johnny as it reaches the top of the stairs, disintegrating into just a swarm of people greeting friends and relatives or running for the ferry. The blonde from the train clatters past him on her heels and jumps into the arms of a guy with a dockworker's muscles, squealing about how the train almost crashed and she almost died but she was so brave and she was thinking of him all the time, and her words fade back into the hum of the crowd. Taggett lopes away from the scene, wanders around the shiny tile floor, wonders if all the train stations in the country are big open cathedrals like this, and eventually drifts to a stop. "Made it," he says, even though he can't hear himself in the echoing hall. "Now what?"

Then he notices a strange disturbance, a ripple in the crowd, and it's headed his direction: guys jumping out of the way of something, girls squealing as they're bumped by something Taggett can't see yet. His scar gives a twinge and he starts to reach for his forty-five, until he sees what's causing the hub-bub. It's a little fireplug of a man dressed in a slick brown pinstriped suit complete with matching vest and derby and limping jauntily through the mass of humanity, lurching into passersby as he goes. Johnny's whole face lights up and he can't help yelling "Walt!"

"Johnny!" yells McBride.

The crowd seems to make a little clearing around the two men as they shake hands, Taggett grinning deep into his partner's liquid brown eyes. "You look like a million bucks," Johnny says.

"And you look like a giant pile of crap," says Walt. "Railway travel doesn't agree with you, I can tell."

Johnny lets out a snort of laughter. "Brother, if you only knew."

"Well, let's figure it out over coffee or something. You still drink coffee, right? Riding the rails with the Rockefellers hasn't gotten you hooked on champagne, I hope." Walt reaches up to slap Johnny on the shoulder. "Welcome home, you bum."

"Yeah, I guess this is home now," growls Taggett as he returns the slap, almost knocking unsteady McBride off his shiny gumshoes. "Better be something stronger to drink than coffee, though, or I'm on the next train back to New York."

Walt lets out a bellowing bark of a laugh that turns a few heads even in the random anonymous human noise bouncing around the terminal. Hushing himself with a smile that belongs on an adorable schoolboy up to some naughtiness, he says, "Old buddy, I think I know a place or two that can help with this horrible thirst you've developed. Just put yourself in my hands."

Taggett shrugs and follows the smaller man out through a pair of glass doors set into a wall big enough to remind Johnny of the barracks the army kept him in. McBride bobs and weaves through the mob on the sidewalk, bouncing off oncoming pedestrians like a cork in a stream, and Taggett follows on a fairly straight path, as the citizens who were about to yell at the little squirt who just bumped them take a look at the massive lug behind him and suddenly change their minds. The pair takes a right and a left and another left and some kind of diagonal downhill then uphill to get to a narrow alley paved with dirt between a couple of red wooden buildings tall enough to trap the sun into a little strip of light down the alley's center. McBride stops suddenly and turns to his left, knocking on a wooden door with no knob and painted exactly the color of the wall. Johnny would have walked right by it. A panel opens in the door, a pair of eyes peers out, and Walt mumbles a password, barely moving his lips. The door opens just enough to let him through and then a little wider to let Taggett into a long dark hall. At the end is a flickering lamp, revealing another featureless door with a smiling old Chinese man in front of it dressed in a blue robe, his shaggy goatee dripping down from his chin. "Ah, Mr. McBride," he whispers, bowing. "Welcome back, honorable friend, and may I have the pleasure of being introduced to your companion?" Walt vouches for Johnny and pulls a bill from his pocket, passes it to the doorman. Without a word the old fellow slips the bill into his robe somewhere and opens the second door, gesturing the partners into a surprisingly plush sitting room, walls covered in velvet that might be purple or black, candles in sconces leaking a little bit of dirty yellow light. McBride makes his way to a table in the corner, taking a seat with his back to the wall, and Taggett sits with his back to the corner's other wall, stowing his bag under the table. The partners spend a moment or two in the quiet dark of the speakeasy, just the murmurs of drinkers and a hint of opium smoke in the air.

    McBride gets a shiny silver flask out of his coat and holds it up in the air in front of everyone in there. "To crime!" he says. Taggett chuckles and follows suit with his own flask. After a few drinks they trade flasks, then a Chinese kid comes over with some thick, bitter beer. "On the house for Mr. McBride," says the kid, and that's the last that Taggett remembers for a while.

CHAPTER TEN

After a while the light starts hitting him right through his eyelids, so he pulls them open. It takes a little effort: they're stuck shut, and every muscle in his head is throbbing with the effort of opening them. His reward when he does is a shaft of light the color of an old chicken hanging from a butcher's hook. It's pushing through a little dirty window high in a blank wall directly into his throbbing eyes as he sprawls over the edges of an old army cot. A grinding grumble shoves its way up through whatever's lodged in his throat and whatever died in his mouth into speech: "Jesus, what the hell was in that beer?"

The crappy little apartment, one big room above the speakeasy where Taggett thinks he may have left his brain, fades in around him. Shabby furniture huddles in various clumps around the floor: a couple of mismatched chairs flank a table that's trying to lean away from both of them at once, and in a corner a couple of stools are holding up under the weight of a coffee pot and a hotplate plugged into the wall. There's some kind of dark wooden cabinet next to the door, squatting there like a forgotten pet. The cot Taggett's on lies along the wall opposite the window, and between them a giant Murphy bed hogs up most of the space. A smelly pile of dirty blankets takes up most of the bed.

"Shitter's down the hall," comes McBride's voice from somewhere deep in the pile.

Taggett makes some kind of noise to respond, stumbles out of the room in his t-shirt and shorts, and steps back in a minute later, saying, "Damn, who's been using that thing?"

The pile of blankets has grown McBride's head by this time, and he chuckles. "Yeah, those Chineses have a pretty wild diet. Amazing the smells they can make."

"Whatever, where's the coffee," Taggett's grumbling as he looks around the place. "And what the hell happened to my clothes?"

"Relax, Princess, I stashed your suit in the chest of drawers, over there by the door. The coffee's in the pot in the corner. You can warm it up on the hotplate, unless you're worried about messing up your manicure. Christ, didn't you use to be a tough guy?"

Laughing, Taggett tells him, "Tough enough for your gimpy ass any day of the week." The big man squeezes between the Murphy bed and the cot to get to the coffee pot, which is half full of a black liquid that shimmers like an oil slick as he swirls it around. "You sure this is coffee?"

McBride's still digging himself out of the blankets as he grins over at his partner. "Complaints, complaints, it's only three or four days old." Finally naked, he's rooting around for something on the floor between the bed and the windowed wall, giving Taggett a view almost as nauseating as the coffee starting to bubble on the hotplate with a noise like a lip-smacking dog. Taggett swallows and finds a random direction to look in for a moment until McBride comes up with some pants and screws his legs into them. Over the sound from the coffee Johnny can hear his old buddy hiss with pain. Glancing back, he sees Walt slip a hand into his pocket, as if he's checking for something in there as he limps toward the door. Walt catches Johnny's eye and grins: "Please, I get so self-conscious when you make those wolf-eyes at me. I'll just giggle like a schoolgirl or faint or something. Come on, Sarge, we're burning daylight." With a hiccuping chortle he staggers through the door.

Johnny looks at the door for a second, than he shrugs, finds his suit folded at the bottom of a drawer in the cabinet along with his hat and his forty-five, and gets himself dressed. Pulling on his coat, he checks to see if the ring is still in there. It still is, and his fingers get a little shock as they brush over it. He shudders and stands there for a moment, then he straightens out the blankets and pushes the Murphy bed back up into the wall. After a little search, he even finds a pack of smokes and a matchbook from someplace called the Lotus Club. He lights up and exhales stands there waiting.

The little man bounces back into the room after about half a cigarette. Hustling over to another cabinet Johnny can barely see in the gloom, he hauls out a clean shirt, a tie like an explosion in a paint factory, and a snubnose thirty-eight. "I see you're still carrying that buffalo gun around," snickers Walt. "What a bruiser you must be to need that kind of firepower. Police issue's always been good enough for me."

"Yeah, and your winning personality. Are we going somewhere? Today? I need to work off some of this haze in my head." Taggett can't help glaring down at the smaller man. "Is the office far from here?"

"Just a hop and a jump, old pal. We can get some noodles on the way. You've got some money, right?"

A creaky wooden staircase leads back down to the speakeasy, where McBride has a quick argument with the kid from last night. Taggett settles it with a five-dollar bill, and soon enough the partners are pushing their way through Chinatown, carrying little cardboard boxes full of thick noodles steaming with smells of spices Johnny can't identify. McBride's bouncing off the citizens, some dressed in shiny silk pajamas, others in suits like Taggett's, and the bigger man's shoving on along behind him, breathing in the hundreds of strange scents and trying to keep up. The city noise almost reminds him of New York, except that the babble of a thousand voices buying or selling or just carrying on life is in Chinese instead of Italian. The air's chilly, and he picks up his pace. McBride bobs and dodges around a couple of corners, then almost falls back into Taggett's arms as a wagon full of squawking chickens rumbles past, pulled by a guy losing his sweat in a fine mist around his fleshy head, a guy way too big to be running that fast.

Johnny can't help a little chuckle as he steadies his friend. "What's the rush? We don't punch a clock, do we?"

Walt's breathing heavy, and there's a muscle fluttering in his cheek as he says, "No good staying out in the open too long. You never know who's on your tail, know what I mean? This is the Wild West, old sport, where all the tough guys like us come to make their fortune, and they'll be happy to make it out of your skin if you're not careful. Anyway, this is it."

They're outside some sort of big wooden barn-like structure. "Used to be for grain storage when the cattlemen were in charge," Walt tells him as they step through a dusty glass door and into a bare lobby with a buzzing overhead light and a couple of threadbare couches flanking a weathered coffee table. They head through a door that says "OFFICES" and start up a long shallow flight of stairs. Even as Taggett starts to lose his breath, Walt's continuing the history lesson: "They tell me that after the big fire in oh-six the place was still standing somehow. They called it the Miracle Building, but any kind of real estate in Chinatown gets divvied up pretty quick." They make it to a landing labeled "2ND FLOOR," and Taggett goes for a green door to the left of the next flight of stairs going up, but McBride just turns the corner, pushing himself up the stairs and gabbing on about the rich heritage of whatever. Taggett follows, taking off his hat for a second to mop the sweat from his forehead, and they eventually get to the third floor landing. There's no sign, but the stairs stop: Taggett catches his breath and lights up a fresh smoke.

"Jesus," he says. "You do this every day?"

McBride lets out one of those weird laughs of his and says, "Sure, it keeps me in fighting shape. Besides, a big strong fellow like you should—"

The door they're heading for opens and a couple of Chinese guys step through it, dressed in sharp black suits with skinny ties. There's a splat as two little boxes of noodles hit the floor and burst, and then a moment of absolute silence while four right hands slip into four suit coats. Taggett's fingers are edging onto the grip of his forty-five, and he's guessing everyone else is feeling some steel right now. He takes a breath at the same time the other guys in this little box of a landing take a breath. The air in there's as thick as a glass of blood. The Chinese guys move a little to their left, toward the stairs, and Taggett and McBride slide a little to their right, toward the door. No one seems to have anything to say: careful breathing and the scrapes of shoes on the floor sound louder in the charged quiet. The spilled noodles are still steaming. Finally McBride gets to the door, gets his left hand on the knob, and opens it just enough to slip through. Taggett takes a moment to look at the tough guys standing at the top of the stairs and nods. One of the tough guys nods back. Taggett relaxes a little and steps back through the door.

McBride's standing a few feet down the hallway, looking like he's bracing himself for a fight. Taggett has to lean against the door and gawk at him for a second or two before he can find it in him to say as much as "What the hell?"

McBride relaxes a little and stands up as straight as he can. "Don't worry your pretty little head, partner. We're not the only ones with offices in this building, and some customers are just real sensitive about surprises. You know how it goes. I told you, this is the Wild West."

"Well, I didn't expect a gunfight my first day." Taggett straightens himself out and follows his partner down the dim hall, lighting up a fresh smoke as they walk between rows of plain doors with labels in English and Chinese and what he thinks must be Polish, until they get to the one that says "McBRIDE INVESTIGATIONS." Walt pulls out a key and opens up, explaining how he's gonna get that sign changed first thing. Johnny shrugs and looks around.

The office is a big dusty room with a window that looks out onto the buzzing street. Two desks occupy the room at right angles to each other: the one that faces the door, with a rusty old typewriter and two or three photos of hot dishes on it must be Walt's. The other one, Johnny's, faces the window across the office. It looks like the brother of the black and battle-scarred desk he left at the precinct. Johnny snorts, "You do all your furniture shopping at the dump?"

"Laugh it up, smart guy, I do just fine." As he's settling into his chair, squirming around a little and grimacing until he's leaning to the proper angle, McBride pulls open a drawer and shows Johnny the bottle inside. "In case you need a jolt. Sometimes the days get pretty long." He digs around in another drawer, finds a deck of cards, and starts dealing himself a hand of solitaire.

Taggett has a seat, his big hands flat on the desk in front of him. "Hey, I'm pretty sure I saw those guys from a minute ago at the train station when I came in yesterday. They looked like they were looking for someone," he says. "Are you in some sort of trouble?"

Walt's eyes stay on his cards. "I'm telling you, those guys are just another couple of shady bums from one of these offices. Come on, don't you know they all look alike?"

Taggett watches his partner play solitaire for a while, then he starts thinking about the future.

CHAPTER ELEVEN

And then a few weeks go by, and the future turns into the present. That crazy San Francisco fog is getting thicker in Taggett's head. The partners have settled into a routine: days in the office waiting for a job, nights drinking until one or the other passes out or gets in a fight. Usually it's Taggett who passes out and Walt who gets in the fight. Johnny knows how he solves his partner's problem, being tougher than most of the waiters and bartenders McBride explodes at, but he has no idea how that gimpy little guy drags home all the dead weight of big Johnny Taggett on the nod. As long as the money holds out he supposes he doesn't care much.

But the money's going pretty fast. Some afternoons he mutters to Walt about trying to get more work, like going out and wearing down some shoe leather looking for problems to solve, but Walt just tells him to relax and let the big time come to him. Johnny wonders if the big time will manage to get up all three flights of stairs, if the big time can even find the building, and if the big time will be speaking English when it shows up. He keeps his mouth shut, though: he's trying to develop the patience of a real gumshoe.

At least Walt managed to get the sign changed. Taggett can't see it through the cheap wood of the office door, but he knows he's officially part of McBRIDE & TAGGETT INVESTIGATIONS. Some nights after he's poured Walt into bed and shoved his own body as best he can into that crappy cot, he gets a little misty about his name on the sign. "My own," he mumbles as he drifts off. "Home of my own."

So time shoots forward as fast as a getaway car just before the alarm goes off, and it also crawls along as slow as a bad smell. The partners spend whole days waiting for that knock at the door that's not the mailman sniffing around for gossip. The air in the office gets thick with boredom: Taggett even starts to hope they run into those Chinese dudes with the skinny ties just to break up the endless wait for something to happen. He hasn't seen them lately, though, so he guesses that Walt was right and that the characters at the train station were someone else's deal. That's just fine with Johnny. After all that crazy stuff on the train from New York, he doesn't need to be caught up in anything Walt might be dealing with. Even though McBride can explain all the little changes in his behavior—why he seems so twitchy and secretive, where he disappears to every couple of days or so, how he manages to pay rent on the office without doing any kind of work he'll tell his partner about—Johnny can't help wondering if something's got hold of the smaller man's tail. He knows McBride's no gambler, but he's acting like one—a steadily losing one.

Right now, though, that's not Johnny's problem, as the tough detective sits alone in the office, smoking at his desk. Walt and all his troubles are in Los Angeles following a letter from the little sister Taggett never knew his partner had. Johnny offered a couple of days ago when Walt got the letter to go down there with him, but McBride just smirked and said, "No dice, partner. Someone's got to do the glamor work and stay to watch the office. Never know when the big time'll show up, right? Anyway, you can have the bed while I'm gone. Gotta be better than that army cot, right? Don't wait up for me, partner, I'll be back before you can forget my name." Taggett remembers that crazy bark of a laugh still echoing in the office as Walt slips out.

So there Johnny sits, his eyes following the big fat fly that's buzzing around McBride's desk. "Bet you're hoping for a little spilled booze," he tells the buzzing insect. "Sorry I'm not such a sloppy drinker." He reaches into his drawer and pulls out his own bottle, uncapping it, taking a pull, and wincing as the harsh whiskey hits his stomach and explodes. When he's satisfied, he tips the bottle over the corner of his desk just long enough to let a drop splash onto the black wood and almost soak in. The fly settles on Johnny's desk, and he lets out a little grumbling chuckle. "Drink up, why not, can't see what else goes on here anyway."

A soft knock at the door makes him twitch a little and spill another few drops right onto the fly. It shakes and tries to take off and falls to the floor as Johnny gets up from his desk. He drags his fingers through his hair, checks his tie, and breathes into his cupped hand just in case that noodle sauce is lingering. "First client," he tells himself. "Too bad Walt isn't around for this, but here goes." He clears his throat and yells, "Come on in!"

Nothing but silence answers him. His scar starts to heat up as three more knocks make their muffled way to his ears. The ring in his coat pocket, the ring he hasn't thought about in weeks, is heating up too. There's a little catch in his voice as he yells again, "Come in!" More silence, so he pulls his forty-five out, steps to the door, and puts his free hand on the doorknob. In one motion he turns it and pulls the door open, ready to blast whatever's on the other side.

What's on the other side looks at first like a featureless black statue, something carved out of ebony to be some crazy tribe's idol. As Taggett keeps looking, he realizes that the idol seems to be made out of velvet, then that it's breathing, then that it's Mrs. Foulsworth. Just as he puts it together, that familiar creepy chuckle comes across the door jamb. "Hello again, Mr. Taggett. You won't be so rude as to fail to extend a lady an invitation to enter, will you?"

"Uh, yeah. I mean no. I mean, uh, come on in." Stammering, Taggett holsters his forty-five and steps out of the way. Mrs. Foulsworth glides in and stands at the chair in front of Walt's desk. She reaches into the little black clutch she's carrying and comes up with that long ivory holder with one of her weird little cigarettes jammed into it. Johnny hustles around to the other side of the desk, finds a matchbook in Walt's chaos, and lights her cigarette. After she fits her holder into her veil, she holds out a hand until Taggett figures out he's supposed to take it and help her into the chair. He lowers her, feeling the strength of the talons beneath that velvet glove, and steps back around the desk, uncomfortable fitting himself into Walt's chair. "What, uh, what can I do for you?" he says.

"You seem surprised to see me, Mr. Taggett. Did you think that I had abandoned you? That I'd given you custody of the Violet Diamond and simply vanished? By the way, you do still have the ring, do you not?"

"In a safe place," Taggett tells her. In his coat pocket the ring flares white-hot for a fraction of a second. He almost flinches. Talking fast to cover, he says, "Is that what's on your mind? Do you need it back?"

"Have you worn the ring, Mr. Taggett? Have you slipped it onto your finger and felt its power?" The black figure's leaning forward in its chair, and Taggett can hear a snarl of hunger in her questions.

He takes a long steady look at the blank where her face should be and says, "No, I don't really go for that kind of look. The only kind of jewelry I go for is brass knuckles."

"Oh, Mr. Taggett, I'd forgotten how utterly droll you can be." As that chuckle emanates from her once more, she leans back a little in her chair and seems to look around the office. "And you furnish your office with such exquisite taste. I see that you insist on surrounding yourself with the trappings of success. You must be simply dizzy with all the action in your new business, serving so many of this lovely neighborhood's upper crust."

Taggett feels his lips tighten. He takes a moment to light a smoke of his own. "We might not travel in your circles, lady," he tells her, "but someone has to help the poor dopes who can't buy their own cops. We do just fine."

"You most certainly do not 'do just fine,' Mr. Taggett." He can hear the sneer in her voice as she sits perfectly still in the flimsy wooden chair. Just the way it did on the train, her playful purr has frozen into gunmetal. She carefully takes the cigarette from its holder and stubs it out on Walt's desk, leaving a little pockmark in the wood, leaving the stub where it lies. "Although the charming gentlemen who followed you from New York seem to have somehow fallen to their death from a moving train, your debt remains, does it not? Might not the Russian extract an even more sever penalty from you? And what about your pitiful existence here? Do you not find yourself three flights of disintegrating steps up from a festering mob whose language you don't even speak? Have you not pledged your future to a sick, pathetic cripple? Are you starting to understand what a terrible mistake you've made, what a horrible travesty of your dream you've allowed your life to become?"

Outside in the hall a door opens and closes, and that's the only sound in the office. Taggett's eyes have narrowed almost shut as he considers his reply. After a long few seconds his throat works and he manages to speak: "You're quite a piece of work, aren't you?"

"I indubitably am, Mr. Taggett. I'm a piece of work that could make your life worth living." The featureless black figure leans forward again. "When we last spoke I made you an offer, and it still stands. I like the way you handle yourself, even when you're being so directly insulted. A lesser man would have evicted me from his office, while you clearly have the perspicacity required to hold your temper and continue listening. You know what I can do for you, and you don't want to miss your chance at the shiny brass ring." She takes another cigarette from her clutch, fits it to the holder, and waits until Johnny lights it for her to keep going. "I suppose that I can see a certain amount of honor in the way that you cling to your friend, as if he has anything to offer you. I value such dedication, and I'm prepared to pay handsomely for its exercise. You must see the attraction of my proposition's generosity."

Taggett blinks. Those crazy whispers that started scratching around the edges of his consciousness around the time she mentioned the ring just now are distracting him, and the smoke from her cigarette just hangs between them in the room's still air, smelling a little like the opium from the speakeasy downstairs. His voice comes thick and slow as he tells her, "I can't just ditch my partner. Listen, I have to talk this over with him when he comes back—"

"From Los Angeles, yes, I know. You can't imagine that I would allow myself to remain ignorant of your Mr. McBride's fascinating situation." The ember at the end of her cigarette glows bright red as she takes a breath. "Mr. Taggett, you must comprehend the extent of my resources. I came here to offer you the opportunity to become one of them, to connect yourself to the power at my command." She takes the gnarled stub of her cigarette from its holder, lays it next to its dead comrade on Walt's desk, and lets out what must be a sigh: "Do you recall what a pleasant experience we had together on the train from New York? Perhaps we should try that again some time, a private little personal conversation over an intimate little dinner. You do strike me as a ladies' man, Mr. Taggett, unless I'm underestimating you."

Johnny can't think of anything better to say than "Yeah, I guess I do all right."

"I'm sure you do. But tell me, how was your luck with that blonde? You know, the one with that fetching little satin negligee. When I saw the two of you there on the deck of the sleeping car together, I felt sure you would take advantage somehow, but you seemed to lose interest. Do you fold under pressure, Mr. Taggett? Do a younger woman's charms intimidate you?" She's sitting on the edge of her seat as if she's ready to leap across the desk and tear him apart the way a wild dog tears up a package of ground beef. "Tell me, do you lie awake some nights and wonder what it would be to have the strength and vitality of your youth to serve the wisdom you've acquired with age?"

The cigarette nearly falls out of Taggett's mouth as he puts his hands flat on the desk and leans forward to match her, nearly coming out of his chair. He speaks slowly and carefully, trying for the most soothing tone he can manage: "Lady, what the hell are you talking about?"

The black figure relaxes back into her chair with another of those creepy chuckles. "Such vulgarity. You'll shock an old lady, sir. But I can detect your sincerity when you say you need time to think." Her posture straightens as Taggett stands and walks around the desk to take the hand she's extending. He has no trouble helping her out of her seat, but he can feel the bony fingers under the velvet glove clutching him the way a parrot clutches a seed it's about to crush. "I shall return in one week's time," she tells him, "and I shall expect your answer. Consider it carefully, as it determines your entire future. Good day, Mr. Taggett. Do give my regards to your partner." Without waiting for his reply, she opens the door herself, and then she's gone, and the silence settles back in.

Taggett settles back into his own chair and spends a little time contemplating the fly drowned in whiskey on the floor by the corner of his desk. After a few minutes of that, he growls, "Oh, the hell with this," stands up, jams his hat on his head, and starts the trek downstairs toward a real drink and some human company.

CHAPTER TWELVE

The sun's going down behind Taggett's building, casting a big flat shadow over him as he pushes his way through the evening crowd. Once he gets to the other side of the street he lights up a smoke and takes a look at the old grain warehouse he just came out of. Then he turns around and meanders deeper into the shadow. He doesn't really know where he's going, just following his nose to the nearest clip joint. After he wanders around for a while through the thickening dusk, he ends up stumbling down a narrow dirt alley with a shaft of dying sunlight painting a yellow stripe down its spine: he's back at the speakeasy downstairs from Walt's apartment.

After exchanging the password with the first doorman and giving up a fin to the second doorman, he sinks into the cool dark of the little barroom. He raises his hand to signal the waiter, and the boy comes over with one of those crazy dark beers, just the way Taggett likes it, but he doesn't even make it halfway through the glass before he's up and out again into the night. "You need a woman," he tells himself as he stomps down the alley.

After not too long he's in another alley, down at the bottom of some hill. Broken glass crunches under his feet. Jazz from a jukebox is drifting through the unlit air, guiding him around a corner and down a little further to a dirty little storefront nestled like a mass of toejam between a couple of white marble office buildings abandoned for the night. He gives the grimy wooden door a knock. At the first tap of his knuckles it opens right up. A smell of cheap gin and cigarettes billows out at him, and he mutters, chuckling, "Holy hell, this town is just wide open, isn't it? I guess Walt was right about the Wild West." Licking his lips, he steps through and lets the door swing shut behind him.

The place is even darker than the basements Walt's been taking him to, but it's definitely populated. The light comes from a surprisingly modern jukebox playing a scratchy old Benny Goodman record. Smears of red and yellow taint the wall behind it and pool on the floor where a couple of couples are leaning on each other, too tired or drunk to do anything but sway. A ring of mismatched tables and chairs around the perimeter defines the dance floor, and most of the chairs hold what seem to be bums on the nod. Taggett finds an unoccupied seat and drops his big body into it.

After a while the record ends, then it starts again. The couples on the floor don't seem to notice. They just keep swaying together, holding each other up as if they're in the course of losing a marathon. As Taggett sits there and watches them, wondering what the hell is going on in his life, a leathery woman in a white ball gown ambles toward him. The gown's got some weird stains on it, and the woman's eyes look like the marbles in a stuffed vulture, but Johnny can't take his eyes off her sway as she approaches. She gets to his table, leans down so he can get a better look at her shiny cleavage, and says to him, "So, ya gonna order a drink or are ya just gonna let that big body of yours keep holding down your chair?"

He gets an eyeful and gives her a chuckle. "Yeah, sure," he says, "drink's what I'm here for. What can I get?"

"Mister, in here you can get pretty much anything you want." She gives him back his chuckle with all the good feeling drained right out of it. "The boss is in tight with the mayor or the chief of police or someone. I dunno, I don't ask questions. Just tell me what you're drinking and get it over with."

Taggett wastes a second or two blinking at her. She just stares back until he says, "Uh, whiskey," and hands her a sawbuck. Then she shoves the bill down her dress, wiggles away to a bar he can barely see in the gloom, and comes back with a bottle and a passably clean glass. Without another word she disappears back into the darkness. Taggett cracks the bottle open, pours himself a drink, and grimaces as it hits his gut. "This'll kill the pain for a while," he tells himself.

So there he sits, staring at whatever his face is pointed at while he pours and drinks and pours, until he notices the fresh ripe tomato standing next to the jukebox, the red and yellow light caressing over her curves. She's wearing a silk dress of some color that Johnny can't make out in the darkness, and he's getting a little jealous of the way it's clinging to her, so tight he has to wonder what her skin feels like under it. He squirms a little in his seat and pours himself another drink. The record finishes. The girl leaning against the wall is staring at Johnny through a pair of smoky, heavy-lidded eyes, and he's staring right back. As the record starts up again she pushes herself forward and moves across the floor toward him, stepping around the sloppily shuffling dancers. She's gliding like a boat in a dream. He can't stop gawking. "Hope this isn't just another waitress on the make," he grumbles to himself. Finally she gets to his table and has a seat in the other chair.

Her voice drips like honey from her mouth as she purrs, "Hello there, Hercules. Been waiting for me?"

He's just slick enough to come up with "Only all my life" in return, and that gets a soft laugh out of her, the kind of a laugh most women can only manage in the bedroom. Johnny manages to keep himself from jumping over the table, but he can't help twitching a little. Her big green eyes catch a drifting fragment of the jukebox's light and flash black for a second. Her perfume, some kind of deep and promising scent probably only half store-bought, probably mostly the smell of her soft hot body, isn't helping his self-control.

"Well, aren't you a cutie," she says. "I like a man who's good with his . . .mind." She gives him a wink that would make old Edgar Foulsworth stand up out of his chair. "So, Sampson, what are we drinking tonight?" She reaches across the table between them and picks up Johnny's glass, takes a swallow, grimaces. "Battery acid, nice. I hope you don't mind having to drink from the bottle, but I'm sure you can tell I'm a lady." Another one of those laughs floats into the bar's thick air, as she pulls out a smoke and puts on a show of waiting for a light.

Taggett figures it out, lights a cigarette for her and one for himself while he's at it. "Don't worry about that, I'm a Wild West buckaroo just off the trail. You're a pretty fast worker yourself, I see."

She stops smirking for a moment and beams those eyes right into his. "When I see what I want, I go get it. Why waste time?" She takes another belt of Taggett's whiskey, squirming from the heat as it goes down. "I guess it gets smoother as you drink more. Must be good stuff." Her deep red lips curl back into a half-smile, the grin of a cat who's found a slow canary. Taggett likes that kind of grin: he likes it when the prey thinks it's the predator. The two of them sit there for a lingering moment, drinking and sizing each other up as the record starts and stops and starts and finally doesn't start again. In the weird silence as the slouching couples start to mutter and the waitress heads toward the jukebox, she says, "We should find some other place to be. Got any ideas?"

"Lady, I got all sorts of ideas."

Many drinks later they're staggering up the stairs to Walt's apartment, and he isn't quite sure how they got there, but he knows the night air on the way didn't do a thing to sober them up. He's got a hand cupping one of her soft round cheeks, feeling the warmth of her skin through that dress, to keep her from pitching over as they climb. She doesn't seem to mind. In fact, about halfway up she turns, raises a hand to his face, and kisses him, her lips lingering for a long warm moment, opening his mouth with hers, her tongue darting in and playing around. She tastes like whiskey and cigarette smoke. Johnny makes a caveman kind of growl deep in his throat and hustles her up the stairs and down the hall to the crappy little room he's been sleeping in. Tonight he gets the bed.

Tangled up in each other, they make it to the door. He stabs a couple of times with his key at the keyhole until she takes it from him, makes a couple of stabs of her own, and manages to open the door. They tumble in together. In the dark they make it toward the bed that Johnny hasn't bothered to close into the wall, and then they fall in, flailing around and getting more and more naked. Soon enough, he's down to his boxers, she's down to her stockings, and they're just about ready for heaven when he shocks himself with a yawn he can't help. He recovers and looks down and notices that her eyes have drifted shut. Her body, warm under his, is twitching a little, moving in the underwater patterns of the dreamer. Rolling off of her, he manages to let out a little chuckle before the whiskey turns everything soft and black, raven's wings carrying him away.

CHAPTER THIRTEEN

Some time later his eyes snap open in the dark. Something he can't put his finger on is wrong. He lies there frozen for he doesn't know how long, trying to figure it out. Some little sound, some tiny shift in air pressure. The warm body next to him snores a little and turns over with a soft sleepy moan, and then he notices a faint grey sliver of light from the hall. Walt's door's an inch open. Somebody's in there with them.

As he rolls off the bed the room explodes. The grinding of a machine gun splits the night open. The air above his head's on fire with bullets, and it smells like basic training in the little apartment, like the night Flagely got killed, that hot metal smell he can't forget. He's on his hands and knees, sweaty palms slipping on the floor's cheap tile as he crawls under the bed, scrabbling for his forty-five. He finds it in its holster on the floor where he must have tossed it last night when he came in. The thunder doesn't stop. From his belly on the floor he can see what might be a pair of legs obscure the open door, striping the grey light with black. He takes aim, but the shadow flickers out of view. Fire's flashing around him. Blinking as the muzzle-flashes blind him, he gets a snapshot in his mind of a pretty girl across the table from him drinking his whiskey. He can't help snarling deep in his throat. He puts his back flat against the bottom of the bed and straightens his legs, pushing it back into the wall, hiding her in there, exposing himself against the crappy little room's back wall as he sights down the barrel, blasting a shot to either side of the door. Then he drops back to the floor and spins out of the way as another burst of lead flies over him, and then another. He squeezes his trigger again and blows the door out of the jamb with the force of his weapon. A shadow slips through the dim rectangle into the hall, and then the little room falls silent again. A shout from the speakeasy downstairs, another couple of hammering bursts and someone's trapped-animal scream tell him that whoever was here has either faded into the night or gotten murdered by now.

"What the hell?" mutters Taggett as he comes fully awake? "Someone after me? But who knows I'm here, this is Walt's place. So is someone after Walt? But who, what's he into? Is it those Chinese characters? Where the hell is he? What the hell is going on? Who'd sneak in here like this, why didn't he just kill me in my sleep? That creep could've shot me dead; I know I was right in his sights. He couldn't have missed. Why didn't he . . . oh, no." He turns his head away from the door to see the bottom of the folded up Murphy bed full of holes and dripping blood. His growl nearly a moan, his eyes open so wide they're bulging out of their sockets, he reaches up to pull it down, and there she is. There's what's left of her. That creep must have been carrying a Tommy gun: the high-powered bullets have chopped the girl into various cuts of wet meat strewn over the wrecked bed, cooling to room temperature and smelling like a butcher's shop in early May. Her eyes are open, as if the noise of the gunfire woke her up just in time to make her feel the pain. Somehow he's bent close enough to her face to see his reflection in them. He can't seem to catch his breath. It's not the first dead body he's seen, but he can't stop staring. He can feel the cold sweat oozing out of his scalp, and his scar's on fire. The forty-five weighs heavy in his hand, just a lump of metal, as he pulls his eyes away from the mess on the bed and starts glancing around Walt's apartment, interrogating the scene for some clue to what just happened.

The room's as dead as the girl is. The force of the flying bullets has smashed the coffee pot and the stool it sat on. The table and chairs have joined each other as a pile of splinters. There's another pile of rubble over where Walt's chest used to be: the light from the hall is making little pieces of glass glisten in the chaos of black wood and shredded gaudy rags. "Crazy," he murmurs. "This is way too much firepower just to murder someone. Doesn't make any sense." He turns back to the corpse, takes another long slow look, this time with his detective skills engaged, and doesn't see anything that tells him anything. "Maybe someone's after her, not like she had a chance to tell me much." He blinks once or twice as he realizes: "I never even knew her name. Shit, I wonder if she has anyone to miss her." Pacing back and forth around the bed, he's still talking to himself. "Get a grip, flatfoot. Whatever the hell just happened, it's over now, time to figure out your next move before someone blows up the goddam building."

    A draft through the big hole that used to be the front door reminds him that he's still standing there barefoot in his boxers. He can't help shivering a little. It takes him a minute or two of searching to find a pair of pants and a shirt that aren't blown full of holes or made for a much smaller man: he has to try on a couple of Walt's crooked trousers before he finds a pair of his own. He gets into some trouble putting on his shirt because he doesn't want to put down his forty-five, but he figures it out, manages to get his hat onto his head and shrug into his coat, and even stumbles over a pack of smokes. "Nice piece of luck for me," he catches himself chuckling, and the back of his tongue burns like acid. He grimaces, shoves his feet into his shoes without even looking for socks, and gets out of there, staggering down the hall toward the staircase with an unlit cigarette stuck to his bottom lip.

    He notices about halfway down that the screams haven't stopped. They're more like wails, really, not so much the sound of someone with a bullet wound as the sound of someone with a torn soul. The shrieks are enough to slow him down a little, but just a little. "Got to get to the office," he's telling himself. "Got to get to the office, find that phone number for Walt's sister, make sure he's okay, no time, what if they know where he is," he keeps muttering as he gets to the bottom of the stairs. The screams are coming from behind the door to his left, the backdoor to the speakeasy. Usually it's locked, but tonight it's hanging open, a jagged hole where its knob used to be. He tries the door to his right, the one clearly marked EXIT, and it doesn't budge, so he follows the killer's path into the speakeasy.

As he steps through the door he can see the second doorman, the old guy he always has to pay off to get in, crumpled in a bloody heap with a red hole in place of his heart, half in the lap of the big guy, the first doorman, who's kneeling in front of the entrance, howling his grief to the otherwise empty room. It's darker in there than he's ever seen it: all the lights are out, and just a glow from the street outside crawls in down the hall to outline the figure kneeling and shrieking. The sight stops Taggett in his tracks. "Damn," he grumbles to himself. "Only one way out of here and it's through that mess. I don't have time for this shit."

The soft rasp of Johnny's voice must be carrying tonight: the wailing man in front of the door breaks into shocked muteness for a second. He turns his face, tracking Johnny's voice. Then his cry comes back, even louder, the big doorman's eyes blazing blindly into Taggett's: "You! You white devil! He say this all about you! All your fault! He say you lousy deadbeat gambler! He say you pay his money or next time he don't just kill your girlfriend, he kill you too! He kill everyone! He kill Wong!" The harsh yells dissolve into more sobs as the doorman bends down and kisses the forehead of the corpse he's holding. Taggett's never heard him speak before, never seen the doorman's round face twisted like this into a gaping mask of melted rubber. The shouts echo off the little room's walls like a series of slaps to the tough detective's face. "Wong never hurt no one! Wong never done nothing! Why Wong have to die for you? Why you no pay the man's money? You nothing! You no good! Damn you white devil! You get out! Never come back! Get out this place! White devil! Get out!" He's screaming curses straight from hell, and then something in Chinese, probably even more horrible curses, and then just the cries and whimpers of a tortured animal. Taggett can't move. He can't stop staring. He can't say anything. Slowly, the cries get softer and die in the big doorman's throat. A spasm shudders through his body like an electric shock. He sniffs, swallows, and gets up, carrying the body of the smaller man away from the entrance and into the depths of the wrecked room's darkness. A door opens and closes and Taggett's completely alone.

The unlit cigarette's still clamped between his lips as he staggers across the room and down the hall and out into the alley. A cold wind cuts through his skin and blows the cigarette out of his mouth. The sirens he can hear coming toward one end of the alley, toward the front of the building he could have thought of as home, make him head the other way, into the dead of night, headed for the office and a phone, scar throbbing on his face, ring pulsing in his pocket. He doesn't even glance back at the building he's never going into again. He can't do anything for anyone in there.

CHAPTER FOURTEEN

The morning sun punches him in the face through the office window. He's slouched in his chair across from it, feeling like someone's rubbed the inside of his eye sockets with sandpaper, his right hand resting on the desk over his forty-five. The office is as wrecked as the inside of Johnny's head, all the contents of Walt's desk—his bottle, his Tijuana funnybooks, the photos he keeps of all the showgirls he's plowed, notes in some kind of cramped scribble Taggett can't decipher—scattered all over the floor like sawdust and peanut shells in a barroom. The big detective groans as he remembers pulling his partner's desk apart, looking for that phone number, finding nothing but junk. Blindly, he reaches for a smoke, lights it, and tries to figure out his next move. On the other side of the window, the city goes on about its business.

The sudden ringing of the phone makes his whole body jerk like a hooked fish. He nearly spits out his cigarette. His eyes dart around the room until he spots the little black cylinder vibrating with its own noise on the floor next to the bottle Taggett emptied last night as he was ransacking the office. He dives for it, yanks the earpiece from its cradle and yells into the base: "Hello? Walt? Are you okay, did they get you?"

Nothing comes back for a minute but the underwater noise of a crowd milling around. "Must be a pay phone," Johnny grumbles to himself. "Damn things never work at all." Into the featureless sound he yells again: "Hello! Walt! Tell me what's going on! Say something, damn you!"

Out of the earpiece comes a voice that eerily reminds Taggett of his partner's, except for its weird tremble and faint Chinese accent. "Is that Johnny Taggett?" it says. "I'm calling for Johnny Taggett. The private investigator." Whoever's on the other end of the line sounds like someone swallowing a rotten piece of meat and trying not to puke on the dinner table?

Taggett feels his jaw get tight as he growls, "Who the hell is this, the creep from last night? Listen, punk, when I find you—"

"No, no, Mr. Taggett, I'm not—I don't—whatever happened to you last night, I had nothing to do with it." The voice pauses. Johnny can hear the deep breathing of someone trying to keep from breaking down. "I'm, uh, well, Mr. McBride told me I should try to find you if there's any trouble. He said they'd probably attack the apartment, so you'd probably be in your office, so I called, and—"

"Enough!" Taggett bellows. "Who the hell are you, what do you know about last night, why isn't Walt on the phone, why aren't you answering my question?" As he yells he can feel his scar burning like a thin stream of acid dripping down the side of his face. He's gripping the phone so tight his knuckles are creaking and popping.

Nothing comes out of the earpiece for a long moment but that shuddering breath, and then the voice comes back a little more softly but with a little more steel in it. "Mr. Taggett, my name is Chen Hao Ye. Mr. McBride's my boss, I do little jobs for him like following creeps and keeping my eyes open for whatever happens on the street. I don't have any idea what happened to you last night, I got your office number from the business card Mr. McBride gave me. And he's not on the phone because . . . because he's dead. I saw them kill him." The quiver in the voice breaks into a trembling sob, then works itself back into speech. "We were . . . we were at Midlands Hospital, waiting for . . . sitting next to each other on the bench there, waiting for a doctor Mr. McBride needed to talk to, and these guys in black suits and skinny ties came over and asked him if he was the Walter McBride from San Francisco, the private investigator. I thought it was weird to see a couple of Chinese guys dressed like that, especially down here, but I was concentrating on something, I don't know, I should have been—" Chen sucks in another breath. "I should have been watching. He didn't make a sound. I just happened to glance back at them when I saw the, uh, when I saw their switchblades, saw them . . . they stabbed him, like, four or five times before I could even get my legs uncrossed, I couldn't do anything, one of them just smashed me over the skull with something. They could've killed me too, I don't know why they didn't. They were gone when I woke up and I, I, oh, Jesus, he was bleeding, I had to leave him propped up there on the bench, had to get away before the cops got there, I couldn't let them . . . well, that doesn't matter. He's dead, Mr. Taggett. Mr. McBride's dead."

Sitting on the floor, hunched over the phone, Johnny has nothing to say. He swallows a few times, notices his smoke's gone out, and puts down the earpiece for a moment to light up a new one. He can hear a faint voice calling his name from the little black hollow of plastic on the floor next to him, but he takes his time getting the flame to the tip of the cigarette. His hands shaking. He stares at the flame of the match until it steadies, then blows it out and picks up the phone again. "Okay," he grits out. "Where are you?"

"I'm, uh, I'm at a payphone by Union Station. I figure if I want to see these jerks coming the safest place for me is in a crowd of white folks."

"Okay. Okay." Taggett's mind's racing the way a rat would run around a shrinking cage. "Let me figure this out. You got a safe place there, somewhere you can hide until this all blows over?"

"No, I'm from San Francisco, I don't know anybody here but Mr. Mc—I guess I don't know anyone."

"Shit, that complicates things." Taggett glances around the office, waiting for the answer to come to him. It doesn't come. A chime sounds in the earpiece, then an operator talking through her nose asking for five more cents for the next three minutes.

"Mr. Taggett," Chen says, "I'm running out of nickels. Maybe I should join you there. I've still got my return ticket; I can get on a bus and be up there in a couple days."

Taggett relaxes his grip on the phone a little bit. "Yeah, okay, good idea. I'm gonna be hiding out until then, I'll figure out some hole in the wall to lay low in. You had been to the office here before?"

"No, I always meet Mr. McBride in a little speakeasy he knows, the door's in an alley off Martinez. Maybe we could—"

"I don't think I'm welcome back there," Taggett interrupts with a dry attempt at a chuckle. "The doorman probably wants to kill me."

A more realistic laugh comes through the phone. "Mr. McBride told me a little about what a winning personality you've got. Is it true that you once took a swing at your chief of police?"

"Yeah, but he swung first. He thought he was tough." The detective blinks once or twice, and the room seems to come into focus for the first time in days. "I told him he'd be crying like a little girl if he had to go through half the shit I've taken, and he gave me one in the jaw. I remember I just winked and gave it back to him. He ended up on the deck. I ended up at my desk for the next month. It was worth it." He takes a look at the empty desk in his office, the job waiting for him. "Thanks for reminding me of that, kid. Listen, I figure if you've got enough on the ball to work for Walt, you can find our office without too much fuss. I'll see you here day after tomorrow, first thing in the morning. We'll figure out the next move together." Holding the phone, Taggett stands up.

The quiver's completely gone from Chen's voice: "We're going to get them, aren't we? We're going to get those creeps that killed him, aren't we, Mr. Taggett?"

"Yeah. We're gonna find them, and we're gonna get them." The tough guy takes a long drag from his cigarette. Just before he puts the phone back on its hook and gets ready to start, he remembers to say to the kid, "And call me Johnny."

CHAPTER FIFTEEN

A couple of days later he's looking at the old grain warehouse his office is in through the greasy plate glass window of Lee Ming's, the noodle house across the street. He's been staying in old Ming's back room, smoking and thinking and letting the office stay empty. In the back of his mind he can hear Walt giving him a hard time for the business he's missing, but he tells that ghost, "My only business now is to stay alive long enough to send whoever killed you to Hell." He hasn't changed clothes or shaved. He's starting to look like just another bum, the guy you don't even see as he's following you, learning your secrets. Hat tipped over his eyes, he's hunched over a table, fumbling around with his chopsticks in a bowl of some kind of spicy noodles, when he notices a figure in black cutting through the crowd outside the way a raven cuts through air currents. He coughs and drops his chopsticks: "Oh, shit, what's she doing here now?" By now he's learned to recognize Mrs. Foulsworth. Slouching down into his seat, he watches her glide toward the old grain warehouse. The ring in his pocket gives a sharp, hot pulse.

"Wonder if she saw me," he mutters to himself. "Can't tell, the way she's all shrouded like that, can't even see which way her face is pointed, really." He keeps watching as she slips into the building. "Okay, guess not." He breathes a little sigh of relief until he realizes that she's probably going to haunt his office door for a while. "Shit," he says again, and calls to Ming for another bowl of noodles and sausage.

For a few hours he watches the parade of citizens back and forth beyond Ming's dirty window. He recognizes a couple of the local working girls who've squeezed themselves into drab sweaters and skirts to go shopping, one of them pushing a stroller. He sees a thin man fall into step behind a guy wearing a suit, a white guy obviously lost, and keeps looking as the skinny local boosts the white guy's wallet so gracefully that the white guy never breaks stride. A gravelly snicker pushes through Taggett's lips at that sight. A minute later, the pickpocket almost strutting in the other direction, some passing goon just punches him in the face, knocks him to the sidewalk, and takes the white guy's wallet. Taggett has to put a hand over his mouth to stifle the laugh. Nursing that bowl of sausage and noodles, the tough detective watches the light in the street change from morning white to afternoon orange to the blues of dusk.

Soon enough, night comes on. The street starts to empty as the day people pack up their stalls and head back to their homes for dinner, then it fills up again as the night people come out, mostly whores and johns, and get to work. He's been staring at the crowd all day, and he hasn't seen Mrs. Foulsworth leave the building. He grumbles, "Jesus, what is that old lady made of? Has she been hanging around my office door all this time?" Stubbing out his last smoke onto the table, he pushes his chair back and stands. "Guess I'll have to go find out what she's doing. Hell, maybe she's got something to do with what happened to Walt. Way my luck's going, she's just here to finish the job from the night before last." He chuckles. "At least that'll give me an excuse to shoot that freak, see if she bleeds."

By now he's made it to Ming's front door. He glances back and tells the old shopkeeper, "Keep my room for me one more night." Without really hearing the reply he opens the door and finds himself facing a wall of flesh in a sweat-stained grey suit. The fat boy on the other side of the door just stares at him, shifting from foot to foot the way a sailor stands on deck, not saying a thing. He seems to be smiling, but Johnny can't tell through the grime on the creep's mug. "What the hell," says Taggett, and El Gordo just pushes out a big doughy paw, palm up like a bellboy waiting for a tip. Ming's behind Taggett in the shop somewhere, being a great big help by staying out of it. It's just one tough detective and the fat boy standing in his way. "Listen," Johnny tells him, "it's not like I'm a big hurry, but I just finished my last pack of smokes and I need to get some more and do some business. I'll ask you nicely if you'd mind getting out of my way."

The fat boy just keeps standing there and swaying. His eyes, little pools of blankness in the big pink pool of his face, look like they're staring down into Johnny's. They don't betray a flicker of response. The hand stays out. A silence stretches between the two men on either side of the door, a silence thick enough to mute the street noise around the scene. Taggett's scar's starting to tingle. The fat boy's starting to look like that grasshopper back in New York, the creep that used a hidden razor to mark Taggett's face. El Gordo here's got that same kind of glassy stare. He doesn't move, but his jowls are starting to twitch up into what might be a smirk.

Taggett snarls, "I can see how you might be local color around here, but I'm not in the mood. I got nothing for you. Step aside." The grin on the boy's face just gets wider. His lower lip, the color of raw veal, is getting shiny with spittle as he drools. The paw he's sticking out looks just as moist, all sweaty, though there's a cold wind pushing around him into the noodle shop. Taggett can hear himself growling low in his throat. His scar on fire, the ring in his pocket burning his hip, those crazy whispers scuttling around the back of his skull. "I'm warning you," he hisses.

The fat boy sways hypnotically, like a half-demolished building ready to give up. There's a noise like a chuckle bubbling out from between his lips. The extended hand moves forward, and the other hand twitches toward the grimy grey suit jacket stretching over his belly.

Taggett's right fist shoots out into the meat of the fat creep's shoulder. El Gordo bleats and drops the straight razor he was pulling out of his jacket. He doesn't keep bleating for long: Taggett's left fist smashes into the middle of his soft wet face. The force of the blow drives him a couple steps back, so Taggett takes a couple steps forward and hits him again, two jabs to the gut, then grabs a fistful of the doubling over fat boy's hair and brings a knee up into the bloody mess he's making of the creep's face. El Gordo goes down, hits the asphalt and stays there in a twitching heap.

Johnny squats down and rolls the fat kid over on his back, the effort gritting the tough guy's teeth and forcing a grunt out of his throat. He opens the jacket, looking for some clue about who he just had to knock out, and finds only a bent pack of smokes. Someone in the gathered crowd mutters something like, "Didn't have to hit him so hard."

Standing up, grinning into the mob as it loses interest and breaks up, Johnny says, "He was in my way." He reaches back into the noodle shop for his hat and winks at the old man he's leaving in there, and then he's strolling along the sidewalk toward the old grain warehouse. It takes him a minute to realize that he's whistling a little tune as he wipes the kid's blood off his bruised knuckles. The night people are staying out of his way. The fat boy's lying in the street staring up at the sky.

As Taggett gets closer to the building's front door, he notices a couple of shadows flanking it, trying to blend into the darkness and not quite making it. He stops in his tracks and groans to himself. "Sweet Christ on a crutch, how much more of this shit do I need in one night?" Taking a breath, he slides his hand into his jacket, into his holster, curls his fingers around the cool handle of his forty-five, pulls it out, lets the thugs in front of the building have a good look. From half a block away he yells at them: "I'm coming in! I'll come through you if I have to, I don't even care! Is she paying you enough to take a bullet?" He's steadily walking forward as he's barking, and the shadows dissolve into the night.

Holding his forty-five ready, he pulls the door open and steps inside. The lobby's as empty as it always is. Those elderly couches are still holding down the yellowing linoleum, the potted palm trees just as dead, and the door to the stairwells closed. He slams it open against the wall behind it. No one's there. It takes him ten minutes to get up the three flights to his office floor, and when he slams the door from the landing open against the wall behind it, no one's there. No sign of Mrs. Foulsworth. He can't even smell her perfume, just the industrial soap that the janitor no one ever sees cleans the floor with. "What the hell," the detective mumbles. "I was watching all day, she never left the building. What kind of ghost have I been dealing with?" Though the ring's not doing anything in his pocket, he can feel it there as he unlocks his office door and steps inside.

It's the same place he left it the day before yesterday, except that it smells a little worse, like stale booze. He lights up one of the fat boy's cigarettes and stands for a minute with his back against the door, observing the mess. Then he straightens up and starts to go through Walt's crap, organizing it into the stuff that'll help figure out who killed him and the stuff that won't. A little after he puts the phone back on his desk it rings. He lets it. He's got no time for another mystery: "Too much work to do," he tells himself, and somewhere in the back of the tough detective's imagination, the ghost of Walt McBride is cracking a hint of a smile.

CHAPTER SIXTEEN

The morning sun's casting shadows from the city into the bay as the tough detective lights up another smoke and takes another long look at the crowd parting around him. He's gotten rid of the suit he's been wearing for the last couple days, just left it in a bloodstained pile of rags stinking of whiskey sweat in an alley somewhere, and now he's dressed just like a citizen, hat tipped down to cover half his face as he waits on a bus bench across the street from the Ferry Building for Chen. According to the schedule in the paper, the bus from Los Angeles is due in about fifteen minutes: Johnny's there early to see who else seems interested in Chen's arrival. So far he hasn't seen any sign of those strangely dressed Chinese guys. Behind the paper he's holding he mutters to himself, "Wonder if they know he's coming . . . whoever they are. I hope this kid can help me figure out what's chasing me." He keeps watching the big glass doors across the street as they open every five minutes or so to let out a new flood of travelers.

After about ten minutes he notices a dirty bus growling its way into the big doors at the side of the building. "Looks like road dirt on that one," he tells himself. "Better look sharp, see if this Chen kid's bringing any new trouble." Straightening his posture on the bench he sneakily slides his forty-five out of its holster and puts it down next to him, his right hand over it. A babe walking past glances at it and cocks an eyebrow at him. He winks at her, letting his lips curl up into a grin he saw once on a wolf at the zoo, then turns his attention back to the doors opening up across the street. As far as he can tell, she just keeps moving. "The Wild West," he chuckles to himself.

The incoming crowd pushes through the doors like flood water breaking through a dam. Most of it seems to be Mexican laborers, rough brown faces and clothing and the stooped posture of the farm worker. Some of the people coming out are white, a couple of families carrying beat-up cardboard suitcases, mothers and fathers looking worried about the future and children looking too tired to care. Johnny can see three or four Chinese faces and doesn't recognize any of them: either Chen's got no tail on him, or the thugs that killed Walt aren't ones that Johnny's seen before. He tightens his grip on his forty-five, slips his finger over the trigger.

As he keeps watching, the few Chinese guys go their separate ways, one of them coming right at him. Johnny's finger flexes a little, just enough to feel the weight of the trigger against it. The guy comes closer, stands over the seated tough guy, says, "You're Johnny Taggett, aren't you?" The voice is Chen's. Johnny's finger relaxes.

Chen's not quite as big as Johnny, but he looks just as tough. He's got the same square jaw, the same straight slash of a mouth. He's even got a scar going through his right eyebrow. A greying bandage peeks out from behind his hat like a bald spot his short black hair grows around. He stands there looking at Johnny, the faintest hint of a smirk twitching around his thin lips. "Mr. McBride told me you were a tricky one. I thought you said we'd meet in your office."

Putting his gun away, Johnny looks up at the younger man. "Yeah, that's what I said, but I thought it'd be better to see if anyone came with you before we all got stuck in that little room." The tough detective takes out a smoke and lights it up, then he points the open pack at Chen, who takes one and holds it to Johnny's match. They take a minute to smoke and look each other over. The crowd dwindles around them.

Finally Chen says, "So what's going on here, Mr. Taggett? You said someone attacked you in Mr. McBride's apartment? How did you get away? Who's after you—us?"

Taggett stands up to find out that he's only about a head taller than Chen. "I don't know yet, kid, and I told you to call me Johnny. I've got an idea or two, though. Let's head to the office, I'll tell you what I know." The two men walk together through the maze of streets and alleys that leads to Taggett's office, the tough detective talking as they go. "I don't know if Walt told you, but I'm out here in front of some heavy debt, had to quit the police department back in New York."

"Yeah," says Chen. "Mr. McBride told me that you were even worse back there than he was. Said you never knew when to quit. So you think it followed you here? You think it came after Mr. McBride?"

Taggett furrows his brow for a moment. "No, that doesn't make any sense. I can see why a guy would kill the girl I was in bed with as some crazy kind of warning—"

"In bed with you?" Chen stops right there in the middle of the sidewalk and gapes up into Johnny's face. "How could they have missed you? Did they use a knife or something?"

"A machine gun," says Johnny. "Killed one of the guys that worked downstairs, too. I guess the killer hollered something about the money I owe as he was lamming it, so I just figured it was this crazy hit man, the Russian they call him, doing some weird thing to scare me into paying." As they start walking again, he has another thought. "That doesn't explain what happened to Walt, though. And it was his place that creep came to. Do you know if he owes anybody?"

Chen barely has to think before he says, "Yeah, probably about half the dealers in town. Mr. McBride was a great detective, but he had some real problems. He was going to get clean in Los Angeles, said he was getting ashamed of himself with you around. Said he was sick of hiding."

This time it's Johnny who has to stop in the middle of the alley they're crossing. He stands they're like a fighter just about to fall until a truck's horn jolts him across, and then he stands there some more on the sidewalk. "Jesus," he says. "I had no idea."

Chen reaches out and lays a hand on the bigger man's shoulder. "It's okay, Mr. McBride was very good at hiding things. He knew how you would get if you found out. He figured you'd probably try to beat up someone who could do you real harm."

"Yeah, well, plenty of losers have tried to do me harm, and I'm still here." Johnny returns Chen's gesture, then his arm drops back to his side and he starts walking again. Chen sticks right by his side.

After a little silence, Chen speaks up. "It still doesn't make sense. It's like you say, you don't kill a guy because he owes you money, you scare him. If those creeps in L.A. were trying to collect a debt from Mr. McBride, they'd've killed me to send the message, right? I think they just knocked me out so they could get away. And if they were trying to send a message, wouldn't they, you know, say something? They just seemed too weird to be enforcers, you know?"

"Yeah," says Taggett. Another silence falls as the men walk past Lee Ming's. The old man's face peers fearfully out through the window at the big white man as they pass, but Taggett doesn't notice. They're almost to the old grain warehouse when he stops and snaps his fingers. "That crazy Foulsworth dame!" he shouts. "She's just weird enough to set all this crap in motion."

Chen squints up at Johnny. "Foulsworth? You mean like Edgar Foulsworth?"

Somehow the sunny morning turns into a cold shadow. The butt of Johnny's cigarette falls out of his mouth as he gapes at the younger man. His mouth closes and opens again a time or two, and then he manages to say, "What the hell do you know about the Foulsworths? How can you possibly—"

"I just know the name Edgar Foulsworth," says Chen. "That's the name of the doctor Mr. McBride was going to see the doctor who was going to help him get clean."

"Did you see him?" Johnny's eyes are almost bulging past their lids. He grabs Chen by the shoulders, almost shaking him. "Did you see this Foulsworth character, a creepy old party in a wheelchair?"

Chen just looks at him for a long minute. "Mr. McBride got killed before we could see him, so, uh, no," he says evenly and waits for Taggett to let go. Finally Johnny drops his hands. Chen says, "The name must mean a lot to you. What's it all about?"

Calming himself, Johnny fishes out a cigarette and lights it. "I met a guy on the train from New York who called himself that—or that's what his wife called him, anyway. He never really said anything to me, just showed me some kind of scribble I couldn't really make out. His wife's even weirder, does all the talking, seems to be in charge. I think she's trying to hire me into some kind of mob, or maybe she's trying to get into my pants. I really can't figure her out, can't even see her face through that black veil she's always wearing. Hell, I've only ever seen her all in black, like she's some kind of Lon Chaney creature of the night." He glances at the citizens passing around. He doesn't see anyone looking back, so he reaches into his coat and shows Chen the Violet Diamond. It flares warm in his palm as he holds it. "She gave me this crazy little trinket to hold on to as some kind of loyalty test, I think." As Chen reaches out he pulls his hand back. "Better not. It's supposed to have some sort of mystic attachment to the one holding it. Probably she's got it coated with some sort of drug or fingerprint powder or something that'll tell her I let it go."

"Whatever," Chen shrugs. "I'm not in the jewelry business, and I don't want to be anyone's legbreaker. What have you been telling this Mrs. Foulsworth?"

By this time they've started walking again and made it to the door of the old grain warehouse. As they're crossing the lobby and climbing up those creaky stairs, Johnny says, "I've been putting her off. She's just too weird for me. This thing with the ring, I don't know, and to hear her husband's name mixed up with Walt's death—well, let's just say I don't want to get on her bad side until I know how bad it can get." He opens the door to the landing, and the two men walk down the hall to Johnny's office.

"Well, it can't get any worse for Mr. McBride," Chen says. "I think we need to find out about the Foulsworths and what they want with you."

Johnny smirks and says, "No argument there, kid." He opens the office door to usher the younger man in and then follows and then stops short before he quite gets through the door.

The eerie black figure of Mrs. Foulsworth is standing in the middle of the room, right between Johnny's desk and Walt's. Taggett can't tell which way she's facing: she might be looking out the window or right into his eyes. "Mr. Taggett," comes that menacingly seductive purr. "And Mr. Chen. I'm so glad you've arrived at last. I've been waiting for you."

CHAPTER SEVENTEEN

"Let me make something very clear to you both," says Mrs. Foulsworth a few minutes later in that distantly intimate voice of hers. She's sitting in the same chair she had for her last visit, that ivory cigarette holder projecting from her veil, one of those weird little brown cigarettes smoldering away at the tip. Taggett's managed to make it into Walt's desk chair. Chen's standing beside him. They're both staring at her, speechless. "The negotiations have ended, and you're entering my employ immediately, both of you, despite any plans I might have had to the contrary. Mr. Taggett, since you have chosen to include your young friend in the situation in which you find yourself, his fate has become your responsibility. You've place his life in your hands. Fortunately, we have a use for him."

Chen flinches at this. He glances at Taggett, and the older man gives a little shake of the head. Chen stays where he is, but Johnny can see the way his muscles are flexing, the way he's trying to keep his breathing still and the fire out of his stare. The cryptic figure of Mrs. Foulsworth gives the impression that she's politely but impatiently waiting through this exchange of glances before she goes on.

"I've been enjoying our little flirtation, Mr. Taggett, but the line of endeavor we pursue in this life sometimes makes demands on us to which even the most powerful among us must accede. Simply put, the work I'm employing you to do, the service I'm calling upon you to provide for me, is one that simply will not wait upon the whim of a helpless romantic such as myself. Therefore, I have come to this uncivilized outpost to claim you and end this protracted engagement you seem to desire. You're mine, Mr. Taggett, and I'm here for you." A noise like a chuckle comes out of that black figure. It goes on until it turns into a weird coughing rattle. The cigarette holder falls to the floor as Mrs. Foulsworth bends over, pulls something from a fold in her skirt, slips it under her veil. The coughing stops, but a noise like a dog licking the last drops of water from a dripping nozzle replaces it. Taggett glances at Chen. A grimace of disgust is twisting up the features on both their faces. After far too long, Mrs. Foulsworth slips the thing back into her skirt somewhere, picks her cigarette holder up off the floor and puts it away too, and straightens up in her seat. As if nothing more than a sneeze just happened, she turns slightly and says, "But first let's consider your case, Chen Hao Ye."

Chen's eyes widen a little, and his voice has to push its way out of his tightening throat.. "That's the second time you've used my name, ma'am. I don't think we've been properly introduced."

Another of those mirthless laughs: "Oh, Mr. Taggett, where could your manners be? Has no one taught you to introduce a lady?" Still chortling the way an engine idles, she takes her ivory cigarette holder back out, plugs another of those odd cigarettes into its tip, and holds it up, waiting.

As Taggett strikes a match he growls, "Chen Hao Ye, allow me to present Mrs. Edgar Foulsworth.." He lights her cigarette, then one for himself, but he blows out the match and strikes a new one to light Chen's.

"Charmed, I'm sure," she says, holding out a hand for Chen to take. He takes it, and Taggett sees him start to blink and stagger a little as his gaze falls into the glittering trap of her jewelry. She lets this go on for a few seconds then takes her hand back and goes on. "You must imagine that we've taken notice of you, Mr. Chen, as we've paid attention to your departed mentor, Mr. McBride. You're quite a handy customer in a dockside brawl, wouldn't you say? A man accustomed to a certain amount of, shall we say, carefully applied brutality? Wasn't that Mr. McBride's interest in you? We are completely aware of the type of

situation in which he employs your talents, antisocial as they may be."
The ring in Taggett's pocket gives a sharp little pulse of heat.

Chen's standing there like a tree struck by lightning. His eyes seem to be staring through Mrs. Foulsworth's head as he swallows and starts to say something that Taggett just talks over through the taste of ashes at the back of his tongue. Standing up from his chair, looming over the desk, Taggett shouts, "How the hell long have you been following Walt? Did you have him killed? You bitch, did you kill my partner?"

Her voice comes back with the same alien calmness as ever. "Mr. Taggett, your hat seems to have fallen off. Please do compose yourself. Let me assure you with the utmost sincerity that I am completely ignorant of the circumstances regarding Mr. McBride's demise, for which I extend my sympathies. It is true, however, that our organization has had you and your talents under consideration for some time. Perhaps you remember Joey Sakal, the fight promoter. Perhaps you remember the events at Madison Square Garden about six months before your abrupt retirement from such a promising career as a member of the New York Police Department, the shooting of poor Sandman Jackson right in the middle of his match. No doubt the incident sticks in your mind due to the crazed rantings of the man you arrested, his complete lack of apparent motivation for such a bizarrely random crime. Now what if I were to tell you, Mr. Taggett, that Joey Sakal attended that fight, had paid Jackson to lose that fight, had pulled the trigger himself in a fit of rage at Jackson's failure to comply, had seen you looking his way at just the right moment. You didn't see him, did you, but Sakal didn't know that, did he." She interrupts herself for a moment with a fit of that creepy laughter, then continues. "You've been a marked man for quite some time, Mr. Taggett, pursued by the Russian and by Sakal's men simultaneously. You must have the luck of the perfect fool. You know, Sakal had arranged for your execution in one gang fight after another, but somehow you managed to evade him—temporarily." Another chuckle as Taggett's face gets paler with shock after shock. "Oh, did you think those clowns on the train from New York were your only pursuers? Did you imagine that you were safe with your damaged little partner—or he with you? No doubt one of Sakal's men or one of the

Russian's wanted you to know just how precarious your position remains, that no one you care about will be safe from the repercussions of your improvident behavior. I warned you, Mr. Taggett, and you chose to ignore my friendly advice. Now you have nothing. Your friend here has nothing. Your imprudent way of life has severed every single one of your connections to what you may have thought of as your society. You're in a corner, Mr. Taggett. Your ability to survive to this point has occasioned our interest in you, but you've reached the point where our help is crucial to your continued existence. Simply put, Mr. Taggett, Mr. Chen, your lives are mine."

The two men are standing they're staring at her, paralyzed with helpless rage. After a long moment of silence, Chen speaks up. "Mrs. Foulsworth, I don't know who you think you are, but we—"

"Do you get seasick, Mr. Chen?" Her question cuts him right off.

He goggles at her a moment, then manages to say, "Uh, no, I was brought up around the bay here, but I—"

"And you, Mr. Taggett?"

Johnny's sunk back down into his chair, hand raised, fingertips resting along the line of his scar. He looks across the desk at the pitiless black figure, and his voice comes out flat: "I don't know, I've never been on a boat."

"Well, then," she chortles, "you have an exciting adventure ahead of you. You'll be leaving for Shanghai two days from now."

Chen's still standing, fuming, getting ready to speak again when she says something to him in what Taggett guesses is Chinese. Whatever she says stops him dead: the color drains from his face and he just says, "Okay."

Unscrewing her the stub of her cigarette from its holder and laying the wrinkled brown butt on the desk in front of her, she rises from her seat. "I'll return tomorrow with more detailed instructions," she tells her two new employees. "Of course, Mr. Taggett, you may consider yourself your own supervisor, with Mr. Chen responsible to you. That's the way of nature, wouldn't you agree?" As she glides to the door she adds, "I'm sure you'd hate to see yourself involved in anything unnatural." She opens the door and steps through it, and that eerie chuckle echoes for a minute or two behind her in the office with them as her footsteps fade down the hall.

Chen finally breaks the awkward silence, pulling out a cigarette and lighting up. "You weren't lying, Johnny, that is one strange bird. Looks like she's got us cornered, though."

Still sitting, but tipping his hat back on his head, Taggett holds a new cigarette to Chen's match. As the tip of it catches fire he winks at the younger man. "Cornered is the best place for a street dog. I figure the sooner we know what she's got planned for us, the sooner we can do something about it."

"So you're letting her think she's got you?"

"Oh, she's got me," chuckles Johnny, leaning back in his chair. "Now she'll just have to see if she can keep me."

CHAPTER EIGHTEEN

"So she'll be back for us in a couple of days," says Chen. "What do we do till then?"

Johnny smirks and leans back in his chair, propping his feet on the desk. "We wait, kid. All we know about this job is that we're going on a boat. That could mean across the bay or across the damn planet. Can't get ready for something we don't know anything about." Chen scowls and smacks his right fist into his left hand. "Relax," Johnny tells him. "If she's the one hunting us, we're off the hook. Probably we're off the hook with Sakal and the Russian too. I haven't been around for them to find, so they probably think they've scared me underground. All we can do is wait for that weird spider of a woman to make the next move."

So the two men spend the next day in Johnny's office, waiting for the word from the shadowy dame. Right around sundown, Chen sneaks out to Lee Ming's to get some noodles and some of Ming's backroom whiskey, and the new partners spend the night drinking and telling stories about Walt McBride, laughing and crying at the same time. For the first time in what seems like months, Taggett falls asleep with a smile on his face.

Sooner or later they wake up with the clear light of a San Francisco winter morning stretching itself in stripes across them. Taggett groans a little and lights up a smoke, then he passes it to Chen and lights one up for himself. Glancing around, he finds the last of the whiskey puddling the inside of its bottle. He takes a hair of the dog and passes Chen the last swallow. The younger man bolts it down, winks at Johnny, and says, "We gotta get some more of this."

With a chuckle, Taggett tells him, "I think we're on a diet for a while, kid." He pulls out a deck of cards. "You ever play Marriage Rummy?"

"Of course," says Chen as Johnny starts to shuffle. "I learned it from Mr. McBride, same as you." That gets another chuckle out of the older man, and the two of them spend the rest of the day trading nickel bets back and forth as the light in the room fades from white to orange, then from orange to blue. Just as Taggett turns on the desk lamp, three faint knocks come from the door. Both faces suddenly lose their smiles. Taggett puts his forty-five on the desk, his hand over it, and nods to Chen. The younger man nods back and steps to the door, opening it. The black shape of Mrs. Foulsworth stands framed like a photo in the doorway. Chen steps aside to let her in.

She's already snickering as she glides to her usual seat in front of the desk that used to be Walt's. "I notice you haven't yet made the necessary alterations to the sign on your door, Mr. Taggett. Such beautiful loyalty, but perhaps counterproductive for the line of business you've chosen. Anyone attempting to employ McBride and Taggett Investigations would surely suffer disappointment to find only half the promised personnel available, don't you think?" By this time she's got her ivory cigarette holder out and screwed a butt into it. She holds it up and waits for Taggett to light it. Once that twisted brown cigarette is smoldering away, she reaches into what must be a pocket somewhere in her old-fashioned widow's weeds and pulls out a white envelope. "You'll find in there the documents required for your passage," she says.

"Passage to where?" growls Taggett. "Lady, I don't know what you're expecting but—"

Mrs. Foulsworth talks right over him, her cigarette holder bobbing hypnotically up and down as she goes on. "You'll also find five hundred dollars and a list of supplies you'll need for your voyage. Two days from now at dawn you'll report to Captain Ramirez of the *Salvador*, and he'll expect you to be fully provisioned. We're hardly proposing to send you on a luxury cruise, gentlemen. However, I can with great confidence promise you a reward at the end of your odyssey. Simply put, I can offer you freedom."

Chen grunts and scowls. "Freedom," he snarls. "Looks to me like you've taken away everything in my life just to get me to play your twisted little game. Where's the freedom?"

"I can make you your own man, Mr. Taggett." It's like she doesn't even hear Chen. "You can finally set your own pace, perform your tasks just the way you think you should. You'll even have an assistant besides your rude companion here, who should know better than to attempt to interrupt when his superiors are conducting business. We've arranged, along with what we're assured is the most efficacious automobile available, for a driver, a native called Jie Chio, to meet you in Shanghai."

Taggett grins into what ought to be her face and manages to break in to her onslaught of babble: "What's in Shanghai?"

A moment of awkward silence fills the little office. Taggett can hear Chen breathing hard, controlling himself. Mrs. Foulsworth's cigarette makes a little hiss as it goes out, smoked up. Finally a strange sound comes out of the veiled figure, an almost girlish giggle. "Oh, dear, I seem to have given away the surprise. What a pity. I must admit, though, that brief look of shock on your face entirely justified my indiscretion, at least to myself. Well, I suppose, now that you've so cleverly torn the secret from me, I shall have to explain further." Unscrewing her dead cigarette from its holder and dropping it on the desk in front of her, she takes in a breath as if she's ready to launch into another of her speeches. Instead, she says, "Why have you never offered me a drink, Mr. Taggett?"

Taggett can only stutter something like, "What?"

"A drink, Mr. Taggett. I'm not mistaken in assuming that you're a man who knows his way around a liquor bottle, am I?"

"Uh, I don't see what—"

Her voice has turned stern again, but in a strange playful way, the voice of a cat with a caught mouse. "Really, Mr. Taggett, this is the third time you've had me as a guest in your delightful establishment, and you have yet to extend the simple courtesy of offering a lady a drink. Has no one ever taught you manners?"

Taggett just stares at her, the hint of a smirk tugging at the corner of his mouth. "Lady, a few people have tried to teach me manners here and there. I never really took to it." He lights up a smoke for himself and then one for Chen, then he blows out the match as she's fitting a new cigarette into her holder. He makes her wait for him to strike a fresh match for her. After he lights her smoke he makes her wait another minute while he finds a glass, pulls a bottle from the bottom drawer of Walt's desk, opens it, pours, and slides it across the desk to her.

She takes it in her gloved hand, jewelry sparkling in the lamplight. "Well, thank you, Mr. Taggett. I have no doubt that a man of your intellectual capability will one day learn impeccable manners, perhaps one day sooner than you think." The hand holding the glass disappears under the veil, comes back out with about the whiskey gone. "I must admit your partner had excellent taste. In liquor, at any rate."

The chair under Taggett slams back into the wall behind it as he leaps up to get in front of Chen. The younger man is already lunging forward, almost has his hands around her throat before Taggett can push him back, Chen's muscles straining hard against the older man's. Chen's shouting,, "Bitch! You don't ever say his name again!" and it's all Taggett can do to get him pressed up against the back wall of the office, pinning the smaller man's wrists to the crappy plywood. He's got his lips to Chen's ear, whispering, "Don't let her get to you. We can't get back at her for Walt if we scare her off." After a long moment the fire dims in Chen's deep black eyes and he relaxes.

Breathing hard, Taggett turns around to see Mrs. Foulsworth still at ease in her seat, taking the last sip of her whiskey, the glass coming out empty from under her veil along with that familiar mirthless chortle. "You're wise to control your subordinate, Mr. Taggett," she tells him. "Perhaps you should ask your Mr. Chen some time about his temper. You might find your new friend just as dangerous as your vast array of enemies has been. Then again, you now have an ally—indeed, a benefactor—to warn you of such potentialities, assuming that you haven't made use of your impressive skills as a private investigator to find out anything about this boy before inviting him into your office, into the center of your miserable stump of a life. I'm so happy that I can perform that service for you." She sets her glass on the desk next to the stub of her cigarette and holds out her hand. Shooting a glance at Chen, Johnny steps forward and takes it as she makes him help her out of the chair, those talons of hers gripping Taggett's arm through his coat. Her blank of a face is so close to his that it takes up his whole field of vision. He sees nothing but black as she hisses, "I own you, Mr. Taggett, just as you're beginning to own the Violet Diamond." As he gapes, she keeps whispering: "Oh, don't you worry, I haven't forgotten. It'll make a lovely excuse to visit you again sometime. I just can't bear to say goodbye." She loosens her grip, and he staggers back against the desk as she takes that creepy laugh of hers to the door.

"Good luck on your voyage, Mr. Taggett. Never forget your responsibilities." Her sinister chuckle fades away down the hall as she leaves them there.

Taggett stands back up, rests his hand on the back of Mrs. Foulsworth's chair, takes a long look at Chen. The smaller man's still quivering against the back wall, taking long deep breaths, slowing himself down. He looks back at Taggett without a word.

The tough detective finds his smokes on the desk, lights one up, and reaches one over to his partner. "Kid," he says, "I guess we've got some shopping to do before we start."

CHAPTER NINETEEN

The rising sun's lighting up the Art Deco buildings along the expanse of the Huangpu River, painting them gold. Taggett's staring down into the shadow the *Salvador* makes on the dark river water and shivering in his peacoat, his breath fogging out in front of him. The ship's bobbing a little on the river's waves, not as badly as it did on the ocean he's been puking his meals into, but enough to make him grip the rail. "Christ," he mutters to himself, "that weird old bat wasn't kidding, this isn't any kind of luxury, don't think I've ever been this tired . . . but here we are." He raises his eyes to the buildings along the shore as the *Salvador* drops to the bottom of a wave and his gut jumps into his throat. "For you, Walt. This is where I find out why they croaked you."

"Damn right," says Chen, suddenly next to him along the rail.

Taggett flinches for a second, then grins. "You're a sneaky one, aren't you? Did you get all that?"

Laughing, Chen says, "I guess I got enough. You're just not seafaring material, are you?"

"I can take it," Taggett grumbles. "If it gets me closer to Walt's killers I can take it." He straightens up and turns to face his partner. "I'm ready for anything."

Chen reaches out to pat the older man on the shoulder. "Good, anything might happen." Leaning a little closer, he murmurs, "For instance, have you noticed the guy that's been watching us?"

Johnny glances around and says, "Yeah, I've been catching a guy at mess every day looking my direction, trying to act casual, but he looks away every time he sees me looking back. Same little dark guy always working on some little patch-up job whenever I'm on deck. Real amateur hour stuff, I'm not surprised you caught him too. Haven't seen him the last couple of days, though."

"Yeah, that's pretty weird, where could he have gone to?" Chen pulls a pack of smokes from his peacoat, lights one, hands it to Taggett, lights one for himself. "You run into a lot of people that just disappear, don't you?"

Taggett chuckles, "Yeah, lately. That Edgar Foulsworth on the train and now this guy. Think I should change my aftershave?"

"Maybe you just need to meet a better class of people," Chen laughs. "Anyway, we're nearly to port and Martinez has us on gangplank duty. If we hang around while the rest of the crew gets off, maybe we can get a look at this shifty creep, maybe follow him into the city, see what his story is. Did you get a good look at his face?"

As they turn away from the rail Taggett thinks for a minute and says, "No, he always managed to have something in front of his face every time I looked his way. Like I say, amateur hour, the guy just made himself look shifty." He swerves back to the rail to flip his cigarette into the river. "And it doesn't make sense, anyway. Who'd put a tail on me in the middle of the ocean? Where'm I gonna go?" The motion of the boat makes him stagger a little, and Chen catches him.

Settling the bigger man back on his own feet, Chen says, "Maybe this guy's not as amateur hour as you think. Sounds to me like he wanted you to catch him watching you, just not so much that he wants you to know what he looks like. I'm thinking if this guy's got that kind of control he must be pretty good."

"You're thinking this guy's a message from someone."

Chen takes Johnny's elbow, down the stairway to the lower deck. "I'm thinking that crazy whatever-she-is we're working for wants us to know what kind of leash we're on."

As they go down into the hold Taggett lets out a laughing snort. "Good. That way we can pull her whole operation down when we yank that leash. The tighter their grip, the harder they'll fall."

The boat shudders as it pulls into the dock. Taggett can hear the shouts of the sailors above them on deck throwing out ropes or lines or whatever they're called. The shrill voice of the captain cuts through that noise the way a bullet would tear through a two-by-four: "Gangplank! Where the hell is the gangplank?" Johnny hustles to undo the knots holding the sliding panel to the deck while Chen slides open the big door in the side of the boat. Together, they push the plank onto the dock, where a couple of workers on the other side tie it down. One of the workers signals up to the deck, and Martinez's holler shoots back down to Chen and Johnny: "Finally!"

A little while later the partners have made it across the gangplank themselves, and they're both staggering a little as they walk away from the *Salvador*, solid land rolling and tilting under their sea-legs. They've changed out of the peacoat and heavy canvas pants they had to wear onboard and back into the snappy three-piece suits they treated themselves to that last night in the States. Taggett adjusts his fedora to shade his eyes from the morning sun casting long shadows in front of the two men as they push their way through the humming crowd of workers and peddlers until they can't push any further. "This must be the line for the ferry," Chen says.

"Ferry?" Taggett almost drops the cigarette he's lighting. "Didn't we just get off a damn boat?"

Chen laughs gently and holds his cigarette up to Taggett's match. "Maybe you didn't notice, but all the hotels are on the other side of the river, and it might be too cold to swim. Don't worry, it won't be much of a trip, you probably won't puke more than once or twice."

"Cute," says Taggett. The crowd pushes them slowly to the ferry, a big flat barge with a roof made of a canvas awning stretched between poles sticking out of the barge's sides. The two men, bigger than most of the mob chattering around them, push their way to an edge and turn their backs on the passing river. "We want to keep an eye out," Taggett tells Chen. "See if anyone's paying us too much attention."

About halfway across Chen gives Taggett a little jab in the ribs with his elbow, then points with his chin to a little dark guy who's standing in the middle of the big flat deck and looking right at them. Almost without moving his lips, Taggett mutters, "Don't do a thing yet. This crowd's no place for a shootout. Let's let this guy make the first move." Chen nods, and the two tough guys stand ready. As the crowd mills between them, Taggett's eyes lock on the little guy's mild gaze. He's dressed in the same kind of suit Taggett's wearing. He's moving closer. His eyes are fixed on Taggett's. The tough detective can feel Chen beside him radiating nervous energy, the younger man's breath speeding up. "Careful," says Taggett as the little guy picks his way through the crowd toward them. Taggett can see the flat nose, the straight line of a mouth, the serious expression on the little guy's face. Breathing in through his nose, out through his mouth, Taggett keeps his right hand from inching toward the forty-five in the shoulder holster his coat's concealing. Chen's hands are curled into tight fists. The little guy stops right in front of Taggett, looking up into his eyes.

"Pardon me for intruding, but might you be Mr. Taggett?" says the little guy in a weird kind of English accent.

Johnny shoots a glance at Chen, who's almost quivering, the way a racehorse shivers a little just before the starting buzzer. Johnny squares his feet, getting ready, and snarls back, "Yeah, I might be. Who wants to know?"

"Pardon me, sir, I certainly don't mean to alarm you." The guy takes a step back and bows a little. "I believe you were informed that my services would be at your disposal. I am Jie Chio."

Taggett stares blankly for a moment, than his body relaxes as he snaps his fingers. "Right, the driver." Next to him, Chen's still on edge, fists still clenched. Taggett turns to him and says, "Listen, this guy's with us. Remember? We got the word just before we shipped out." That calms his young partner down a little, so Johnny turns back to Jie and says, "I figured you'd be meeting us at the hotel."

Jie's straight mouth curves up into a smile that doesn't quite get to his eyes. "Please excuse my impertinence, sir, but I felt it better to introduce myself here amongst a large group of people in case your understandable caution were to get the better of you. I've been told you have a temper that sometimes causes you to act regrettably." Chen snorts with laughter at that. Jie takes a moment to regard him then makes some kind of comment Taggett can't understand.

Chen stares at Jie for a second and mutters, "Yeah, that's not really a dialect I speak. Sorry."

"Think nothing of it, sir," Jie replies. "I was merely attempting to convey my anticipation of a close working relationship with one of my countrymen."

Chen's pale face darkens. "Listen, I'm from the USA, and—"

"Relax," says Johnny, stepping between the two of them. "Jie, this is Chen Hao Ye. We're working together on this thing, whatever it is."

Impassively, Jie says, "Yes, sir, I've been fully briefed, if, perhaps, not as fully as I might have hoped. Please be assured nonetheless that I had no trouble recognizing either of you." He turns his head as the sailors stationed at the corners of the ferry toss ropes to the sailors on the rapidly approaching dock. "Ah, I see we've arrived. Gentlemen, if you'll accompany me, I'll show you to your accommodations at the Palace Hotel. I strongly advise you to take advantage of the opportunity to rest, as I'm sure you'll want to be at your best tomorrow morning when I take you to meet your new employer." As the ferry bumps to a halt, Jie bows again. "Right this way, gentlemen."

CHAPTER TWENTY

Taggett's suite at the Palace Hotel is bigger than his apartment in New York. "Hell," he mumbles to himself as he relaxes, "this bed is almost as big as that old rat trap I lived in. A fellow could get used to this kind of treatment if he's not careful." He's stark naked for the first time in months, skin all smooth and warm from the first hot shower he's had months, between clean sheets, under a thick soft blanket. In that luxurious darkness he thinks back to that afternoon, the conversation with Chen in the back of that amazing car.

"You think we can trust this guy?" Chen's asking as the engine gently vibrates the cushioned back seat there riding on. "He seems a little off, don't you think? Maybe he's driving us into some kind of trap."

Taggett has to chuckle. "What are we gonna do, jump out of the car and start wandering around Shanghai? We'll just have to see where he takes us and deal with what we find. Anyway, I get the feeling he's just a working stiff like you and me." Gazing out the window, he lets out a yawn. "Anyway, it looks like we're pretty well within the hotel district. Damn, look at these buildings, it's like I'm back in New York." As the big black car they're riding in makes its stately progress along the wide street, windows glisten in the wall of brightly colored hotels reaching up like a cliff face to Taggett's left. He winks at his younger partner. "I'll tell you this much, kid, I've definitely never been in a car like this before."

From the front seat, Jie says, "It might interest you gentlemen to know that you're currently occupying the Rolls Royce Phantom II, an automobile of which only three models exist in the world. It seems apparent that our employer has spared no expense for your luxury. Let me assure you that the pleasure of driving this fantastic machine has already begun to reward my service to you."

Chen gives the driver a long flat look as Taggett coughs. "Uh, yeah," says Johnny. "Glad to hear it. But speaking of our employer, what can you tell me about this guy?"

"Regrettably, sir, not a thing. Mr. Wang never shows himself to anyone. His willingness to meet you personally indicates a deep respect for you—both of you—and your skills, a respect for which I'm sure you'll show, as gentlemen, appropriate gratitude." Jie eases the Phantom into an alley that reaches inland from the broad river road like a tendril reaching from a fern. A chorus of horns and shouts announces the turn as the car, shiny and black as an oil slick, slips between buildings and backs up, returning to the loud traffic along the river then sliding into a parking spot. Jie turns around and addresses the men over the back of the car's front bench. "Gentlemen, we have arrived at the Palace Hotel. Please allow me to concern myself with your baggage, which you should find in your suites within the half hour. In the meantime, perhaps you'd care to refresh yourself at the bar." The little man slides out of the car and takes the long walk around to the back to open the door for Johnny and Chen. "I'll call upon you at six o'clock tomorrow morning to take you to meet our employer, and you can ask him all the questions to which, alas, I have no answers."

Taggett steps out of the car and looks down at Jie. "Alas?" he laughs. "Does anybody really talk that way?"

Jie gets a little taller as his posture stiffens. "Sir, I was educated in the finest finishing school Hong Kong has to offer, which is to say the finest finishing school in the entire Orient. I can assure you with great confidence that people do indeed, as you so colorfully put it, talk that way."

That gets a laugh out of Chen and makes Taggett look down at his shoes for a second. "Yeah, I guess you talk like you talk," says the tough detective. "Sorry, I don't mean to make fun of you."

"Very good of you to apologize, sir," says Jie, recovering his cool, "but completely unnecessary. Indeed, I must extend an apology of my own, having overreacted to your tone. I'm terribly sorry to have caused embarrassment." By this time he's got the trunk unlocked, handing the two little suitcases Taggett and Chen have packed their lives into to a guy in a bright red bellhop uniform. He says something Taggett doesn't get to the bellhop, slips the kid a bill of some kind, then turns back to the partners. "Gentlemen, you'll be established on the fortieth floor momentarily. Until then, please allow me again to suggest that you pass your time at the bar."

Lying there in the dark, drifting, Taggett remembers that barroom, the amber light pouring through big panes of glass into the long ranks of bottles shelved behind the bar with a mirror behind them to bounce out into his eyes, dazzling him the way Mrs. Foulsworth's rings always do. He's got a cool glass in his hand, drinking out in the open, not hiding in some kind of dirt-floored crap shack. There's a band playing over the happy hum of a big crowd getting mellow. He takes a last bite of the dripping hamburger in front of him on the bar, looks over at Chen and yells, "This is the way it oughta be!"

Chen's leaning on his elbow, posing with his glass, giving the eye to the barmaid dressed in a kimono so short the two Americans can almost see the lower curve of her pale ass when she rises up on her toes to get a new bottle. Every now and then she catches his gaze and giggles and gives him a wink. "China's treating us all right," he says. "This beer they've got here, I can't get enough, it's like nothing I've ever . . ." He seems to forget what he was going to say as the barmaid sways past and his eyes look like they're trying to bust out of his skull so they can follow her.

Taggett chuckles and takes another sip of the best whiskey he's ever imagined in his wildest dream of boozehound heaven and tells his partner, "Take it easy. We don't want to be too out of it when we meet the man tomorrow." He finishes his drink and sets it on the bar, feeling the satisfying response of the thick glass to the solid wood of the bar, a sound like the carpentry his daddy used to do. As he puts on his hat he reaches into his jacket for a fresh smoke, and the barmaid's right there with a light before he can quite get it to his lips. He smiles and flips her a quarter, then turns back to Chen. Reaching out to clap the younger man on the shoulder, he says, "I'm gonna go upstairs, take a nice long hot shower, scrub some of the ocean scum off my skin, get myself nice and rested before whatever happens next." Chen, still staring at the barmaid, just flaps a hand at him, so Taggett makes his way to the elevator and up to the fortieth floor and the lush comfort he's lying in right now. He can feel his eyes shutting, can feel himself sinking into a blissful sleep.

And then his eyes snap back open. The room's just as dark, just as quiet. No way to tell how long he's been out. He starts to notice that the bed's just a little warmer than it was, and before he can think to grumble about never getting a full night's sleep he's reaching under the pillow next to his head for his forty-five. The gun's not there. He sucks in a breath, ready for a fight, and smells some kind of lilac perfume just as the whisper hits his ear: "There's no need for that kind of weapon tonight, Mr. Taggett."

The heat of that whisper goes to Johnny's head the way his first shot of whiskey did. He can feel the heat rising in him as a soft hand reaches around his body, reaches down for his stiffening dick. A hot wet tongue tickles his ear and there's that whisper again, decorated by a light Chinese accent. "Compliments of Mr. Wang. Just relax and enjoy." Fingers curl around his shaft as it thickens, lazily stroking, making Johnny moan.

"You," he stutters, "you work downstairs . . . in . . . in the bar," as the hand grips him a little tighter. Lips drift over the back of his neck as a soft warm body presses into his back. He can feel her nipples, so hard they're almost pressing into him. His hips start to pump into her strokes, and he can feel her hair bristling against his ass as her leg pushes between his. He can feel the heat of her on the back of his thigh. He can barely get the words out as he groans, "Who…who are you?"

The tongue slides into his ear and out again, and the hot whisper blows cool over his skin. "It doesn't matter who I am, Mr. Taggett." The soft hot hand grips tighter, strokes faster, the voice going a little higher, a little breathier. "After tonight you'll never see me again, never have to think of me." Little sharp teeth bite into the side of his neck, a hot wet mouth sucking his skin. She's humming, and it's vibrating through him, shooting sparks in every nerve. Pleasure pulls a long loud moan out of Johnny's chest as his body writhes and jerks. That clever little hand keeps pulling, caressing his length, the breath in his ear coming faster, the girl behind him cooing and sighing. "Yes, Johnny," she whispers. "Let yourself go." He can feel the pressure of his explosion rising along his spine, a growl he can't contain pushing up through his throat, his eyes rolling back as he loses control. His body shakes and shakes.

He can feel himself fade back into that warm dark pool of sleep as the lips tease a playful little kiss over his ear. "Sweet dreams, Mr. Taggett," she giggles. "Your new employer looks forward to meeting you." Before he can think of a question to ask she's gone and he's asleep anyway.

CHAPTER TWENTY ONE

"You didn't get a wink of sleep, did you?" Taggett has to chuckle as he gets off the elevator to find Chen slumped in one of the lobby's plush wing-back chairs with a hand draped over his eyes to block the morning sun glittering off the river. The younger man just groans and gropes for his hat as Taggett sits down across the little glass table from him, lights a smoke, and passes it over. "Get a visitor last night?" he asks, winking as he lights one for himself, takes a nice long drag, blows out a plume of smoke that hangs curling and twisting around itself in the still morning air.

Chen jams his hat down over his eyes and groans again. "Met a girl at the bar, took her back up to my room, had some more beers, and then I don't even know what. All I know is she was gone when I woke up and whatever's in that beer is giving me a head full of broken glass." He takes a long drag of his cigarette, blows out a cloud to join the one forming around Taggett. "I'll be all right, don't worry, I've had a hangover before." Straightening up, he pushes back his hat and looks deep into Taggett's eyes. "Seriously, don't worry about me. I can see that look on your face. I'll be just fine to meet the big boss."

Taggett takes a long look back at his partner and says, "I trust you, Chen. You say you'll be all right, you'll be all right." He glances around the lobby and doesn't notice anyone looking too interested in him, so he turns his gaze back to Chen. "Just remember, we don't really know where we're going or what's gonna happen. This guy, Wang or Wong or whatever, he'll be waiting for us. We need to be ready for anything. You made sure to load your gun, right?"

"Come on," Chen snorts. "You know I don't carry one of those. They make it too easy to kill a man, and that just gets me in trouble." He laces his fingers together and arches his hands backward. His knuckles crack like little pistol shots. "Besides, I don't need one," he smirks. "I can just take care of myself if I have to."

Taggett chuckles again. "Yeah, I guess you can." Far off across the lush expanse of the lobby's carpet a door opens and closes, and Taggett's smile switches off. "Okay, look sharp, here comes Jie."

The little man's coming right at them, wearing a shiny silver-grey double-breasted suit and a hat about half a size too small for his head. His ears are sticking out like rudders to aim his approach, as direct as a friendly torpedo. The partners stand up as he nears and stops a few feet away. "Good morning, gentlemen," he says. "I trust your stay has allowed you to recuperate successfully from the stressful endeavors of your voyage and that you've made yourself adequately prepared for your first meeting with our mutual employer."

Chen just glares while Taggett mumbles, "Uh, yeah, looking forward, sure." The three men cross the vast floor, headed toward the hotel's entrance, but Jie makes a sudden left before they get there, leading them through a door labeled STAFF ONLY and into a narrow hall that smells a little like stagnant water. They follow it through a few sharp turns and end up in the little alley between hotels. The Phantom II is standing there, taking up almost the whole space. Jie opens the back door, nearly nicking it on a concrete wall. As Chen and Johnny duck their heads to step into the car, the little man pulls out a handkerchief so clean it's almost blinding and wipes a speck from the door, then shuts it behind them. In the moment of silence after the *thunk* of the shutting door, Taggett turns to his partner and murmurs, "What's your problem with this guy?"

"I just don't like the way he talks," says Chen, and then Jie's got the front door open and he's slipped inside, started the engine, and got the car gliding along the alley, away from the river. When he gets to the back of the Palace he makes a left and a left and a right and then that fabulous car is back on the river highway, hunched-over workers pushing big carts of fish and ice along the sidewalks and into the alleys as the Phantom II makes its stately way upriver.

Johnny watches through the window as the buildings to his right get smaller. The fancy hotels turn into cheaper hotels, and the cheaper hotels turn into block after block of low flat warehouses. Jie makes a right, leaving the highway. The Phantom II starts to jolt as its wheels leave the paved road and dig into the packed dirt of the streets Jie's driving down, streets narrowing into not much more than alleys. After more turns than Taggett can keep track of, the car pulls to a stop beside a wide blank plaster wall with a little door set in it. There's a sign over the door, but Taggett has no idea what the curlicues printed on it might mean. Chen snores a little beside him. Taggett jabs him in the ribs with an elbow. "Look alive," mutters the tough detective. "I think we're here." Chen jerks himself awake, blinking as Jie steps from the car into the muddy little street and walks around to open the car's back door.

"Gentlemen," the little man says in his oddly mellow voice, "we have arrived." He holds the door open as Taggett and Chen slide out into the crappy little lane and look around. The neighborhood's deserted. Something that sounds like a crow is making an invisible racket somewhere, the only sound Taggett can hear over his own breathing. He sniffs the still air and smells the river. He can tell it's nearby, but he can't see it. Jie closes the car door and steps past the partners to the little door in the wall to press the button it's got instead of a knob. After a second or two the door opens and a goon almost too big to fit through it steps out, blocking the entrance with his body. The big thug grins wide enough to show everyone how many teeth he's got. He's got a lot of teeth.

In a strained whisper, the guy says to Jie, "The master's been expecting you." That's when Taggett notices the thick red scar straight across the goon's throat.

"The master give you that cute decoration on your neck?" says Taggett, and the goon turns and looks at him. The guy's so big he has to turn his whole body like the spotlight in a lighthouse. Taggett swallows and keeps going. "I mean, is this the kind of guy we're gonna be working for, the kind of guy who just slashes a guy across the throat? What the hell's his problem, some kind of discipline deal?"

The goon reaches toward Taggett, holds his big hand next to the detective's head, makes a fist the size of a bowling ball. "I am the master's discipline," he whispers. "When he commands I obey. My commands are his. When I command for him you must obey. Now give me your gun."

"What?" Taggett blinks at the big guy. "You're crazy. First thing they taught me at the precinct house was never give up your gun, never to anyone. You'll get my forty-five when you can swallow it, Baby Huey. Come on, yell if you don't like it."

It's the goon's turn to blink, but not for long as that massive fist starts to pull back. Taggett braces himself to take the hit, stepping back, getting ready to duck and roll and pull out his forty-five and blast a hole in the goon's big melon. In the corner of his eye he can see Chen moving into a fighting stance, just a little too slow to get involved before that big thug punches Johnny's head off.

Then Jie's standing between them. Taggett didn't even see the little man move. Jie's looking up at the goon, saying something Taggett doesn't get, and the goon's backing up, relaxing that massive fist back into a massive hand. As Taggett relaxes, Jie turns around and says, "Please, Mr. Taggett. You really must surrender your firearm to gain admission to the master's presence. Otherwise, your employment may come to a sudden end."

Taggett snarls, "You threatening me?"

"Not at all, sir," Jie says, his tone staying as even as the table at a board meeting. "I merely point out that you find yourself here far away from the world you've known. Without Mr. Wong's protection, his guidance, your situation could very well become untenable. I'm sure you have no wish to throw off that protection and guidance, to isolate yourself in a country where you have no friends and no prospects. You strike me as a man with too much wisdom to pursue such a foolish and self-destructive course."

Beside him, Chen murmurs, "Come on, Johnny. This is our only shot at finding out why they killed Mr. McBride."

Taggett growls. The three other men on the sidewalk stand there looking at him. The goon cracks his knuckles. Chen bounces on the balls of his feet, flexing his fingers, still ready to fight. Jie stands still, a look on his face as if he's waiting for a bus as he extends his hand toward Taggett. "Please, sir," says the little man. "I can assure you that your firearm will be well taken care of in my custody, but you must pass it into my care before Banh here will allow you entrance." Banh grins again, and Taggett has to wonder just how much damage those jagged teeth can do. That invisible bird is still yelling about whatever bothers birds. Taggett shrugs, reaches into his coat, and hands Jie his forty-five. "Congratulations, sir, you've made the right decision," Jie murmurs and tucks it away in the pocket of his jacket. Straightening himself, shooting a stiff look at the goon, he bows a little and gestures toward the dark space just beyond the door in the wall. "Gentlemen, if you'll be so kind as to step inside."

Taggett takes a moment to light up a fresh smoke. He stands there puffing idly, as Chen lights one up for himself. Finally, in their own good time, the men walk through the door into the darkness. Their footsteps click on the concrete floor as the door slams shut behind them.

They stand there for a minute in the silent darkness. The tips of their cigarettes glow red, getting brighter as the partners keep smoking. Then, with a thick dull clank, a spotlight flares on. Both men throw a hand up, trying to shield already dazed eyes. Chen yells something and the spotlight switches back off. Taggett sways a little in the sudden darkness, little spots swimming all around him as he blinks. Just as suddenly as the spotlight did, some tall lamps in the corners of what turns out to be a room about the size of Johnny's at the Palace blink on. "Jesus," Johnny mumbles, "it looks like a Tarzan movie in here."

The walls look like they're made of bamboo rods tied together with vines. There's a deep red rug on the floor a few feet ahead of them with a couple of bamboo chairs that look like thrones and a glass-topped bamboo coffee table holding it down. On the other side of the rug stands an Oriental girl in a tight dress that hugs her curves into an invitation, its skirt reaching all the way down to the floor but slit twice all the way up to her hips. As Taggett blinks the last of his blindness away, she winks at him and says in a soft voice that sounds like she's just about to giggle, "Honored guests, please make yourselves comfortable. You will soon meet our master."

Taggett cautiously takes a chair, and Chen takes the other. The girl lightly steps forward and kneels on the rug. "If this one can be of assistance to you in any way," she breathes, and just lets the men finish that thought on their own.

"Oh, honey, you're definitely a professional," snorts Taggett, "and a good one, but you'd better just slide back to wherever you came from and get your boss. We've come a long way and—"

"THE WAY YOU HAVE COME IS FAR, BUT YOU HAVE FAR TO GO," blares a voice from a loudspeaker somewhere. The raw power of the amplification makes both men jump and twist around to try to see what made that harsh noise, so distorted it could be anyone talking. "JOHN FRANCIS TAGGETT. CHEN HAO YE. I AM YOUR EMPLOYER. YOU MAY ADDRESS ME AS MR. WONG."

The girl, still kneeling, sighs, "The master shows his face to no one."

"NO ONE," the mechanical voice agrees.

Taggett reaches into his coat, pulls out a pack of cigarettes, shakes one up through the top, offers it to Chen. Chen reaches over to accept. Taggett takes one for himself, puts the pack back in his pocket, light his, lights Chen's, puts his matchbook away, and says into the air, "Are you that ugly?"

The hidden speaker hums and then erupts into a set of explosions that sound a little like someone laughing then clicks. "PERHAPS, JOHN TAGGETT. IT IS NOT YOUR CONCERN. YOU ARE A KILLER. I HAVE BROUGHT YOU HERE TO KILL."

"Uh," says Johnny, "I don't know what you've heard about me, but I've never—"

"YOU WILL. YOU WILL KILL FOR ME. YOU HAVE NO CHOICE. ANY WHO STEAL FROM ME MUST DIE."

Johnny tries a chuckle, but it sticks in his throat. "Don't you have killers in Shanghai?"

"YOU ARE THE KILLER FOR THIS JOB, JOHN TAGGETT. BOTH YOU AND YOUR ASSOCIATE POSSESS THE NECESSARY SKILLS FOR THIS TASK. IT IS MY DESIRE THAT YOU PERFORM

IT. YOU WILL PERFORM IT. YOU MAY NOW RETURN TO YOUR HOTEL AND AWAIT INSTRUCTION." The hum of the loudspeaker abruptly turns back to silence.

Chen looks at Taggett. "What the hell," says the younger man.

"Son, I have no clue on earth what that was," says Taggett.

The girl kneeling between them says, "The master has dismissed you, gentlemen. Time for you to leave." With that, the lamps shut off, exploding the room back into total darkness before the partners can quite get out of their chairs.

Behind them, the door to the street opens, and a big block of sunlight pushes in. Taggett looks around for the shadow of the girl, but they're alone. From outside Jie's voice announces, "This way, gentlemen. We have instructions to wait." Blinking, Chen and Johnny make their way back out to the Phantom II. The big goon grins at them, and Chen grins right back. Holding open the big car's back door, Jie blinks and says to Taggett and Chen, "Welcome, gentlemen, to the organization. Welcome to Shanghai."

CHAPTER TWENTY TWO

They ride back to the hotel in a silence as thick as the dirt on a grave. Taggett stares out the window at the river and its crowd of little boats dodging around the big freighters, but he's not seeing any of that. His fingers are drumming on the armrest. By this time of morning, the tourists are wandering around the edges of the road, scurrying in and out of the hotel doors like ants in a maze. The big Phantom II eases its way down the river past the ferry landing, and takes its wide swooping left across traffic into the alley next to the Palace as Taggett gazes at whatever's going on in his head.

Jie comes around to open the door. "Gentlemen, you may expect a representative of the master to appear this evening and explain to you the details of your mission. As before, of course, all the entertainments of which the Palace Hotel is capable of provision are at your disposal while you wait. Please do enjoy yourselves. Mr. Wong firmly maintains that a man works best when he knows that the organization of which he finds himself a part considers his pleasures as well as its own needs. I'm quite sure that you gentlemen will find that a most congenial philosophy." By the time he's through all that Chen and Johnny have made it out of the car. They're standing there staring down at him. Taggett absentmindedly, almost automatically, gets out a cigarette and lights it as Jie pushes the door closed and stands between the partners blinking. Chen lights up one of his own. The three men stand there for a moment as the city makes its noise around them, cars rattling along the river road, boat horns blasting into the air, tourists clattering past the mouth of the alley on their own business, barely noticing the Phantom II, not even seeing the men standing next to it, two big guys staring down at a smaller one.

About halfway through his cigarette Taggett finally says, "So what the hell, Jie? What is it with this Wong character? Is he nuts? Why the hell would he ruin two lives—wait, three or four lives—just to get an amateur hit man from half a world away? None of this makes a damn bit of sense."

Jie keeps blinking. "The master's ways are his own, Mr. Taggett. He commands and we obey."

"Nuts to that," says Chen. He throws his cigarette to the ground and steps closer to Jie. "I'm sick of this game. What if I just start shaking answers out of you, you little puffed-up excuse for a taxi driver? Think you'd talk a little better then?"

Jie doesn't back up. His spine straightens and his hands drift out from his body a little. "I assure you, sir," he says, "that although I of course regret your unfavorable opinion of me, I will by no means be threatened. Because the master has need of you I cannot cause you such damage as to incapacitate you. I can, however—forgive me, I forget myself." His hands fall back to hang at his sides, then come together under the little man's chin with their palms together. ""Sir, I apologize for my outburst. Please understand that I simply have none of the answers you seek. Like you, I await instructions."

Johnny has to hold Chen back as the younger man lunges for Jie. "Come on," says Johnny, lips to Chen's ear. "We need this guy. He's the only way we're gonna find out what's going on here. Let's try not to kill each other before we do what we came here for." He gives Chen a little shove back and turns to the smaller man. "Listen, Jie, I'm guessing that Wong's got hooks in you like he's got in us. We're all in this together, right? Isn't there anything you can tell us about what he's got going on?"

Jie blinks up at Taggett and slowly smiles. "Sir, we all attempt to proceed with honor. I can see that our paths have indeed joined for a time and that our interests have become as one. On that basis, perhaps I can elucidate our employer's expectations. I have become aware that the master's efforts in supplying opium to various markets in the United

States have been obstructed here in Shanghai. I can only assume that he wishes you to somehow remove that obstacle." Slipping a key into the little door in the alley, he opens it, explaining, "But perhaps this conversation will better serve in the more convivial surroundings of your suite. I must suspect that the master would respond most unfavorably to the details of his business being discussed here in a public alley." He gives a harsh whistle, and a kid in a snappy red uniform steps out through the door. Jie says something to the kid and hands him a bill. The kid gives a little salute, gets into the car, and drives it away as Jie shepherds the larger men inside.

A few minutes later they're sitting around the low mahogany table in Taggett's suite. Jie's mixed up some martinis from the bar that's right there in the room, and Taggett has to give a little contented sigh as he sips. "These are amazing, Jie. Where'd you learn to mix drinks like that?"

"You'll find I have many unsuspected talents, Mr. Taggett." The little guy's almost smirking.

"I'm counting on it. But what more can you tell me about Wong's opium business?" Taggett glances over his scowling partner across the table. "What the hell could he possibly need with a couple of small-times like Chen and me?"

"Alas, sir, my knowledge is deeply limited." Chen twitches a little, lips starting to pull back from his teeth, but a glare from Johnny keeps him under control. "I do know that the master makes a habit of the most extreme caution. This is why he lets no one see his face. Perhaps he wishes to insulate himself from the consequences of the actions he asks you to perform."

Taggett chuckles. "Perhaps." He lights up a smoke and offers one to Jie, but the little man just shakes his head. Taggett shrugs and offers it to Chen. The younger man takes it and lights it and goes back to scowling across the table at Jie. Johnny takes a long look at his partner. "Perhaps we can do something about that," he says, and then he takes another sip of his martini and grins. "Jie, how would you like to be out from under this guy? I figure he's got the same kind of hooks in you he's got in Chen and me. How'd you like to get unhooked, be your own man?"

Jie suddenly becomes very still. He takes in a long slow breath of air and stops blinking. Finally he says, "Sir, I find myself at a loss for words. I suspect that honor demands that I reject the proposal you implicitly put forward."

"Maybe and maybe not," says Taggett. "Seems to me this Wong guy doesn't have too much honor, the way he treats the people who work for him. What's he done to deserve your respect, your loyalty?"

Jie takes a sip of his martini and looks steady into Taggett's eyes over the rim of the glass. There's a grandfather clock in the corner of the room, and its ticking is the only noise in there, like slow steady knocks with a hammer to the side of a coffin. Taggett's holding his breath, waiting for Jie's response. The little guy looks like he's planning his way through a minefield as he starts to speak. "Sir," he says, "you strike me as a man conversant with the difficulties of the honorable life. The ways of honor often compel a man into situations he would not otherwise have made for himself. You seem to have ascertained my predicament, and you speak persuasively to indicate a possible escape from it." He takes another sip. "Indeed, sir, you appear to be offering me a chance I can hardly refuse to take, bound to serve the master though I may be. However, your partner's evident dislike for me may prove an insurmountable obstacle to the kind of communitarian exercise you appear to have in mind."

"I can get over that," says Chen. "I don't think I'm ever gonna get used to the weird way you talk, but I'm here for a reason, not just to get all worked up all the time. I'm trying to follow Johnny's example."

Jie nods. "That seems wise. Your Mr. Taggett seems to possess uncommon awareness of his priorities."

"Thanks," Taggett snorts. "You're gonna make me feel like someone's dad." The men around the table laugh together as they finish their drinks, and Jie gets up to make another batch.

After a while the light in the suite starts to get all golden as the sun starts going down. As Chen's turning on one of the gilded lamps a knock comes from the door. Taggett slides a hand into his jacket, fingers brushing the handle of his forty-five, and nods and Chen. The younger man steps to the door and opens it.

The white guy on the other side's wearing a porkpie hat with his black suit and skinny tie. He holds up a hand and says in a voice that comes squeaking through his nose, "Greetings, partner. It's Chen, right? Welcome to the team. I'm Smith. I'll be explaining things to you. Gonna let me in, or should we do this in the hall?" Chen steps back, almost growling, his muscles taut and ready as Smith steps into the room and pushes the door shut behind him. The slick character makes a pistol out of his finger and thumb and points at Johnny. "And you must be Taggett, the tough guy. We hear a lot of real fascinating things about you, tough guy."

Taggett slides an empty hand out of his jacket, relaxing a little. He smirks into Smith's eyes. "I can see you're trying to be impressive. Good for you. Maybe some time we'll see just how impressive you are, but tonight you're just here to tell us what's going on. Right?"

Smith seems to shrink a little in his snappy outfit. "Yeah. Right. Okay." He tosses his hat on the table and takes a seat at the table next to Jie. He doesn't say anything to the little guy, and Jie doesn't say anything to Smith. They barely seem to notice each other. As Chen sits down next to Taggett, the tough detective grins like a shark into Smith's eyes. Smith returns the stare for as long as he can, then drops his gaze back down to the table and starts talking. "The opium trade's been nice and fat for us until the law around here went crazy and started busting our transport system. We just can't take our cargo over the roads anymore, can't even get it on a train. So we've been using barges, shipping down the Grand Canal through the countryside, paying off the captains, hiding our packages in their freight—you know, food, animal shit, whatever. We don't even put our stuff on every barge, we pick loads at random just to throw off the kind of scum who'd try to steal from us. And that's been working pretty good for us, but lately our cargo's been coming up short. The boss doesn't like it when the cargo comes up short." The snappy character stops to take a breath, glancing around the table at the empty martini glasses in front of the three other men. "Say, all this talking is thirsty work. Mind if I—" Taggett interrupts him with a shake of the head. Smith sighs and goes on. "Anyway, we figure someone from the Zhang organization has doped out our scheme. Those bastards are always trying to one-up the boss. We don't know how they're doing it, but those scumbags are somehow lifting our product off the barges. We can't figure it out—we know the crew's on our pad, and we've tortured a few of them anyway, just to make sure they're not filling their pockets on our dime. They're not. If they were they would've been begging to tell us about it, trust me." Smith lets a nasty little grin stretch out under his letter opener of a nose as the three men sit there and stare at him. He takes another look at the empty glasses and rolls his eyes toward the bar and smacks his lips like a desert pilgrim dying of thirst. No one moves, so he starts again. "Someone from the Zhangs is getting on our barges and taking off our goods. That's gotta stop. The boss seems to think you're the guy to stop it. So what you gotta do is find out how those Zhangs are getting our product and make them stop. You might have to kill one or two of them. The boss'll probably give you a bonus if you do." The nasty smirk hasn't gone away, and now Smith's aiming his dead blue eyes right at Taggett. "You're not afraid to get your hands dirty, are you?"

Taggett chuckles a little. "Like I say, you might find out some time. I do what I gotta, don't worry."

Smith chuckles right back. "I never worry, flatfoot. I'm just a bluebird of happiness." He leans back in a chair and lights up a cigarette, slipping the pack right back into his pocket. "Any of you mugs got any questions about the mission?"

Chen says, "Ever think about getting one of your own guys into one of these crews? Just to figure out how you're getting screwed?"

"Yeah, we thought of that, Mr. Genius," says Smith. "Somehow they always end up getting dead by the time they get to Shanghai. I'm guessing the boss doesn't want to lose any more useful guys, so he hired you and your pal, a couple of mopes no one's gonna miss anyway." He cracks his knuckles one by one as he stares Chen in the face, then sneers, "Any other bright comments?"

Chen's starting to push his chair back a little, so Taggett speaks up before the fight can break out. "No, I think we got it." The tough detective lights up a smoke and passes it over to Chen. "Here," he mutters to his partner, "keep your hands busy." Turning his gaze back to

Smith he says, "You got anything else to explain, or are you just waiting around for a free drink?"

Smith lets the comment hang in the air for a moment, then settles his hat back on his head. He makes the finger pistols again, pointing at Taggett, then at Chen, then he slips out of the room without another word. The three men look at each other, and Jie says, "I suppose the master takes his help where he can find it. Don't worry, gentlemen. I know the Grand Canal very well. In the morning, I shall drive us to the city of Suzhou, near the head of the canal, and we can begin our investigation."

Taggett smiles at the little guy. "We?"

"Yes, sir," Jie smiles back.

CHAPTER TWENTY THREE

And that starts a solid couple weeks of trouble. Taggett finds out pretty fast that Shanghai doesn't look much like its tourist district: that four-lane highway that follows the river turns into a bunch of dirt paths once you get a little inland, and the road that runs along the canal is mostly made of mud. He and Chen manage to ruin a good suit or two dragging the Phantom II out of some kind of Chinese muck, so Jie has to tell the cleaning staff at the Palace that the men are on some kind of government surveying team. The maps Jie gets from his people turn out to be from before the War: the little villages along the wandering scribble that's supposed to represent the canal seem to keep moving. Some just don't exist anymore. The canal itself leaves the side of what passes for the road so many times that the partners keep losing it. Jie stops every now and then to ask one of the villagers about it, but no one knows anything, like the canal is some sort of secret legend they're keeping from the outside world. Taggett tries spreading out a few fistfuls of Wong's money to loosen those clenched jaws, but the partners get nowhere. Sooner or later they give up and just start making their own map, scrawling with a scrounged crayon on the wax paper that the hotel wraps their sandwiches in as the Phantom II pokes around the little paths from village to canal. "Not quite as easy as we thought it'd be," says Chen.

"Nothing ever is," says Taggett. They're jittering around in the big back seat of the Phantom II as Jie maneuvers it over a dirt road that heads through some village they can't quite figure out the name of on the map. The glossy black surface of the fancy car has turned all mottled and pitted, looks a little like the surface of the road it's trying to handle. Chen's been staring off to the left through Jie's old British Army binoculars for hints of where the canal might be. They lost sight of it a few hours ago, and the sky's getting dark, the shadows of the shacks they pass starting to stretch into the crappy little road like pits an outsider could fall in. Taggett squints down at the mess of black lines on the greasy paper in his lap and says, "This is getting ridiculous. We're never gonna map this whole canal. Probably why Wong uses it in the first place, you can barely get to it from the land. There's just no way to get at those barges after they're launched."

Chen takes the binoculars away from his eyes and glances at his partner. "Must be some way," says the younger man. "I mean, they're doing it, right?"

"Yeah," scowls Taggett. "I just don't see how." Reaching out for the binoculars, he scans the horizon on his side of the car. The scenery sways like a hangover as Jie steers around the ruts in the road, and then it jumps and hops as the Phantom II hits the ruts Jie can't steer around. Through his headache, through the thickening dusk, Taggett notices something. Without moving his head, he says, "Hey, Jie, make a right, I think I see something . . . yeah, I think I've got an idea."

Jie finds a place to make a turn and swings the Phantom II into a wide right. Taggett almost falls over onto Chen as the road gets even worse. Jie sounds like his teeth are chattering as he says, "Ah, sir, I believe I understand the stratagem you're contemplating."

Chen rolls his eyes and groans a little. "Stratagem, really, come on, Johnny, what's on your—oh, I get it." Along with the other two men, Chen looks through the dusty windshield and sees what they're driving toward. The setting sun's casting the shadow of a wooden bridge that spans the canal maybe a quarter mile from where they were looking the wrong way for it.

Winking at his partner and somehow lighting a smoke in the bouncing back seat, Taggett says, "Yeah, this might be something. I figure if I can—" A sudden swerve throws him against the back door, almost knocks the cigarette out of his mouth. "Damn it, Jie, what the—"

"Forgive me, sir," says the driver. "I found myself impelled to take evasive action due to the prospect of gunfire from the party that's been following us since approximately the moment we entered the village through which we've just passed." The older man twists the wheel again, throwing Taggett all the way into Chen. The younger man gives Taggett a shove and grabs on to the door handle next to him. "Again, gentlemen, my apologies," come the words through Jie's clenched teeth. "I thought it wise also not to alert our pursuers to our consideration of the canal bridge."

A little explosion goes off, the kind of explosion Taggett remembers from boot camp, and then another, and then something ricochets off the side of the car with a little spark. Chen yells, "Jesus, shut up and drive, they're shooting at us!" He and Johnny have twisted around on the back seat to peer through the Phantom II's back window at the pair of headlights that's all they can see of whatever's chasing them. Jie makes a quick left, and the deep blue sky of evening turning into night fills their vision and then the headlights again, growing as the creeps get closer. There's a flash from the car behind and another *ping!* as the Phantom II takes another bullet. Taggett growls and unholsters his forty-five. He grips it in his right hand as his left rolls down the window and he gets ready to lean out. Another swerve knocks him on his ass.

"Goddamit, Jie, hold steady," he snarls. "I'm gonna mark these mothers so they'll leave us alone."

As the Phantom II speeds away from the shadow of the bridge Jie says, "May I advise an alternate course of action, sir, especially as you consider the inhabitants of the small village we're about to once more pass through." Taggett turns back around to figure out what Jie's talking about and discovers that in the two seconds he's had his eye off the car behind him the sun's vanished completely. The world's gone black except for the little patch of real estate the headlights on the Phantom II reveal and the lights of the big hotels a mile or two off ahead to their left. Jie's leaning forward a little, his eyes fixed on the road, the mirror, a gauge on the dashboard, the road again, his movements precise as he dodges the pits in the road. "An exchange of gunfire could have unpleasant ramifications," says Jie over his shoulder, as if he's making conversation while keeping track of the tea service. "Many of the people who live in these primitive conditions have astonishingly up-to-date firearms. In any event, I have total confidence in my ability to evade our, as you would say, shadow. I suggest you allow me to do so, thereby prolonging our chance to successfully complete our mission." Without waiting for an answer the little man twists the wheel again and stomps on the gas. Taggett flies back as the Phantom II digs into the crappy road and shoots forward.

Chen's still twisted around, riding lightly on his knees, adjusting to the car's crazy twists and turns like he's kneeling on the floor next to his bed. "Looks like you know what you're talking about," he says. "We're losing them, whoever they are. You're a hell of a driver."

"Learned it in the War," says Jie. "Now let's see about getting you back to your accommodations, and perhaps Mr. Taggett can explain his thoughts more thoroughly."

Taggett's putting his forty-five away. He looks up and says, "Uh, yeah," then sits back in the seat, head on a swivel, not talking as Jie sneaks the Phantom II into the alley next to the Palace. The tough detective's mind is buzzing with the ideas he's putting together as the partners make their way down the service hall, through the bar, into the elevator and into Taggett's suite.

Chen and Taggett have a seat at the big mahogany table, and Jie busies himself mixing up the martinis. The younger man lights up a smoke and passes it to Johnny, lighting one up for himself on the same match. "So what do you think?" says Chen.

"They're using the bridges," says Taggett. "They've got someone on the inside to tell them what barge to pilfer, and someone's dropping from one of those bridges to do it."

As Jie steps from the bar to the table, and places cool glasses full of nerve medicine in front of Taggett and Chen, he says, "Your hypothesis has a plausible ring to it, but can you account for your presumed bridge-jumper's ability to escape undetected from the targeted craft?"

Taggett smokes for a minute and stares into space. "I don't know," he finally says, "but I think I know how I can find out. We gotta map out where those bridges cross and figure out a timetable for the barges. Jie, you think we can get some help on that from Wong?"

Jie sips the martini he's served himself and blinks for a minute into Taggett's eyes before he replies, "I believe I can endeavor to obtain some information from Mr. Wong. Shall I represent the request as coming from you?"

"Yeah, you better do that," says Taggett. "I'd hate for him to torture me to death just because he thinks I'm the thief I'm chasing."

CHAPTER TWENTY FOUR

The Phantom II's parked about half a mile from a little village somewhere between Wuxi and Suzhou around sunset a couple days later. Taggett's finishing up the big ham sandwich the hotel wrapped up for him as Chen keeps his binoculars trained on the grey rock arch of the bridge the car's pointed at and Jie sits with his hands on the wheel, his gaze darting all over the scene. "Nothing yet," Chen says.

Taggett swallows and says, "Keep watching. If I've got it figured right, one of Wong's shipments should be cruising along any minute now. I wanna see what happens when it goes under that bridge."

"So the schedule I was able to produce for you proved to be of use?" Jie inquires. "I did assure the master that you'd be up to no sort of funny business. I believe he trusts you—and you, Mr. Chen—approximately as much as he expects the sun to rise in the West." That gets a snicker out of Taggett as the tough detective crumples up the wax paper his sandwich came in and lights up a smoke, offers one to Jie. The older man holds up a hand without taking his eyes off the scenery and says, "Forgive me, sir, but it's a habit I've never acquired. It may distract me from the task at hand, and I would find it hard to forgive myself were my lack of vigilance to provide an opportunity for our pursuers from the other night to establish our position and attack us unawares."

Taggett nods. "Yeah, I guess that makes sense. I'll tell you this, though, a lit cigarette's a good thing to have if some creep's getting too close and needs a hot little reminder to back off." Chen snorts a laugh, and Taggett turns his way and says, "Anything doing over there?"

Chen reaches back for a smoke and Taggett lights one from the tip of his own, passes it over. The younger man takes a drag without taking the binoculars away from his eyes. "Not a thing," he says. "Plenty of barges, but not the one we're waiting for, and no activity on the bridge. You think we got bad information?"

For a long moment no one has anything to say until Taggett speaks up: "I think Jie knows what he's doing. He hasn't steered us wrong yet. Except for you, he's the only guy in this whole crazy town I can trust." The tough detective takes a long drag on his cigarette and turns back toward Jie. "You got this timetable straight from Wong, right?"

"It would be more accurate to say that I dealt with the master's odious associate, that character who insists on calling himself Smith. If you'll forgive my saying so, the temptation was nearly overpowering to shut that miscreant's mouth with one or two applications of my knuckles." Chen and Taggett both nod and chuckle at that. "However, despite the man's distasteful mode of behavior, I know him to be a faithful servant of Mr. Wong, and as such highly unlikely to supply us with intelligence unlikely to promote the success of what we do here for him."

"I don't know about that," says Chen. "He didn't seem to happy to meet us, especially Johnny. I can see how he'd give us fake information just to make us look bad, maybe get us killed. I get the feeling he's the kind of guy who likes to throw gas on fires." Taggett cracks his knuckles and grins. Without turning around, Chen says, "I can hear that, Johnny. You're thinking about what you'll do when you see that snappy-talking squirt again."

Taggett taps some ash from his smoke into the armrest's ashtray and thinks for a minute. "Yeah," he finally says. "There's just something about that guy that rubs me wrong. I knew dozens of jerks like him in New York, weasels who think they're tough because they've got a big man behind them. I used to make a hobby of smacking punks like that around till they'd squeal."

"I can see that you have quite the strong sense of honor, sir," says Jie.

Taggett snorts, "Yeah, I'm a shining knight." Lighting up another smoke from the butt of his last one, he leans back and gazes out the window. "No, I just hate fakes. Never could stand a soft character acting tough. That's the kind of shit that gets a man killed." The three men sit in silence for a moment, Chen still observing the bridge and Jie watching everything else. The sky just keeps getting darker.

Suddenly, for the first time in months, Taggett's scar starts to itch as Jie clears his throat to say, "Pardon me, sirs, but I believe that the unpleasant character we were just discussing is coming toward us." Taggett turns around in the back seat and there's Smith, picking his way across the muddy track between his car and the Phantom, that same grin resting on his face like a knife balancing on its blade. The tough detective glances at Chen. The younger man's already got the binoculars stowed somewhere as Taggett's hand slides toward his forty-five. Jie sits motionless.

Smith takes a while to get to the car, looks like he's being careful not to get the cuffs of his pants messed up. He's wearing that same black suit, that same porkpie hat, that same skinny black tie. By the time he reaches the men the sun's a dull halo behind him. His face is just a field of shadow until he lights up a smoke, the flare of the match flickering over his sharp features, his dead eyes. "Greetings, boys," he says. "I was just in the neighborhood when I noticed you parked here all alone. Not interrupting some kind of orgy, I hope."

Chen growls, and Taggett holds a restraining hand back. "No such luck," he says with a little chuckle. "You'll have to get your thrills some other way."

"I keep forgetting what a cute sense of humor you've got, tough guy. Quite the comedian. You might start singing a different tune if I see without your little crew to back you up." Smith leans into the window, cigarette stuck in that grin, and blows some smoke at Taggett's face.

Taggett squints and grins back and lights up a new smoke of his own, passing the pack to Chen. The younger man lights up and slides the pack into his jacket and says, "I'll get you a new pack later."

"Yeah, no problem," says Taggett, his eyes not leaving Smith's. "As for you, Smith or Jones or whatever you want to call yourself, you gotta know that no one here is happy to see you. We're trying to get some work done, so why don't you take your cowboy act and scurry along before someone has to get hurt."

The grin turns into a snarl for a second and then recovers itself. "Listen, Sluggo, you've got it all wrong," says Smith. "It's not like I'm here for the pleasure of your witty banter. The boss gave me a job to do, just like he gave you one, right? Only my job is to make sure you mugs don't screw up your job." He taps his ash into the ashtray Taggett's been using. "Get it? Whether I'm welcome, whether you like me, I'm part of your life. You're what they call an investment. You know the boss'd hate to lose you the way he lost your buddy McBride." Smith snickers.

Chen lunges across Taggett before anyone else can move, reaching around the tough detective and grabbing Smith by his skinny tie to pull the punk deeper into the car. Taggett locks eyes with his partner and cradles the younger man's face in his big hands. "Not yet," he says. "This isn't the time. We need to figure this out. Just killing this one punk won't get even for Walt. Let him go. Let him go. You can let go." He manages to crowd Chen over to the other end of the backseat, up against the window, and looks back.

Smith's back outside the car, hands in the air. For a second Taggett wonders where Jie's gone to in all this, then he sees the old driver behind Smith. He's got the weasel locked in a full Nelson, arms curled around the slightly bigger man's shoulders, fingers laced behind Smith's head. Jie's got his lips to Smith's ears, murmuring something. Smith shakes his head like a wet dog, then winces as Jie tightens his grip. Finally, Smith nods and Jie lets him go. Smith staggers forward a few steps and looks around on the ground for his hat in the thickening dusk. Jie's a few paces away, watching him. Finally, Smith finds his hat, shoves it back on his head, and starts back across the track. "This ain't over!" he's yelling. "I'm on to you, you son of a bitch! All of you! The boss is gonna hear about this!" In the darkness there's the sound of a car door slamming, then Smith turns on his headlights, fires up his car's engine, and makes a rooster tail of mud as he spins his back wheels getting out of there. Jie jumps gracefully out of the way and slips back into the Phantom II, taking his place behind the wheel.

Taggett's been pressing on Chen's chest all this time, keeping his partner in the car and out of trouble. Now he looks back into Chen's face and finds him perfectly calm, a little smirk curving his thin lips. "You can let go now," says the younger man, "unless you just can't take your hands off me."

The tough detective leans back and takes a long look the man who's shaking a new smoke out of the pack and lighting up. After a moment Taggett has to laugh. "You wily son of a bitch," he says. Chen grins and passes his partner the pack of cigarettes. Taggett lights up. "You were just trying to get rid of Smith."

"Hey, I'm supposed to be the crazy one, right? I figured I may as well use that to get us a little space to work in." Chen chuckles as he takes a drag, blows out a long plume of smoke. "Did you see the look on that rat's face when I went for him? They're gonna have to wash more than mud out of his suit tonight."

Taggett keeps laughing. "Yeah, I guess we're gonna have to start calling you Mad Dog Chen. Good thing Jie was here to handle that creep."

"It seemed the best course of action, sir," says Jie as the darkness settles in around the car. "I felt it necessary to endeavor to deter Mr. Smith from his course of action, one which could jeopardize not only our mission but also, indeed, and his well-being. He seemed convinced by my argument." That just cracks up the guys in the back, Chen laughing so hard he actually slaps his knee. Jie says nothing for a moment, then comes up with, "I wonder if our response will cause further distrust on the part of Mr. Wong. Perhaps our treatment of Mr. Smith was injudicious and ultimately detrimental to the success of our larger plan."

That shuts them up. The sounds of the village shutting itself down for the night seep in through the open windows. Taggett can hear what must be a lullaby coming from one of the shacks on the village's outskirts and a scraping of chopsticks against wooden dishes. Somewhere crickets are calling to each other as the night gets darker. After a few minutes of this, Chen says, "It occurs to me, that might not be a problem. I got so busy laughing I forgot why I was so hot to get Smith out of here." He stubs out his butt in the ashtray in the backseat's other armrest. "Listen,

Johnny, just before Jie noticed that jerk I saw what we were looking for. Wong's barge passed under the bridge and I could swear some guy jumped down onto it. You were right, that's how they're doing it." Chen's eyes are on fire as they stare into Taggett's.

Taggett grins back. "May as well take us home, Jie," he says as he lights a new smoke from the end of the old one. "Tomorrow we'll find the bridge up the canal from this one, and maybe a smuggler'll get a little surprise."

CHAPTER TWENTY FIVE

"Now," says Johnny, "let's figure out what we're gonna need for this trick." They're sitting around the mahogany table in Johnny's suite as thick clouds gather around the slowly rising sun. "I'm gonna need some practice, so we're gonna have to grease one or two of these barge captains, have them cruise under the bridge so I can drop and then pull into the next village and let me off. Think we can do that?"

Jie takes a sip of water and thinks for a short moment. "Yes, sir, I believe that is within my abilities. In the course of our worked I've managed to develop some relationships among the traders that ply the waterways here, and I've found them quite amenable to monetary persuasion. Very little effort should be required to convince one or two of these hardy mariners to alter his course to meet our requirements. I shall endeavor in that regard and return to you with information later this morning, if that suits you."

Taggett swallows a cool mouthful of his breakfast martini and says, "Yeah, suits me just fine. I'm gonna take a little stroll, see if I can find out where Smith is staying, maybe keep him off our backs today. Meet back here at eleven?"

"I'm with you," says Chen. "I wouldn't mind another little conversation with that punk."

Taggett chuckles. "Good idea, Mad Dog. It'll be fun just to watch him flinch when he sees you." The tough detective finishes his drink and pushes back his chair. "Let's go have a laugh." He lights a cigarette for Chen and one for himself, and the two of them head for the bar in the lobby to start asking questions.

And a couple hours of that gets them exactly nowhere. No one they describe Smith to has any idea where he might hang his stupid little hat. No one even admits to recognizing the little creep. One of the maids just turns and walks away the second she hears the punk's name. Chen watches the sway of her hips as she goes, the way she makes the little skirt of her maid's uniform flip back and forth, and gives Johnny a nudge. "Maybe we should follow her, you know, just to see where that sweet ass ends up."

Taggett takes a look at his watch and shakes his head, saying, "No time for that now. We gotta meet Jie back in the suite. We can find out about Smith another time."

"If he doesn't crawl out of his hole while we're working today," Chen snickers.

Taggett doesn't laugh in return. "If he comes after us," he says, "we'll deal with him. We've got more important things to worry about than swatting a fly." The tough detective lights up a fresh smoke. Chen lights up one of his own, and the two of them find their way back to Taggett's suite.

Jie's waiting there behind a table crowded with steaming bowls of noodles. Taggett and Chen have to take a deep breath as they come in, just to get as much as they can of that deep aroma before they shuck off their jackets and sit. They don't waste a minute grabbing plates and piling on the chow mein and sucking it right down. As Jie's asking them to pardon his presumption in having a brief repast delivered in order that Mr. Taggett might furnish himself with sufficient energy for his exertions, Johnny's finishing up a second plate and leaning back into his seat with a hand on his belly and his eyes a little glazed. He lights up a smoke and says, "So I guess this means you didn't have too much trouble getting us some practice barges."

"None whatsoever, sir," Jie smiles. Glancing at the clock behind Taggett's head, he continues, "I also took the liberty of purchasing some supplies you may need, especially if you intend to take advantage of the cover of darkness for this endeavor. However, if we're to arrive at our rendezvous at the designated hour, we'd be well-advised to make our departure with speed and dispatch." Chen lets a mouthful of noodles dangle over his chin and blinks at the little driver. Jie blinks back. "In other words, gentlemen, we should leave soon so we'll get there on time."

Taggett chuckles. "Shouldn't be a problem. Those noodles smelled so good we never even got around to taking our hats off. Okay, I'm ready. Let's go."

By the time they get out to the Phantom II the rain's coming down in thick drops, spattering on their hats like bugs, painting stripes in the dirt on the car's body. Jie guides the big car through various twists and turns into the countryside. Taggett's in the front seat with him, checking the map to get them to the right bridge, while Chen kneels in the back, scanning through the back window for any sign of company. "You suppose that was Smith shooting at us the other night?" he says without turning around.

Without taking his eyes off the map Taggett says, "Even for such a weird jerk as Smith, I don't see why he'd want to do that. I'm pretty sure he still thinks we're all working for the same guy."

"I don't think that guy's working for anyone but himself," Chen snickers. "Doesn't look like anyone's following, though." He's doing his trick again, staying balanced on his knees as Jie swerves the Phantom II around the bigger potholes and through the endless mud puddles. The rain's coming harder, smacking like bullets into the excuse for a road. "We're probably the only sons of bitches foolish enough to go out in this weather," Chen says.

Taggett says, "Turn right here and park. I'll have to go the rest of the way on foot." Looking out the window, he shudders. "Did I ever tell you guys what happened to my old pal Sergeant Flagely?"

"Huh?" says Chen.

Johnny shakes his head like a wet dog, shaking off memories. "Doesn't matter. I'm just not a big fan of heights and rain."

Jie looks levelly at Taggett and says, "If I may be so bold, sir, I can—"

"No you may not," says Taggett. "This is what I gotta do, so I'm gonna be the one doing it. If everything goes right, I'll meet you a couple miles down the canal at however the hell you pronounce this." He stabs a stubby finger at the map, and Jie nods. The tough detective opens the door and says, "Be ready. Anything can happen." Then he's out, slamming the door and pushing through the thick hot rain toward the shadowy arch of the stone bridge.

He's muttering as he stomps through the sucking mud. "Of course it had to rain today . . . doesn't matter, it'll make a good test . . . but I'll be glad to get onto those stone steps, out of this muck . . . hope this works . . . can't think of another way to get at those thieves . . . give Wong what he wants, get him trusting me, find out what his deal is with Walt . . ." His heels click as he makes it onto the bridge. He can feel the weight of his thighs as he climbs up. "Steeper than I thought," he says to himself. "Taller, too, and these steps are slippery. Better remember this when I'm trying to do it in the dark." He gets to the top of the bridge's arch, looks up the canal into the grey wall the rain's making. He can't help groaning a little: "Come on, be on time, show your buddy Jie you're worth what we paid for you." The rain taps on his hat and splashes in the canal below. He can hear it like a radio stuck between stations, then he hears a low hum that turns into the buzz of an outboard motor. The shape of a barge fades in black from the featureless scene. It's getting closer to the bridge, and he sees a light blink on and off from it. "Time," he mutters.

The bridge has wide stone guardrails to either side. Taggett turns around and takes the seven steps to the further rail, grabs it, lifts himself up the foot or two to get on it. He stands there for a second, blinking in the rain, the rocks slick under his feet. "Jesus," he grumbles, "there's got to be a better way. Oh, well, here we go." He turns around again, facing the bridge, and gets on all fours. Inching backward, he feels the surface disappear under his feet, his shins, and then he's on his belly, still worming himself backwards. The sound of the barge is getting louder. He figures the front of it must be under the bridge as his body bends over the corner of the rail. Gravity starts to take over, pulling him further back until he's dangling from the bridge by his fingers. He's not looking down. The buzz of the barge's motor develops an echo. "Now or never," Taggett grits through his teeth. He lets go.

Pain shoots up his legs as they hit the deck of the barge. He rolls and gets back to his feet, glancing around wildly, hand straying toward his forty-five. The deck rolls and Johnny staggers as a leathery old fellow wearing a captain's hat comes toward him. The captain's grinning and holding out his hand like a bellboy. Standing there and keeping his balance, Taggett figures it out and reaches into his pocket for the roll of bills Jie handed him earlier. "Good job," says Johnny. "You stay bought."

The captain grins into Taggett's eyes. "Also, I speak excellent English," he says in a voice like a choking Doberman. "So don't insult me while you're on my ship."

"Sorry," says Johnny.

Still grinning, the captain bends down, picks up the tough detective's hat, hands it to him. "Don't worry about it. You Yankees don't know any better. We'll be dropping you off in about half an hour. Try not to get in the way." Taggett notices that the captain's grin looks a little more like someone's pulling his lips apart with fishhooks. He doesn't have too much time to wonder about that as the captain just turns and walks away across the shifting deck. Taggett lights up a smoke and tries not to fall over.

The Phantom II's waiting on the dock as Taggett jumps off and winces just a little from the spark of pain still teasing up his legs. As he slides into the front seat he says to Jie, "That fellow you found is a real charmer."

Jie allows himself a chuckle. "With all due respect, sir, the personality of a man in that particular trade hardly ever lends itself to conviviality." He starts the car and they head back up the canal.

Chen passes Johnny one of the hotel's ham sandwiches over the back of the front seat and says, "So, other than the new friend you made, how'd it go?"

Taggett unwraps the sandwich and takes a big bite, then takes Chen's canteen and a big swig of that excellent hotel whiskey to wash it down. "Went good," he says. "I was right about how the sound changes when the barge goes under the bridge, so I shouldn't have any trouble in the dark. I just gotta make sure I land in something a little softer, though. That wooden deck just about splintered my shins when I hit it."

As Jie maneuvers the car through the mud the rain starts to let up. Huge's orange shafts of light break through the iron dome up there. The driver glances up. "The evening light appears already to have begun to assert itself. Clearly, I have underestimated the extent of the day and of our time between your arrival here and our expected arrival at our second rendezvous point. Gentlemen, brace yourselves." Jie presses down with his foot and the Phantom II lunges forward, its engine growling as he expertly shifts its gears. The scenery turns into green and brown streaks. "As to your concern for the intensity of your landing, Mr. Taggett," he continues, "I can assure you that the barge you'll be dropping onto will be piled high, as is the custom for many of the barges making night voyages, with raw fertilizer, a substance which, I can tell you from unpleasant personal experience, is remarkably soft and yielding." Though he has to raise his voice a little over the car's deep rumbling, his tone's as calm as it always is.

Chen's back to kneeling on the back seat scouting for a tail, but he turns around for a moment, twisting his torso to squint at Jie. "Uh, I'm no walking dictionary or anything, but did you just say that Johnny's gonna jump in a big pile of shit?"

Eyes on the road, Jie says, "Exactly, sir."

Taggett tears another bite from his sandwich and mutters, "Great."

By the time they get back to the bridge the dusk is turning everything into shadows. Taggett's had time to change into more appropriate gear, black sweater and pants and hat, his forty-five strapped to his shoulder. The rain's started back up, and there's Johnny forcing his way through it again, pulling his shoes out of the same thick mud that almost got them the last time he tried this, muttering through his teeth. "Genius, Taggett, just had to make sure you could do it at night . . . like it's not cold enough during the day . . . well, maybe that pile of shit I'm jumping into'll be nice and warm." He chuckles. "Guess the laundry staff'll just have to hate me a little more." The steps are a little slipperier under his shoes than he remembers. As the dark folds itself around the scene he stumbles, gets himself back on his feet, and waits.

"Rain's killing all the other sound," he can't help saying to himself. "Jesus, wish I could have a cigarette . . . don't want the light to give me away . . . gotta do this like it's for real, like I'm sneaking onto a drug shipment . . . wait a minute." He can hear the faint buzz of the barge's motor. He turns around and gropes forward through the dark for the edge of the rail, hoists himself up, lies down on his belly, waits. The sound grows, getting closer. He pushes himself backwards, hangs by his fingers, waits. The sound echoes. Taggett drops.

The shit's as warm as he was hoping and as rank as he expected, but it cushions his fall just enough to let him roll back to his feet without seeing yellow flashes of pain behind his eyes. As he gets up he reaches to rub his shoulder. "Ouch," he says, "gotta roll better next time." A spotlight comes on from somewhere, blinding him for a second. He blinks it away and there's a silhouette in front of him, between him and the light. He can see what looks like the outline of a captain's hat as he reaches for the guy's payoff. "Here you go, and I meant to say thanks for—"

Something brushes the deck just behind him to his right. Before he can even flinch something smashes the back of his skull. He drops to the deck. A groan tears its way up his throat as he rolls over on the shoulder he just hurt. He's on his back. The black sky's hanging over him, then something even blacker leans close and fingers curl around his throat. He manages to plant his fist into something soft. There's a grunt and the fingers come loose. He scrambles backward and pulls out his forty-five and fires and fires again. The weight of his head turns his face to the road along the canal. He can see the headlights of the Phantom II flickering and jittering as the car chases the barge. Then the lights turn into yellow streaks and then fade to velvet black along with everything else as the tough detective mumbles something about the god-damned rain and passes out.

CHAPTER TWENTY SIX

Someone's calling his name from the other end of a long dark hallway and he's trying to run toward the sound, but the floor keeps jumping up behind him and dragging him back down into the same night that ate up Flagely and that girl in San Francisco and Walt. He can feel himself sweating and crying. For some reason everything smells like shit as he starts to recognize Chen's voice, as the hallway starts to open to a sky made of harsh white electricity. The tough detective blinks and hears a groan coming out of his throat. Chen's face is hovering over him, the barge's floodlight making a halo around the younger man's head. "Come on, Johnny, snap out of it," he's saying. Taggett blinks again and flinches as his head swells up with pain. Finally he holds up a hand. Chen grabs it and pulls him to his feet. Taggett sways, but his partner catches him before he can fall.

They're on the vacant barge tied up to the dock. The rains dried up and the clouds have all blown away: the stars crowding the sky stare down from their distance. He can feel the weight of the forty-five dragging his right hand down as he glances around wild-eyed. He's starting to notice that he's been muttering: "Drop on me . . . got the drop . . . son of a bitch . . . knew I was coming . . . set up a dummy . . . where . . ." His throat dries up and he chokes. In the sudden quiet the water laps at the edge of the barge. Taggett looks down to see a two-by-four lying on the deck, one end glistening darkly in the Phantom II's headlights. By itself, his right hand rises to the back of his head. His whole body shakes with pain as the fingertips brush over some kind of sticky mess back there.

Chen's still holding on to him. "We heard the shots," the younger man's saying. "Got here as fast as we could, the barge was tied up when we got here. Did you see him? Did you see the guy that hit you?" His voice is cracking. Taggett just blinks and staggers back and forth. "Jesus," says Chen, "what's that smell?"

Jie's suddenly there on Taggett's other side, helping Chen hold him up. "That would be the fertilizer, sir," says the driver. He sniffs again and furrows his brow. "Fertilizer and . . . and blood. More blood than could possibly be coming from Mr. Taggett's wound." The older man gasps, his face changing expression for the first time since Johnny met him, lips curling back to a black, jagged set of teeth. "Someone has slaughtered this barge's entire crew, left their bodies to rot, for the police to find you here with them," he growls. "Vile." As his face gets back to its professionally calm expression, he tells the two men, "We must abandon this scene immediately, gentlemen. If my suspicions are correct, the authorities have been alerted to the carnage around us. The further possibility exists that they possess Mr. Taggett's name and description and are prepared to charge him as the obvious suspect in the murder of this barge's crew."

Taggett starts to nod as they drag his body from the barge to the dock, and the darkness swells up and swallows him again.

Some time later the back seat of the Phantom II fades in around him, his head a big balloon full of pain. He can see the sky getting lighter through the window as he lies there, streaks of grey clouds turning pink ahead of them. Chen's in the front seat yelling at Jie: "Can't you see he needs a doctor?"

The driver's voice, calm as he wrestles the big car along the mud track that leads to the main road, replies, "A doctor is exactly what he shall have, sir, but I have no intention of exposing him to the tender mercies of the police investigation that would surely follow his appearance in any of Shanghai's public hospitals. I regret the necessity of reminding you that both of you gentlemen have come to this city under circumstances that any officer of the law would find highly suspicious, on an errand of which you most certainly would have great difficulty attempting an innocent explanation. Mr. Taggett is the victim of an assault that would require the same kind of explanation, one to which my poor powers of falsification are hardly equal." He makes a swerve and Taggett moans a little, starts to fade again as he hears Jie tell Chen, "Among my acquaintances is a doctor who asks few questions in return for proper remuneration. Fortunately for us, he lives in one of Mr. Wong's suites at the Palace." Raising his voice a little, turning his head a fraction, the driver says, "We'll be there soon, Mr. Taggett. Hold tightly to your resolve, sir."

Everything turns black again with a throb that makes Taggett feel like he's inside a heart and the next thing he knows he's draped between Chen and Jie, each man holding him up by an arm and helping him stumble through the back entrance of the Palace. The smell of the food cooking in the kitchen they're pulling his body through is making him gag. Chen's babbling into his ear, "Just a little further, Johnny, you can lie down, we'll have a guy look at you, Jesus, you're gonna be okay, Johnny, just stay with me, stay with me."

Taggett turns his head to look into Chen's eyes, grunting with the effort and somehow keeping his feet moving at the same time. He growls, "Not going anywhere," and pukes a thick yellow mess onto his shoes and passes out again.

And then somehow he's in a big soft bed with the morning light gently flooding in through the picture window to his left. He can feel the smooth coolness of the sheets under him as he squirms, the back of his head a patch of numbness. He takes a breath, smells the clean laundry, notices Chen and Jie sitting in straight-backed chairs by the side of the bed. Their heads are both tilted over in sleep. Chen's got a little black stubble lining his jaw. Taggett tries to swallow, tries to say something, but all he gets is a kind of low squawk. Somehow that's enough to make Chen's eyes snap open. The younger man's face develops a smile like the sun burning through clouds and nudges Jie. "Hey, he's awake!"

Jie manages to open his eyes without changing his facial expression and says, "Indeed, sir, and may I be so bold as to assert my unequivocal pleasure at this development." The older man leans over the bed. "It's good to see you once again among the living, Mr. Taggett. I've taken the liberty of ordering some ice from the bar for the purposes of lubricating your throat." He reaches back to pull an ice cube out of a bucket Johnny can't see and rubs it over the tough detective's lips. As the cool trickle slides over his shriveled tongue and down his tight throat, Taggett moans like a dog getting its belly rubbed. "There you are, sir," says Jie. "This should help, yes. You should feel able to converse momentarily."

Taggett sucks ice and coughs. The sound that comes out of his throat reminds him of a dog he once found in an alley with a mouthful of broken glass. Slowly it starts to sound like his own voice saying, "How long have I been out?"

"A couple of days," Chen says, a little choked up himself. "Jie's doc said you should've died from getting hit like that."

A rusty chuckle comes out of the patient. "Probably, why the son of a bitch didn't finish me off? He had plenty of time, too. Must have thought he killed me with one shot. Poor creep must not know me too well." He starts to sit up in bed, grabbing the covers. "Listen, it looks like we've got some time till tonight, so I'm . . . uh . . ."

"Most sincerely begging your pardon for the interruption, sir," says Jie, "but I'm assured by the physician who treated you that your physical activity must be severely limited to allow your recuperative process to take place. He prescribed at least a solid week of bed rest for you, sir. I'm afraid our mission will just have to wait."

Taggett curses and winces as the pain shoves into his head. "I guess you're right," he says, and then waits for the room to stop spinning before he goes on. "I just hate to lose a whole week of work now that we've finally figured out what we're doing."

"Actually, sir, in your convalescence I've been considering how best to use this otherwise non-productive time," says Jie, still leaning forward to watch Taggett's eyes, "and I believe that I have discovered a course of action that will allow our scheme to progress in your absence." The little man looks back and forth between the Americans. "Perhaps this seems obvious to you gentlemen, but I was wondering just how the low character that assaulted Mr. Taggett could possibly have formulated a plan of attack, considering that we ourselves had no idea just which barge he would be occupying until that very morning."

Chen looks hard at Jie, then gives a little snort of a laugh. "Someone bought off the captain you bought off. Doesn't exactly take Sherlock Holmes to figure that one out?"

The laugh Jie gives back sounds like he's humoring a senile uncle. "Yes, of course, sir, that does indeed seem obvious. However, the question remains of just how the person we might call the winning bidder knew exactly which captain to approach and how that particular trap—I believe Mr. Taggett spoke of some kind of diversionary mannequin—could have been set with such haste and precision. Some sort of preparation lies behind this attack."

"That's crazy," says Taggett from the depth of his pillow. "No one even knows what we're up to except the people in the room."

Chen leaps out of his chair to smack his left hand with his fist. "Smith! I told you! That bastard's playing some kind of game on his own!"

"Yeah, just like we are," Taggett chuckles. "Only problem is, his game's getting in the way of ours."

Jie nods, snapping his fingers. "My thought exactly, sir. Thus, I propose that Chen and I go about ascertaining the scoundrel's whereabouts while you take the required rest. We may quite possibly be able to eliminate the obstacle represented by his extracurricular interference by the time you've become sufficiently capable to proceed along the path of our planned endeavor."

Chen says, "Oh, yeah, I'm ready for that, I can't wait to see what that smirk of his looks like with a nice fat lip." He smacks his hand again and bounces a little on the balls of his feet. Jie looks at him blankly for a moment, then does something that looks suspiciously like slipping Taggett a wink.

"The activity will most certainly occupy our time while our friend Mr. Taggett regains his strength," says the little guy. "I would imagine that the lack of strenuous distraction can only aid in his recovery. May I suggest we begin immediately, Mr. Chen?"

Chen whips his head over to glare down at Jie. "What? Uh, yeah. Let's get going. Let's get that guy. See you later, Johnny." The young man bounces out of the room, and Taggett hears a door slam.

Jie looks down at the tough detective and says, "Do get your rest, sir. The success of our mission depends on your well-being. In addition, I've wagered my freedom on that success. Let's not fail one another, shall we?" The older man bows and leaves the room, closing the door carefully behind him. In the silence that fills the room after that soft click, Taggett feels himself slipping into sleep.

When he wakes up its dark. The room could be the size of Madison Square Garden for all he knows. The tough detective squirms between the soft sheets, lets a hand slide up under the pillow next to his head, feels the butt of his forty-five as his fingers curled around it. Smiling, he goes back to sleep.

CHAPTER TWENTY SEVEN

His bladder wakes him up sometime the next day, and he manages to stumble all the way to the toilet before the fireworks start going off in his head. He stands there and takes it and makes it back to bed just about the time there's a soft knock at his bedroom door. He answers with the kind of noise a Model T makes when it's stuck between gears. He takes a breath and tries again: "Come on in, you guys. I'm decent."

A low giggle sneaks through the door as it slowly swings open, followed by a vision from one of Taggett's teenaged dreams. The woman standing there fills the door frame with her broad shoulders, but the shelf of breast in front of them really gets the detective's attention. She's dressed in some kind of nurse's uniform, a little something of gauzy white fabric that clings to her curves, to the way her hips flare out, giving up somewhere around the top of her sturdy thighs. A pair of eyes as deep and black as a hot summer midnight flashes into his, and a pair of blood red lips curls up into a smile that makes him take a sharp breath. That gets another of those low giggles. "Good morning, Mr. Taggett," she murmurs. "I am Olga. I come for . . . I mean I come to give you . . . what is term . . . physical therapy."

Taggett watches her tongue make its way around her molasses-thick Russian accent and feels a grin spread itself over his face. He sees her eyes drift down from his and realizes at just that moment that his partners put him to bed naked last night. His grin gets wider. "I think that's just what I need," he tells her.

Her grin matches his as she sways her soft body toward the bed. "My clients are not usually so . . . how is it . . . so masculine," she purrs. "Usually just flabby old men." She's taking her time getting closer, and he's shivering a little as he stares. He can see the muscles moving under her skin, rolling the way he saw a lion's do in a circus once. She finally gets to the bed and just crawls right up into it, her eyes back on his, blazing with hunger. "I think I will like serving you . . . and I know you will like it," she whispers, slipping between his thighs. The heat of her breath on his skin makes him shiver and moan. She grins into his gaze, lets her tongue drag slowly along her thick lower lip. She leans down. He feels her lips caress along his length, feels them take him in. Lights explode behind his eyes.

The next thing he knows he's waking up again, staring at the chandelier above his bed. He groans a little and lets his hand fumble over the nightstand for a cigarette. What his hand finds instead is a piece of paper thick enough to be hotel stationery. With another groan he pulls it into his field of vision.

It says, "M. Taget you no worry. Olga cleen you good. I come back tomorow, give you more theripy. Next time you stay awake whole way thru." The paper smells like someone's flower garden around midnight in the middle of summer. Taggett breathes it in and chuckles, then goes back to groping around for that cigarette. He finds one and a match, lights up, and lies there, thinking. After a while he falls asleep again.

She shows up the next morning, and he definitely stays awake. Her skin's hot and smooth under his big hands as he puts them all over her, feeling those muscles push her body over his. Over the course of the next few days their bodies get to know each other. He learns the smell of her, the way her smoky giggle gets him stiffer than the Empire State Building, how she forgets her English when he's distracting her. She tells him that he's the best of the clients Mr. Wong sends her to, that she'd do him for the sheer joy of it. In those drifting moments afterward, they talk about her job. Mr. Wong treats his girls like daughters, she tells him, except for her friend Arianne, who Mr. Wong found out was stealing from him and had her thumbs cut off and her tongue pulled out. Arianne works out in front of the hotel at night, Olga tells the tough detective, trying to use her hands and mouth to earn back what she owes her boss.

So this goes on for about a week, the sex and the stories, and there's Johnny in bed, smoking and trying to put it all together into something he can use. There's a soft knock at the door and Taggett grins and shouts, "Yeah, come on in, baby, I been thinking about ways to get you—"

Chen's smiling face interrupts him as he steps in, followed by Jie. "I missed you too," say's the younger man, "but you don't have to call me baby." Behind him Taggett sees Jie's throat tighten a little. The little driver's either coughing or laughing as Chen strides into the room. "Been keeping yourself busy while we do all the work, I see," says Taggett's partner.

"Picked up a hobby," Taggett chuckles right back, handing Chen the cigarette out of his mouth and starting up a new one. "I gotta tell you, I feel a lot better, you should try this treatment I'm getting."

Chen can't stop grinning as he and the driver have a seat by the bed. "Yeah, I hear hobbies are real good for focusing the mind. You must've turned into Sherlock Holmes by now, right?" He takes a drag and lets the laughs hang in the air for a moment, and then comes out with, "So maybe you want to know what the two of us have been up to while you've been . . . uh . . . studying or whatever."

Jie's been sitting there watching this with a look on his face like a rich guy falling asleep at a tennis match. "We've actually had some success, sir," he says. "We devoted our efforts to ascertaining the habits a denizen of the underground such as Smith must surely have acquired. At first, alas, we found disappointment." Taggett flicks a glance at Chen, but the younger man barely flinches at the crazy way Jie talks. The detective smiles a little as Jie gets up and steps toward the bar, still explaining. "The rascal has, I must admit, an impressive amount of discipline. Although we endeavored to trace, for instance, his regular employment of a particular prostitute or a necessarily punctual visit to a regular purveyor of narcotics, we found him to be utterly abstemious."

That gets Chen coughing. "Abstemious? Are you kidding? I spent a whole week with this guy and he still pulls out these—"

"He means Smith doesn't have any nasty habits," says Taggett. "He's a careful guy."

Jie nods as he pours the martinis he's been mixing. "Quite, sir. Very frustrating for the erstwhile tracker. However, Mr. Chen was able to contribute greatly by convincing one or two of the local subterraneans of the wisdom they could display in alerting us to any proclivities the bounder may successfully have hidden." He hands Chen a cool glass, one bead of perspiration sliding down the slope of its outside, and smiles. "We found one." He serves Taggett a glass and settles back into his chair with a drink of his own.

The men sip their drinks for a moment until Taggett finally says, "Well?"

"He likes jazz," Chen grins. "Word is he's all gaga for this band that plays once a week at the Dreaming Blossom, this club a few miles downriver in the red light district. They say he doesn't miss a show, has a regular table in the back where he thinks no one can see." He finishes his martini, licks his lips, makes a little moan of pleasure. "You really know how to mix this stuff, Jie."

Jie tips his head in a discreet nod. "Very kind of you, sir, thank you. One likes to believe that one has picked up one or two skills in the course of one's life." He takes a last sip and reaches for Chen's glass, takes the two empties back to the bar. "I have found, sir, that the secret to correctly preparing the martini involves the careful preservation of the integrity of the ice in the decanter. While some prefer the modern convenience of the stainless steel shaker, I have concluded that to shake the martini merely weakens the overall effect of—"

"Are you kidding me?" Taggett bursts in. "Are we really talking about how good these martinis are? I've been trapped in this freaking bedroom for a solid week, I don't need to know how Jie makes his martinis so good. I need to get this Smith creep out of our way so we can do what we gotta do. When does Smith have his jazz date?"

Jie returns from the bar with another couple of glasses and hands one to Chen. "As luck would have it, sir, considering your quite understandable impatience, the Parker Dalton jazz band is appearing at the Dreaming Blossom this very evening. All the information that we've been able to gather indicates that we will finally have the opportunity to confront the man who calls himself Smith at a time and place of our choosing rather than his."

Taggett leans forward, finishes his drink. Chen hands him the fresh glass. As the detective sips he says, "We don't even have to get in his face. If it all works out, we can follow him, trace him back to whoever he's working for, figure out what his angle is."

"Indeed, sir," says Jie. He takes the glass from Chen and walks it back to the bar. As he pours the last drink from the carafe, he allows himself one of those dry chuckles. "I'm happy that your convalescence is concluding with you in such eager spirits."

"Well, I've had plenty of time to think," says Taggett. "And now I'm ready to get this guy and bring down his whole house of cards. He's been a pain in our ass for too long." As he grins at his partners he glances at the bedroom door and wonders if it's been closed all this time, or if that click he thinks he just heard means that his night is about to get even more interesting.

CHAPTER TWENTY EIGHT

The buzzing red and blue neon sign outside the Dreaming Blossom makes a purple halo for itself in the rain as Taggett and Chen pull up in a rickshaw. Taggett hands a couple of bills to the shivering guy who pulled the little cart they're getting out of all the way from the Palace Hotel. "Too bad Jie couldn't make it," Chen says. "I get the feeling that the little fellow doesn't get out much." The two men wait for a few cars to speed past then sprint across the slick asphalt of the highway. They make it under the pink awning that leads to the club's ornately carved front door, then they light up a smoke and take a good look around the perimeter.

His eyes darting all over the scene, noting all the parked cars a shooter could be hiding in or the ornamental bushes one could be hiding behind, Taggett says, "I don't think this kind of thing is really what Jie likes. He reminds me of a few of the guys I've met who've been in the War. I guess once you've seen that kind of thing you get pretty serious."

"Yeah, I've seen plenty," says Chen. "And I'm too young to be that serious. Let's get in there and settle that creep's hash for him."

Taggett flicks away his cigarette and says, "No time like the present." He and Chen turn and walk along the red carpet the pink awning's keeping the rain from. Soon enough they get to the door. Taggett gives the hard wood a good solid shave-and-a-haircut and they wait as the faint buzz of jazz trumpet filters through the door's thickness. The rain makes little snare taps on the awning, playing along. The partners stand there smoking.

"I meant to say," says Chen. "Nice suit."

"Thanks," says Taggett, looking down at the flannel double-breasted number he's wearing. "Custom made. Some guy named Hong, works in the hotel. Jie had to translate, but I got what I needed." Taggett opens his jacket to show off the way his forty-five's holster fits right in without showing a lump in the suit. Chen whistles, and Taggett closes his jacket and taps with his knuckles just over the breast pocket. There's a clank. Chen whistles again. "Pocket for my flask," says Taggett. "You never know when you might get thirsty."

Chen laughs. "You're the only guy I've ever heard of who'd bring a flask into a bar."

"If we ever get into the bar," smirks Taggett. He gives the door another knock, this time cop-style with his fist. Lighting a new smoke from the butt of the one he's just finishing, he mutters, "Guess the door man just fell asleep or something."

Chen flips his butt away and reaches for the wrought-iron handle. He gives the door a little pull and it just swings open, letting a blast of brassy chords out into the night. "Guess the clubs don't need to lock their doors if they're not worried about getting raided," he laughs.

"Guess not," says Taggett, and the two of them step into the smoky darkness of the Dreaming Blossom, pulling the door shut behind them. The stage is in the middle of the room, with spotlights on it bouncing off the bright trumpets and saxophones and turning the rest of the room, the tables ringed around the stage, into blank shapes and outlines. The noise coming from the stage blasts Taggett into memories of New York City traffic jams. He shakes it off and stands just inside the door, scanning the scene. To his left, he senses Chen moving to the other side of the door.

He can feel his throat constrict and his lips move as he mutters, even though he can't hear himself through the metal yelling of the band. "So Smith's got a VIP seat . . . probably facing the door, the guy's a pro . . . one of these corners in the back . . . watching the door . . . but if he's here for the band he wants to see it . . . so a view of both . . . come on,

Taggett, club's not that big, he's got to be here somewhere . . ." His eyes are shooting from table to table, looking for a silhouette that could be Smith's. Nothing registers. He shoots a glance across the door to Chen and gets a frown and a shake of the head from his partner. With a tilt of his head, he moves a little further into the club.

The darkness has a thousand tiny holes in it as the lights on the band shatter themselves against the instruments. Taggett keeps looking around. For some reason no one's dancing, just sitting there drinking and listening to the noise, even though the drummer's working so hard he's wrapped in a little fog of his own sweat. The tough detective stands there for a minute watching the band and wondering what's wrong with this crowd. "Probably scared of Smith," he says to himself. "I bet that little creep think this place is his own private kingdom. He'll think different soon enough, soon as Chen and me can get to him. We need to find out if he's got a private room somehow. I get the feeling that this place is bigger than it looks." He moves toward a wall. "Let's see if we can't find some kind of hidden door." He starts to grope over the flat hard surface, flaws in the concrete ripping his palms a little. When his hands hit wood he trails one down in search of a knob, finds one, turns it: locked. The band's still making that crazy sound behind him as he faces the door he can't see in the darkness. He reaches into his pants pocket for his set of lockpicks. Working blind, he slides one of the thin strips of metal into the slot he can feel just below the knob. He wiggles the strip around and waits to feel a click vibrating up its length. He gets nothing. The band keeps wailing. He stands there a little longer working at it until he realizes he's got his back to the room, and by that time it's too late.

The hot breath on his ear makes him twitch before he realizes it's a whisper, a sexy Russian accent saying, "Am so sorry, Mr. Taggett. He make me lead you here, he threaten my family." A soft hand slips something into the side pocket of his jacket. "Maybe this help you when he attack." He whirls around, hand rising to his holster, just in time to see Olga's back as she fades back into the club's leopard-spotted darkness. His breathing gets fast and shallow, his scar itching furiously. A trumpet screams a piercing high note.

And then the lights in the room come on and everyone's looking right at him. He squints, his eyes water, in a little while the blurs turn into familiar scowling faces. The place is crowded with thugs, bruisers at every table, guys he recognizes from back in New York. He can feel the scar on his face itching and crawling. His hand's in his jacket, but he's not bringing it out. Not yet.

From a fancy booth in the middle of a side wall a man stands up. He's tall, dressed in a jet black suit, and bald as a mountaintop. The long black beard he's wearing doesn't quite mask the smirk twisting his lips. When he starts to speak his voice rumbles like a forest of trees coming down. "We finally meet," he says. "So rare that I travel around the world and around the world again for the hopeless likes of a degenerate gambler such as yourself, but here we are." A wolf's chuckle fights its way out of the Russian's throat as Taggett stands there gaping. "My men and I have waited far too long for this," says the enforcer. The goons keep staring. No one but the Russian is moving. Even the musicians on stage are just standing there staring, still holding their instruments until the Russian snaps his fingers. Then they just run out the front door.

That's when Taggett notices that Chen isn't in the same spot as before. He glances around to see that a couple of the goons aren't staring at him anymore. Their heads are down, chin to chest. He snaps his eyes back to the Russian, who's still chuckling. A second later a faint creak cuts the chuckle off. The Russian's head whips right and left, and then one of the thugs lets out a groan and falls out of his chair and there's Chen standing behind him a weird little grin on his face. He's bouncing on the balls of his feet, smacking his left hand with the blackjack he's got in his right. "Look around, boys," he shouts. "I'm here for every last one of you!" Suddenly he's standing on a table and then he's in the air and his feet are smashing into some creep's face. As the creep goes down Chen's in the air again, the sap in his hand smacking into some other guy's forehead and his feet driving yet another one's jaw crooked. No one else has even started moving yet.

The Russian lets out a bellow and the whole place explodes. The thugs start coming at Chen almost as fast as he can knock them down. Taggett just stares as the younger man's fists and feet blur into streaks like wild propellers mowing down the crowd closing in on him. Absently, while the Russian roars on the other side of the room and the fight boils between them, the detective slips a hand into his jacket. There's a folded piece of paper in there. Taggett pulls it out and glances at it as the Russian's gang keeps going after Chen, like they've forgotten all about the detective they came here for.

The piece of paper's a note: "Johny, he make me lead you in to this trap but I never want to hurt you. I help you insted. Find secret dore in bathroom, in wall akross from sink. Hurry Johny to make eskape, you never beat him." She didn't sign it, maybe thought she could get away with warning him. He glances up from the note to the Russian and his eyes go wide as the assassin pulls out some kind of bazooka, aims it right at the tough detective's head. The noise the Russian's gun makes echoes through the club over the meaty sounds of Chen's fists and feet hitting goons in the gut and face.. Taggett hears the bullet hit the wall behind him and sharp little pieces of wood sting through his jacket. The explosion seems to wake up the thirty or so rough types that Chen hasn't already knocked out. They stare at the Russian for a second until the big bald assassin barks something that turns them toward Taggett. They start pulling out knives and brass knuckles and leather saps as they advance on the detective the way a fog bank blots out the houses along the street it's pushing itself along. Taggett glances at Chen, but the younger man's busy. Making a sound in his throat that he doesn't like, Taggett turns around and runs into the bathroom, smashing the thin door open with his body.

He's just enough ahead of the mob to get a flash of the layout: toilet across from the door, sink to the left, blank wall to the right with a little change of color to show him where it's been knocked in and replastered. He swerves fast to his right, pushes the faded patch with his fingertips. The wall opens and he slips through and swings the secret door back shut as the thundering footsteps of the crowd get louder, closer. He stands there in the dark with his ear to the black wall, listening to the confused grunting of the thugs. "What the hell?" he hears someone say. "Where'd he go?"

CHAPTER TWENTY NINE

He stands there in the absolute darkness, listening to the goons fumble around on the other side of the hidden door like a bunch of zoo monkeys. Then there's a bang like a door slamming open and Chen's voice hollering, "Where's Johnny? What did you do to him? I'll tear every last one of you greaseballs limb from limb!" The detective hammers with his fists on the wall he just pushed his way through, but it doesn't budge, even when something that sounds like a big bag of meat smacks into it from the other side. After a few minutes of Chen yelling and thugs making little strained whimpers of pain, there's a silence. Taggett stands there in the blackness and pounds on the wall a few more times, yelling Chen's name. Nothing happens. He can't push back through.

Taking a big whiff of the rotten-fish-scented air, he has to laugh to himself. "Just like always, the only way out is through," he mumbles, lighting up a smoke and letting the match burn to get a look at what he's shoved himself into. Little streams of water glisten in the flicker as they drip down the rough rocks behind the club's wall. Directly in front of him it just gets darker. The floor he's standing on turns out to be just a big concrete slab that ends where the tunnel slopes down. He steps off the slab onto packed earth, muttering, "At least it's not more mud." Then he hisses a little as the fire from the match gets to his fingertips and sputters out. He drops the matchstick and stands for a minute or two to get his eyes adjusted to the return of such deep darkness it's almost solid. Blinking, he puts his arms out Karloff-style and gropes along the slimy tunnel walls.

After a while the smell of rotting fish fades. Now the darkness smells like a swamp in New Jersey, the way ahead of him sloping downward. The cherry end of Taggett's cigarette bobs in front of his face as he feels his way along. "Jesus," he grumbles, "maybe I should have stuck around and fought that Russian . . . not like I haven't got firepower of my own . . . wonder where he got that sidearm of his . . . and what the hell he's doing here . . . I thought he was supposed to be bought off or something . . . what the hell kind of set-up is this . . . where the hell am I—"

The twinkle he sees shuts him up. In that total darkness, the little glimmer of light that's coming from the hole in the wall a few feet ahead of him is as bright as a spotlight. He puts his back to the wall, pulls out his forty-five, and slides himself along until he's almost opposite the round bright spot. Then he lowers himself, pushes back his hat, very slowly rises to take a peek.

The room on the other side of that wall has a little couch in it, covered in red velvet a little darker than the red velvet wallpaper. A woman lounges on the couch, her black stockings and garters and bra defining her soft white skin. Taggett can't help gasping a little at her beauty. The hungry look on her face is getting him a little sweaty in the cold tunnel. Her deep black eyes are turned to something off to Taggett's left, and then a guy comes in from that direction. He's already loosening his tie and throwing his hat into a corner as he settles onto the little couch with her. Their mouths come together. Taggett can almost hear the animal noises as she kisses the man the way a cannibal might eat the face off a missionary. The man's leg pushes between the woman's thighs, pushing them open. Taggett lowers himself back to the ground and crawls a foot or two away before he straightens up in the dark.

"Jesus," the tough detective tells himself, "this tunnel must go through the whole red-light district, maybe some kind of back door for the bosses . . . wonder if Wong knows about this . . . probably had it built, him or some guy before him . . . some way to keep tabs on the workers . . . bet there's a secret door to the whorehouse around here somewhere . . . no place for me to just show up, though . . . better keep following this trail . . . see where I wind up." His fingers keep scrabbling over the cool wet wall. He spits out the butt of his cigarette as he feels his way toward whatever's waiting for him, hears the hiss as the stub hits the floor.

The surface under his fingertips turns from rock to wood at the same time his ankle hits something. He flattens his hands against the wall to keep himself from falling over and lifts his foot to explore. His toe finds a flat place about the height of one step up. Taggett sucks in a breath and takes that step, then the next, the wooden staircase under him creaking a little from his weight. The darkness around him seems to close in a little. Slowly he takes the invisible stairs until his foot comes down a little harder than he intended. He stumbles at the top of the stairs, his hands still on the wall to his side, bracing him. Even so, the head of a nail bites into the seam of his suitcoat. "Damn," he says, "I just can't keep a suit together," and blinks to see the circular trace of another peephole a little way down the line. Trying to keep his big mouth shut, he drops to the floor and crawls toward the light.

He's getting splinters in his hands as he braces them against the wall and carefully raises himself up to where he can see through the hole. What he sees makes his eyes go wide. It's an office like the one he had back in Frisco, two desks and two chairs and not much else. A guy with an old Colt revolver in a shiny leather holster strapped to his leg is sitting at one of the desks, counting money, moving the bills from one pile to another and making little tick marks on a pad of paper next to him. Taggett can't see anyone at the other desk. As the detective watches, the guy at the desk stops counting and sits very still for a moment. Then he's whipping the gun out so that it's pointing right at the peephole, right at Taggett. No one moves for one of those minutes that stretches out into hours. Taggett crouches against the wall, waiting for a twitch, waiting to dive out of the way. Then the guy at the desk chuckles a little, puts his gun back in its place. He draws again, aiming up into a corner of the office, and then quick draws toward a door in the far wall. The door opens and a guy comes through and starts yelling at the gunslinger in the chair. Taggett tries not to let himself breathe a sigh of relief. As soon as he thinks the guy's not looking his way, he lowers himself again, crawls back along the floor into the thick heavy darkness.

"Did that guy see me?" he asks himself. "Couldn't be, he'd just plug me right through the wall . . . wonder whose money that was . . . maybe Wong's, maybe one of the other bosses around here . . . they've really got it carved up in big pieces, this tunnel must feed into three or four buildings . . . hell of a lot bigger territory than anyone in New York . . .so why bother with me . . . why pay that Russian and his whole damn army to come all the way out here . . . I must be stepping on someone's toes . . . good . . . shake someone up, get them off base, maybe I can do some damage around here." He straightens himself up against a wall and lights up a fresh smoke. In the flare from the match he can see what a tight space he's in, the wall he's about to bruise himself on looming up in the light. Before the match goes out he whips his head left and right. "Okay, right turn," he mutters, and keeps his hand on the rough wood wall as he stumbles along. "Wonder if there's any way out of here. Just keep going, Taggett, you'll come to the end soon enough."

After what seems like too long, the wood under his hands turns back into rock. It's not the slick, slimy surface he was feeling back toward the Dreaming Blossom. This stuff is dry, sandy, crumbling as he brushes his fingers over it. He blinks a few times and then stops and blinks again. He can see a hint of light somewhere up ahead, too much light to be just another peephole. It might be the crack between a door and a wall, a tall thin line of flickering light he can follow to somewhere that makes any damn sense, anywhere but underground the way he's been for all this time, however much time that is. He steps toward the light and then suddenly stops himself.

At about the level of his waist there's another light, another one of those peepholes. If he wants to get past it without blocking it, without letting whoever's on the other side know he's there, he'll have to crawl on his belly. So he does. Once he gets under it, though, he just has to take a peek. Rolling over on his back, he stiffens the muscles in his belly, bends up a little to get his eye to the right angle.

That's when he feels that scratching at the back of his mind, those crazy whispers he barely remembers from the train to San Francisco starting up again. The ring he's been keeping in his hat all this time gets as hot as a rivet. He clamps his teeth shut to keep out a groan of pain. Somehow he knows what he's about to see.

The room on the other side of the peephole could be in Shanghai or San Francisco or New York, anywhere there's a party of people who have too much laughing at the people who don't have any. A bunch of guys in tuxedos are holding up champagne glasses, guffawing through faces the color of rare roast beef at something or another. Taggett barely sees them. He barely sees the big ice swan in the middle of what must be some kind of banquet hall, barely sees the squad of whores starting to glide toward the tuxedo crowd, barely sees the little army of muscular creeps along the room's edges keeping the line strong between their bosses and the poor suckers who never get to see a big swan made of ice.

What he sees is a figure dressed entirely in black velvet and gesturing with a cigarette holder made of ivory so white it leaves streaks on his vision. He can't hear what the figure might be saying, but he remembers that purring laugh, the way it turns into a snarl so far from human it can chill even the toughest tough guy. He can almost feel the grip of deceptively strong fingers on his arm. It takes all his self-control not to gasp and blurt out the name of the woman he thought he'd never see again.

Mrs. Foulsworth is pointing at one of the hired goons with her cigarette holder, then she points it right at the hole Taggett's peeping through. He throws himself to the ground and stays there for a long moment, breathing fast and shallow. The sound of his breath fills his ears with a sound like a broken radio before he can calm himself down a little. Then he rolls over in the dark, over the rough hard floor, until his body hits the opposite wall. He lies there on his back, looking up at the circle of light the peephole's letting through. "What the hell," he whispers to himself.

CHAPTER THIRTY

A sudden cool draft of air blowing up his body from somewhere past his feet reminds him how close he must be to a way out of here. The spot of light above him has quit flickering and turned into a steady blue circle burning into the black wall as he stares up at it. Taking a breath, he rolls himself back across the floor, takes out his forty-five, levers himself back into position to take one more quick look through the peephole. His thumb's on the hammer of his gun, his finger on the trigger.

The room on the other side of the wall is empty. The big ice swan is dripping itself to death into a copper bowl of some kind with no one there to appreciate its effort. Taggett snorts another "What the hell" and stands up in the darkness, fingers still gripping the butt of his forty-five. His other hand finds its way back to the wall as he steps carefully toward the thin strip of light ahead of him.

Before too long he's right in front of it. His free hand flattens against what feels like a brick wall and starts to press. Nothing happens, so he pushes a little harder, and still nothing. "Must be some kind of catch," he tells himself. "They wouldn't have built this without some way out . . . these clever bastards wouldn't just let anyone know about it . . . probably want to keep me trapped in here till I starve . . . or till they come to get me . . . damn, I need to get out of here." He starts feeling with his fingers over the flat surface, looking for a crack or a button or a loose brick he can push. He doesn't feel anything give.

Then he hears a faint sound behind him, something like a bottle of champagne opening. It's the first sound he's heard in all this time in the dark that he hasn't made. He whirls around from the wall he's facing and stares back along the tunnel, but he can't see anything. Another popping noise, a little louder. Holding his breath, he turns back around and crouches to feel at the base of the wall for some kind of switch. He scrabbles to the left and right of the narrow split letting that little bit of light through, his thick fingers pressing and scraping along the surface. The next sound he hears is more a bang than a pop. He's starting to sweat. He presses his slippery hands to the wall, pushing hard at each change in texture. "Gotta be a way out," he's muttering. "Come on, come on . . . there!"

A soft section of the wall gives under his hand, and the whole thing swings open. He falls forward onto something that smells like wet asphalt in the rain and rolls as the door slams back behind him, the wind of it knocking his hat off as it goes by. He lies there, on the ground in an alley that reminds him too much of home, and stares at the blank shape of the brick wall he just tumbled through. The cold rain keeps poking him in the face as he glances around to find his hat. He finds it, shoves it back onto his head, and scrambles back on his ass to brace himself against the opposite wall. Teeth chattering in the sudden cold, he pulls out his forty-five and waits for the wall to swing open again. He takes a glance at either end of the alley he's in, the vice trade of Shanghai passing back and forth on its way to the next whore or a high. Taggett sits there alone, finger resting on the trigger, waiting.

The sounds of a trumpet band in one of the other clubs around here drift into the tough detective's ears. He can still smell the rotten fish smeared all over his suit, but also the smoke from the fire some hoboes must have set up in an oil can. The alley he's in is deserted, though, like someone cleared it out. "Cops?" Taggett asks himself. "Or . . . oh shit."

"Is correct, yes, Mr. Taggett. Oh shit: you step in big pile, yes." Stepping out of a shadow, the Russian grins at him. The rain's coming down hard, smacking the assassin right on his shaved dome, but the guy doesn't even flinch. He just lets the water drip down his weird little goatee, lets Johnny stare down the barrel of that crazy giant pistol he's got pointed right at the American's forehead. "I see you staring at my gun. You like, eh?" The grin turns into a sneer as he steps closer, waving it in the detective's face. "I take it from a lowlife punk in Chicago. He try to run three years, change name, get new job with new boss, does not matter. I find him, I kill him, I get this beautiful gun, has taken many lives." The Russian chuckles, comes closer, the grin coming back, the same grin Taggett felt on his own face when he was beating up that poor dummy in Frisco. "I think it takes your life tonight, yes?"

"No," says Johnny and kicks the Russian's knee sideways. The killer yelps and tries to pull the trigger of his hand cannon as he goes down, but the pull on the trigger is too heavy when the hammer's not cocked. Taggett rolls out of the way as the Russian's body slams into the asphalt, then he pops up to his feet, hands curled into fists, ready.

The Russian recovers quickly, sending a sharp kick back Taggett's way. The detective jumps away, but that gives the Russian time to get back up. He hasn't got his gun. Eyes wide, the crazy hitman glances over the dark ground. Taggett charges forward, punches the killer hard in the gut. He gets an elbow in the face for his trouble, goes staggering back. The two of them look at each other, breathing hard, skin glistening with sweat in the light from the street. Under the hum of the passing cars Taggett can hear a growl pushing its way out of the Russian's throat. The tough detective plants his feet as the Russian charges and takes the force of the murderer's hard dense body. They're grappling, throwing each other back and forth until Taggett finds himself on his back again in a pile of trash that smells worse than the tunnel. He groans, tries to lift his head, feels it fall back again.

An explosion of thunder shakes him back to life; his body squirming as the flash of lightning that comes right after shows him the Russian, who's turning to see the glint of his huge gun where it lies on the ground. The crazy bald creep goes for it, and Taggett pulls a bottle out of the pile of trash and throws it at the killer's shape. It connects. The Russian goes down again but gets up fast, just as Taggett makes it back to his own feet. The cold rain's coming down hard, soaking the detective's new suit. The two tough guys hold still for a moment in the dark, and then they both scream and charge. Taggett gets a knee between the Russian's legs, pushes up as the Russian gets a big hand around Taggett's neck. Thunder goes off around them again. The lightning shows Taggett, the bloody cut on the Russian's head where the bottle hit. The tough detective grins, pushes an arm up to knock the killer's hand away, and butts the wound, then butts it again, smashing his skull into the Russian's blood. The Russian falls back, moaning, and Taggett kicks him in the gut. The Russian slips on the wet pavement, falls back against the wall Taggett came through, and another shot of thunder rattles the alley. Taggett blinks in the lightning but sees the strobe flash on the backs of his eyelids of the Russian's hand falling on his gun. The detective throws himself to the ground as the Russian's shot plows into the soft brick of whatever club this alley's behind. Taggett crawls forward on his belly till he can grab one of the Russian's ankles then punches with his other hand straight into the crazy killer's balls. The roar of another blast of thunder drowns out the Russian's howl of pain, but the lightning reveals his grimace. Taggett grunts and punches again with all his force. When he pulls his fist back for a third shot the Russian manages to kick him away. Taggett rolls out of range. Lying on his back, he slips his hand into his jacket, pulls out his forty-five, points it at the Russian, stares down the barrel of the bazooka's the Russian's pointing right back at him. Taggett's finger pulls. An explosion of thunder fills the alley. The lightning freezes the scene into a snapshot of the two men on the ground mirroring each other, arms extended, eyes bugging out and red with rage and fear, and then the alley goes black as the men fall back, as both guns roar and spit fire. Cars hum past at either end of the alley as the rain smacks the asphalt.

After a moment a low groan comes out of Taggett. His thick body rolls over on the wet pavement, his hands grope around for his hat. As he's shaking the water from it and pasting it back on his head, the rain stops. A cold wind blows the clouds away from the moon to let a little pale light down into the alley. Right next to him in the alley a light he hadn't seen before snaps on over the wall the tunnel's behind, and then it fizzles back off again. The detective staggers to his feet and reaches into his suitcoat, poking around in the pack to find the last cigarette that's not mangled to shreds. He plants it in his mouth and flicks a match to life with his thumbnail, never once giving up his grip on the forty-five in his right hand. Once he's got his smoke lit, he turns to look down at the Russian.

The assassin's sprawled on the asphalt, squirming and bleeding. The gash on his head has covered his face with a dark stain of blood, and there's more coming out of the new wound in his hip where Taggett's bullet punched through the bone. That giant gun is just out of reach of the Russian's hand, fingers clutching at nothing as Taggett steps closer. The ex-cop kicks the gun down the alley. "You know," he says, "I never killed anybody. Not in the war, not on the street, not even in self-defense. I've beat some punks so bad they wished they were dead, sure, but I always figured that the good guys don't kill, that's how you tell them from the bad guys." The Russian's face is turning pale in the moonlight. His eyes are starting to roll back, so Taggett pokes a toe into the guy's hip. The Russian lets out a breath that wants to be a scream. His eyes lock on Taggett's. "Good, I've got your attention," says the detective. "I wanted to make sure you know how seriously I'm taking this. I'm not a killer. But you're never gonna stop, are you?" The Russian's head shakes, either saying no or just out of control in the cold night. It doesn't matter. "And I know how you work, you'll just come after one of my friends or a lover or something. No good. This has to end." He takes a long drag of his cigarette, cocks his forty-five, aims right between the Russian's eyes. The two of them just stare at each other for a moment, then the detective pulls the trigger. He sees the bullet smack into the Russian's skull, sees the hitman's head explode into a dark stain on the dark pavement. Swallowing, he steps back from the mess and holsters his pistol.

The light sizzles on again in the blank wall that hides the tunnel and stays on this time. Taggett glances over at it, sees it flicker, then notices that the wall is moving a little. When that light bulb finally pops, he can still make out a little vertical line in the wall's surface, something behind it swinging up and down like a flashlight. The detective's eyes go wide. "Jesus," he mutters. "Someone got in there behind me." He glances around the alley and then runs toward the traffic. Behind him he can hear a little explosion and then cursing and then a scream. He risks a glance back to see a crowd of the Russian's goons hovering around the assassin's corpse and a guy who must have gotten caught in the closing door yelling his head off and holding a hand to what's left of his ribcage. Then the mob of thugs notices him and starts to thunder in his direction.

The alley seems to stretch as Taggett runs. His shoes are splashing in the puddles, almost slipping, his eyes darting left and right for a door he can slip through. There's a pop behind him and in front of him a chip leaps out of a wall. Another pop and a sting in his ankle as the bullet just misses his foot. He jumps forward, almost stumbling, keeps running. His legs are starting to feel like wood. His side's starting to tighten, getting ready to cramp. The street's too far away. His breath is burning in his chest, his throat. He can feel himself slowing down. He can hear the crazy mob getting louder behind him.

Then a door swings open to his left. He makes an old football move, cutting with his left foot then jumping back to his right to make the turn before any of the mugs behind him can plant their feet to catch him. "Thanks, Murphy," he gasps as he flies through the frame and onto what feels like a rough wooden floor. The door slams shut behind him, and he hears the crashing yell of the Russian's army go on down the alley. He can't do anything but lie on his belly for a few minutes, breathing and shaking. Finally he manages to roll over on his back in the darkness. He reaches into his jacket for a match and a smoke but he's out. "Shit," he says. "Back in the dark. Well, can't be as bad as getting carved up by that crazy goon squad."

Somewhere in that thick darkness, just a little too close to Johnny's ear, a voice says, "Don't be so sure."

Taggett twitches out of the way. "What the hell," he shouts. "Smith?"

"No," says the voice. "Worse."

CHAPTER THIRTY ONE

"Last week you made a terrible mistake, Johnny," says the voice in the dark.

Taggett rolls over onto his belly, gets his feet under him, stands up. "Listen," he growls, "whoever you are, you don't know me well enough to—"

Something hits him hard behind the knees and he drops back down to the floor. "And you do not know me well enough to rise before me without permission," the voice says. It's a deep rumble, full of barely restrained violence, the voice of an almost tame bear. "Your second attempt will be your last. As I was saying, you made a terrible mistake last week. You boarded one of my vessels and slaughtered the entire crew. Worse, you stole from me. I do not take such trespasses lightly."

The detective can't get a bead on where the voice is coming from. The guy seems to be moving around in the room, but Taggett doesn't hear any footsteps. He sniffs and gets a hint of that fish aroma from the tunnel. "I didn't steal from you," he says. "I didn't kill those men. I was set up."

"Of course you were, Johnny," comes the voice from a spot a foot or so away, and then a hard slap to his face puts him down on all fours. From what could be the other side of the room the voice continues, "And I think you can guess who has done that to you."

"Yeah. Smith. He's your man." Taggett spits on the floor and gets what feels like a kick in the ribs for his trouble. He takes it and straightens back up to his knees. "He's spying on Wong for you. I'm guessing that was him on the boat that night. Let him know he shoulda killed me," the tough detective tells the darkness.

Then he takes a shot to the kidney and goes back down to his hands and knees. "He thought he had," the voice rumbles in its thick Chinese accent. "The man you call Smith is . . . what is your word . . . nervous, jumpy . . . he is a coward. Perhaps I should say he was a coward. He failed to accomplish the task I gave him. Nobody fails me twice." What must be a boot to the ass knocks Taggett the rest of the way to the floor.

"Dammit, enough!" Taggett yells and slams his open hands onto the floor, the pain that shoots up his forearms sparking him back up to his knees. "Why do you keep hitting me? What's your problem? You had me set up, you've had Smith on me all along, you know I didn't kill your guys or steal your cargo or whatever, so what the hell is all this Dracula shit about? If you're gonna kill me, just do it and quit dancing around!" The tough guy on his knees can't help flinching just a little.

The silence lingers too long in the dark, and then the voice comes from right in front of Taggett. "No, Johnny, I do not kill what I can use, any more than you would burn your American dollar bills." Whoever's talking is close. Taggett can smell the fish sauce on the guy's breath. "You have value for me. You can complete the assignment Smith could not. I think you have no choice."

Taggett can't help smirking. "You offering me a job?" he says.

"An opportunity," says the voice. "For a stranger in this city, a man with no friends and no connections, such an opportunity does not often present itself. There is a man who must die. Johnny, you will kill that man for me."

"Well, that's nice, but you're barking up the wrong tree," says Taggett. "I've already got a boss, so I don't need a job, and I'm no killer anyway. So turn on a light or something and let me out of here. If that was all you had to say to me, we got nothing to talk about."

A hard strike, a fist blasting into the top of his spine just below where that two-by-four opened him up, sends him back down to his belly. The voice hasn't gotten louder or softer or calmer or angrier. "It is because you already have a boss that I can offer you this mission," it says patiently. "And as to your being a killer, I think your actions in this very alley this very night make you a liar. You kill. I put you in the tunnel, I let you see Shanghai's whole operation, I give you the Russian to kill, and you kill him. Now I give you Mr. Wong to kill. You will kill him for me."

The tough detective struggles back to his knees, groaning a little. He can feel some blood dripping out of his nose, hear it splatter on the floor in front of him. "I will not," he growls. "I'm sick of getting shoved around by every half-bit Lamont Cranston in this town. Wong, Foulsworth, you—it's like you're all playing some sort of crazy chess game, pushing me around like a damn checker. I won't take it. I'm done. I'm not killing anyone for any of you bastards." The floor presses against his knees as he makes his little speech into the empty air. The voice doesn't say anything. Taggett kneels there, breathing hard. The room stays silent. He can hear the beating of his heart as it pushes against the inside of his chest. His scar's on fire, but that might just be from all the punches he's taken to the face. He gropes around the wooden floor for his hat, finds it, settles it on his head. The silence in the room swells into his ears. "Still here?" he says. Only silence answers. "Figures. These creeps are all the same, trying to scare me with this fancy talk in the dark, just folding up when I push back a little. Probably no one ever pushed back before." He gets one foot flat on the floor and starts to stand. "Just a bunch of hot air and-"

The blow to his chest knocks him right off his feet. His back slams into a wooden wall that creaks and gives a little as all the breath leaves him. The second blow knocks him through that wall, must have been the door he came in through, and back into the alley. The rain has stopped, the clouds are gone, the sky's developing a little hint of dawn. The detective is lying on the ground trying to suck in a breath. He's looking down his body at the rectangular hole where the door was into a field of blackness so dense it looks like a heavy velvet curtain blocking the world behind it. The lines of the buildings around that area of absolute darkness bend and waver the way that curtain would in a strong wind. Taggett lies there staring. Inside the darkness something moves like a shadow on a black wall. The figure of a man seems to step forward, seems to raise an arm, seems to throw something at Taggett. Something glitters for a moment in the air between the detective and that area of darkness, and then his chest explodes with pain. He lets out a weak moan. The darkness expands and swallows up everything.

But there's still a hint of light, a candle far away in the fog. Taggett's eyes are just open enough to see the figure step out of the dark room. He's pulling some kind of black hood off his head, and the detective observes the weird excuse for a face on whoever just beat him up so bad: a road map of scars, and one of the eyes covered over by flesh. The guy's face looks like a piece of melted tire stuck to the road. The one-eyed man moves closer, gliding over the asphalt of the alley floor without a sound. He's dressed in some sort of black pajama outfit. Even in the rising morning light Taggett can barely see him drift closer. A watery groan drools out of Taggett's mouth as the scenery fades. He rattles out a last breath.

Something's sparking in his brain. A world of whispers is bringing itself together. He can't see in the dark behind his eyelids, but his ears are keeping him on the planet. The whispers are scratching the back of his mind. Something's hot and throbbing against his scalp, under his hat. The throb takes a shape. It's a ring. Just then, the way you might see a face come up from under a still lake, a voice rises above those crazy whispers in his head. "And so we have arrived, as we always knew we must, at the conclusion of our brief and ultimately disappointing dance, Mr. Taggett. You had such potential, had you only known enough to refrain from too closely examining the source of your livelihood. Halfway around the world, to discover at the end of your travels merely the degrading posture of one of the countless throng of street scum above which you lacked the capacity to pull yourself. Such a sad testament to the sorry state of these modern times, don't you think, One-Eye?" As he struggles to keep his eyes closed, to keep from jumping into another one of whatever One-Eye threw at him, he listens to Mrs. Foulsworth give out another one of those dead chuckles.

"No man can withstand the shuriken. No man can withstand the ninja. When the ninja wields the shuriken, there can be no resistance," rumbles One-Eye. Taggett can feel the mutilated creep's breath on his skin, smell that fish sauce even as he tries to keep from breathing. "But we should not leave him here for the police. Allow me to drag the remains back into our warehouse."

Taggett keeps his eyes closed as no one says anything for a moment. He can hear the creak of the big wooden carts the night workers are pushing home. The morning sun is starting to pull his skin tight. Somehow the throbbing heat of the ring under his hat is helping him to stay still. Finally, Mrs. Foulsworth says, "Abandoning his corpse to the tender mercies of the local constabulary would alleviate one or two of our current discordances with them. However, this wretched example of deluded persistence could serve us with perhaps even more efficacy as a mysterious figure to whom can be attributed any number of activities with which we may not wish ourselves associated. Yes, One-Eye, drag him back into the warehouse, and do it with all the alacrity that you can summon from your Oriental soul. The day has barely begun, and we have many arrangements to make." With his eyes closed Taggett can hear the soft clicks of her shoes as she walks away.

The detective feels hard hands clutch his ankles, then the scrape of the alley floor along his back. "You could have been a noble opponent," he hears One-Eye mutter, "but, like you, I have honor enough not to contradict my word to my employer. And now you have died, as we all must. I wish for your sake that you had died in a proper battle." Something rough drags heavily down Taggett's face in some kind of brutal caress. "Good luck in the afterlife, Johnny Taggett." The detective listens to the door getting propped back up in its hole, and then everything is darkness and silence.

CHAPTER THIRTY TWO

It's a beautiful morning in Shanghai. Once you get away from the clump of buildings the red light district lives in, you walk through the cattle-fields along the canal, smelling the thick solid musk of all that manure as you stumble along. Even though he's not dressed for this kind of walk, even though his body feels like one big tired bruise, Taggett's grinning as he goes. No one gets in his way as he hikes through the mud. He's taking the long way for just that reason, keeping shy of the city area with the big boulevard running through it. The way he's limping and pulling himself through the wet ground that's trying to suck his shoes off, it takes him almost till noon to get back to the river. The respectable tourists get out of his way as he staggers down the big sidewalk in front of the hotels. He doesn't stop grinning. "I might look like some kind of hobo," he tells himself, "but I'm alive . . . finally know just what I'm up against . . . what Walt died for . . . no more damn games . . ." Finally the muttering bum makes it to the Palace.

As he reels in through the front door he gets the dim eye from the brave soul in the uniform manning the front desk, a look like Taggett is some kind of nuisance. He grins in the guy's face. "I'm a guest," he says. "Give someone else that high hat." The guy keeps looking at him, doesn't make a sound. The two of them are just staring at each other. Taggett takes a step closer. He's growling. "I said take that attitude elsewhere, monkey. I've had a hard night." Still, the guy doesn't flinch. The detective's getting ready to slide a hand into what's left of his jacket and pull out his forty-five when he feels a hand on his arm. He spins to the right, fist cocked.

Chen's eyes beam up into his, the younger man's face just glowing. "You're alive," he says. Taggett glances over at the desk to see Jie murmuring something in the guy's ear while Chen keeps going. "I lost you at the club last night. What the hell was that, anyway? That guy with the beard, was that the Russian? You just vanished. I must have put out twenty or thirty guys looking for you. Jesus, you really know how to make friends. That Russian guy ducked out right after you disappeared. I tried to get to him but his crew slowed me down. Did he catch up with you? Holy shit, what's that in your jacket?" By this time Jie's gotten back around the counter to put a hand on Chen's shoulder. Chen glances at the little driver, swallows, and shuts up. One of Taggett's arms over each man's shoulders, they manage to steer him to a set of chairs in the lobby.

He drops into a seat, and Jie runs a pair of practiced hands over him, stopping at his chest. "Oh my," says Jie. "You've had quite an eventful night, sir. I don't believe that I've seen a shuriken since before the War." Between the older man's fingers a star-shaped knife glistens in the lobby's mellow light.

The detective's eyes go wide. "Shit, that was in me?"

"Not exactly, sir," says Jie. He reaches out and taps on the breast of Taggett's jacket. Even in the soft buzz of the lobby's business the three of them can hear a clank of metal hitting metal through the tatters of his jacket.

That gets a snort out of Chen. "The only man who'd take a flask to a bar."

"Never know when you'll need it," Taggett winks back.

Jie's expression hasn't changed. "Sir, such a weapon as this is wielded only by the ninja, a secret organization of almost inhumanly trained assassins. Am I to understand, then, sir, that you've encountered a ninja? Remarkable. Very few men have survived such an encounter."

"Ninja?" Taggett asks him. "Far as I can tell, I got my ass kicked by some kind of dancer in a set of black pajamas. Got the impression that he's one of the bosses around here."

Jie frowns. "With all due respect to your observational acumen, sir, that state of affairs would seem to have a high degree of unlikeliness. Ninja very rarely take command positions. They prefer to serve a strong lord, acting as an invisible weapon against their master's enemies. Their strict code of honor demands it."

"And you think this One-Eye character from last night is one of these ninjas?" says Taggett.

Jie stops moving entirely, except that his jaw literally hangs open for a moment. "One-Eye?" he says. He looks down at the shuriken in his palm, squinting a little as he studies the shining weapon. "Then he's still alive," the old man mutters to himself, as if Taggett and Chen and the whole lobby had just faded all the way out. "Still alive and in Shanghai. I can barely believe it. All this time? Impossible, I'd surely have heard of him before." He's talking straight into the shuriken, and Taggett can see his face lose all the blankness he expects from the calm old man: the eyes are getting darker, the lips are setting into nearly a snarl. Those dark eyes suddenly snap into Taggett's gaze. "How did you establish your attacker's identity?" The question comes out like a bullet from a gun. After a moment Jie adds, "Sir."

Chen and Taggett sit there staring at the old man who just turned into a tiger in front of them, then the tough detective clears his throat and says, "I guess they thought I was dead. They definitely didn't think I was listening."

"They?" says Jie.

"Yeah," says Taggett. "This One-Eye character and Mrs. Foulsworth."

Now it's Chen's turn to gasp. "Foulsworth?" he almost yells. "What the hell is that crazy old bat doing here?"

With both his friends staring at him the way hungry dogs look at a steak, Taggett can only say, "I don't know. Once that freak thought he'd killed me, she just suddenly appeared. They went back and forth a little bit about what to do with my body, and she finally told him to drag me back into the warehouse. He definitely waited on her say-so. It looks like they're trying to shake things up around here. I guess One-Eye was pretending to be Wong's enemy, said he wanted the guy killed, said I was the man to do it. Guess he didn't like my answer."

Chen grabs Taggett's lapels so hard that one comes off in his hand. "What about Foulsworth?" he demands.

Jie puts a hand on the younger man's shoulder and starts talking in his usual bland tone. "Clearly, sir, this Mrs. Foulsworth you refer to has developed an aspiration to control at least a portion of Shanghai's considerable market in sin. Her employment of One-Eye, apparent from your description of their conversation, suggests to me that she, rather than Mr. Wong's rival, bears responsibility for the opium theft we're currently investigating. I suspect a campaign of subterfuge, an attempt to play one faction against the other so as to leave the entirety exposed to predatory attentions. Sir, this Mrs. Foulsworth demonstrates an amount of tactical wisdom almost unheard of in a female."

"Yeah," says Taggett. "She's definitely a different kind of dame. Smart as she is, she made a bad mistake, though. Same one they always make. She left me alive."

Chen laughs and relaxes back into his seat. "You don't die too easy, do you?" says the younger man, still holding onto the scrap of fabric he pulled off Taggett's new suit.

Grinning like a wolf, Taggett just shakes his head.

Jie also sits back, his impassive eyes examining the shuriken he's still got on his palm. Looking back up at Taggett, he says, "Again I must beg your pardon, sir, for the amazement I cannot seem to forbear expressing, but I find your having survived a meeting with One-Eye a complete astonishment. I have heard his name whispered for decades by the kind of half-educated cases one encounters in the pursuit of one's less savory duties, but I have never once heard of anyone surviving a personal encounter. He has a reputation as such a painstaking master of disguise that he will, as he follows the track of his target, take a position as one of his target's trusted associates, only to assassinate his prey and leave the associate to take the blame. That he would reveal himself to you to the extent of allowing you to hear his name simply beggars the imagination."

"Like the man says, I take a lot of killing," Taggett chuckles. "By the way, either of you guys got a smoke?"

Chen leans back forward, holding out a pack and laughing. "If it'll keep you from trying to wipe the floor with the help, take a few." Taggett takes one and holds it to the flame the younger man's got cupped in his palm. Chen lights one for himself, offers one to Jie. Jie shrugs it off, and everyone rests for a moment.

"Well, sir," says Jie. "I presume our first course of action to involve the finding of some new clothing for you. If you'll pardon the potential effrontery of my assumption, that suit appears to have crawled through every gutter in the red-light district."

"You're probably right," laughs Taggett. "The way I feel right now, I need a new suit, a steak sandwich, a shower, and a nap. I'll settle for the nap. You guys should probably get some rest too. We've got work to do tonight."

Jie leans forward, still hanging on to One-Eye's shuriken. "Most respectfully, Mr. Taggett, you've obviously been involved in something beyond my poor ability to comprehend, some series of events that has transformed the lovely suit so exquisitely tailored for you by Mr. Chang into the—and I characterize them thus without reference to your character—noisome rags you currently inhabit." Even Jie can't help squinting a little as he describes what the detective's got on. Taggett just raises an eyebrow, so the older man goes on. "Sir, if the condition of the suit serves to reflect the condition of your body, then you must find yourself in serious need of, if not medical attention, then at least an extended period of rest."

Taggett shakes his head violently, almost throwing off his hat. "No way," he growls. "Rest is just where you sit still long enough for someone to catch you napping."

"Now you're talking," says Chen, leaning forward with sparks in his eyes.

Taggett takes a drag off his cigarette and looks at his partners. "Jie, you need to find out what's shipping tonight. Bribe who you need to. I've got a feeling Wong's money's gonna give out on us pretty soon one way or the other. Chen, you know the supplies we need. Get 'em. If these creeps wanna smash up the underworld, I say we smash it up for them. And we don't leave them anything to play with."

Chen tosses his butt, smacks his hand with his fist. Jie nods, his jaw square, his lips flat against his teeth. The three of them look at each other for a quiet moment, then they get to work.

CHAPTER THIRTY THREE

Two of them go to work, anyway. Taggett's in a haze as he stumbles through the lobby to the elevator, up to the suite for a change of clothes, back down to the bar for one of those delicious hamburgers and three or four beers, back across the lobby to get a new suit from Mr. Chang. "Make sure you put a pocket in there for my lucky flask," the detective mumbles. Mr. Chang grins and nods and hands over a slip of paper with some Chinese writing on it.

"Tomorrow," says Mr. Chang.

Taggett blinks and nods and staggers back through the lobby to the elevator to the suite and falls deep into that big soft bed without even undressing, without even taking his hat off. His eyes are drifting closed, his body relaxing, sinking into the bed. He can feel sleep closing in on him like a fog bank.

Pulsing like the yellow glow of a lighthouse far back in the cloud that's folding around him he can feel the heat of the Violet Diamond. He can feel it in his brain, almost hear it like slow Morse Code. His right hand twitches toward his head but flops back down. His body squirms a little. The pulsing in his brain speeds up, turns into the sound of a radio stuck between stations, the swooping whistle, the fuzz of static. As his body gets heavier the static starts developing a pattern. He can hear whispers in it. Something's whispering to him. He can feel his body roll over and his hat fall off, but the throb's still in his brain, the whispers keep coming. They're telling him the story he can start to see as he slides deeper along the chute that leads down into dreamland.

A dingy little office fades in around him. It could be in San Francisco or Shanghai or Sweden for all he knows. Light through a window casts bars of shadow on the dim room's floor, in front of a desk like the one he used back at the precinct house. It's even got the same black tower of a telephone. He hears himself mumbling, "Damn, this is a lot more real than anything I've dreamed before." He can feel the floor solid under his feet, feel the still air warm on his skin. Then he looks down at the floor and notices that he can't see any sign of his feet or his legs. He waves his hands and feels the air drag over his fingers, but he can't see the hands he's waving. "Guess I'm invisible," he shrugs. "Every flatfoot's dream." Snickering a little, he glances at the door to see what might happen next.

Right on cue, it opens and Mrs. Foulsworth steps through. He flinches as she glides past the spot where he's standing by about half an inch, but she just keeps going until she's behind the desk. Once she's taken a seat, she takes out that weird ivory cigarette holder and screws in one of those brown cigarettes. She takes a lighter out of the same secret pocket she got the holder and cigarette out of and lights up. Then she just sits there, featureless black figure absolutely still, only the glow of the cigarette's cherry revealing as it brightens and dims that she's breathing. Her figure sits there, a little less dark than the room around it. The ember's almost touching the tip of the holder by the time the door opens again and One-Eye slides into the little room. The detective holds his breath as the ninja steps close. That wrecked face seems to twitch a little in his direction under its blank black mask, but the solid dark shape of One-Eye just takes a parade-rest position in front of the desk, the bars of shadow on the floor nearly touching the blunt ends of his feet. The two dark profiles face each other silently for a long moment.

Finally the ninja speaks up. "You called me here for a reason," he rumbles, "not just to pose for photographs."

"Such an inappropriately impertinent tone to take as the opening gambit in a conversation with one's superior," she replies in that distantly mocking tone. "The incisiveness of your wit betrays an unseemly

Western influence threatening to corrupt the purity of your service. Perhaps that would explain your actions last night."

One-Eye doesn't flinch. "I am unaware of a need for explanation," he tells her.

That gets one of those chuckles that you could mistake for the sound of a lion cub getting ready to tear into a gazelle out of her. "You damaged a significant asset, one for the preparation of whose part in my design I have spent considerable time and fortune. Your decision last night to deviate from the plan laid out before you by your superior—by your master—has necessitated corresponding adjustments to my design."

"You informed me of your desire to test the American's loyalty," says One-Eye. "I tested it. You informed me of your expectation that he would fail my test. He did not. You gave me no instructions regarding my response to his strength of character. I assumed that your intention depended on his disloyalty. I assumed that he had therefore become useless to you. He had become what you call a loose end. For that reason I eliminated him."

The strange woman's voice crowds the room with its mechanical harshness. "You placed your wisdom above mine and proceeded without understanding, presuming vastly beyond your place. In doing so, you have caused perhaps irrevocable damage to the project for which I have contracted your assistance. Clearly the incompetence of my employees is of limitless capacity. Smith's incompetence has cost me one assassin, and now yours has cost me the use of Johnny Taggett." Out comes another one of those stunted brown cigarettes. She screws it into her holder, lights it herself before the ninja can move to offer to do it for her. When she starts talking again, her voice has gone back to its regular tone of dry mockery. "You poor mangled wreck, I really should exercise my prerogative as your lord and find a way to punish you for your disappointing lapses in judgment. Had nature not already done so with such severity, I might be inclined to have you mutilated to such an extent that you would never dare show your face in public. I might condemn you to a life in the shadows, to the half-existence of a monster whose legend petty criminals whisper to each other in the night—if, as I say, nature, something that happened in your misbegotten mother's womb or some fascinating event from the recent War, had not already exacted just that revenge upon you."

One-Eye stands there and takes it.

"You realize, do you not, that at this minute I could have been on the brink of cementing my personal control over the entire underworld of this quaint little outpost you people insist on describing as a city. I could at this moment have been receiving the news that Wong and Zhang have destroyed each other, leaving my scrupulously clean hands to safely grasp their combined power." She pauses to take a drag from her holder, the tip of her weird cigarette flaring like a stab at the darkness. "The only thing standing between me and my assumption of my rightful place as absolute ruler of this squalid little empire, the sole obstacle to successful execution of my plan to employ this brainless gumshoe from New York as my catspaw, has been you and your continuing failure to fulfill the promise of relentless efficiency expected of an instrument such as yourself." She opens the drawer of the desk and pulls out a small black revolver. Aiming the barrel at the middle of One-Eye's ruined face, she inquires, "Do you see the truth in that statement? Do you have the effrontery to attempt some sort of exculpatory response?"

One-Eye hasn't flinched through any of this. He barely seems to notice the gun pointed at him. "A plan that relies to such an extent on the actions of one man risks failure," he tells her. "No one can predict the actions of one man. You seek to evade your responsibility. I will not accept it. I have agreed to help you. I will not betray my principles for your profit."

The black velvet talon tightens on the trigger. One-Eye still isn't moving. "You have agreed to serve me, and serve me you shall," says Mrs. Foulsworth. "I have not released you from the bond into which you have delivered yourself, as I continue to require your services, such as they are."

"Then probably you will not shoot me." The ninja makes a sound that might be a chuckle. "You make yourself feel better with insults. That is your privilege as a woman. I do not allow your insults to affect me. You accuse me of disgracing my code. Woman, you do not know my code. You speak of my obligation to you. You speak of yourself as my master. A true master knows the use of his tools. A true master understands the realities of the world. Certainly a true master does not behave with such recklessness as you show at this moment."

The finger on the trigger tightens a little further. One-Eye stands there silently. A sound like gears grinding starts to come out of Mrs. Foulsworth. She puts the gun down on the desk as she bends over the surface, coughing and pulling in big ragged gasps of air. One-Eye watches her do it. After a minute or so of this, her body shakes once, the way a landed fish's body shakes when it finally gives up, and then she settles back in her seat. The gun stays on the desk. The voice that comes out of her has its usual calm. "I'm master enough for you, you unspeakable embarrassment. The only other man who has dared to address me in such an insolent manner as you here display lies rotting in our warehouse. If your misdirected hand had not prematurely deprived me of his usefulness, Taggett would surely have perished at mine at the conclusion of his task. You continue to breathe my air only because I continue to require things done that only you can accomplish. Your failure to accomplish my requirements, the very failure that I have been describing to you, must for that reason have a decided effect upon your ability to lengthen for the space of a single day your stunted and hardly human existence. Do you understand me?"

"You use many words to threaten my life." That sound that might be a chuckle barks out of the ninja again. "My life has been threatened many times." The two of them stare at each other for a stretching minute, then One-Eye says, "You require something done."

"I do," says Mrs. Foulsworth. "However, I doubt your ability to do it. Although many have repeated the proverb that the world fears a masterless ninja, I know to the contrary the lack of direction, the rudderless drifting, that occurs when a ninja forswears his master. You simply cannot choose your own course of action without the guiding hand of a strategist capable of using you as the tool, the weapon, you have made of yourself, and here you stand rejecting the strategy with which I, your master, am doing you the favor of acquainting you." She reaches for the gun, only to slide it back into its drawer. "What use could I possibly have for a rudderless boat?" She reaches down to pick the cigarette holder off the floor where it fell during her fit.

One-Eye bows, his right fist smacking his open left hand. "Your honor or lack of honor does not determine my actions," he tells her. "The terms of my contract with you have not been fulfilled. I remain in your service. I pursue your goals as my own. What do you require done?"

She takes her time fitting a new cigarette into the holder. Finally she says, "I require the return of the Violet Diamond. In the wake of Taggett's demise, I shall have to find it a new host. The mental training you performed in the course of your development as a ninja should, I believe, render you impervious to the charms exerted by the gem's peculiar qualities." She lets the tip of her cigarette glow for a moment, then stubs it out on the desk in front of her. "The imbecile keeps it on his person."

The room's getting darker somehow as the bars of light on the floor between the two of them fading into the black surface of the floor. "Remove the Violet Diamond from the corpse of that ultimately redundant moron," she says, "and return it to me." Her voice is getting softer the way the room's getting dimmer, the sound of her words fading into a noise like far-off traffic. As the invisible detective feels the scene slip away from him he can barely hear her say, "And while you're at it, bring me his tongue. It will serve as a delightful souvenir."

Taggett's eyes snap open to darkness. A sound like a rusty gate getting pulled open comes out of his throat. He rubs the sandpaper out of his eyes with his fingers and gropes for a smoke, telling himself, "Damn, must've slept the whole day away. Better get down to the lobby and meet the—"

A faint purple glow at the foot of the bed derails his train of thought before he can light the smoke. He can't really tell where that glow could be coming from, but it's revealing in silhouette the soft curves of Olga, the massage therapist. He can't see her face, but he can hear the grin in her voice as she says, "You have a little time, Johnny." It sounds like her voice, anyway, but she's lost her accent. "The Violet Diamond has another present for you."

CHAPTER THIRTY FOUR

Everything about the sexy body outlined in shadows on that weird purple glow tells him that it's Olga talking to him, except the way she's talking. "Don't worry, Johnny," she's saying, "Olga has come to no harm. You distracted the Russian and let her get away. You did a good deed, Johnny Taggett. You deserve a reward." He can feel a wave of heat come off the curvy shape he's staring at. His whole body feels it. The purple glow's getting stronger, but the shadow that looks like Olga stays dark. The voice is whispering directly into his brain. "Go ahead, Johnny. Take what you need. Give yourself to me."

The tough detective squirms back toward the big headboard and fumbles for his forty-five. "This is too weird," he mutters as his hand gropes for the holster under his coat, can't find it. "What the hell is going on here?"

The laugh that gets feels like a tongue sliding into his ear. "You don't have to be afraid," says the shadow, only now the voice sounds just like the girl he picked up in Frisco, the girl that got killed just to send Johnny a message. "There's no need for that kind of gun with me. Not tonight. You took such good care of me, Johnny. It's time for me to take care of you." His body's hot all over except for the cold sweat he can feel on his face. The shadow's changed shape, thickening a little as the glow keeps getting brighter. He can almost see her face the way it looked in that crappy little gin joint.

"I didn't take care of you." He can feel his eyes going wide as the words come out of him in a shaking moan. "I got you murdered. You'd still be alive if you never met me." He glances left and right the way a fugitive looks around a dead-end alley for an open door, but there's nothing in the room but the purple light and him and the woman. "You're not even real!"

And now she's Olga again. She's smiling right into his eyes as she crawls up on the bed, crawls toward him. "Of course I'm real," she says. "And of course you took care of me, Johnny. You kept me away from that horrible woman and her plans. You carried me across the ocean, almost to my home." She's close enough by now for Johnny to smell. The air between them is thick with some kind of desert musk, the breath of a powerful beast as it gets ready to touch you with its mouth. "Now that you know what she's up to you can end it for me, can't you?" she purrs at him.

Now that he can see her face he can see that it's not Olga or that girl from Frisco or his ex-wife or any woman he's ever seen, even in his dreams, even though she looks a little like all of them. Her eyes are the same color as the light that's flooding the room. They're looking right into his, and he can feel all his muscles relaxing. "That's right," she tells him. "I know you're my friend, Johnny. Let's be friendly." He can feel the heat of her skin on his over the inch or two of space between them. That's how he suddenly realizes that he's naked, just as naked as she is.

And he's hard, as hard as he's ever been. His hands rise on their own and find her hips. He can hear himself growling a little as the heat of her plays over his skin, as she squirms under his hands. She moans. The sound of her voice slips into his ear with a feeling like a strong shot of whiskey. His hands slip back to grip a soft firm pair of cheeks. He squeezes, and she moans again, and now he's moaning with her. The purple flames of her eyes are taking up his whole field of vision.

She reaches between them, curls long fingers around his throb. Her touch makes him jerk and twitch. He can feel her breath on his lips as she whispers, "Take me. Make me yours, Johnny, yours forever." She's guiding him into her. Her wet heat's gripping him, drawing him deeper and deeper as he can't help leaning forward to take her lower lip between his teeth. It tastes a little like blood under his tongue. His big hands are pulling her onto his body. His hips are pushing up, pushing deep, pushing into her. His eyes are closed, but that purple light is so bright he can hear it buzzing in his brain. He's thrusting into her, deeper, harder, arching under her, driving into her. He can see her with his eyes closed burning like a purple flame. He can feel the flame inside him and around him. She's riding him, growling with him, pulling him deeper and deeper into the light. He can feel his mouth gaping open. He's breathing in her fire. Pleasure starts to explode at the base of his spine, pushing itself up his back toward his brain. He's crying out from the pressure of his orgasm. Even over his howls he can hear her whisper, "Yes, Johnny. We are one."

It feels like he's floating above the surface of the bed. There is no bed. There is no surface. The girl, the shape, the ghost or whatever is inside his body, looking out through his eyes at nothing but pleasure. They're moaning together in his voice. His body has disappeared completely. His body is a purple fire. He's exploding. The girl is gone. He's absorbed her. The world is nothing but purple light.

And then his eyes snap open into darkness. He's in his clothes, sprawled on the bed, as the shadows around him start to fill in. "Still in my suite at the Palace," he tells himself. "All just some kind of crazy dream. Guess getting killed so often really takes it out of a fella. Have to admit, I got beat pretty bad by that . . . hey, wait a minute, I'm not feeling any of it. I feel great! That must have been some excellent sleep!" He gropes on the night table for a cigarette, lights up, breathes in deep. He can feel the smoke drifting thickly back along his tongue and down his throat. A clock somewhere is making its back-and-forth noise. He lies there looking around the dark bedroom. "Be a shame to kiss all this luxury goodbye," he mumbles. "Never mine to begin with, I guess. Just let me wreck this Foulsworth woman's plot, I'll get back on the street where I belong."

A knock at the door sends him grabbing for his forty-five. As he fills one hand with the cold steel he uses the other to stub out the giveaway glow of his smoke. He lies there in silence, not moving, as the knock comes again. He risks the click of pulling back the hammer just after he hears the faintest hint of some skilled hand jimmying the front door's lock. There's a creak as the door opens, a whisper of breath hissed in and held. Taggett trains his eyes on the rectangle of the suite's bedroom door. Careful footsteps patter over the floor beyond it. The detective's index finger tightens.

"Mr. Taggett. Sir?" Jie's voice sounds a little muffled from the other side of the door. "Mr. Chen and I have arrived to accompany you on tonight's mission, but only if you feel yourself sufficiently recovered from the ordeal to which you subjected yourself last—"

Taggett shuts him up by leaping out of bed and yanking open the door, grinning down into the smaller man's face. "Oh, I'm up to it," he says. "I'm up above it. I'm ready to smash that crazy creep's whole operation to dust." He winks over at Chen. "She's gonna get just what's coming to her. We're gonna pay her off in spades for killing Walt." The big man strides into the suite's main room and looks around. "Chen, you'd better pick up anything you think you'll need. I've got a feeling this place isn't gonna be so welcoming after tonight."

Chen grins back. "I'm ready, Johnny. Let's burn her down."

"Come on, guys," says Taggett. "I'll tell you in the car what we're doing."

CHAPTER THIRTY FIVE

The Phantom II's headlights are cutting jagged holes in the night as the car bounces along the beat-up track that shadows the canal. Jie's driving. Taggett's next to him in the front seat, explaining. Chen's in the back next to a huge stuffed burlap sack about the size of the tough detective. The Phantom II shakes and jolts as it hits the holes and ruts in the road.

"So you paid the captain to burn a yellow light for us?" Johnny's asking Jie.

The driver nods. "Indeed, sir. I felt it prudent to invest the remainder of the stipend provided for us by Mr. Wong to influence the success of our endeavor by making the target of your efforts fully evident. If I understand you correctly, sir, failure tonight would signify the complete destruction of our ability to achieve the objective necessary to completion of our mission. Thus, I felt justified in the large expenditure I undertook to assure the captain's good will and access to his schedule."

"Good will or not," Johnny says, "we'd better be ready for a trap. If Wong's letting this guy get bought, then that means they're still trying to set us up, probably want the cops to catch us red-handed with a bunch of dope."

Chen snorts, "More like catch Jie and me red-handed. Aren't you supposed to be dead?" He puts his hand on the ceiling to keep from smacking into it with his skull as the Phantom II slams over another little rise in the road.

"They'll find out soon enough," says Johnny, "which is why we have to do this now. Good job on the dummy, by the way."

"I've made a few friends on the cleaning staff," Chen smirks. "Wasn't too hard to get one of the maids to stuff a sack for me? It's probably your torn-up old suit anyway."

Hunched over the steering wheel, his eyes focused like crosshairs on the road unwinding in front of the headlights, Jie speaks up: "I must ask your forgiveness for this interruption, gentlemen, but perhaps one of you could be so kind as to divert your attention from the admittedly well-manufactured decoy for the purpose of informing me of our destination."

Johnny turns back to the driver. "Sorry, Jie. You'll see it when the road swings a little closer to the canal. There's a double bridge a few miles up from there, about at I think it was, how do you say it, Soo-zoo?"

Jie lets out a little dry chuckle. "Suzhou, sir. And I know the double bridge of which you speak. It looks as if the designer became confused and added two bridges side-by-side where the rest of the canal features single bridges." A shock to the Phantom II as the road turns for a moment into a bunch of random cobblestones makes everyone cough, then Jie goes on: "A very picturesque location, sir. The gap between the bridges provides admirable balance in the scene."

"Uh . . . yeah," says Johnny. "I figure the two bridges together are wide enough for us to set up a little distraction. It'll take a while for the barge to get under both bridges, so there'll be time to make a double drop. While everyone's at one end of the barge trying to figure out what's going on, I can drop down on the other end as it crosses under the farther bridge. You guys'll run alongside in the Phantom II, and when the time's right I'll pitch the goods to you and you can get out of there."

Chen's frowning in the back seat. He says to Johnny, "So where does that leave you?"

Jie has the same frown. "It leaves him on a barge with a fully armed crew who will soon discover him as the purloiner of their valuable merchandise, and it leaves him at their mercy, which I fear will be dubious at best." He wrenches the wheel right then left then right again to get around some kind of pit in the middle of the road. Chen's got a hand on the fake Taggett, keeping it from falling over. "Sir," Jie goes on, "have you fully considered the implications of your strategy?"

Now Taggett's chuckling and grinning that wolf grin of his. "Yeah," he says, and for a long moment the only sound is the roar of the Phantom II's engine, almost echoed by the creaking of the car's chassis as the road beats it to death from underneath. Finally, just before Chen can explode, he says, "I got two things going for me. One is you guys and this hardware." He takes a second to readjust the tommy gun between him and Jie. "Nice artillery, by the way."

"Thank you, sir," says Jie. "It seemed prudent after the War to preserve to the best of my ability my skill, and the clandestine practice required to achieve that goal required the purchase of a weapon."

Taggett keeps chuckling. "Well, lucky for us that you're so ambitious with your knowledge." He leans back to look at Chen. "You ready for this?"

Chen looks right back at him with a face just as blank as Jie's. "If there's a chance I'll help one of the goons that got Mr. McBride get killed, then you know I'm ready. Guess this is why Jie's been teaching me to handle the Phantom II, eh?" Taggett just nods. "So what's the other thing?" says the younger man.

"Huh?"

Chen smirks into the tough detective's eyes. "You said you had two things going for you. What's the other thing? "Heh. Right. The other thing is that I got hardware of my own. And those poor bastards on the barge are gonna have their backs to me. Here's the turn, Jie."

"I see it, sir." Jie pulls hard at the wheel just as the car hits a deep rut. The headlights stab up into the sky for a moment and then back ahead into the night. Just at the edge of their range the darkness seems to somehow be flowing, a stream of black velvet under the black marble of the sky. The car keeps growling forward, and the flow in the darkness gets broader, shows itself as the canal.

"Nearly there," says Taggett. The road bends again, and Jie twists the wheel to keep up with it. The Phantom II digs into the road with its tires and flings mud all over itself. A red light swells out of the darkness, coming closer, then passes right on by, bobbing a little on the canal's waves, a barge on some kind of business that no one in the car has to care about. Taggett notices that his hand's been in his coat, fingers brushing his forty-five, ever since he saw the light. He chuckles a little and makes himself relax, and then the headlights pick out a couple of shadows looming against the night. "Here!" he says.

Jie pulls over. He cuts the engine. The quiet of the night settles in around them as they step out, Chen with the burlap dummy, Jie with the machine gun. No one says a word. With a look toward Jie, Taggett and Chen start walking across the road, toward the side-by-side arches of the twin bridges. "Wait for the yellow light," Taggett mutters to Chen. "And be ready. It's gonna get nasty."

Chen just looks at him and totes the dummy. When they get to the stone steps of the bridges, the tough detective lights a smoke, offers one to Chen. They stand for a minute in the night, then Chen flips his half-smoked cigarette away. "Let's get this done," he says.

Taggett chuckles, "I'll see you downstream." Then he flips away his own smoke and starts climbing the stairs. Thick stone walls hide him and Chen from each other as well as the darkness does.

By the time he's gotten to the middle of the bridge a breeze has kicked up, cold over his face. He braces himself against the wall in front of him and stares upstream. The dirty-aquarium smell of the canal drifts up to meet him as he peers into the horizon, his brain making yellow lights flare up and vanish in the distance. Finally one stays on, gets brighter and bigger. "That's it," he can't help muttering. "Come on, Chen, be ready."

The buzz he remembers from the last time he tried this is getting louder. Along with it he can hear men talking Chinese, trying to keep quiet. "Yeah, that's the one all right," he chuckles to himself. "Too many guards for a regular barge. Wong or whoever must want to make sure this gets through." The buzz of motor and chat gets louder. Taggett ducks and crawls across the width of the bridge, reaches up from his crouch to let his fingertips grab the ledge of the wall in front of him. He starts counting the seconds as the sound grows stronger.

At seven he hears a thump and the chatter cuts itself off with the light. A spray of shots from the shore covers the sound of Chen running back along the bridge and down the stairs, and then the back of the barge erupts in reply. Taggett hoists himself up to the broad top of the wall, rolls over and squirms to hang from the far side, waiting. The gunfire stops as the barge crosses under the first bridge. Taggett waits. His fingers start to cramp and weaken. He keeps waiting. Jie fires off another round at the barge as it passes between the bridges. A guy lets out a grunt and topples forward off the back. The night lights up yellow with the blasts coming from the barge. Under the explosions the detective can hear the Phantom II starting up. He smells the gunpowder from the thugs' artillery at the exact second that he starts to smell what the barge is carrying. "Oh, shit," he growls as Jie sends one more burst along the waterline and the cramping fingers let Johnny's heavy body drop.

CHAPTER THIRTY SIX

He feels his feet hit the deck a second before the firing stops. He stands there as still as he can, trying not to breathe in the foul-smelling darkness. He figures he's facing the back of the barge, and he might have hung a little too long, so he's probably not quite at the front of it. Chinese whispers are coming from ahead of him, one of the voices whimpering like a stuffed dog. He can catch glimpses of the moonlight reflecting from the Phantom II's, its headlights dark, but he can't hear its engine over the throb of the barges. He stands there, letting his eyes adjust, and then a shot from behind him makes him dive to the deck. As another round of fire comes from the Phantom II, he rolls toward what he hopes is the middle of the barge. Face down, he listens. Someone's yelling in Chinese behind him. The noise the guy's making covers Taggett as he crawls on his belly, making his way toward the most horrible part of the stench. The yelling stops, so Taggett does too, and then another burst comes from the road alongside the canal, and another thug screams and splashes.

"Better get this done soon," he mutters to himself. "They're gonna run out of road—" A blast from the guy that was yelling a second ago shuts him up, gets him crawling forward as the guy starts hollering again. A spray of bullets from the Phantom II interrupts whatever he's saying. As everyone's firing back at the invisible car, Taggett crawls forward into something soft and warm. The pile of shit he's crawling into surrounds him, seems to suck him in even as he turns himself around to face the way he came in. His ears are full of it, muffling the gunfight going on around him to a concert of faraway snare drums. He can feel the deck under him vibrating, and then it stops as someone cuts the barge's engine. There's another faraway drumroll and another splash. He's holding his breath, his fingers on the butt of his forty-five. Someone's walking on the deck. Through his clenched-shut eyelids, through the inch or so of shit in front of his face, the detective can sense the beam of a flashlight playing back and forth. He pulls his feet up under his body. The footsteps are coming closer. Under his coat, Taggett's thumb carefully pulls back the hammer. He can't hear the footsteps, but he can feel them through the wood of the deck, getting closer still. Another drumroll, another splash, and the footsteps stop. Taggett can feel the breath pushing against his chest, trying to push out through his mouth. His fingers curl around the butt, around the trigger. The wood under his feet transmits the feeling of those footsteps coming just a little closer, almost close enough. The darkness of his closed eyes is getting red around the edges. The footsteps pause just out of range. Finally they get closer and Taggett leaps out of the pile of shit, draws his forty-five, rolls on the deck, fires three times in the dark. He blows out as hard as he can, then takes a giant breath in, gagging on the smell of himself. His ears are still clogged with shit as he waits for the return shot from whatever the other guy's holding. What he gets is a thump he can feel across the boards of the barge's swaying deck. He crawls forward until his hands hit flesh and hair—the guy's head, must be—and then keeps going until he can feel the warmth of the guy's blood making a puddle under him. Taggett gets a handful of hair, pulls the head up, jams the forty-five into the soft part under the chin, fires. Then the tough detective gets a hand wet with blood and wipes the shit from his face so he can pull his eyelids apart.

The Phantom II's still shadowing the barge. He can see its headlights making vertical stripes in the night as the car jolts along the ruts of some poor bastard's field. Spitting, he stands up with his hands in the air, swaying a little as the barge keeps drifting downstream. Ahead he can see the lone light of a little dock. "Hope the tide'll get me there," he mutters.

His luck's holding. The canal's current pushes the barge full of shit and corpses right up to the soft wood of this dock out in the middle of nowhere. On his hands and knees, Taggett manages to find a line and toss it to Chen, who's jumping out of the Phantom II and running toward him. The detective can almost hear the younger guy's voice yelling something that sounds like a cheer. Chen ties off the barge and jumps over the gap between it and the dock, grinning.

"Johnny, we did it!" says Chen. "I can't believe how good Jie was with that—oh, shit, Johnny, can you smell yourself?" He backs away a little from Taggett, his face curdling. "What the hell have you been doing?"

The detective chuckles so deep in his throat it's almost a growl. "Sometimes you have to get dirty, I guess. Let's look around and find that stuff before someone comes after it. Or us." The light from the dock is so bright that it makes the shadows thrown by the piles of raw shit even darker. As Taggett looks around the barge he notices that there's a little hut on the very front. If his timing hadn't been a little off, he would have fallen from the bridge onto its roof. He jerks his head toward it and tells Chen, "That must be where they keep the engine controls. Probably where they keep the special cargo, too."

"I sure hope so," says the younger man. "Otherwise, you've got a lot more of this fertilizer to plow through."

Jie's voice comes from the dock: "And not much time to do it, gentlemen. I believe I can see the glow of someone's headlights approaching quite rapidly." Taggett glances downstream and sees the white light coming toward them, getting brighter and bigger. His eyes dart around the barge, nothing but those shit piles, and then back down to the guy he shot. The corpse lies there on the deck, black blood seeping from what's left of its head. Taggett gets back on his knees and runs his hands over the dead guy's body. A spasm shoots through the detective, like he just had a big slug of castor oil, and he swallows a lump of something he hopes isn't shit. He can feel the heat the body's giving up through its rough canvas clothes. It's belching and farting a little as he pushes on it, letting out a smell just a little worse than Taggett's. Finally his hands find a flat rectangular bulge of some kind in the guy's pants pocket. He slides a hand in and finds a pack of cards wrapped in wax paper. He pulls out the wad and tries to read what's on the cards through the blur of the paper as the light from whatever's coming after them gets stronger.

There's a yell from the hut: "Nothing in here but leftover noodles," hollers Chen. "Looks like we've been suckered again." The younger man comes out of the little building smacking his left hand with his right fist. "I can't believe they're always a step ahead of us," he complains.

"Maybe not this time," says Taggett. "I've got a pretty good feeling that these aren't just playing cards." He nudges the corpse on the deck with his toe. "This guy's working way too hard to protect them." Grinning at Chen, the detective lightly taps his palm with the pack of cards. "This might just be what we didn't know we were looking for."

Jie's raised his voice a little. "Gentlemen, I really must insist that we depart with all possible haste." Taggett looks up to see that the oncoming glow has gotten close enough for him to see both headlights individually. He shoves the cards into his jacket's inner pocket, just over his forty-five, runs a step or two and jumps onto the dock. Chen thumps right after him. Taggett dives into the back of the Phantom II, and Chen leaps into the driver's seat. Jie's on the passenger side, his tommy gun already aimed back at whatever's chasing them. Taggett rolls down the window on the driver's side as Chen brings the car to roaring life and stomps on the pedal. The tires shriek against the wood of the dock and then grab the ground and shoot the Phantom II forward into the night.

The darkness cracks in front of the car to let it through. Jie and Taggett are both turned around to face behind, and the headlights back there are getting bigger. Taggett leans out, cold wind dragging at his face, sights along the line of his forty-five, shoots one of those headlights blind. From the other side of the Phantom II, Jie lets off a sharp controlled burst and takes care of the other headlight. An answer from the car behind them takes out one of the Phantom II's tail lights, then the mirror next to Chen's head. Without flinching he swerves, and the next shot goes wide. Taggett takes another shot and hears his bullet smash through some glass back there. He ducks back into the car as one of their shots flashes past. He can hear Jie murmuring something in the front seat, then the older man leans back out and rakes a line of fire across the road just in front of the car that's chasing them. Looking back, Taggett sees it dip forward as its front tires explode, the grille digging into the ground and flipping the car over on itself. That's when Chen throws the car into a sudden skid, turning it around to face the wreck that a couple of thugs are already crawling out of.

They're wearing black suits with white shirts and skinny ties, but their outfits are all stained with blood and the mud of the road. Three more guys join them, one on his hands and knees, tie dragging in the mud, blood spurting from his head. It doesn't take him long to drop to his belly and vanish in the dark. The Phantom II's headlights pin the rest of them to the night's thick black background. They stand there like they're getting pictures taken, staring into those lights, blinking, then one of them raises a pistol, aiming blindly at glare. He yells something in Chinese, his voice shaky and cracking. The night fills up with the sound of the wrecked car creaking as it settles, a back wheel whirring as it keeps spinning for no good reason. The guy yells again. There's a pop, and then a red flower blossoms in the middle of the creep's forehead. His eyes roll up to see what just happened, and then his body folds down onto the road.

From the back seat of the Phantom II, Taggett gawks at Jie. "I've never seen someone fire just one shot from a Tommy gun. How the hell do you do that?"

"Practice," Jie says, his trained gaze not leaving the scene in front of them, three thugs frozen around the corpse of a fourth, their hands drifting up like they were tied to balloons. "If I may offer a suggestion, sir," he goes on, "these oddly dressed characters could prove a valuable source of information if asked the appropriate questions in the appropriate manner. Perhaps I could arrange a conversation?"

Taggett spits out the window, tasting the shit he's been crawling through. He feels the weight of the cards in his coat pocket as he gently uncocks his forty-five. "No," he says. "I think we know enough. I'm tired and sore and I need a shower."

"As you wish, sir," says Jie, and he shoots the goons down in one long burst. They don't even have time to scream before they fall. The quiet that comes after the explosion of gunfire fills Taggett's ears. Even the wrecked car has stopped making its little noises. The corpses in the road just lie there and bleed, the smell of their blood so strong it even penetrates the shit the detective's still trying to blow out through his nose. The two younger men in the car stare for a minute at the driver.

Chen breaks the silence with a long slow whistle. "That's crazy," says Chen. "How the hell did you do that?"

Jie's voice seems to come from far away as he tells the younger man, "As I say, sir, it gets easier with practice. After a while one hardly feels it at all." In the back seat Taggett can't help nodding as the slime all over starts to dry and crack.

The tough detective has to clear his throat a couple of times before he can say, "All right, let's get out of here and see what we've got." Chen steps on the pedal and maneuvers the Phantom II around the bodies.

CHAPTER THIRTY SEVEN

So Chen drives for an hour or two as Jie talks him past the Palace Hotel to a little area downriver with small neat houses in rows along a dirt road so smooth it might as well be paved. They stash the Phantom II behind one of the houses and find some buckets of water to wash the crust of shit off Johnny. Soon enough the tough detective's dressed in some Chinese guy's robe, laid out on the floor of a house Jie says belongs to a friend from the War. He's looking up at the thatch of the ceiling as his eyes drift shut.

And that dark office fades in around him again. It still looks like a room he's been in a hundred times, but packed somehow with creepy shadows for furniture. Mrs. Foulsworth's already at the desk, motionless as some kind of weird idol. Invisible Taggett stands where he's been put and watches her not move, a darker shadow in a room full of night. After a while the door opens and a little Chinese looking guy dressed in a double-breasted shark-grey suit so shiny the light slips right off it walks in. He's holding himself very straight, like someone's idea of a general, and he manages to come off like the assistant overseer on the graveyard shift of a downtown brothel. His soft and well-polished skin glows pale in the dark room as he steps to the front of Mrs. Foulsworth's desk. He stands there between the chairs, his face angled down a little bit so that he can stare into where her eyes would be. Little dust motes of silence thicken the air. The little guy looks like he's having a staring contest with a wall.

Finally he blinks. "Mrs. Foulsworth," he begins in a voice that sounds almost like he's playing a flute, "let me express my gratitude at your finally notifying me of your presence in my city. Did you find the accommodations aboard my vessel to your liking?"

Mrs. Foulsworth silently removes that ivory holder from a fold in her dress, fits one of those wrinkled brown cigarettes into it, holds it up between the two of them. The little guy looks at it and wrinkles his nose, then reaches into his pocket for a book of matches and lights her smoke for her. The end glows and dims as she breathes a number of calm slow breaths. After a pause that goes on a few seconds too long, she says, "Mr. Wong, the so-called accommodations on your little smuggling craft barely reach the level of storage, having only the virtue of secrecy to recommend them. The comfort of my voyage, however, is utterly immaterial. You brought me here to solicit my assistance in the destruction of your rival and your assumption of the reins of the illicit economy the city of Shanghai continues to allow you to construct as if it were some kind of temple to your skill as a procurer of life-destroying substances and behaviors. I have assured you of the efficacy and availability of the assistance you desire—based on certain considerations." The idea hangs for a second in the thick dark air.

Wong blinks like someone's shining a floodlight on him. "My men were to meet you at the dock, Mrs. Foulsworth. When they returned to me without you, I disciplined them most severely, but I now must believe the story that I could not believe two days ago, that you did indeed avoid them. This was very unfortunate for the children of the men I sent to meet you, the children that I have had to orphan based on my disbelief." His fluty voice has developed a discord as his throat gets all tight. "The considerations you refer to were in the hands of those men whom you have avoided. Now they are in my hands, and I will relinquish them to you no sooner than you have explained your behavior to me."

The fire at the end of Mrs. Foulsworth's cigarette glows a little brighter as some ash drifts down out of sight to her desk. The grating mechanical sound of her chuckle fills the room. Wong steps back as if the laughter's hitting him in the face. She finally stops laughing and says, "I rarely indulge in the temptation of explaining myself to anyone, especially to an inferior." Wong gets a little red and starts to object, but she just keeps going. "Your inferiority has demonstrated itself conclusively in your inability to deal with the threat of the American who seems to continue finding weaknesses in your shipments. How many of your workers have you allowed this single man to eliminate? How can you not find him in what you so grandly refer to as your city? Perhaps my purposes will be better served by my offering to assist your rival, Mr. Zhang, against you."

"No, no," says Wong, putting up his hands, his voice getting up into the piccolo range. "The guardian of the Violet Diamond has such powers of influence that I dare not reject your offer of aid. You have my deepest gratitude, I assure you." He folds those soft hands together in prayer. "The knowledge you gain of our enemy's operations through the powers of the Diamond you hold can make the difference between success and failure, and as you know—"

"Failure is death," she says, finishing his sentence for him. "I know with a deeper intensity than your mundane and petty mind can possibly conceive the truth of that statement." She takes the holder out of her veil and stubs the cigarette out on the desk. "Nonetheless, failure seems inescapably to be your destiny. You have come to me with empty hands, have you not?" Wong's gaze drops to the floor. "The jewels that I have requested are not in your possession, are they? Indeed, your promise of recompense for my assistance was completely fraudulent, was it not?" Wong snaps his stare back up into hers, his eyes on fire. In return she lets out one of those humorless little chuckles of hers. "I suppose your perfidy makes no difference in the end. Very little of the minuscule trappings of power that you claim to possess, the glittering prizes of your life of crime in this little excuse for a metropolis that you claim as your city, can be unattainable to me. You must have realized that when you went so far as to offer me items that you have no ability to deliver. You must have realized further the consequences of such rash action." The head veiled in darkness seems to tilt a little bit forward, as if she's nodding.

Wong's eyes widen, and his shrill voice breaks into a squeak. "Please! No! I have information!" Even as the little guy tries to bargain, a shadow behind him is breaking out of the office's darkness, taking the shape of a short muscular body. "The American!" Wong's shrieking. "I can tell you of his movements! I have a man in—" The shadow has wrapped a forearm around the little guy's neck, shutting him up, bending him back over a knee. Wong's face darkens, starts to turn red. His arms flail around as if he's trying to keep his balance. The featureless mass of darkness lets out a little grunt of effort as it keeps squeezing the life out of the little gangster. Wong's making some sort of quacking noise. On her side of the desk, Mrs. Foulsworth doesn't move, but a strange lingering moan seems to be coming from her, almost a moan of pleasure. Wong's body jolts. A pop like the sound of a walnut cracking fills the dark little office. Wong's body goes limp. The shadow lets the meat fall to the floor then reaches up to its own head to pull off a hood, revealing a blasted landscape of scars where its face should be.

"Satisfactory?" rumbles the thick voice of One-Eye.

Mrs. Foulsworth pats her left hand's palm with her right hand's fingers. "I would go so far as to characterize your performance as impressive," she says. "You positively excel at sneaking up behind defenseless and unsuspecting victims to murder them in the dark. You must take such pride in yourself." One-Eye stands there over the corpse and says nothing. Mrs. Foulsworth lets out that weird laugh for a moment then goes on. "Tell me your opinion of what our former friend there was trying to convey."

"He knows nothing," says the ninja. "You had me kill him for no reason."

"I had you kill him to make a point, and I do devoutly hope that it was not lost on you despite your heritage." One-Eye hasn't moved a muscle through all this. That wreck of a face doesn't even smirk. "However," Mrs. Foulsworth says, "he has claimed to have knowledge of the whereabouts of that fool from New York, the fool you seem to have failed to kill, and the possibility that the former lord of crime lying lifeless between us was more than a small bag of wind demands further investigation. You Orientals have such devious and sophisticated minds. I would not be at all surprised to find that the late Mr. Wong has installed some sort of counterspy within the ranks of Taggett's confidantes to report on that silly so-called detective's blundering actions and perhaps guide him away from the prospect of serious jeopardy to the main operations." She screws another cigarette into her holder and lights it herself before One-Eye can move to do it for her. The black figure cocks its head. "Come to think of it, Wong seemed quite insistent that I connect Taggett with this Jie Chio, recommending him as a driver who could be counted on—"

The ninja's voice interrupts with a sound like the side of a building collapsing. "Jie Chio? In Shanghai? I would never have thought—"

"I don't pay you to think!" Mrs. Foulsworth makes an even harsher sound, her voice breaking into One-Eye's speech like a thrown knife. He shuts up and stare at her as she keeps going. "I pay you to serve my will," she tells him. "My will now is that you find this Jie Chio and find out what he knows about Taggett's plan." She's been rising out of her chair as she's been talking, and now she's got her hands on the desk, her body bent toward One-Eye, the cigarette in that ivory holder burning a hole in the room's thick darkness. "The potential of a double agent within the operation that strange silly man is trying to compose against me offers great possibilities in terms of at last turning a profit from this ghastly series of mistakes into which the shortcomings of my employees have thrust me." She folds herself back into the chair and drops the stub of her cigarette on the desk in front of her. One-Eye keeps standing there in front of her until she barks, "Go. And find someone to get rid of that." One-Eye looks down at Wong's corpse and grunts, then he bows and slips through the door as the dark office starts to dissolve.

Taggett blinks, feels himself get lighter, and just as he feels the surface of the waking world break around him, he catches what might be a glimpse of Mrs. Foulsworth turning her head to face the area where his invisible self has been standing. That goes in a flash, though, and he finds himself lying on that stranger's floor, staring up at the thatch of the ceiling, remembering everything that happened while he was sleeping. "Jie," he mutters to himself. "I guess you just can't trust anyone."

CHAPTER THIRTY EIGHT

Taggett doesn't have much to say that next morning at breakfast. He and Chen and Jie have nailed down a table in the restaurant two hotels down from the Palace. "Nice idea," Chen's telling Jie, hiding close enough to keep an eye on whoever comes after us at the Palace. They'd never think we'd be bold enough to stay so close."

"Indeed, sir, and thank you," says Jie as Taggett keeps looking at him. The tough detective's got his hat down over his eyes, and his whole face is a flat black shadow with a cigarette sticking out of it, smoldering. The little driver is buttering every inch of a piece of toast, bland-faced as always. "I must say, gentlemen, I never can get used to the ready availability of this wonderful butter," Jie tells them. "It is the one vice I must admit to. Something about it reminds me of the simpler days before the War."

Taggett grunts out a chuckle. "Seems like you learned a lot in that war old-timer. Don't think we ever quite learned which side you were on, though." Chen drops his spoon into his saucer with a clatter and stares at the detective, and Jie's eyes shift from the window he's been examining the crowd through to focus on the shadow covering Taggett's face. In the silence hovering over the table Taggett goes on, "It's pretty obvious you've done some dark business, the way you handle yourself. I guess we just need to know how dark you get." The detective stubs out his cigarette and lights a new one, the flare from the match burning for a moment's flash deep in the dark gaze he's got trained on Jie's eyes.

Without any kind of expression at all on his face, Jie gazes right back. He holds the look for a moment then finishes buttering his toast. Once the whole surface is covered with slick yellow shine, he turns his eyes back up to Taggett's and says, "Sir, I wish to express myself with the utmost clarity at my command, so I must beg your pardon for the perhaps inappropriately protracted moment I require to completely formulate a reply to the unexpected accusation implied by the line of conversation you appear suddenly to have introduced." He casts his eyes back down to his breakfast plate as Chen takes a sip of coffee, the younger man's eyes darting back and forth between the other two faces at the table. Taggett smokes and says nothing. Still looking down at his toast, Jie says, "Perhaps you have no recollection of the time before the War. I remember it as an opportunity. I became educated by the cream of Mother England to the extent that I began to consider myself one of their own, a member of the greatest empire this world has ever imagined, rather than the orphaned charity case that I must admit myself to have been. When the War came, I enthusiastically volunteered to prove myself on the field of honor for what I felt deep within my soul to be my country." He flicks a glance at Chen, who's letting his jaw slack a little as the older man tells his story. "As you can imagine," Jie goes on, "I was rejected. The Master of my academy, to whom I presented myself as a candidate for the defense of our great nation, could barely restrain himself from laughing directly into my face as he explained that I was nothing like an Englishman and should never expect to become one and was therefore irrelevant to the War effort." He's still looking at Chen as he's telling them this. "I found myself a man with no past, no cause but such cause as I could make for myself. For that reason, I determined to make my own honor my cause, and I have devoted all my actions since then to the effort of maintaining such honor for which I can demonstrate the capability." He turns his eyes back to Taggett's, finding them in the shadow the detective's hat's been casting. "How, sir, can you suppose that such a cause would allow me to betray a confederate as close as you have become?"

"Don't think I ever said I did suppose that," Taggett snickers. "I just wanted to know how far you can go."

"And, you imply, for whom I will cover that distance," says Jie. "Am I mistaken in my inference, sir? Has something occurred to inspire doubt in you as to my loyalty to the enterprise that we both have undertaken?"

Taggett stubs out his smoke and lights a new one. "You're too smart for that." No one talks for a moment, then Taggett keeps going. "You fought your own War, I figure. Hung around the lines, dodged those shells, cut down whatever got in your way. Must have been some crazy way to live." Jie goes completely still, turning into a statue Taggett keeps talking at. "I just want to know what that might do to a man's mind," says Taggett. "I know what it's like when you gotta do what you gotta do, so I just need to know what that is for you lately." He reaches into his jacket and pulls out the forty-five, puts it on the table with the business end pointing right at Jie. "How did Smith keep finding us? That guy that clocked me with the two-by-four, how was he waiting for me? Who were those creeps we had to mow down last night, how did they track us down?" He puts his hand on the forty-five, his eyes not leaving Jie's. "I'm sick of crawling through shit in the dark. If you don't tell me what's going on I'll cut you down where you sit."

The older man's fingers slip over the handle of the butter knife as Chen slowly puts down the cup of coffee that's been cooling in his hands. "I think you know as well as I, sir," says Jie. "To the extent, that is, if I may be allowed to continue, that I know nothing. I cannot help but agree that the attentions of Smith and that crew from last night displayed a disturbing level of familiarity with our movements. However, this familiarity does not, if you can pardon me for contradicting you so boldly, necessarily imply my treachery." Chen's got both hands palms down on the table. Taggett's hand is still on the forty-five. Jie glances back and forth between them for a moment and keeps talking to the tough detective. "Perhaps, sir, you may not have considered the idea of a microphone hidden in your suite at the Palace with a wire leading to another room from which an enterprising character such as Smith could have surreptitiously taken note of our plans. Mr. Wong, as you may be aware from your earlier interaction with him, has a predilection for such imaginative applications of modern technology, as does, I suspect, this

Mrs. Foulsworth who has been giving you such trouble." Jie's fingers rest on the handle of the butter knife like guard dogs faking sleep.

Taggett's watching those fingers as he growls, "But what about the car? We did our share of planning in there, and I didn't see any wires coming out. And what do you know about all this electronic stuff anyhow?"

"As you say, sir," Jie replies, "I performed many tasks in the War. Your romantic image of my exploits notwithstanding, I undertook several missions requiring a collective effort and thus was able to take advantage of the experience of specialists in numerous fields. Among these fields was that of radio technology, an interest pursued in secret by various of the contending forces, including, Mr. Taggett, your own." He looks down at the length of metal his fingers are playing with and moves them away from it to lie on the table. "A sufficiently small transmitter could even have been concealed in the boot of the Phantom II, revealing not perhaps our specific plans but rather the movements of the automobile, enabling our adversaries to locate us by locating our conveyance. Again, sir, no treachery on my part is necessary to explain the obstacles we have faced in our endeavor."

Chen clears his throat and speaks up. "I've been with him every minute since you've been laid up, Johnny. I don't see how he could be reporting on us to anyone."

Johnny doesn't move. Over Jie's right shoulder he's seeing that weird purple glow around the curved and ornate edges of the restaurant's old-timey tables and chairs. There's a waitress headed toward their table. The detective's eyes get a little wider as he recognizes her from his suite at the Palace. It's the girl who called herself the Violet Diamond, the girl he must have dreamed up in his delirium after that night in the tunnel. She's getting closer and looking right at him, her eyes like little purple gems catching the lobby's light and shooting it into him. He can't quite shift his gaze from her back to Jie, who's just sitting there like someone watching a slightly boring cliffhanger. He doesn't even seem to be breathing. That's when Taggett notices that no one in the whole lobby is moving except for the Violet Diamond girl. She's getting closer, almost to their table. When she gets there she stands over Taggett's chair and murmurs his name. "Don't lose your friends," she tells him. "No matter what you think you've seen, you know that this man is helping you. Listen to him, Johnny." Her whisper fills his head. His face is tilted up to hers, those eyes shooting deep into his. "You're so close, don't lose yourself now," she breathes, and then she starts moving again, her soft bright body gliding out of his range of vision as the people in the lobby slip back into motion, the room filling again with the buzz and clink of breakfast conversation. Taggett looks back at Jie. The older man blinks.

"Okay," says Taggett. He takes his hand off his forty-five and extends it to Jie for a shake. "I'm sorry for flying off the handle like that."

Jie takes Taggett's hand. The older man's touch is cool and a little leathery as he says, "No apology necessary, sir. I quite understand the pressure under which you find yourself operating, such pressure as must cause a rupture at some point. Allow me to applaud you, if I may, on the degree of self-control that you have exhibited by questioning me rather than simply shooting me in the alley behind this hotel."

"Uh, yeah," Taggett says. "Sure." He lets the driver's hand go, picks up the forty-five, slides it back into the holster. "Let's just forget it."

Chen laughs and picks his coffee back up, telling his partners, "I'm forgetting it already. So what was on those cards, Jie?"

Letting Taggett's hand go, Jie takes a delicate sip of his tea. "They were encoded," he says. "However, I can happily claim to have had some experience with the particular code used by Mr. Wong's organization, it having been derived from a British code with which I made myself familiar as part of my self-assigned duties during the war." He takes a nibble of his butter-slick toast and another sip of tea. "The documents recovered from our escapades of last night detail the time, date, and quantity of a month's worth of shipments. Gentlemen, we hold the key to the entirety of Mr. Wong's operation."

Taggett grins. "Good. Now let's start wrecking it."

CHAPTER THIRTY NINE

After a while they give up on watching the Palace. Separately, each man makes his way out of the restaurant as the sky starts turning the color of an old bruise. They meet up again in that neat little house on the outskirts where Jie's friend lives. The sky gets uglier as the day gets older, and then the rain starts coming down in thick sheets the wind blows around. Taggett peeks out at the weather through Jie's friend's door and smirks, "Nice night for a boat ride."

Jie looks up from cleaning his machine gun to say, "Perhaps for some, sir, but I fear that it might become quite unpleasant for a number of others." He goes back to polishing the barrel of his tommy gun with a soft cotton cloth, and then loads a new magazine into the slot with a solid click. Glancing back at his friend, he says something in Chinese. Jie's friend, a serious-looking guy a lot younger than you'd think he'd be, nods and replies and makes a gesture like a bowing headwaiter's toward a wooden box. Jie opens it. It's full of dynamite. "I trust, sir," says the small quiet driver, "that this will suffice for our purposes."

"Wow," says Chen, and whistles. "You've never really left the War, have you?"

Jie looks back at the younger man and says, "No, sir." He places his gun carefully on the floor beside where he's kneeling. Turning to his right, he picks up a pack of little throwing knives and slips it into a pocket. "The War has never left me." He slips a couple extra clips into another pocket hidden so deep in his black outfit that Taggett can hardly even see the bulge the ammo makes once it's in there. "Even in my service to Mr. Wong," Jie murmurs, "I have kept within myself the dream of atonement for what the War has led me to, what I did then and what I have failed to do since. I cannot forget, nor have I been able to put to rest, the obligations the War has placed upon what I find myself compelled to characterize as the remains of my integrity. I owe you gentleman a large debt of gratitude for providing me the opportunity to set into action the recompense that I have been for so many years merely contemplating."

"Life works in funny ways, I guess," says the tough detective. He takes out his forty-five, works the action, slides it back into the holster. "Ready to drive, Chen?"

Chen cracks his knuckles. "Ready for anything. Let's go."

Taggett and Jie's friend pick up the box full of dynamite with all the caution you'd expect from a couple of guys with a box of dynamite and baby it out to the back seat of the Phantom II. The detective shakes hands with Jie's friend and slides in beside the box as Chen and Jie get into the front. Chen turns the key and the engine roars to life like the sudden blast of thunder that goes off at the same time. A bolt of lightning flashes down into the dark landscape. Chen steps on the pedal and the Phantom II leaps away from Jie's friend, from the pretty little suburb he's managed to make a home of, and into the traffic along the river, past the big hotels and deeper into the country, into the night.

Jie takes a look at the notes in his lap and tells Chen to pull off about half an hour later. With its lights off, the black Phantom II's invisible in the black rain. Even the beam from the flashlight Taggett's switching on just gives up before it can get to anywhere anyone can see it. The detective lights up a smoke, trains the flickering yellow circle from his flashlight on the box next to him, raises the lid just enough to pull out a doughy stick of the stuff that's lurking in there for its chance to break something. He pulls a fuse out of his pocket and shoves it into the mass, then turns the light back off again. Jie's got the binoculars trained on the canal they can hear brushing against its banks as it rushes past under the pressure of the storm. The three of them wait.

Taggett's almost through his smoke when they see the little dot of red bobbing deep in the black background. They keep watching as it gets bigger, the red light on the back of a barge, the only light on it. "Bastards are trying to kill themselves in the storm," mutters Taggett, and then he can't help chuckling. "May as well help them out." As the red light keeps getting closer, the tough detective takes the butt from between his lips and holds the tip to the fuse sticking out of the sweaty stick of death in his hand. Keeping his movements smooth, he steps out of the Phantom II, and the brim of his hat presses down under the weight of the rain. Shadows make the light flicker a little as the poor suckers on the barge pass back and forth in front of it. Taggett stands in the cold rain smacking him in the face with its little needles for a moment, then he braces himself against the wind, hurls the dynamite at the little red light on the canal.

The grey thing he throws disappears in the darkness, and a second later a heat from a fireball blossoming over the barge spreads across the detective's face. A second after that comes the body-shaking thump of all the air in a small space emptying out. He lifts a hand to keep his hat on his head. By the harsh orange light of the flame he can see thugs jumping off the barge into the canal. He watches for a moment then sees the one of the shadows pointing something his way just in time to duck as someone over there starts shooting. The guns over there make puny little pops like echoes of the earlier explosion. From the passenger window Jie shoots back, and Taggett can hear more screams and splashes. He pulls out his forty-five and finds a thrashing shape in the reflection of the fire taking over the barge. He aims and pulls his trigger and the shape stops thrashing. He only has to do it two or three more times before no one can hear any more screaming.

The rain steams a little in the flames eating the barge. As Taggett reloads he watches for a moment then reaches back into the Phantom II with his free hand. Jie hands him another stick of explosive. The detective fits it with a fresh fuse, leans his face down to light it with the last of his cigarette, reaches back and throws the thing into the fire. The explosion cracks the barge in two .The black canal water starts to swallow up the pieces, and in a few more minutes there's nothing there but darkness and rain. Taggett holsters his forty-five and slips back into the Phantom II. "One down," he mutters.

"One down," Jie agrees as he pulls the spent magazine out of his tommy gun and fits in a fresh one. "I rather doubt anyone will have survived our intervention with sufficient perspicacity to warn anyone further along our route of our actions. We should, I think, have plenty of time to complete our endeavor." He sets the tommy guy back on the seat beside him and settles in to keep going over the cards in his lap.

Chen steps on the pedal, and the Phantom II pushes itself back up along the road. "All the way to Suzhou?" he asks.

"Yeah," says Taggett. "With a few more stops along the way. We should be thorough, shouldn't we?" He gives the box beside him a little pat on its lid as the big car rockets through the night. He's peering out through the window at what passes for scenery in the blackness of the night as it rushes by, and then he lights a cigarette to pass to Chen over the younger man's shoulder and one more for himself. Chen barely turns his head to take the smoke in his mouth. As the tough detective's waving out the match he tells his partners, "We're finishing Wong tonight."

Five stops later the box is almost empty and the canal's got a few more wrecks and dead bodies decaying in it than it did that morning. Once or twice Taggett lets Chen throw the dynamite. "Kid's got a pretty good arm," the detective mutters to himself.

"Yeah," Chen chuckles back. "Too bad the kid's so Chinese, or there might be a big baseball career in the cards." Taggett laughs a little but doesn't reply, popping another shot from his forty-five at one of the thugs that just leaped off the hell the dynamite has turned the barge into. A burst from Jie's tommy gun catches another goon in mid-air. The three men watch as the flying shadow twists around itself and splashes down into the thick black water to disappear from history. "Almost beautiful," Chen says.

That gets the detective to smirk. "Even prettier when we're done," he tells the younger man. "When the whole operation's a pile of ashes, then you'll see something."

"Can't wait," says Chen, walking around the Phantom II to slide back in behind the steering wheel. "Let's go."

Jie takes a look at his notes and says, "We appear to have one more shipment to intercept, gentlemen. Having had the opportunity as we have been in transit to further study the documentation our work last night made available to us, I have determined that Mr. Wong appears to be transporting his entire inventory for reasons I am as yet unable to ascertain." Chen gets the big engine growling, and Jie keeps talking as the Phantom II charges up the road. "If I have interpreted these notations correctly, the next barge to distinguish itself with the red lanterns we have observed should contain the remainder of Mr. Wong's supply of contraband. It may, perhaps, contain Mr. Wong himself."

"Not too likely," mutters Taggett, chuckling a little and reloading.

Jie glances back over his shoulder and takes a good long look at the detective. Taggett looks right back at him. Chen's humming something as the darkness whips past, as he peers through the sheets of rain that blur the Phantom II's headlights on the road into a yellow void. The two older men keep inspecting each other until Jie finally looks down and gives his Tommy gun another once-over. After a minute he takes a breath and looks back up into the shadow over Taggett's eyes. In his usual careful tone he says, "Sir, how do you—"

A jolt from under the Phantom II interrupts him. The few sticks of dynamite left in the box thump as they bounce against its bottom. Taggett finds himself pressing against the lid with his forearm at the same time his body's trying to squirm away into a corner of the car. "Jesus, Chen!" he barks. "Who're you trying to blow up, them or us?"

Chen's hunched over the wheel, doesn't turn around to respond, but his voice leaps right back. "This isn't exactly Market Street, I'm doing the best I—oh, shit." Everything lurches forward as the Phantom II shrieks to a sudden stop. Taggett's got his arm against the front of the box now, bracing it back against the back of the seat as his head bounces off the back of the front seat.

He straightens up, looks through the windshield, and mutters a curse. The ricochet of the rain is outlining the panel truck parked across the road. Five guys wearing black suits with white shirts and skinny ties are standing shoulder to shoulder in front of the truck, each of them holding a Tommy gun like Jie's, each Tommy gun pointed right at Chen.

He wrestles the gear shift into reverse, but another truck pulls across the road and stops before the Phantom II can move more than a couple of feet. Five guys get out of that truck and stand in front of it in their dark suits and skinny ties, pointing their Tommy guns at Taggett's head. "What now?" says Chen?

Carefully, Taggett reaches into his jacket for his forty-five. He slides it out of the holster and sets it on the seat next to him. "Now we go where they want to take us," he says. "That'll tell us where the real action is." As the goons advance on them, the tough detective grins at his partners. "And once we get where we want to go we kill every single last son of a bitch we see. This shit ends tonight." A thug opens the door next to Taggett and the tough detective steps out into the darkness. He winks at the armed creep standing next to him. "How do you like this weather?" he says. The creep winks back and smacks him between the eyes with the butt of the Tommy gun. A deeper darkness swells up in Taggett's head and takes him away.

CHAPTER FORTY

He's running along a dark tunnel toward a locked door. Of course the tunnel's stretching as he runs, of course that door's getting further out of reach the closer he gets to it. That's just the way it works. You'd think he'd wise up and stop running, lie down and stop worrying about the nonsense he's been walking through the way a sleepwalker walks through spider webs. He doesn't. He can't. The floor of the tunnel has turned to mud, sucking at his feet and slowing him down. Little growls force their way out of his throat as he pushes harder. The growls are turning into words. He can hear them from up ahead, from behind that door, someone screaming questions. It's not his voice. He can't quite tell the words the voice is yelling from the noise the tunnel's filling up with, a deep throb like a big engine picking up speed. His little growls are blending in with all that other noise. That door's getting closer. Light's bleeding around it into the darkness of that tunnel, and the voice coming from behind the door is making more sense, asking over and over about the diamond. He mutters something as he's running about never really following baseball and the tunnel suddenly gets longer, a jolt passing through him as he stumbles. But he can't stop running forward, getting closer to that door, that voice, those questions. He can see the knob. He's reaching forward. He's got it in his hand, clutching the cool metal the way a drowning man clutches whatever's closest. He turns the knob. The door opens. The light comes through. It almost blinds him.

He fights his eyes open, squinting against the light he was expecting, to find himself in the dark office from his dreams. He's tied to the chair he's in. The rope around his wrists has them raw and itchy. He turns his head to the right to see Chen with fresh bruises staining his face, tied up the same way Taggett is, then he turns his head to the left and there's Jie in the same shitty pickle. The three of them are in a row in front of that big black desk like students brought in to face the principal. No one's in the chair on the other side of the desk.

Chen lets out a groan as he comes to. He turns his head to see Taggett and says, "Wow, Johnny, you really know how to have fun. I've seen guys get smacked around before, but you take more of a beating than a guy should live through." He takes a moment to swallow, tongue tracing over his puffed-up lips, and stares a little at the older man. "I must be punch-drunk," he says. "Doesn't look like there's a mark on you. What the hell is going on?"

Taggett blinks in the darkness and growls a little. "Looks like you take a pretty good punch yourself. They ask you any questions, or did they just work you over?" He shifts his shoulders, pulls a little at the rope behind his back. It gives a little, but not enough.

"They started with questions," says Chen, wincing as he does a little squirming of his own. "Something about some kind of diamond. Damn, whoever tied these knots is a pro! They were asking you first and knocking you around like batting practice, but you weren't coming through, so they decided to play with me for a while. You've got some cute friends. They were shining a light in my face while they were hitting me and some guy back in the shadows was going on about a violin and a diamond, didn't make any sense, so I just took it until they put me to sleep."

A discreet clearing of the throat turns Taggett's head the other way. "Perhaps I might be able to elucidate Mr. Chen's explanation, sir," says Jie, somehow sitting in a chair with his hands tied behind his back the way a sleepy businessman might wait for a shoeshine. "The interrogation concerned the Violet Diamond. I presume, sir, that you may have some familiarity with that subject." Taggett just blinks at the little man. After a moment Jie continues, "I do hope, sir, that my presumption does not betoken an overinquisitive familiarity with matters you have until now chosen to consider private and thus have not spoken of to either Mr. Chen or my unworthy self, but I find myself regrettably forced to broach this perhaps uncomfortable topic of conversation in the light of its sudden and undeniable relevance to our current endeavor." Chen coughs and groans. Taggett keeps listening. "Your recent actions, sir," says Jie, "in conjunction with the research that professional necessities have required me to undertake, have led me to the consideration that you may perhaps have crossed paths with the legendary Violet Diamond, a stone that is reputed to have effected significant changes upon certain of its owners. Might you, sir, perhaps be one of those owners?"

"Exactly my question," comes a nasal voice from behind them. "I got an employer wants to know all about it, and you birds just ain't singing the right tune."

Taggett snarls, "Smith. Your buddy the ninja told me you were dead."

"A lot of people say a lot of things," says the weasel, stepping around the black desk to relax in the chair behind it. "You'd think a guy who calls himself a detective would figure out that people lie," he snickers. Chen's leaning forward against his ropes, dark eyes trained on Smith, and the sharp-dressed little guy keeps laughing. "I've been threatened by scarier dogs than you," he says as he pulls out a little pistol and lays it on the desk in front of him.

Now it's Taggett's turn to chuckle. "So now we're supposed to be scared? That's not the first cute little gun we've seen a jumped-up little errand boy wave around."

The two of them trade laughs for a moment, then Smith says, "Such a comedian this tough guy is. That's why I like you, Johnny-boy, that's why I'm gonna kill you last." His hands on the gun, twisting it left to right and back again, letting it point at Jie, then Chen, then Jie again. "You gotta ask yourself how much that secret's worth to you, tough guy. You've seen cute little guns like this before, so you know what the cute little bullets in here can do to a man's brain." The gun keeps twisting back and forth. "Who gets to die for you, killer? Which of your buddies gets his brains all mushed up so you can keep your tough mouth shut?"

Taggett's taking a breath to answer when Jie's calm voice interrupts. "Perhaps I can volunteer for that task. If, that is, you think you have the capability."

Smith snickers some more. "I never took you for the suicidal type, grampa. What's the matter, nothing left to live for now that you're off Wong's tit?" The snappy-dressed character grins at Jie, who just stares back without any kind of look at all on his face.

"You poor lost soul," says the older man. "It astounds me that you can speak of having something to live for. I have observed your behavior in the service of our mutual employer for a number of years, and I have ascertained that you concern yourself with nothing but your physical appetite and the exertion of power over those weaker than you. You play at sophistication but lack the ability to discern your self-deluded notions of importance from the reality of your existence as a mere pawn, an errand-boy, as Mr. Taggett points out, to those who, unlike you, possessed the strength and ability to seize their advantage." Jie's voice has been getting slowly louder all this time, until the measured tones of his speech are filling the little dark office. "You have lived for nothing," he informs the man across the desk, "and you will soon die for nothing. I find myself compelled to pity you."

And the grin has slipped off Smith's face. His eyes have been getting glassy as Jie's been explaining the slick little chiseler to himself. He stops the speech by slapping his hand on the desk and barking, "Enough!" Jie falls silent; the veteran's dark eyes steady on Smith's. "You don't know a thing about me," the little guy yelps. "I'm the guy that's been two steps ahead of you all this time, don't forget. I know all about you, war hero, so you can just climb down off that high horse. I'm the guy that's gonna end you. Don't you get that?" Slowly, the grin slides back up onto his lips but still don't quite get to his eyes. "Don't suppose it matters," he says, picking up the little gun and rising from his seat. He walks around the desk and touches the tip of the barrel to Jie's temple, standing in front of the older man. "Soon enough you're not gonna have to worry about learning anything about anything ever again," he snickers.

Without a sound Jie bends forward, and opens his arms. Some pieces of cut rope drop to the floor behind him as his left hand jabs into

Smith's kidney. The little guy drops his gun into Jie's lap as the older man straightens up. Smith has time to start to scream before the knife in Jie's other hand plunges into his throat. Jie holds Smith's body by both handles and stands up so that each can look into the other's eyes. Smith's are wide with pain, darting about the room as if he's tracking a trapped bird with them. Jie's are darker than the unlit office and as steady as a sniper's aim. "I know everything about you, you vulgar little man," he murmurs."I know what you lived for, and I know what you are dying for, and my tolerance of you has come to an end. Goodbye." He lets the body drop to the floor, where it shakes for a moment and then stops. Sliding another thin flat knife from a pocket that might be on his back or in his sleeve, Jie turns from what's left of Smith and cuts his partners loose. They stand up, Chen rubbing his wrists and Taggett looking down at the dead little clown. Then they both turn away and start looking around for the door.

Taggett finds it first, thumping on the wall to get a hollow sound. He runs his hands over the surface. "Can't find a catch," he tells the other two. "This has to be the door, but I can't see how it works."

"Perhaps its operation requires a device designed to produce some sort of electronic signal, sir," Jie says. He walks over to the pile of meat on the floor and rifles through its pockets. "Alas," he says, "The man who a moment ago was going to end me does not seem to have seen it fit to have equipped himself with such a device." He wipes his bloody fingers on Smith's hair and moves to search the desk. Opening the largest drawer, he comes up with Taggett's forty-five and a little collection of black cigarette butts lining the bottom of the drawer like a colony of dead beetles, but he doesn't find anything that looks electronic. None of the other drawers is holding anything more secret than a thick soft layer of dust. It doesn't take the little veteran too long to step back around and hand Taggett the forty-five.

Taggett takes the cool weight of the metal in his hand and winks at the older man. "Looks like you found the skeleton key," says the tough detective, and then he pulls back the hammer and blasts a ragged hole in thin wood that makes the wall. The noise and light of the shot fill the shadowy little office and leave the three men blind and deaf for a moment. As the scenery fades in, Taggett's the first to realize that behind the brimstone smell of the gunshot there's a hint of rotten fish. He glances back at Chen. The younger man's cracking his knuckles, bouncing on the balls of his feet, flexing his neck. Jie's a little further back in the gloom of the office jacking a fresh clip into the Tommy gun he found in a corner. Jie looks back at Taggett and gives a nod. Taggett grins and plants his foot just under the hole he made, kicking hard. The wall bursts open on hidden hinges. The three of them leap through the opening. They run down a short hall to another dead end that Taggett's forty-five burns right through. A gust of cold wet air pushes through the new hole, so they push back and jump through it into the dark.

And then they're outside, standing under the black sky on a wooden surface that sinks under their feet and then rises back up. Chen's in a fighting stance, ready for anything, and Jie and Taggett both have their guns out sweeping across the vista. There's a yell and a clank, and then brutally white light floods the scene, and there they are on the standing like gun range targets on the deck of Wong's biggest barge. Taggett looks behind him to see his shadow looming up the front wall of the small square hut they just got out of. Ahead of them there's another one. A panel slides open in it, and a goon in a captain's hat comes out cradling some kind of double-barreled pistol about the size of bazooka. He grins, raising the gun, and then staggers back against the wall that just closed up behind him. The artillery drops to the deck as the captain raises both hands to clutch the handle of the flat knife in his throat. Taggett throws a glance back to see Jie dissolve into a shadow cast by the building behind them. Chen's already gone. By the time the guns he can't see start going off, the tough detective's dropped to his belly, forty-five drawn, elbows pulling him over the wet deck into the nearest patch of darkness.

He finds a wall of the little structure they busted out of and sets his back to it. Looking around, he notices three or four buildings just like the one he's leaning on casting their big square shadows over the deck. "Like a crappy little town on water," he mumbles to himself and then uses a bullet from his forty-five to knock down the goon running toward him out of one of those shadows. Across the barge he can see the shape of Chen flying through the air to take out three or four more of Wong's creeps, and he can hear the mechanized growl of Jie's Tommy gun mowing them down somewhere to his left. The detective pops another bullet into another charging thug.

Underneath the sounds of the fight comes a deep rumble. The deck under Taggett starts to vibrate. The cold wet wind pushes harder against his face, so he has to squint a little. "Speeding up," he mutters. "What the hell, better find somewhere else to hide?" Forty-five in his hand, he crawls from the structure's shadow into the flat white area the floodlights are bleaching. He sees the divot spring up from the deck in front of his head just before he hears the smack of the pistol shot behind him. He rolls over on his back, raises his own gun, squeezes the trigger. Someone grunts in pain, and then the deck thuds as someone's body hits it. Taggett keeps rolling, finds another block of shadow. "Jesus, still speeding up," he tells himself. "Who's driving this trolley, anyway?"

Above them the sky's starting to get light. Taggett glances to his left and sees the landscape in silhouette rushing by way too fast. He starts to look around for something he can hang on to, but the deck is bare except for a few corpses and their guns sliding back and forth over the slippery wood. He hears Chen and Jie calling his name at the same time and yells, "Over here!"

They get to him on their hands and knees as the barge keeps speeding up, the engine starting to shake and squeal under the deck. Jie crawls close to the tough detective's ear and hollers, "Sir, we have to get to the bow!" Taggett nods and holsters his forty-five and shoots a look at Chen. The younger man nods back. The three of them start crawling forward. The deck keeps dropping out from under them and then smacking back up into their knees and elbows. The wood's starting to get hot under their palms as the splinters drive a little deeper. The men get to the front of the barge a little after the punishment has made even Taggett start to groan. The day's gotten bright enough for them to see a bend in the canal coming at them the way a subway train comes at a hobo sleeping on the tracks.

"Shit!" Taggett barks. "Get ready to jump!" They get to their feet, knees bent, hands out for balance, trying to ride the bucking deck without getting knocked into the canal's stinking depth. The rocky bank of the canal keeps coming. Taggett glances back for some reason and sees a man-shaped shadow standing on the roof of one of the square huts. The shadow reaches up, pulls off its hood, reveals the melted face of One-Eye. The ninja smirks, waggles his fingers in a bye-bye wave. A weird deep moan from Chen jerks Taggett's head back around. The barge is shuddering under him. He bends his legs, coiling his muscles like springs. The rocks the canal wall's made of look like they're lunging at him. He jumps.

CHAPTER FORTY ONE

Something's burning. Johnny's laying face-down in a field of stinking mud. He can feel thick heat pressing down on his back the way a heavy blanket hangs on a fever patient. The mud smells like rotten fish and cow shit. He lies there for a while, lets himself breathe it all in. A high-pitched tone is buzzing around in his brain, bouncing back and forth between ears that feel like they're packed with cotton. He lets out a groan he feels in his chest more than he hears. Someone's yelling his name. Somewhere in that tuning-fork drone he can make out a voice that sounds like someone he should know standing at the back of a big crowd. He groans again, pulls his face out of the mud, rolls over onto his back.

The morning sky is smeared orange with fire. Flaming fragments of the barge are still floating in the canal, making the putrid water hiss as it gives off foul-smelling steam. Other pieces of the barge are littered around where Taggett's lying. They're burning too. Something along the imaginary line from the top of his head to the horizon is spewing out thick black smoke that's fighting with the orange smear across the sky to turn the scene back to night. It's doing a pretty good job of it. The voice calling his name starts coughing as the sound between the detective's ears starts to fade, the low hum of the fire taking its place. That voice keeps yelling through the fits of coughing until he realizes it's Chen. He breathes in to answer and Chen's voice cuts off in a flurry of weak gasps, the way a dog will stop barking when you kick it hard enough. He pushes his hands down into the mud, feels the cool slime slurp around his fingers, gets himself to his knees, then up to his feet.

The only other man standing in this twisted landscape of mud and fire is One-Eye. The ninja's standing over Chen's body, just standing there like a guy waiting for the next bus. Taggett charges him and flies right past, body skidding to a stop back in the mud. The detective fights his way back up off his belly, whirling around to face One-Eye, groping in his holster for his forty-five. It's not there. One-Eye stands there and watches him, the scars that make up the ninja's face wrinkling into something that might be a smirk or a smile. Taggett pulls an empty hand out of his jacket and braces for the attack.

One-Eye keeps standing there. "Please do not be alarmed. I have done nothing to your companion," he says in that subterranean rumble of a voice. "A warrior with honor does not use an opponent's personal connections as an avenue to attack."

"Why tell me?" says Taggett. "You're just talking to a dead man, right?" The greasy black smoke billows over them. Some faraway traffic starts humming as the tourists start to wake up downtown, but between the two men a heavy silence thickens.

One-Eye breaks it. "I do not wish to be misunderstood by a fellow warrior." He backs away gracefully from Chen. The younger man's lying there in the mud, body squirming a little, light whimpers pushing their way out of his throat. "Your companion's leap from the barge was less than nimble," says the ninja. "He seems to have injured himself. If you will allow me I can render some assistance."

Taggett looks around at the wreckage. Most of the fires have gone out, but that veil of smoke still blocks the rising sun. Aside from the two men standing and the one on the ground there's no one visible. "Where's Jie?" says the detective.

"Your other companion? I do not know. I may have lost sight of him in the explosion." The maskless ninja has his hands up and his good eye focused on a fixed point deep in Taggett's gaze. "The man before me would appear to have more urgent problems," he says. "Will you allow me to help?"

Staring right back, Taggett says, "Why should I trust you? Seemed like you had a pretty good time beating me half to death the other night! Maybe you enjoy your work a little too much to keep from killing my friend."

One-Eye seems to wince, and then he gives a little bow. "Your suspicion, though deeply insulting, has merit. I cannot deny the unpleasantness of our last encounter." The ninja takes a breath and goes on. "I apologize for that. Our meeting resulted from the cause I followed at the time. I regret that cause. Please allow me to make amends by attending to this man's injuries. I give you my word as a warrior. I do not seek harm to him or to you." Neither man moves, but the way Chen's writhing in the mud is starting to look like a seizure. Taggett can see the paleness of the younger man's skin through the mask of mud and blood covering it. "Time may be running out," says One-Eye.

"Help him," says Taggett.

One-Eye takes off his black gloves and kneels in the mud over Chen. The skin on the ninja's hands looks like melting wax as he applies them to Chen's chest, some kind of mutter coming out of One-Eye's twisted mouth as he works. The younger man moans a little and calms down. One-Eye stands back up, puts his gloves back on. "Your friend's condition should improve now. Soon he will be ready to leave with you." He takes a few steps back away from Chen and stands at parade rest, hands behind his back.

The tough detective pats himself down for a pack of smokes, finds it, takes one out and lights it up. One-Eye doesn't move. "I guess I owe you one," Taggett says.

"It is I who am in your debt." Taggett blinks at that, and the ninja goes on. "My attack on you was unwarranted, dishonorable. By allowing me to help your companion you help me make up for that dishonor." One-Eye bows, then bends at the knees and comes up with Taggett's hat. "Perhaps we will meet again," rumbles the warrior as he tosses the detective his hat. "Perhaps we will have a chance to truly test ourselves against each other." Taggett doesn't reply, just keeps smoking. One-Eye goes back to his parade rest stance. The two of them stand in the mud. Chen, lying between them, mumbles in his sleep.

The canal has swallowed up the last of the wreckage that was floating in it, and the black billow of smoke has drifted apart. The morning sun's washing the scene with pale light, stretching shadows over the muddy field. The faint buzz of traffic from the hotel district is getting louder as the two men stand there staring at each other. The noise keeps growing, turns into the sound of a car getting closer. Taggett glances away from the ninja in front of him, notices a dark fountain of dark churned-up mud coming their way. "Your people?" he snarls at the ninja.

One-Eye makes a sound that might be a laugh or a low answering growl. "I have no people," he says and twists his neck to look over his shoulder. "I believe that to be the sign of your other companion coming to your aid." The ninja shifts a little and suddenly he's somehow facing both Taggett and the cloud coming toward them. Taggett's lips pull back from his teeth. The plume of mud gets closer, close enough for Taggett to see the dark thrusting shape of the Phantom II at its bottom.

"What the hell," the detective says. "How could he—"

One-Eye interrupts him. "Your life has taken a strange turn. You have entered a world that your experience cannot explain. Not all men have the strength for what you have endured. For what you will endure."

Taggett draws in a breath to say something, but the Phantom II's already in shouting distance. Jie's leaning on the horn, even as the car's close enough for Taggett to see his face. The usually half-closed eyes are open wide, as wide as the mouth he's shouting Johnny's name with. The detective glances back from the oncoming mass of car to One-Eye's face. There's no face there to glance at. The ninja's gone. Chen's lying there with his eyes closed, taking slow deep breaths while the mud dries around him. The Phantom II growls to a stop beside them.

Jie throws open the door and jumps out, breathing hard and sweating. He looks wild-eyed at Taggett for a second then bends to pick Chen up, even though Chen outweighs the smaller man by about fifty pounds. Taggett takes a few quick steps to open the car's back door and Jie slides the unconscious younger man into the back seat. By the time the door has thudded shut, the driver has recovered himself. "Based on your current physical integrity, sir," he says, "and that of our enthusiastic confederate, I must presume to speculate that our erstwhile adversary has somehow metamorphosed into, if not an ally, at least a sympathetically neutral party."

"You mean, because he didn't beat me up he must be on our side?" Taggett snickers.

Jie looks blankly back at him. "Yes, sir, I believe that to be a fair estimate of the point I had been attempting to make." The veteran slides behind the wheel of the Phantom II, and Taggett gets in next to him. As he pushes the pedal down and the car lunges forward, Jie keeps talking. "It may perhaps be germane at this moment, sir, to congratulate you on your remarkable resilience, considering the force of the explosion you have just experienced. Many other men, having encountered an event such as the violent destruction currently receding in our rear-view mirror, would be in a position even more distressing than that of our mutual friend in the back seat. If I may be so bold as to inquire, sir, to what do you attribute this astounding state of affairs?"

Taggett glances back at Chen, who's just lying there, breathing easy but shaking with the motion of the car as it jitters along the road. Then the detective takes a long careful look at Jie. The little old guy's leaning forward just a little, his hands on the wheel making tiny adjustments, keeping the Phantom II on a straight line. "I don't know," says Taggett. "Maybe I'm just tough."

"Forgive me, sir," Jie says, "but I rather doubt that mere toughness could explain your having survived such a cataclysm without having sustained serious physical injuries, much less the full retention of consciousness that you display simply by participating in this conversation."

Taggett chuckles, "I guess not. On the other hand, I don't get what might explain how you got from that same cat-whatever into this car to show up when you did. Looks like we've both got some weird shit to explain." He reaches into the glove box and pulls out a fresh pack of smokes, lights one up.

"Wanna go first?" The huts and farms of outer Shanghai whiz by as Jie begins to speak.

CHAPTER FORTY TWO

The end of the War (says Jie) left me, as it did so many of my compatriots who found their purpose by clinging to a sense of honor that the senseless turmoil of the conflict would seem to have obviated, rudderless. The world had lost its ability to distinguish right from wrong, and, though I exerted all the effort of which I was capable to make of myself a still point in that chaos, I found myself drifting, without any sense of direction whatsoever. I allowed myself to become no more than an attack dog, a weapon available to any who desired my service against a given enemy.

I kept my squalid headquarters in a dark cell deep in the slums of Shanghai, in a neighborhood only the bravest, most foolish, or most desperate would dare to enter. I neither spoke to nor saw any of my fellow denizens of that shadowy corner of Hell, nor did any of them see or speak to me. I occupied my time by sitting in the dark and contemplating the failures of my honor to which the War had led me.

In retrospect, I can only assume that I was endeavoring to become nonexistent.

My physical ties to the world, however, retained their tenacity; I especially suffered from the bondage of hunger. To ease those bonds, I was forced to take such employment as filtered down to me from the world of ordinary humans. To acquire such employment, I made my skills as a supplier of pain, and death known throughout the neighborhood I inhabited. I did this through actions, to the detriment of one or two of my fellow sty-dwellers. I had no reason to injure them other than my need to demonstrate my facility at the tasks I expected to be assigned to and paid for. My demonstration bore fruit. A day or two after I beat one of my neighbors to pulp with my bare hands and left his pulverized body sobbing and moaning at the doorstep of his lover, an envelope slid through the crack between my hovel's front door and the ground. I was quick to throw open my door to catch a glimpse of the envelope's source, but the only recompense I received for my effort was a smell of petrol fumes and the roar of a powerful engine diminishing as it sped away. I stood in my doorway a fraction longer than ordinarily, scanning the area for a clue. Nothing in the darkness showed itself to me. Rather than pursue a phantom, I shrugged and retrieved the envelope, opening it with one of my Filipino daggers.

I found inside a photograph, a slip of paper, and enough money to feed me for half a year. The photograph was of a Caucasian man wearing a suit from the last century, even though he seemed only ten or twenty years older than I, tottering, with the help of a white cane appearing oddly to be made of marble, from somewhere to the left of the photographer into the frame, most of which was taken up by a black void barely recognizable as the wall of an alley resembling the ones I had travelled to reach my little room at the bottom of the world. The accompanying slip of paper had printed on it the sentence HE MUST DIE.

I may have smirked or chuckled, having no difficulty understanding such a clearly expressed mission statement. Without a moment's thought I tore up the photograph and slip of paper, shredding them to unrecognizable fragments, and slid the money into one of my pockets. Although I have no specific memory regarding it, I strongly suspect that I left the door open as I departed. None would dare disturb the territory of a local nightmare the kind of which I had become, and in any case the room held nothing without which I could not continue my drift. I walked into the night in search of my prey.

The following days found me lingering invisibly at the intersection of some local alleys. I had recognized one of them in the photograph, and I determined that my quarry, as a Caucasian, could have had only the most illicit business in these quarters. I had long since discovered that illicit business, the kind of business requiring a man of evident wealth and style to subject himself to the foulness of these narrow smoky alleys, often accompanies an addiction of one kind or another; addiction leads to regularity of habits. I waited, therefore, for the predictable return of the man who, I had concluded, must die for no particular reason.

My wait proved surprisingly short. I heard the man before I saw him, a clicking of ivory against the rough stones of the ghetto alleys and an accompanying shuffle. I faded into one of the plethora of shadows the area provided and observed his slow progress. The photograph had given me no notion of the sense of utter weakness he projected as he felt his way forward into what must have been utter blackness to a man wearing the thick tinted spectacles that obscured the eyes of my target. Beneath the lenses his face resembled the remains left by an avalanche, his facial bones projecting sharply under the tight pale skin. He leaned forward into his limping footsteps as if the cane that supported him were a third leg; I could see him using it as an oar to drag his body along the dark length of that narrow, stifling alley. I crouched in the shadow that covered me, watching his determination take him farther than his failing body could.

I must admit that my curiosity at that moment overwhelmed my sense of duty to my anonymous benefactor. I had seen the effects of addiction to mere drugs, the way the need can turn a man into nothing more than a machine for gratifying insatiable appetites, but the creature I was looking at seemed to demonstrate a different kind of drive. Something exerted an irresistible magnetic force upon this man, a force sufficient to propel him seemingly beyond his capability of voluntary motion. My curiosity began to exhibit a similar force upon me. I followed him, invisibly and soundlessly, although I need not have bothered to exercise my skills, so intent was my prey upon his mysterious goal. We made our slow way through the smells of cheap greasy food and rats and urine to a trap door I had not previously noticed in my explorations. The man bent his knees with such effort I could almost hear them creak, grasped a ring concealed in the ground, and pulled the door open, stepping onto a platform that descended as the door flattened back into the ground with an unnatural slowness. I waited for ten slow breaths and opened the door.

I took the most delicate step of which I was capable onto what revealed itself to my scrutiny as a wooden platform just large enough to support a small human body, as small as mine or as that of the man I followed, and it began to lower itself under my weight. Although I had been on a lift before, the action of the platform on which I stood did not resemble that experience; whereas a lift progresses vertically with the accompaniment of a deafening mechanical racket, my descent that night was soundless. The air through which I slowly dropped got warmer and thicker, and the darkness of the squalid night outside gave way to an increasingly bright purple glow. I crouched, resting on the balls of my feet, ready for anything, as the platform finally met its destination, settling into the ground with a soft thump.

I faced a hallway, at the end of which was a door, the purple light outlining a searing rectangle around its edges. I crept off the platform and whirled around as it rose back to ground level, leaving behind it a smooth wall of marble, the same marble; I thought wildly, that composed my target's cane. I was far beyond my experience, but I knew that the only way out of this inexplicable chamber was through it. I began to move down the hall toward the door at its end, my trepidation slowing me to the pace of a feeble old man.

After what seemed an eternity I reached the door. The glow that illuminated that strange hallway had by this time become accompanied by a low hum of a kind I had never heard before, a sound that seemed to pulse, as if I had somehow found myself within a huge violet heart throbbing around me and between my ears. I felt the door with my fingertips, discovering it also to be composed of some kind of cool stone that seemed to throb beneath my touch, the same stone that comprised the wall at the passage's other end. I closed my eyes and took deep breaths, but even the darkness behind my eyelids continued to vibrate with that purple light, continuing to distract me. Feeling a little dizzy, I explored the surface of the door for the knob or lever that would permit my escape from the steadily increasing intensity of the light and sound that were beginning to leech away my hold on consciousness. I could feel my mind fading under the pressure of that pulsing light as I tried to center all my perceptions in my fingertips, desperately pressing the unyielding marble to find that one hidden point that would move under my touch. My breaths began to adopt the rhythm of that pulse the way a sleeping lover will breathe to the beat of the partner beside him, and I felt the same kind of blissful heaviness begin to drag me into unconsciousness when something under my fingers clicked and the door swung open.

I fell forward into a dim and quiet room with a small electric lamp wasting its muted yellow glow into a bare corner. My target sat in a stiff wooden chair against the wall the lamp was almost illuminating and regarded me through eyes whose color I could not ascertain. He clutched his marble walking stick as he addressed me in a voice that creaked and popped under the pressure of his own breath. "So," he said, "you've come to kill me. At last. At last she's letting me go."

I found my feet and stood over the old man. "Yes, I've come to kill you," I told him, "but I find myself for the first time in many years wondering why. Who are you? What is this place? Why must you die?"

The chuckle that answered me soon became a cough that bent the old man forward and turned his corpse-white face bright pink for a moment. "I used to think we all had to die," he said. "Now I'm not so sure. I don't suppose it matters. She needs a new guardian. I'm too old, too feeble." He coughed again, a little more weakly this time. "The trouble is that I don't even know if I can die. Not anymore."

I stood over him, blinking, unable to speak. I could have reached out at that very moment and curled my fingers around his scrawny neck, gazing deep into those eyes of no particular color until they became the glass marbles of a taxidermist's model. I could have opened his veins with the flat Filipino dagger I carried and let his blood pool invisibly on the dark floor between us. Instead, I stood there as the old man coughed some more and waited for him to regain his breath and make some sense of the fever dream I had apparently fallen into.

"She wants someone ready to kill for her," he told me. "Ready to die for her." He raised those colorless eyes to mine, and I saw in his gaze a lifetime of suffering. "I wasn't strong enough. Never was." He was pushing his words through thick and effortful breath, as if he were writing his last words in his own blood. "She told me. Someone stronger coming to rescue. To avenge." Suddenly, he reached out and encircled one of my wrists with a hand that felt like wet leather, his touch making me shudder with revulsion and attempt to free myself from his grip, which proved inescapable, stronger than any I had felt. "Not you," he breathed. "Your soul is too broken. But you will know. You will know when you see." As I kept blinking, I noticed that the purple glow from the hall had begun to invade the little dark room where the old man held me. "You will know," he said again as the light grew brighter, burning away the details of the scene the way ordinary light fades the ink from a love letter and turns it back to mere paper. His fingers on my wrist began to burn, his unfathomably deep eyes occupying my entire field of vision. As the throb from the hallway began again to fill my ears, my brain, I heard him say, "Violet Diamond," and then I may have closed my own eyes, or perhaps I had opened them to the full extent of their capability. I think I was roaring along with that irresistible pulse, but I could hear nothing more than the beat of that light.

    I began to notice a chill in the air, and then I noticed that I was no longer inside. I had apparently fallen to my knees, beneath which I felt rough dirt that bit into my skin. The night air smelled of a coming storm, the cold wind bearing an electric charge I could feel in the roots of my hair as I groveled on the ground. I raised myself up to a kneeling position and examined my wrist; the old man had indeed left his mark on me, four thin scars I bear to this day and sometimes feel itching and burning when circumstances become especially perilous. With a roar of thunder the black sky began to inundate the landscape, the dirt under my knees turning quickly to mud and threatening to dislodge my shaky equilibrium, to send me back onto all fours into the animal nature to which I had, just before the mysterious experience I am describing, been at the verge of succumbing. I fought that seductive pull, having gained at least a set of questions to which I could seek answers. Though I had failed in my assignment to kill the old man, I had acquired from my encounter with him a reason to attempt recovery of my broken honor.

That transition between the old man's underground apartment and the muddy ground before what proved to be the mansion of Mr. Wong, my impossible journey from one point to the other without passing through any point between, was an occurrence I had thought never to experience again. However, last night, just as Mr. Wong's barge was beginning to collide with the rocks, I found myself surrounded by that blinding violet light, that throb at the very base of my auditory perception. When I could see and hear again I realized that I was already at the wheel of the Phantom II and headed toward you; I realized further at that moment what had caused me to find my purpose all those years ago helped me last night to achieve that purpose. I recognized myself as the guardian to the guardian. Whatever the Violet Diamond is, it clearly has plans for you, sir, and I have told you this story of my regrettable past as an attempt to aid you in understanding the depth of my dedication, such as it may be worth to you. Chen is recuperating already. Mr. Taggett, the next move is yours.

CHAPTER FORTY THREE

But Taggett's not listening. The vibrations of the Phantom II as it jumps along the trail are working on his body, massaging the tension of that face-off with One-Eye into soft sleepy mush. As Jie's been talking the detective's eyes have been drifting shut. The older man's voice and the steady growl of the Phantom II are fading into a kind of background hum as Taggett's mind or his soul or whatever does this kind of traveling drifts off to wherever it's going.

It's a different office this time, bigger and brighter than the dark little closet on Wong's barge. He can't tell where the light's coming from, though. The whole place is draped in big colorful swatches of what looks like silk, throwing everything into a weird kind of blur. Pillowy couches line the walls, and the floor's carpeted in something deep and plush. The only hard surface in the room occupies the middle of the floor, a desk painted blindingly white with a glass top and an enormous easy chair behind it. In front of the desk, on what looks like a metal folding chair, sits Mrs. Foulsworth.

Her featureless black figure still looks like a hole in space, even more so against the soft riot of colors around her. She's sitting as perfectly still as ever, but there's a noise that seems to be coming from somewhere deep in the empty space she represents, a kind of a growling hum like a big machine getting ready to lunge out of its place and start smashing whatever gets in its way. If she's making that sound, then she's the only thing in the room that makes any kind of noise at all.

After a while a hidden door opens behind the easy chair, and something that looks like a circus balloon drifts in through it. The balloon coughs delicately and reveals itself as an enormously fat Chinese guy, his facial features squeezed so tightly together by the fat surrounding his skull that he looks like a badly drawn cartoon. A little fringe of thin black hair surrounds the fez he's got stuck to his head somehow. The rest of what must be a monstrous body is draped in shiny velvet, loud colors that go off like a bomb in the plush and perfumed room. The mass of him floats over toward the easy chair and settles into it, producing a groan of stretched springs. His arms rise, the sleeves of his garment pulling back to expose a pair of hands that look like giant meatballs with Vienna sausages stuck in them. He steeples these puffy fingers in front of his face and looks across the desk at Mrs. Foulsworth. The tiny lipless mouth opens up and a voice like a weak breeze blowing through an empty field filters out. "Quite an honor," the fat guy says, "to receive a personal visit." The mouth closes, and the silence of the room crowds back in, only her weird hum disturbing the quiet. Suddenly, it stops.

"I find myself compelled," she announces, "to admit that certain recent setbacks have forced a change in my usual policy of limiting my personal appearances to locations under my control, a policy which has demonstrated its wisdom on many occasions. However, considering the vast service which I have performed for you, one, I might add, for which I have asked no recompense, I have made the assumption that I have nothing to fear from an encounter with you in your—" the top of that ebony column twists around as if she's using a periscope to survey the room—"fascinating place of business. After all, Mr. Zhang, you are a bit of a clown, are you not?"

Zhang's tiny black eyes blink slowly, and his little slit of a mouth opens to let out a wheeze of a laugh. "An uncharacteristically direct statement," he whispers. "Indication of strong feeling. Of need." He claps those meaty hands together. They hardly make a sound, but the sliding door opens again and a dwarf dressed just like Zhang scampers through, carrying a bottle and two glasses. The little mascot puts them on the table and scurries back through the door, which closes noiselessly behind him. "Perhaps a drink," Zhang says.

Mrs. Foulsworth seems to be vibrating in her chair. "I can barely imagine the circumstances under which I could be less enticed by one of the vile concoctions your enterprise has to offer. I have tasted the so-called drinks of your so-called civilization, and I can assert with absolute confidence that only the short-sighted political desire of the United States to maintain the illegality of more potable spirits could explain the success you have achieved as an importer, considering that hillbillies can make better liquor in the rude wooden vessels that they also employ as tubs into which they scrape the crust of scum that covers their repulsive bodies." Her hands rise from her lap to lay their long black-clad fingers over the edge of the desk, as if she's claiming that white surface by staining it. "As my interest in your quaint little corner of the world has come to its conclusion, I require nothing more from you than transportation away from this land of squalor and weakness in which you pathetically consider yourself a figure of power."

While she's been talking Zhang's been pouring a thick red liquid into his glass. He takes a sip, and a sharp pink tongue slithers between his lips to take care of the stain. That wheeze of a laugh leaks out of him again. "An odd way to phrase a request," he finally says. "Perhaps you cannot help yourself. It does not matter." He takes another sip and another lick of his thin lips. "You speak of a service you have done me. I think you mean the service of removing my competition." Another wheeze. "I think you did not mean to do me that service. You meant to destroy me along with Wong." A third sip finishes the little glass. He puts it down on the desk and flanks it with those little round hands, pressing them down on the flat reflective surface. "What could I owe you?" The whisper's gotten a little stronger, turning into a harsh snaky hiss. "Why should I help you? You are no more than the wind. You blow harm to some and help to others. What help could the wind need from simple Zhang?"

She's almost growling again, her body leaning forward a little in its seat, putting a shadow over the clean white desktop. "Because the situation in which I have allowed myself to become extricated, my pursuit of an artifact with power even greater than that of the Violet Diamond, has impelled my association with the unsavory likes of you and Wong, the controllers of your city's underground market, I can no longer simply arrange a passage for myself away from this cesspool without the unbearable inconvenience of finding myself subjected to a barrage of questions which I have no earthly intention of answering." She straightens a little to reach into her dress's hidden pocket and pull out that strangely gnarled ivory cigarette holder. Zhang's crowded-together facial features contract even further into a dark scowl, and she puts the holder back where it came from. Her voice has gotten back some of its amused distance as she goes on. "The sudden unavailability of Wong's services in this regard has left you as my only recourse. That uncomfortable fact alone accounts for the respectful manner in which I have thus far addressed you, as well as the impertinence I have allowed without comment in your replies. Furthermore, I have, as you must admit, allowed your accession to supremacy in the squalid little market you inhabit. For that reason, I strongly suspect that your deliciously antiquated concept of honor will compel you resistlessly to return the favor I have so graciously granted you." A grating chuckle pushes her veil out a little. "And after all," she tells the fat man, "I am merely a weak old woman, a poor waif thrown upon the mercy of your gracious eminence, a victim of circumstance in need of aid only you can provide. Alternately, perhaps your refusal to come to my rescue in my hour of despair will provoke me simply to destroy you the way I destroyed the other joker who clung with such tenacity to the ludicrous fancy that he somehow mattered in the world I shall soon control. You will learn from your competitor's mistake. You will secure for me a berth on one of your cargo ships, and you will do it with discretion. You will assist me because you have no choice." Those black fingers flex and tighten on the desk's edge, even as her voice is just as calm as ever. "You seem to be laboring under the serious misapprehension that I have come here to make a request of you, as if somehow you could be said to occupy a social level commensurate with mine, as if I do not have a perfect right to what is yours by virtue of my innate superiority. I do not make requests. I explain my requirements and expectations, as I have just done for you at the length required by your underevolved Oriental mind, and those expectations and requirements are then fulfilled, in just the way that you shall now provide the transportation both expected and required."

Zhang lets out that wheeze again, and it just keeps going. His face is getting all dark, his huge body starting to shake and twitch. Still smothering himself with laughter, he reaches for the glass and bottle, pours himself another shot of that thick red stuff. After a moment he gets control of himself and takes a sip. "I have given you my answer," he breathes. "I dislike repeating myself. Perhaps the ailment you veil yourself to hide has affected your hearing." He raises the glass to his lips for a second sip.

A screech comes out of Mrs. Foulsworth the way a train on fire comes rocketing out of an underground tunnel, a sound like a vengeful ghost making nightmares, and she springs up over the desk, her fingers reaching for Zhang's head. Her thumbs sink into his eyes as he tries to scream. Little gasping barks puff his lips out. Her black thumbs push deeper into his eye sockets. Her body's on his, a thin black stain eating away at the carnival tent. He's waving his stubby arms around, battering her weakly, as animal sounds come out of her. She's driving a sharp knee deep into the soft body covered in velvet. The fez drops from his head, soundlessly landing on the plush below. Drops of blood leak out of his sockets around her fingers and make stains on the fez and the lush rug. His body's shuddering like a bug on a hotplate. Then it stops. A long slow hiss of air leaks out of his face. She pulls her thumbs, slick and shiny with gore, out of his head and clambers gracelessly off the mound of Zhang's corpse.

The skeletal black figure of Mrs. Foulsworth stands next to the pile of meat, making sounds of labored breathing. Then she bends over, coughing and gasping, the noise of grinding gears coming out of her. This goes on for almost too long until she straightens up, pulls out her cigarette holder and one of those weird stumpy smokes of hers, and lights up. "Apparently I'm once again cast upon my own resources. I require one more service."

"I will provide this service," says One-Eye, stepping out of a fold in the fabric covering the walls. "I will see that you leave this place safely, and then I will consider my obligation to you complete." Mrs.

Foulsworth waves her cigarette impatiently, and the ninja slips through the hidden door, barely opening it.

Taggett's eyes snap open in the front seat of the Phantom II just as Jie's saying, "Mr. Taggett, the next move is yours." The detective turns to his left to grin at the driver then cranes his neck to look back at Chen, who's already shaking his head and blinking and grunting like the bear who fell asleep in the forest and woke up in the zoo.

"The next move is out of here," Taggett says. "It's about time to end this thing."

CHAPTER FORTY FOUR

By the time they get to the neat little house Jie's friend lives in, Chen's balanced in the middle of the Phantom II's back seat and chattering away about some kind of weird dream he had about flying through the sky back to San Francisco and looking right into Walt McBride's smiling face, the crooked little guy laying hands on Chen's heart, reaching right through his chest to tell him everything would be all right. "And then I wake up and here I am in the car. That explosion, that dream—I should be dead, shouldn't I? But I'm not, I'm still here in Shanghai with you guys, going places, getting to the bottom of stuff," and on and on like that while Jie parks the Phantom II.

Taggett looks back at the younger man and smiles. "Don't worry, kid, you're all right," he grumbles as they slide out of the car and head toward the front door of the little house. The door's hanging open in the way a door hangs when no one's bothered to close it, so the detective slows his pace, glancing at Chen as Jie's coming back around the side of the house. The tough detective slips a hand into his jacket, brushing his fingers over his forty-five, and pushes the door with his other hand.

The rooms wrecked. Splintered fragments of furniture litter the floor, pointing up sharply in various directions like brown volcanic islands from the sea of torn-up books and papers that someone scattered around. Someone has decorated the walls with big holes, the kind you need a sledge hammer to make. And in the middle of all this mess is Jie's friend, lying on his back with his arms and legs at crazy broken angles and a face that looks like a pound or so of hamburger and a small square envelope on his unmoving chest. As far as Taggett can see, nothing in that room is alive.

But there are other rooms. The detective pulls out his forty-five and says to Chen, "Go stall Jie. Don't let him see this." As the younger man heads back around the house, Taggett eases into the smashed-up room, stepping as lightly as he can toward the bedroom in the back. He pushes the bedroom door open hard, slamming it against the wall behind it, and sights along the barrel of his forty-five into all the room's corners. There's nothing in there but more wreckage, a bed smashed to pieces, all the drawers pulled out of the dresser and splintered, shards of the mirror showing his ashen face blinking back at him, so he turns around to get another look at the front room.

Jie's friend isn't any less dead. The detective picks his way through the trash on the floor to the corpse in the center of it and crouches to get a better look at that envelope. "No wires," he tells himself. "Doesn't look like a boobytrap. Poisoned?" He looks around and picks a sharp splinter out of the mess. Planting an elbow in the dead man's chest to hold the envelope in place, he uses the splinter to rip open the flap and lever out a piece of stiff cardboard with some Chinese lettering printed on it in crimson ink.

The front door that Taggett had eased shut slams back open and Jie stands there framed in a rectangle of light. The detective stands up in a hurry, ready to keep the older man from charging, but Jie just keeps standing there, taking slow controlled breaths. Chen shows up behind him, sweating and panting, and says to Taggett over Jie's shoulder, "Sorry, Johnny. This old guy's hard to stop."

"If you will permit my disagreement, gentlemen," says Jie, his eyes not leaving the ruins of his friend, "I rather suspect a lack of necessity for such an apology." The old driver's voice carries the hush of a crowded city square just before the riot starts. "I find myself with an inclination to place the blame squarely upon the shoulders of that wretched Mrs. Foulsworth. My strong suspicion is that the man I met those years ago, that first time I experienced the inexplicable powers of the Violet Diamond, must have been the very same Edgar Foulsworth to whom you have alluded, and I further suspect that his wife, or perhaps widow, has come back to Shanghai to pursue one of his discoveries." He turns his eyes to Taggett's. "You and I and"—he takes a breath and keeps going—"my honored friend have found roles as pawns in her mad game. I blame her for this misfortune." The old man's jaw is jutting out like a gun bunker.

Taggett's found a piece of paper to fold around the edges of the card, so he stands up with it in his hand. "Whoever's to blame left a message," he says and steps across the room to give it to Jie. "Can you make anything out of this?"

The old veteran takes a look at the card and tells him, "Yes. It says, 'I am One-Eye. Shanghai is now mine. All outsiders must die. All those who help the outsiders must die.'" He looks back up at Taggett, his eyes shiny. "My expectation, sir, is that One-Eye will formalize his assumption of power in a ceremony at the Dreaming Blossom. For as long as I have maintained my involvement with the underworld of this city, that has been the established custom in times of necessary succession to supremacy of one faction or another. If we move quickly, I confidently assume that we can—"

"I need you here," Taggett interrupts. The older man stands there in the doorway and blinks at him, mouth still hanging open a little. Taggett reaches out and puts a hand on his shoulder. "Listen, you know as well as I do that you'd be going along just to get back at One-Eye, if that's even who wrote this." His eyes on Jie's, the detective takes a breath. "Don't you think you've done enough to your soul already? Let the kid and me handle this, we're too far in to quit now anyway. You stay here. Clean up. Honor your friend."

Jie's hand rises to cover Taggett's for a moment, warm but hard against the detective's rough skin, then drops again. He turns his gaze to the debris left in place of his friend and then back to Taggett's eyes. "Of course you reason correctly, sir," he says. "As you say, my place must be here among the consequences of my having involved my friend in a mission whose undertaking should, if I had been sufficiently honorable, demand the hazard of no life but my own. By the same token, as you seem to have already ascertained, your mission demands that you investigate the identity of the perpetrator of this atrocity." He looks back down at the card. "On reflection, I agree with your doubt that One-Eye himself committed this crime, and I would go so far as to say that his character as I understand it would prevent his having it done by proxy. Indeed, the very idea of a ninja so publicly taking control of any organization strays to such an extent from the ideals maintained by them, a fact which casts further doubt onto this message's ostensible provenance. I must return my suspicion to the Mrs. Foulsworth who seems to have lurked behind the various machinations to which we have been subjected all along."

"Doesn't matter who left the note," says Chen. "Just give me someone to punch some answers out of." He smacks his palm with his fist and bounces a little on the balls of his feet. "I don't even really care about the answers. I'm ready to finish this underworld bullshit once and for all."

"Then get the car," the detective says. "Looks like we've got a social call to make?" The two men step away from the door, moving fast toward the Phantom II. Jie watches them for a moment then turns around and closes the door as he goes back inside. Chen slides into the driver's seat and brings the big black car to roaring life.

Raw speed's pushing Taggett back against the passenger side as the Phantom II's tires eat up the road, leaving little bit of themselves as Chen whips the car around corners, onto the main road, up the river to the red light district. The detective glances at the younger man driving. Chen's lips are peeled back from his teeth, his knuckles white on the wheel. Taggett nods and turns his eyes back to the windshield. The secretly connected buildings that contain Shanghai's vice market get bigger fast as the men get closer. Taggett chuckles, "I gotta tell you kid; the whole thing looks a lot more impressive at night. Seems a little pathetic in the daylight, don't you think?"

"Whatever," says Chen? His leg flexes as he pushes the accelerator to the floor. "This has got to end. I'm not gonna spend the rest of my life waiting for some creep to try to get payback. One way or another, this is over before sundown." The entrance to the Dreaming Blossom's looming closer, starting to fill the whole windshield. Chen's not stopping. "Brace yourself," he tells Taggett. Taggett takes out his forty-five, holds it in his left hand while he grabs the door handle with his right. The Phantom II screeches as Chen yanks it to the left, then it shudders as it plows along the row of poles holding up the awning and smashes the front door of the Dreaming Blossom into a useless mess of wood and glass.

A big crowd of bruisers stands there gaping in the harsh light streaming through the new hole in the club's front wall. They don't stand there for long. Taggett knocks three of them down in three quick shots through the Phantom II's windshield while Chen explodes through the driver's side window and launches himself into the mob, knocking down thugs like a wrecking ball demolishing a neighborhood. Taggett takes aim and kills three more men, then slams his door into a goon coming at him and rolls out of the car, slashing the guy's ankle with the butt of his gun. The guy goes down and Taggett kicks him in the face until he stops trying to get up. A shout from the other side of the car has him vaulting over the hood just in time to catch Chen. They grin at each other for a second before the grunting wall of muscle that tried to break Chen's spine on the car can get to them, and then Taggett shoots the snarling punk in the head. A couple of the gangsters trip over the guy's body and Chen jumps up and lands on the backs of their necks. The young man makes a sound like a panther escaped from the zoo and flips backward to catch another couple of creeps in the face. Taggett has just enough time to notice that about half of them are wearing the suit-and-skinny tie outfit of Wong's gang, while the other half of the crowd is wearing the same kind of carnival suit Zhang had on, and then he's taking a fist in the face from one of Zhang's old crew. He pops the guy right back and the guy goes down, and then the detective fires an inch past Chen's face to kill the creep sneaking up from behind. The guy at his feet trying to get back up, so Taggett kicks him in the throat and then ducks as Chen throws that muscle-man through the Phantom II's side window, where the thick broken body just jams there, pierced all over by thick shards of the windows broken glass, and bleeds down the driver's-side door. Chen makes another one of those crazy animal noises and suddenly he's holding a pair of shiny switchblade knives. They blur into a few bodies until they're a lot less shiny, dripping gore as he skips over the bodies that fall dead in front of him. For a second the boiling crowd stops to stare at this insane murderous dance. Taggett doesn't get distracted, and that gives him time to reload. He slides himself under the Phantom II and pops up from the other side, shooting down the tough guys that Chen hasn't finished off. After another minute or two the echoes of Chen's yells and Taggett's shots dies down, then there's no sound in the wrecked club but something dripping onto the concrete floor, blood or motor oil, and the heavy breathing of the two men left alive.

"Wow," says Chen. He's lost his shirt somewhere in all this, and his thin chest is bright with a gloss of sweat, ribs flexing as he gets a little closer to catching his breath. He drops the knives and looks at his hands, caked with deep red stuff that keeps dripping off, than he looks back at Taggett. "This really is the end, isn't it?"

Taggett holsters his forty-five, digs into his jacket for a pack of smokes. He just shrugs when the search comes up empty. "It'll have to be," he tells the younger man. "I think we're out of suckers to kill. You feel right about Walt?"

Chen blinks, wiping his hands on his pants, just getting his pants filthier. A moment goes by before he can say, "Yeah. I do. I think. He's still dead, I know, but . . . but I think we did something for him. Something he needed."

"We fixed his memory, kid," says Taggett. "Anyone who thinks he's crooked is dead by now, or they know better." He walks around the Phantom II and grabs the muscle man by the ankles, hauling the corpse's bulk out of the window. The skull makes a meaty thud when it hits the floor. "Now let's finish the job." He opens up the back door and reaches into the box that's fallen between the front and rear benches. His hand comes out with a wad of grey putty that's got a fuse still stuck into it. Grinning at Chen, he says, "Got a light?"

Chen grin's right back. "Not on me, but I bet someone around here has got a spare." He bends over and digs around in the pockets of the bodies closest to him, straightens up with a pack of Chinese cigarettes and a book of matches in his bloody hands. "Lucky for us," he says.

"Too bad for them," says Taggett. The detective waits a second as Chen lights up a couple of the smokes, then Taggett takes one and steps around the bodies and the puddles of blood to the bathroom. He feels around that wall for a second until he finds the catch and pushes open the heavy secret door. Cigarette hanging from his lip, he holds the fuse to it until he can hear that hiss, then throws the dynamite into the secret tunnel and runs back to the car. Chen's already in there with the engine running as Taggett dives into the back seat and yells, "Go!"

Chen throws the Phantom II into reverse. For a second that goes on way too long the tires squeal on the slippery floor, but then they catch and the car flies backward out of the Dreaming Blossom. Chen keeps it in reverse until they get to the main road, then the car skids back to its left to make the right turn just as the sound of sudden thunder echoes through the clear morning sky. Taggett twists around for a moment to watch the cloud of smoke shoot up. He keeps watching as it gets smaller, then turns around to watch the road coming on. "Definitely time to go," he mutters.

CHAPTER FORTY FIVE

Jie's finished burying his friend by the time they get back. Chen pulls the Phantom II around as the older man, skin as brown with dirt as Chen's is red with blood, uses the flat of the shovel he's holding to pat the covered grave smooth. Taggett and Chen get out of the car, not saying a word, and the three of them go back into the house. A red trail stretches over the mess between the door and the blank spot at the center of the room where the corpse was. Without a word, the three of them move to the corners and start collecting papers, making a pile in the fourth corner next to the bedroom door. The afternoon light fades orange into evening as they clean, until they're in a bare room with a pile of debris in one corner. Chen's still working with his shirt off, and Taggett's had to get rid of his jacket. Jie hasn't taken off anything. They've been working in blank mechanical silence, toy robots slowly winding down. By the time the sun's gone from the sky they've shuddered to an exhausted stop.

"We should quit," says Taggett. "We can sleep here tonight; those goons probably won't come back." He allows himself a little chuckle. "Assuming we left any of them breathing."

Leaning against one of the side walls, Chen says, "Yeah sounds right to me. I'm so tired I can't even think of driving somewhere." The wiry young man lets himself slide down the wall until he's sitting on the floor, forehead touching his knees. Taggett takes a look at Jie.

Jie's looking back at him with a face that betrays nothing. "Sir," he says, "I am, as ever, at your service and prepared to do my utmost to protect both you and our mission. For that reason, I shall take the night's first watch, in consideration of the remote possibility that a surviving remnant of the forces arrayed against us has the perspicacity to have anticipated your strategy." He crosses the room and stands framed in the front door as the sky turns black behind him. "With the greatest respect for your strength and endurance, sir, I hope that you will allow me to suggest in the strongest possible terms that you afford yourself a period of rest. I rather suspect that more than our little lives depend on your continued ability to pursue your objective."

The tough detective's lips twitch around a hidden smile. "My objective right now is to get the hell out of here. I can't think too far beyond that."

Jie returns the hint of a smile and says, "As you say, sir. My humble efforts can, I believe, assist you in that endeavor. However, the process of acquiring the necessary transportation will require the passage of time, as I cannot possibly begin such a series of negotiations until a more, shall we say, respectable hour. I sincerely regret any inconvenience this might cause you, sir."

"Don't worry about it," Taggett grumbles. "I feel like Chen looks." He points with his head over to where the younger man has fallen over in a pile of twitching arms and legs braced against the wall. "He's a tough kid, but there's only so much anyone can take all at once."

A suggestion of a chuckle pushes out from between Jie's thin lips. "If you will permit an observation, sir," he says, "I would point out that each of us has had to pass through such a level of vulnerability, and, further, that each of us has had to trade that vulnerability for the toughness that accompanies one's experience of such events as those of the last few days." As Taggett finds his own wall to lean against, the older man goes on. "I have from time to time speculated as to the value of this trade. It has, to be sure, allowed my continued survival, but I have, nonetheless, had occasion to wonder whether a shorter, less protected life might not ultimately have been one more happily lived."

On the floor, sitting next to his hat, Taggett lights up a smoke and snorts out a horse laugh. "Happy. Sure. I remember I used to care about that. Now I figure it's for kids and civilians too dumb to know better." He stubs the cigarette out after a couple of drags. Looking up, he tells the older man, "The happy ones are the ones that die quickest."

"As you say, sir," murmurs Jie. "And here we are, still alive." The two of them stare at each other for a moment, then Jie slips out into the night, easing the door shut behind him. Taggett finds his jacket, bunches it up into a pillow, lets his head drop and his eyes flicker shut.

They snap open again in the dark to the clang of someone's phone. "What the hell," he can't help muttering. "What am I doing in a bed? Wait a minute." A rush of sensation—the smell of the room he's in, the feeling of the air against his face, the closed-in feeling of the absolute darkness he's occupying —is pushing him to tell himself, "This is my bed, my bed back in New York before I—hold on, did I really quit? Was that all a dream?" The phone's still ringing. Taggett gropes over the familiar splintery surface of the night table for his pack of smokes and a book of matches, finds them just where they always are, lights up, takes a moment to stare at the dark column of the phone in the darker little rented room. It keeps ringing.

The guy in the next room bangs on the wall between them, his muffled voice barking, "Answer your damn phone, flatfoot!" Taggett bangs right back and the walls where it's always been, its plaster leaving a little scratch on his fist. He reaches up for the chain that lights up the bulb hanging in the middle of the ceiling and looks around at the room he remembers, his suit draped over the chair facing the Murphy bed he's lying there in, the lockbox where he keeps his getaway stash right against the wall where it belongs. The phone still hasn't stopped ringing.

Growling, he wraps his fist around the phone and picks it up, yanks the earpiece of the hook. Nothing comes out of the phone but the sound of the ocean for a moment, then the noise turns into someone's labored breath, then the breath turns into words. "Johnny Taggett? Is that the private investigator Johnny Taggett?" The voice, a man's voice so soft it's almost a whisper, sounds like its being forced through a pipe so thin it's almost a wire. "I have to talk to Johnny Taggett. Have to warn him. Is that you?"

"Yeah," says Taggett, "but I'm no private investigator. At least I don't think I am. Not yet, anyway. Unless I dreamed it all. What time is it? I need to quit the department and take the train to San Francisco and meet that weird Foulsworth lady and go to Shanghai and kill the Russian and everyone else and—"

The creaky voice stops him right there. "You're babbling, Mr. Taggett, probably disoriented. That damned Violet Diamond. Enough of these visions and you lose track of what's real." Taggett looks at the hand that's gripping the phone. Its knuckles have gone white, and it's shaking a little as the rasp of someone's breath comes through the earpiece. "Maybe it's all real," says the guy at the other end of the line. "I don't know. I don't think I know anything. Death in the river."

Taggett yells, "What the hell are you talking about? What the hell is happening? What do you know about the Violet Diamond? Who the hell are you?" His voice is cracking a little, sweat's thickening on his forehead, his eyes are bulging out. The cigarette in his mouth falls onto the bed, but it's gone out anyway. The tough detective stops himself, picks the smoke back up, lights it again. In a much calmer grumble, he says, "This is just too weird. What the hell do you people want with me?"

"I only want," the guy starts to say, and then the voice breaks into a wheezing cough, that thin pipe closing up for a moment. "I only want to warn you," it manages to come out with. "It's a curse. It cursed me. She cursed me. I am Edgar Foulsworth."

The scene goes a little grey as Taggett blinks at the big round hole of the phone's mouthpiece, and then it all fades back into the sharpness of reality. "That doesn't make any sense," he mutters. "I met Edgar Foulsworth on the train . . . or will meet him . . . or dreamed I met him . . . but I know he doesn't talk, just a mummy wrapped up in a wheelchair, poor old fellow can't even feed himself, definitely couldn't work a phone. Try another line, whoever you are, I'm not buying that one." He taps some ash out in the tray on his night table and takes another long drag.

"You never met me," says that creepy whisper. "Haven't been on a train in fourteen years. Haven't left this room. Maybe an impostor employed by my wife. She does that. The darkness of a tunnel that reveals. I am Edgar Foulsworth. I have to warn you." He's talking faster, almost panting. "The Violet Diamond seeks its mate. You must not allow." He's developed some kind of creepy Lugosi accent. "She will take your youth, take your life. I have to warn you! You must not allow!" Some kind of panting comes over the line as the old man's voice breaks into a squeak.

"Calm down," says Taggett. "You're not making any kind of sense. Just take it slow." His torn-up voice is crooning the kind of lullaby tones he learned to use on some ape he's about to ship off to the monkey house at Bellevue. "Now, why not tell me a little more about this Violet Diamond? What's the story here?"

The breath coming out of the earpiece slows down. After a moment the voice starts up again. "The story is a beautiful woman. I thought the Diamond led me to her. A beautiful woman, irresistible. She thought it would keep her alive." He could be laughing or coughing or sobbing, it's hard to tell. "The way it kept me alive. Centuries. But no youth. No youth without the mate. Only decay. She found out. Caged me here. Death in the river, in the water." The weird voice cracks again, recovers itself, and keeps laughing or sobbing or whatever. "She gave it to you. You let it take you. She won't stop until she gets it.

Taggett takes a moment to pull out another smoke and lights it up, and takes a drag. "Well, that's very interesting, mister whoever you are," he says. "But what's the point? What's an old beat cop like me supposed to do about all this crazy bullshit?" He taps out a lingering ash, takes another drag. "This is all just some sort of dream anyway, right, so what's the big lesson I'm supposed to learn?"

"No lesson. A warning." The voice faces into that ocean sound of an open line, then fades back in. "She has combed the world to find the mate. She has it. I've seen her in visions. She must not have the Violet Diamond. The two will steal your youth, your life. You must keep the Diamond."

"And turn into some kind of crazy vampire like that weird old bat?" Taggett looks around at the room and stubs out the cigarette. "You're not really selling me. I'm awake now, don't need to worry about any of this magical crap you're trying to peddle. I can just hang up this phone and go back to work and forget it all, can't I?" He lights up one more cigarette and blows smoke into the mouthpiece, watches it disappear into the air.

The voice hacks up another sobbing chuckle and says, "Perhaps. You decide. Real or not real, hero or stooge, dreamer or actor. I don't know any more." The open connection buzzes for a moment as the party on the other line takes a shaking breath. "But heed my warning," it says a little more strongly, the sound of someone making an effort to be understood. "Defend the Diamond. Death on the water, on the ocean. She chose you, let her protect you, keep her from her mate." The sound of the phone is starting to get softer, the edges of the stuff in Taggett's room starting to blur. "Kill or die. Live or dream."

Taggett starts shouting, "What the hell are you telling me? What? Tell me what it means!" into the phone, and his own voice sounds tinny in his ears. His fingers curled around the phone are becoming empty fists, the bed under him turning into a wooden floor, the empty room Jie's friend used to live in materializing around him as he keeps yelling. Chen's awake and staring at him and Jie bursts in through the door, then stands there looking at them both. Taggett coughs and swallows and blinks at the other two men.

"Gentlemen," Jie says, "I have, with your permission, taken the liberty of allowing you to take a period of rest sufficient to restore your powers to their fullest extent, and now the sun is beginning to reveal the neighborhood to itself with the concurrent increase in civilian activity. I strongly suggest that we absent ourselves from the surroundings and prepare your return to the more comfortable setting of your native land." As Taggett and Chen pull themselves to their feet, the detective pulls a pack of smokes out of his hat, lights two, hands one to the younger man. They stretch the stiffness out of their arms and legs, and Jie says, "I dare say your adventures in Shanghai are swiftly coming to an end."

Taggett stretches his thin lips into a grin that could be a snarl and says, "Almost. I get the impression there's one more meeting before we can finish this business." Chen looks a question at him. "I don't know about you," says the detective, "but I don't think I'm going to get any rest until we deal with that lousy Mrs. Foulsworth."

"Great," says Chen. "Let's find her and finish her." Jie nods and steps out to start the car.

CHAPTER FORTY SIX

The three of them spend the morning cleaning out the other room in the house, shoveling all the broken furniture and torn-up paper and smashed bits of mirror into a pile in a corner. They work in that same silence, Taggett and Chen smoking and Jie just moving rubble from one place to another. By the time they're done the sun's shooting almost straight down onto Shanghai, and they're dripping sweat. Finally, Jie says, "Enough. We have honored my friend to the extent of our ability, I think, and each of us here has a life that requires attention. If you will permit me, gentlemen, I wish to suggest that we adjourn to the Palace Hotel for a last meal before your departure back to the land of your destiny." The old man bows to them. "We all agree, I believe, that your time here has come to a close."

"Couldn't agree more," says Taggett, lighting up a fresh smoke. "It's just too weird around here for us simple citizens, right Chen?" He glances at the younger man, lights up a smoke for him, passes it over. "We need to get back on solid ground."

Chen takes a drag and nods. "We're done here anyway. Whichever of the bastards killed Mr. McBride is all used up with the rest of them."

"As you say, gentlemen," says Jie, and the three of them walk out of the house into the harsh midday light. Jie carefully closes the door behind them and murmurs something that sounds like a prayer. Taggett takes his hat off to watch him do it. The older man falls silent, and they all stand there for a moment, then he steps around to the Phantom II and opens the back door. With a little bow, he says, "Mr. Taggett? May I drive us to our farewell meal?"

"By all means," Taggett chuckles as he slides into the backseat. Chen opens his own door, settles into the passenger side in the front as Jie closes the back door behind Taggett and moves around the car to the driver's seat, and then it seems like no time at all until the detective's tipping his glass to catch the last drops of that excellent whiskey and licking the last bit of burger from his lips. "I'll definitely miss this back in the States," he says.

Jie says, "Perhaps, then, sir, I should endeavor to obtain a few bottles of this establishment's finest for your journey, perhaps even for your enjoyment in the less than entirely free circumstances to which you shall soon return." The driver takes a small sip of the tea he's been nursing while the other two have been tearing with both hands into the burgers and steak fries and boiled carrots and buttered rolls the older man paid for out of a thick roll of currency from one of his many hidden pockets. "I can, I believe, be permitted to assert my ability to acquire such a commodity," he says.

Taggett chuckles back, "Yeah, that'd be swell. I don't know how I'm gonna get used to drinking that rotgut we call whiskey back home." He lets out a little belch, loosens his belt, lights up a smoke. "We've got a little time before we get aboard, right?"

Frowning a little, Jie gives his head a subtle shake. "Alas, sir, I find myself compelled to beg your forgiveness in the face of my slowness of action. I have been remiss in my duties and have failed to thoroughly procure your accommodations. Recent events appear to have distracted me, although, of course, I would never think of offering such a trivial consideration in the place of an excuse." He takes another sip of his tea, finishing the cup, letting it clink just a little as he places it back onto the saucer. "With your permission, gentlemen," he says, eyes on the empty cup in front of him, "I shall go about the business of securing your transportation along with a case of the Palace's whiskey to provide you with companionship during your homeward voyage." He slides his chair back and starts to rise.

"Hold on a second," says Chen. The younger man glances at Taggett and then back at Jie. "You should come with us." Taggett puts up a hand, but the younger man goes right on. "Yeah, a P.I. can always use another leg man, and you're such an operator, you could have the city just wired, wouldn't be anyone who could hide from us when you—"

Now Jie puts up a hand and the chatter cuts off like a shot radio. "I most humbly beg your pardon, sir," he says, "but I cannot possibly accept you're most generous offer." He closes his mouth so tight his lips go white and there's a shimmer in his eyes for a moment. "Although I believe I may consider myself among friends in your company, a journey across the ocean at my advanced age would, I have no doubt, result in little more than unpleasantness and ultimate futility. I wish to thank you most sincerely, with the utmost sincerity of which I am capable, but I fear that there can be nothing for me in the United States."

Taggett stubs out his smoke and looks up at Jie. "Seems to me there's nothing for you here, old timer," he says. "I think we've killed all your employers, unless you've got some kind of secret we never caught on to."

"I have a number of secrets, Mr. Taggett." The corners of the older man's mouth twitch a little before his face gets its blank expression back. "Furthermore, if you will permit me to dispute you, the very fact of the absence of Mr. Wong or Mr. Zhang offers, I suspect, a great opportunity to the appropriate party." He slides a few coins from one of the invisible pockets in his black shirt and drops them on the table. "I learned in the War, sir, and most emphatically in the time after the War, that honor does not preclude survival." This time the smile gets onto his face for half a second before he can get rid of it. "I shall meet you at the dock for the tourist ferry in two hours, gentlemen, and then we must part ways." He takes a long look at the two men sitting at the table before him and turns around and walks away. After a minute he's vanished into the crowd.

Taggett lights up a new smoke. "Nice gesture, kid," he chuckles. "I like how you figure someone around here's a private investigator who needs a leg man."

"You've already got a leg man, Johnny." Chen's looking right into his eyes. "You know I was trained by the best. Besides, I've lived through all this, what can San Francisco do to me?" The kid leans forward and lights a cigarette off the tip of Johnny's. "And what the hell else am I gonna do?" he says.

Taggett smiles and takes a breath to reply, then his eyes go wide and he clamps his lips around his cigarette, tilts his hat down over his face, slumps in his seat. Barely moving his mouth, he mumbles, "Careful, son, there's trouble behind you, five o'clock." Chen doesn't flinch, but his head twists just a tiny bit, and he gives a little hiss of shock that only Taggett can hear.

Behind Chen's head the black shape of Mrs. Foulsworth is pushing her husband in a wheelchair through the crowd in the bar. "What the hell is she doing here," Chen murmurs as she glides past.

"I don't know," says Taggett, his gaze following her slow progress through the glass door of the bar and onto the big tile floor of the hotel's lobby. As the door swings shut behind her he jumps out of his chair and starts pushing through the crowd with Chen right behind him. "Need to find out where she's going?" the detective growls. They get through the big glass door and into the bigger space of the lobby, ringing phones and shuffling footsteps filling the air with noise as they whip their heads around for a sign of that freakish black figure. "There," says Taggett. "She's headed down that hall, toward the laundry it looks like." The two of them start pushing through bodies again on the way to the unlit utility hallway, its darkness almost throwing a shadow into the bright lobby.

They make it to the hallway's entrance and stop. Taggett glances around and then unholsters his forty-five. "How're we gonna see her in this crazy darkness?" Chen whispers to him.

The detective puts a finger to his lips, and the two of them step as softly as they can into the corridor. The sounds of the lobby seem to fade out once they're a yard or two into the long, narrow space. Taggett puts a hand on Chen's chest, and they stop, standing there in the dark silence.

But the darkness isn't silent. Something in there is squeaking, it's the sound of metal on metal echoing from the concrete walls the two men are pressing their backs to. They creep into the blackness, following the noise, Taggett on one side, Chen on the other, letting the flat cool walls guide them deeper. The noise is getting louder, and there's a soft mumble to go with it. Mrs. Foulsworth is talking too quietly for words to come through, maybe to her husband, maybe to herself. Taggett looks back toward the mouth of the hall they're in, the square of light letting grey shadows play around on the floor, and then the wall he's on makes a turn to the right, and that's the end of that. The wheelchair keeps squeaking. "Free," she's muttering, almost growling, her voice coming thick and deep through the stifling air in there. "I shall attain my liberty at last . . . have transcended my need for assistance . . . all possible allies have proven themselves incapable, traitorous, of no use . . . I shall become myself at last . . . the gems will finally save me, cure me . . . none shall stand in my way . . ." The sound keeps growing as they get closer. Taggett's got his forty-five in one hand as the other spreads itself over the concrete. The sound is close enough for him to hear her soft footsteps as they scrape over the floor. He stops moving. His thumb very carefully pulls back the hammer.

Then the squeaking stops as Taggett freezes against the wall. There's a soft click and a rumble and another click and then silence. He stands there for a stretching minute and then risks a whisper. "Chen?"

"Yeah," comes the whisper from the other side of the hall. Both men wait, then Chen's whisper comes again. "I think she ditched us."

Taggett snorts and puts away his forty-five and lights a match on the wall behind him for a fresh smoke. "No shit," he grumbles. "Probably another damn secret door." Match still lit, he steps forward to examine the wall where the hallway turns right again. Chen steps next to him. The two men use three hands to explore the flat surface until the match burns out and Taggett drops it. "What the hell goes on here, anyway," he growls. "How does this get to the laundry?"

"Jie showed it to me," says Chen as their fingers keep working in the dark. "Said it was from older times, all full of cubbyholes and dumbwaiters for the servants to ride up and down in with dinner or whatever." Taggett grunts and then his fingers sink into a soft spot in the wall and something clicks and the wall moves forward.

The partners jump back. Taggett almost tears his holster off getting his forty-five back into his hand. A section of wall about as wide as the detective slides over to the right, and a blast of cool air ruffles over his face. He can see by the light from a window at its far end that this is another hallway walls made out of greenish stone, leading to an office door. He keeps his hand on his forty-five as the two of them, crouching a little, pad down the new corridor's length. About five steps in the wall slides back into place. Taggett whirls around and takes aim, but there's nothing but blank concrete in front of him.

It takes them another minute or two to get to the door. Taggett glances across it at Chen, who carefully wraps his fingers around the knob. The younger man turns the knob slow enough to keep it from making a noise until it stops. Then he yanks the door back into himself, diving out of the way as it slams against the wall behind him and Taggett covers the opening with the forty-five. The detective squints as the light of the afternoon sun glares into his face, but he keeps his aim steady until the details fade in.

He's looking at an empty alley, hearing the honks and growls of tourist traffic cruising up and down the main boulevard a few yards away. Chen's crouching under him, fists clenched, ready to spring, rolls forward into the mud between buildings.

"Careful," says Taggett. "You'll roll right through those nice fresh tire tracks. Someone drove out of here in a hurry."

"Too fast," says Chen, still crouching. "How could she get a wheelchair and a cripple into that truck faster than we can get down that little hallway? Doesn't make sense at all."

Taggett spits out the butt of his dead cigarette and says, "Yeah." He puts his forty-five away and takes another look around. He stops when he gets to the pile of garbage just to the left of the door they just came through. "Look at that," he tells Chen.

The younger man stares for a second and then starts laughing. "A scarecrow? Really? She was carting around a straw dummy?"

"Someone sure as hell was," says the detective. "Someone wanted us in this alleyway." The two of them whip their heads around, but no one's anywhere near. They stand there for another minute or two and listen to the traffic ignore them as they keep their heads on swivels. Nothing happens. Finally Taggett says, "All right, let's get out of here. We'll take a few extra turns on our way to the docks." The two of them head out of the alley and lose themselves in the parade of tourists clotting up the sidewalk.

CHAPTER FORTY SEVEN

He's still complaining about it to Chen two days later. "It doesn't make any sense," he growls, his voice bouncing around the little metal box of a room the two of them are bunking in across the Pacific, just them and the crate of whiskey and the four cartons of smokes that Jie's sending with them on the smuggler's route to San Francisco. "If she wanted us to follow her to that alley, then what the hell for? Some sort of trap? Or she didn't know we were behind her . . . so why dump the dummy right there? Why have a truck waiting? Was it even her, maybe it was some kind of disguise trick. But why? I don't get it. This just doesn't make any sense at all."

"You said that," groans Chen, lighting a new smoke from the tip of the butt in his mouth. "I heard it. It doesn't make any sense." He looks down from the cherry end of his cigarette into the tough detective's eyes. "Johnny, I can't remember the last time anything made sense in my life. Why should it? Why keep asking questions you can't answer?"

Taggett glares at Chen for a second, then lets a chuckle grind out of his throat. "What else am I gonna do?" he says. "If I'd known Jie was shipping us back as cargo I'd've packed some crossword puzzles to pass the time." He lights a cigarette of his own, shakes out the match, throws it on the pile growing in the corner of the windowless room. "So instead I'm stuck staring at these walls while that crazy old bat runs around in my brain," he says. "A couple more weeks of this and they'll have to pull me off the ship on a stretcher."

Chen snorts a laugh right back at him. "You worry too much about things that don't matter." The smaller man swings his feet back up to the top bunk and stretches out, lacing his fingers behind his head. "You want something to worry about," he says to the ceiling a couple of inches past his nose, "you might try figuring out who Jie's been working for all this time."

The best Taggett can come up with from his spot on the floor across from the bunk bed, his big body squirming a little against the cold flat wall, pressed up against the rough wood of the whiskey crate jammed in there with them, is, "Huh?"

Chen rolls to his side and says, "Think about it," laughing a little more. "Who told us about him? How did he know we were coming? If he's been depending on Wong for his payday, how's he so eager to wreck that? All this driving around and blowing stuff up, who's been paying for that? If he's working for Mrs. Foulsworth, why wouldn't he just wrap us up and leave us on her doorstep?" He taps out his smoke, lets the ash drop on the floor in front of Taggett. "That helpful old guy knows a lot more than he lets on, definitely a lot more than we ever figured out, so what's his percentage? Why don't you wrap your big strong detective brain around that one for a while?"

The older man just stares for a moment. The cigarette in his mouth burns closer to his lips as he sits there scratching his forehead until his hat's crushed against the wall behind him.

"Me, I don't care," says Chen. "He helped us get the sons of bitches that took out Mr. McBride, and that's good enough. My enemy's my friend, right?" He licks the tips of his fingers, snuffs out the butt of his smoke, throws it in the pile growing in the corner on the other side of the hatch from the pile of used match sticks. "Anyway, it's gotta be night time by now," he says. "Time to get some sleep. I've got a big day ahead of me, listening to you keep chewing over this mystery of yours." With a snicker he keeps staring into the older man's eyes until his own gaze goes unfocused and his eyelids drop shut.

Taggett stubs his butt out on the floor and throws it on the pile in the corner. "Maybe I should figure out who taught him that smart lip," he mumbles. Time creeps along as he sits there, his big body folded up to fit the little box he's hiding in. The fluorescent light along the middle of the ceiling buzzes and flickers greenish shadows back and forth over the cartons of cigarettes and the crate of whiskey and Chen. Taggett sits there and keeps staring at the cloud of cigarette smoke that swirls and coils in that sick faint glow. Chen snores a little and shifts in his sleep, that snort and the creak of the bunk the only sounds in the little metal room. The detective sits there listening.

After a while a new sound starts to fade in. It's a squeak of metal on metal, the kind of noise you might hear at the other end of a long dark corridor as you follow someone pushing a rickety old wheelchair. Taggett's eyes twitch back and forth, and then his whole head's swiveling around. The sound's not coming from one particular place but from all around him, getting louder, as if that crappy old wheelchair is getting ready to smash into the room through one of the walls. It's like the vacant scream of a mental patient who's forgotten how to anything but shriek for no reason. Chen doesn't even twitch until Taggett starts hammering on the floor with his fist and making some kind of blubbering racket with his mouth almost loud enough to drown out that squeak.

"Jesus, Johnny, enough," the smaller man moans, rolling over. The wheelchair noise cuts out the second he moves. Peering down from the top bunk, he says, "If I knew you were gonna go all stir crazy I'd've booked myself a private suite. Turn it off, will you? Get some sleep."

Taggett says, "You didn't hear that?"

"Hear what? All I heard was you practicing your act, Caruso. Maybe you should stick to your day job."

Johnny reaches for a bottle, takes a swig. "Something about being on a boat just turns you into Eddie Cantor," he grumbles. "Or Walt, which might be worse. But you're right. I'm starting to crack. I better get some air." He pulls his feet up under him and stands, the room's ceiling pressing down on his hat. Now his head's level with Chen's. "I just gotta get out of this room for a minute or two," says Taggett.

"You think that's a good idea?" Chen says. "We're supposed to be invisible. You know smugglers don't like it when the contraband starts wandering around calling attention to itself." He lets out a little chuckle and rolls back onto his back. "Anyone catches you strolling around on deck, you're gonna get tossed overboard."

The tough detective cracks his knuckles. "I'm not too worried about that. Even if there was anyone around it'd take a few of them to get me over the rail, and I'd take a few of them with me. I'm not exactly a pushover, you know." A faint squeaking sound makes his head swerve toward the little hatch they came in through. He presses his lips together and swallows and turns back to Chen, but the smaller man's got his eyes closed. "Anyway," says Taggett, "we're the only cargo on this ship, right? Who's gonna break himself out of a nice sound sleep just to make sure the cargo isn't making too much noise?"

Without opening his eyes, Chen says, "Sure, whatever gets you to clam up for an hour or two so I can get some nice sound sleep of my own? Give your partner a break, why don't you." He turns over so that he's facing the wall, and after a minute his chest is slowly expanding and contracting as he starts to snore.

Taggett mutters, "Great," as he grabs the wheel in the middle of the hatch. The rusty surface bites his palms and he grunts a little as he pulls against the wheel's resistance. Finally he gets the thing turned enough to open the hatch with a metallic scrape that makes Chen roll over and glare at him. "Sorry," says Taggett as the younger man rolls back over again, grumbling into the wall without quite making words. The detective shoves the hatch closed and pushes out into the corridor. The sweat on his face cools in the air that drifts in from the darkness at the corridor's other end. He strikes a match on the wall beside him and lights a fresh smoke before the flame can give him away on deck, and then he steps down the hallway to its open end and through it.

The cherry end of his cigarette is almost blinding in the total darkness out there. The wind across his face gives the only clue that he's not still inside buried in a closet. He gropes for the rail and finds it and stands there, breathing the cold air and smoking. The deck throbs a little under his feet to the rhythm of the boat's engine pushing it forward through the invisible waves that have the tough detective swaying for balance, holding onto that rail to stay upright. The engine makes the only sound in the night, the little boat he's on the only human presence in the vast space of the Pacific Ocean. All alone, he starts muttering.

"All this weirdness, it's like I've got nowhere to stand. Made more sense in New York, at least I knew who was after me and why. Now I've got some crazy creature of the night on my back, looking for something I don't even know if I have, killing everyone in her way like a wild dog, and it feels like she's still after me. But that's crazy. There's no way she could have followed me from—oh, shit, wait a minute." He flicks his spent cigarette over the side and watches it blink out in the black depth under the little boat. "Did she double back on me? Was all that pointless squeaking around just to get me where she could see me, get me to some point she could start shadowing me from? Or maybe she's just trying to drive me crazy." That squeak starts up again. He whips his head around, but there's nothing in the dark but him and the hum of the engine, the squeaking noise shutting off almost as soon as he's noticed it. A growl sets up in his throat. "Just doesn't make any damn sense at all," he tells himself. "How could a wheelchair even get on here? Mind's playing tricks, gotta be. She didn't follow me, couldn't've, doesn't even know I'm here. Even if she knew, how could she get on the boat? Not like it's some kind of cruise ship, some kind of passenger operation. She'd have to be smuggled like Chen and me, killing time in that little metal prison cell; she'd never do it, not for all the tea in China or whatever the hell she wants. I'm just driving myself nuts. I gotta relax." He stands there gripping the rail and listens to the hum of the engine until it suddenly stops.

And there he is in the nearly silent darkness. The deck under his feet keeps rolling and sliding as the waves from somewhere out there push the boat around. Taggett lets the rail go and keeps his knees bent the way Chen would and holds his breath. The waves slap at the side of the boat. The wood creaks. A faint hiss, like the sound of a lace cloth dragging over a corpse's skin, comes in behind him. He doesn't move a muscle, doesn't even reach for his forty-five. There's nothing to shoot at in the dark.

Cold metal presses lightly at the base of his skull, and then he hears that familiar mechanical purr. "Although your obvious confusion has been a source of highly gratifying entertainment for the span of our acquaintance, your performance tonight has provided particular amusement, rather like a dancing monkey about to be electrocuted." That sick parody of a laugh pollutes the silence and then cuts off like an unplugged radio. "You will accompany to my accommodations, Mr. Taggett, and there we will discuss what you owe me for the services I have rendered you and your destiny, which I have indeed made possible, only to be insulted and denied my due recompense." The gun barrel presses a little harder at the soft spot at the top of his neck. "Our time is at last at hand," says Mrs. Foulsworth.

CHAPTER FORTY EIGHT

With her gun pushing him, he gropes his way along a corridor like the one leading to the cell Chen's snoozing away in, but to that corridor's left, through a door and down a steep flight of shallow stairs until she says, "Enough," and flicks a switch somewhere behind him. The explosion of light swells up white in his eyes then fades to reveal a room at least four times the size of the little box he and Chen are cooped up in. It's got room for a big black desk and a set of chairs, two in front, one behind. Mrs. Foulsworth marches him to one of the chairs in front of the desk and says, "Sit." He sits, and the barrel of her gun's not touching him for a moment as she glides around to the desk's other side. He keeps still long enough to see what's going to happen next.

He can barely make out the black metal of the gun still pointed at him against the black depth of her dress. A rectangular spot of light glints from the barrel, but he's not looking at it yet. He's looking at where her face would be if she had one, staring at the space where you'd expect to see her eyes. Her breath ruffles her veil. It's the only thing moving in the big empty space. The air presses on his eardrums in the silence. Finally, he says, "So? We just gonna stare at each other the whole trip, or do you have something you want to say?"

That laugh fills up the space in its creepy automated way. "Your bravado, the desperate flailing of the lobster as it begins to feel the pain of being steamed, continues to serve as a source of entertainment of the kind that my life makes increasingly rare, Mr. Taggett. However, unfortunately, the diversion you provide, like so many other things, including, perhaps, your miserable useless life, must soon come to an end." The gun stays pointed at him as she talks. The light reflecting from it flickers a little as her finger moves in and out of the trigger guard. Taggett keeps his eye on that slowly flickering light and keeps breathing. "You have been adopted by the Violet Diamond, have you not?" she says.

The tough detective swallows and puts on a smirk. His voice comes out a little rough but not too shaky. "Lady, I thought you were nuts when I met you and now I know for sure. How the hell is a diamond supposed to adopt me?" As the veil moves, as she breathes in to answer, he reaches into his coat and watches the finger on the trigger in front of him tense up as he pulls out a pack of smokes and a matchbook. "Do you mind?" he says as he lights up. "If I'm gonna die, I deserve a last cigarette, right?" He smirks into the space where her eyes should be as he leaves the pack and the matches on the desk.

"As I have inadvertently made apparent, I have no intention to affect your demise before you accede to the inevitable and do my bidding, as all who meet me do eventually. However, your insolence begins to try my patience." Her voice has turned harsh and cold the way it does when she's trying to scare someone, but she doesn't shoot. "Clearly, you understand the import of my statement and all its implications, despite your relentless imitation of someone even more ignorant than you appear, assuming for a moment that such a degree of ignorance approaches the realm of possibility." That weird excuse for a laugh fades in and cuts out again. "The strange events of your recent life cannot possibly have escaped the notice of even such a specimen of mental deficiency as yourself. Despite your obvious shortcomings, you must have recently become aware of the difference in your way of dreaming, you're seeming to bear witness to actual events of which you could in no way have been otherwise cognizant."

Taggett blinks for a minute. "Uh, yeah, I'm sorry I didn't bring my dictionary along. I'll admit I've had some weird dreams lately, but I don't see what some crazy nightmare about a weird old creature shoving her thumbs into some fat clowns eye sockets has anything to do with—"

"Silence!" She slaps the desk with an open hand, the other still holding the gun aimed at Taggett's chest. He doesn't flinch, but he does take the half-smoked cigarette out of his mouth and stub it out on the desk in front of him. As he's lighting up a new one, she seems to calm down a little. "Your attempt at mockery betrays your attempt to assert your obliviousness; a feat which would ordinarily be as natural to a thug like you as befouling a statue is to a pigeon. You cannot fool me, Mr. Taggett. I can see the effects of the Violet Diamond's having embraced you as clearly as you could see your own face had you only the perspicacity to recognize what you were seeing, what you must have been seeing in the mirror every day as you shave and failing to notice, even as you style yourself a private investigator." She's calmed down enough to give out another of those creepy chuckles. "I find myself compelled to admit that I will miss that blank stare of yours once I have removed you from the ranks of those able to form expressions. I refer to your facial deformity, baboon, the scar by which you have for so attempted to advertise your toughness. If you want to continue to claim ignorance of the Violet Diamond's effect on you, then you must answer the question that you clearly have never asked yourself: what has become of your scar, Mr. Taggett?"

He can't help lifting a hand to his face and feeling with his fingers for the line of raised flesh that doped-up punk left him with all those years ago. He finds nothing but smooth skin and a little stubble. There's no tingle or itch or throb. His eyes widen a little.

The gun in her left hand doesn't seem to move as she keeps laughing at him. "Truly, Mr. Taggett, you present a perfect specimen of uselessness. Do you mean honestly to attempt to encourage me to believe that you have simply not noticed your own face?"

"I don't spend a lot of time checking to see how pretty I am," he says. "I guess that's something we've got in common."

That cuts out the laughing. The slick little spot of reflected light on the black flat barrel of the gun jiggles a tiny bit, but the gun stays pointed at him. The detective keeps watching that reflection. "My physical appearance is of no concern to you," she tells him in that mechanical drone of hers. "Nor should it be of concern to anyone.

With the help of the Violet Diamond I have transcended such petty mortal matters as mere appearance, a transcendence that you as well would undergo were I to allow you to continue under the Diamond's influence." She shuts up, her chest expanding and contracting as she breathes heavily, and the silence swells into a minute or two of him sitting there smoking and her sitting there casually aiming that little gun somewhere in the area of his face. His cigarette's turning into a long grey tube of ash that points right back at her. Eventually she says, "There is one other effect of the Violet Diamond's adoption of such a miserable host as yourself. Tell me, Mr. Taggett, how many murders have you committed since you came to this revolting little sty of an outpost? How many living persons have you personally assassinated with that giant weapon of yours, despite your claims to conscience and morality, your outrage at the terrible injustice of the death of that poor little drunken whore in San Francisco?" She pauses to let out a long sigh of a breath, the kind of sigh a smoker makes after the first best cigarette of the morning. "Do satisfy my curiosity as to whether you possess the scintilla of self-awareness necessary to recognize the extent to which you have become a monster no better than the freaks and bats you curse with such inarticulate eloquence, the depth of the moral chasm you have allowed yourself to fall into. Tell me your opinion of yourself, killer."

The ash falls onto Taggett's lap. The smirk's wiped off his face. She keeps talking. "I can perceive that you have indeed managed to continue your enviable state of self-delusion concerning the metamorphosis you have incurred by accepting the advantages the Violet Diamond has offered you, the abilities which you have been granted to perceive the hidden and to absorb superhuman amounts of physical punishment. I must assume that you have been equally blind regarding the influence you have been exerting on your adorable little yellow associate, as you lead him to bathe his hands in the same blood with which you besmirch yours." A sound like the clucking of a tongue comes through the veil. "I wonder if you can still feel the shame that an ordinary human would feel upon having discovered not only that he has allowed himself to sink to the level of a common murdering animal but also that he has allowed his protégée to descend to the same plane of hell." The slick of light on the gun jerks a little bit as her breath catches in a barking laugh.

"That what happened to you?" says Taggett. He spits the butt of his smoke onto the desk and lets it lie there. He's got his face pointed straight at the black shape of the front of her veil as it swells and shrinks with her breath, but his eyes keep cutting back to the gun. "Did you use to be a nice girl, some kind of sweet virgin, then the nasty rock turned you into, into whatever you are now?" He starts laughing as he reaches down to the desk for another smoke from his pack. "I bet you were always the second best, weren't you. Not quite pretty or smart or nice enough to really get the attention you needed." He lights up his smoke, uses the flame of the match to check the angle of the gun she's holding. It's drifting a little away from him.

"The vast quantity of your ignorance concerning the circumstances of my life threatens to stagger the imagination of our most celebrated astronomers, Mr. Taggett," she says, "but I can assure you with the greatest level of confidence that I have never, no matter what offenses to common morality I may have found myself obliged to commit, stooped to such a level as to use an innocent such as your young Mr. Chen to satisfy my lust for destruction."

Taggett keeps on laughing through the smoke streaming up from his cigarette. "Yeah, I figure you can satisfy your lust for destruction pretty good on your own." The match is burning closer to his fingers, the flame swelling as the breath of his laugh hits it. The reflection on the gun is showing him the way her attention's still drifting. The barrel's almost pointed away from him. He gets his feet under him. "You just can't help yourself, can you?" He starts to grin. "Just some poor sad little girl swept up into the harsh cold world, right? More like some kind of spider who shouldn't have crawled out of her hole." The gun's not even reflecting the match light anymore, the business end sagging down toward the desk and away across Taggett's body to his right.

The top of the figure across the desk from him bends a little and the gun snaps back to point at him again as she chuckles, "You have become a strategist, Mr. Taggett. How proud you must be of yourself. How sad it must be for you that you have such a short time to savor this unexpected addition to your miniscule set of capabilities, but I have no more time to indulge your attempts at subterfuge. I gave you the Violet Diamond, Mr. Taggett, for safekeeping, and now the service I have called upon you to perform has come to an end. Relinquish it at once, and I will allow you simply to die from the wound I shall inflict upon you with the firearm I hold in my hand." The little dot of light on the top of the gun is holding as still as a rock in a river. "Alternately," she says, "you can continue your course of mulish obstreperousness, in which case I will immobilize you, take you to see your little slant-eyed buttboy, and disembowel him while you watch, and then you will relinquish the Violet Diamond to me just as if I had taken none of the trouble I am describing to you. I will have what is mine, Mr. Taggett."

"It's not yours." Taggett reaches for a fresh smoke even as he gives the one in his mouth another puff, making the cherry end glow orange. "It never was," he says, and lights the match watching the flame suddenly with precise accuracy he flips it into her face. The veil catches fire as she drops the gun and starts to scream in a voice like a manufacturing plant collapsing, metal scraping over metal, great beams of wood creaking and breaking. Her hands go to the front of her head and catch fire as they cover the smoking hole her face is turning into. Taggett jumps forward, across the desk, his chair shooting back to smack against the wall behind him. He grabs her little gun and throws it behind him and throws a punch straight into the burning screaming stink. A rough yell shoves its way out of his throat as his fist burns. She starts to smoke as he gets his hands around her throat. She's gone limp, but he keeps squeezing as his hands start to cook. His fists close around the black scraps he's tearing apart. There's no body in there. He's clutching rags. The lights go out.

His eyes snap back open and there's Chen in front of him, the younger man's shirt gripped between Taggett's fingers. Taggett's straddled over Chen's body, almost crushing the smaller man's ribcage with his thighs as they constrict. Chen's face is calm but wide-eyed and swelling and darkening. Taggett blinks, breathes in a dry shudder, let's go, rolls off Chen's body from the lower bunk down to the floor. "I'm sorry," says the detective. "I'm so god-damned sorry."

Chen swallows and croaks, clears his throat, tries again, comes up with, "Johnny, whatever's in your head, you can take it. You're the toughest guy I've ever met." He sits up on the bunk, looks down at the older man. "And I'm the second toughest. I can handle what you can dish out." He finds a cigarette, lights up, hands it to Johnny. "If it helps, you were yelling something about Mrs. Foulsworth and that Violet Diamond."

Johnny takes a drag of the cigarette and hands it back to his partner. "Yeah, I think my mind's trying to tell me that we're not quite done with that yet." He looks away from Chen and shivers a little. "Whatever's in my head, we're gonna make some use of it before we get home.

This story's not quite over.

CHAPTER FORTY NINE

So he starts spending nights prowling around the dark boat, feeling the walls, listening to the sounds of his shoes on the deck. He sleeps in the daytime like a vampire. He and Chen get their meals every night just before lights out wrapped up in cellophane in front of the hidden hatch they're cooped up behind. Sometimes there's a little note from the captain, the only one on the boat who's supposed to know they're there, reminding them to stay inside and out of sight. Chen passes the time doing pushups on the floor with his feet on the lower bunk. Taggett explores. He carries around a flashlight he boosted out of the galley a day or two ago, but he doesn't use it. He walks softly on the invisible deck, smelling his way through the black corridors, tapping lightly on the walls he passes. His steps are steady and slow. Sometimes he hears a deeper thump than should be, the sound of something hollow, and then he switches on the flashlight for a second or two and scouts around for something sticking out, something he can push in to open a secret door. He can't look for too long, so he just blinks the flashlight on and off to see if something casts a shadow. Tonight's just like the last week or so. Nothing shows itself.

The sound of someone saying his name makes his head spin, and draws his forty-five aiming it along the beam of the flashlight as he flicks the switch with one thumb and pulls back the hammer with the other. The captain stands there squinting in the glare, holding his hand in front of his heavily bearded face, saying, "Jesus, Taggett, turn it off."

"Sorry," says Taggett and turns it off. He stands there blinking away the ghosts of the light until he can start to see the squat shadow of the captain in front of him. The detective puts away his forty-five and pulls out a fresh pack of smokes, looks away from the flame of the match as he lights one and offers it to the captain. The captain shakes his head and blows out the match, and now the only light in the corridor they're crowding in is the cherry at the end of Taggett's cigarette.

The captain talks from deep in his throat, his words making the sound a dog makes when it's about to start barking. "How many times do I have to tell you to keep yourself hidden?" he says. "You know what kind of attention you can bring down on me? If I didn't owe Jie a favor you wouldn't even be taking up space on my ship. What the hell are you doing out of the hold, anyway?"

"Cabin fever," says Taggett. "You know how it gets."

"Sure," says the captain, "but you've got to be a little tougher than that. Maybe you need some self-discipline." His shoes scrape a little on the floor, and his shadow, the outline of his dense blackness against the more open blackness of the corridor, gets a little bigger as he moves a little closer. "Besides, what does all this roaming around in the dark do for you? Wouldn't you be happier out on the deck with the fresh air? You're just trading a little closet for a bigger one when you walk down here."

Taggett chuckles as he takes another drag of his cigarette. "Fresh air's overrated. I just need to walk around, stretch my muscles a little. A gumshoe like me needs a little darkness to operate in."

"Oh, you're operating?" The captain's voice is coming from a point right in front of Taggett and very close. "And just what would you be operating on?" "My business? What do you need to know, really?"

Taking a step back, the detective puts his hands up and says, "Hey, no, I'm not trying to pry. All I'm doing is looking around your boat, keeping my brain working, that's all."

The captain takes that step forward, staying a little too close. "Maybe you should've packed some crossword puzzles," he says in that growl of a voice.

"I thought of that already." The chuckle that comes with Taggett's comeback sounds flat in the dark space between him and the captain, like it's been crushed by the pressure of the atmosphere. He takes another step back. "This butt's getting stale," he says and spits it out onto the floor where it flares and dies. For a moment there's nothing in there but the two men and the dark that's pushing against every surface, and then Taggett takes out another smoke and another match and strikes. In the flash he can see the captain's face close up, the hat tilted down over his eyes, the thick lined face, the thicket of beard obscuring his mouth and chin. The match goes out as Taggett lights his cigarette and there they are back in the dark again.

The captain says, "That's very disrespectful, Taggett. You are my guest here." He's standing close enough for the detective to smell the fish on his breath. "Do I come into your living room and spit on your floor?"

"Maybe it's not your floor," Taggett snaps, then takes another step back and puts his hands up again and says, "My apologies. I'm just not sure who's who these days. Been through some weird shit, you know."

"Now how would I know that," says the captain, a snicker breaking up the snarl in his deep voice just a little. "You talk like a man who is cracking up. I guess you weren't kidding about the cabin fever. What you need is something to keep your attention from wandering. Take up a hobby."

"This is my hobby," Taggett says. "I walk around; I try to figure things out." He sneaks a hand behind his body to feel how close he is to the wall behind him. He's very close, almost backed up against it. "My other hobby's fighting."

The snicker turns all the way into a laugh that's just this side of the way that growling dog in his throat would sound before it launches into a victim. "You need better hobbies, Taggett. You'll get yourself into trouble." The captain takes a step back, pulls out a pipe and a lighter. He pushes down on the plunger at the top of the lighter with a thick hard thumb. The flame as he sucks it into the bowl of his pipe casts a crumpled map of shadows over his face, black lines moving over the little part of it not covered by hat or beard. Once he gets his pipe going the flame cuts out and they're back in the dark. "You should take an interest in something nice and safe. Perhaps jewelry."

Taggett stays where he is and watches the dark shape of the captain swaying a little against the slightly shallower darkness of the corridor as the ocean shoves the boat around. "Funny you should mention jewelry," he says like just another guy in a bar getting ready to bore the guy next to him. "I've had a little experience along that line. Not as safe as you might think, it turns out." He shifts his weight onto his left foot and gives his knees a little bend and keeps watching that dark shape in front of him.

The glow at the end of the captain's pipe shifts as he tells Taggett, "Perhaps you have been studying dangerous jewels. Some stones may be hazardous to the one who holds them without understanding." The voice is changing, getting somehow deeper, developing a rough burr of an accent that's starting to sound familiar. "Honor may demand one holding such a stone to surrender it to a superior."

"Yeah, I don't have a whole lot of superiors," Taggett says. "Any stones I've got, I should probably hold on to. Like you say, some stones are pretty dangerous and shouldn't fall into the wrong hands." He's got his foot braced on the wall behind him. The shadow in front of him seems to draw in on itself a little. "Besides, I thought you were out of this game, One-Eye."

The dark figure doesn't move. Neither of the men is even breathing. The boards of the ship creak a little to make the only sound in the corridor. After a long moment the captain takes a slow deep breath and says, "What did you call me?"

Taggett says, "I called you One-Eye. You've probably got other names, but that's the one I've got for you. Master of disguise, right?" His tone's staying nice and conversational. "I guess you must be? You even fooled Jie, didn't you?"

"Jie is a good man," says the captain, "with few blind spots. Surely even a master of disguise could not fool someone as wise as he." The glow from the pipe's bowl moves down and then breaks into a scurry of little glowing embers and fades as they drop to the deck. Now there's almost nothing to show where he's standing. "But you are not as easily fooled."

Taggett takes the cigarette out of his mouth and holds it just a little away from his head, letting it dip as he talks. "I like to think I'm learning," he says.

One-Eye's voice says, "Then we begin your next lesson," and Taggett manages to duck the foot that smashes into the wall behind him. The detective's on the floor, rolling out of the way, throwing his lit cigarette at the spot where One-Eye's face should be. The little orange light of the dying butt flies down the hall a little way and shatters. By that time Taggett's grabbed One-Eye's ankle and started pulling the ninja down to the floor with him. One-Eye kicks Taggett in the face and frees himself and then stomps down again, but Taggett's rolled aside, his body smashing against the wall to his right. He scuttles on his hands and knees along the corridor and turns over to squat on the floor and look back. One-Eye's invisible against the dead end. Taggett silently gets back onto his feet.

Something creaks at the other end of the corridor. Taggett braces himself, and the bulk of One-Eye's body crashes into him, pushing him back along the corridor and through the hatch at the end. The detective's lying on his back on the stairs with One-Eye on top punching him in the face, going for Taggett's eyes and nose with probing fingers. Taggett reaches up for the ninja's throat and squeezes tight. One-Eye's breath is hot on Taggett's face, and the false beard is coming off and tickling the detective's chin. The ninja gets a thumb into Taggett's eye. Taggett yells and brings a knee up between One-Eye's legs and does it again and again until the assassin's grip loosens and he rolls off Taggett's body. On all fours, Taggett scrambles upstairs and onto the deck.

After the darkness of the corridor, the light of the moon out here is almost blinding. Taggett squints and puts his back to the rail and waits. One-Eye's voice comes rumbling up from the black rectangle of the stairwell Taggett just came through. "Give me the Violet Diamond, Taggett. I must buy my freedom." Taggett says nothing. "I cannot satisfy my employer any other way," says the deep voice, sounding a little out of breath. "I have sold my honor and I must get it back. I require your help."

"So why all the fooling around?" Taggett yells down the stairs. "Why come at me like this? I know I owe you for Chen." A drop of water hits him in the forehead, then another smacks his shoulder. The rain makes little silver threads in the moonlight, defining the invisible deck with the white mist where the drops splash back from it. The wave's splash against the side of the boat as the rain splashes its deck. The wood creaks. No one says anything. Taggett holds onto the rail behind him with one hand and peers down into the darkness, slipping his other hand into his coat, brushing his fingers over the butt of his forty-five. "One-Eye, what the hell is your problem? Come to me like a man! All you freaks, why don't you just deal with me like a man?" Nothing comes up from the blackness down there. Taggett pulls his forty-five out of its holster, leaning forward, arm straightening behind him as his other hand keeps gripping the rail.

A blast of pain goes off in his left eye like a firework and his body goes down, forty-five skittering along the wet deck into the dark, a piece of the rail coming off in his hand as he drops. The side of his face smashes into the deck. One-Eye's on him, forearm pressing into his cheekbone, breath hot and stinking against his ear. "You are not a man," says the ninja. "You are a mission." The forearm pushes Taggett's jaw against the wet wood. The detective's arms and legs are flailing around, but the ninja's got him nailed down. "You are a plaything for a bored wealthy eccentric insane woman." A battering fist knocks his hat off into the ocean. He gets a hand under him and crawls an inch forward under the weight of the man on his back. Another blow to his head knocks him back down to his belly. "You are redemption for lost soldiers. The fulfillment of my duties." The grumble of One-Eye's voice comes through like a threat of thunder under the hiss of the rain, than real thunder cracks above the struggling men on the deck. The lightning that flares up with it shows Taggett the black shape of his forty-five on the deck just out of reach of the hand stretching toward it. One-Eye leans forward, his black hand covering Taggett's, pulling it back away from the weapon. The detective's other hand, the hand with the piece of rail in it, reaches back toward the ninja and tries to stab with the splintered end. "A collection of ridiculous postures," One-Eye says and grabs the piece of rail out of the flailing hand, throwing it overboard to join Taggett's hat on those invisible waves that are throwing the boat back and forth.

Taggett rolls with One-Eye's throwing motion and gets the thick-muscled assassin under him. One hand spreads over the ninja's throat, holding his head to the deck while the other turns into a fist and smashes into his face again and again. "I'm a man!" Taggett shouts into the shadow over the ninja's face.

One-Eye's knee comes up between Taggett's thighs and smashes his balls. The detective yells in pain and falls back, and the ninja follows him over. Another bellow of thunder and lightning shows him One-Eye's jet black form looming over him, slowing just enough for Taggett to get a foot up and into the ninja's belly and push hard. One-Eye's body twists away but slams into the rail and pushes out a little over the black depth before he windmills himself back forward. By that time Taggett's back on his feet. They stand there on the slippery deck, each man barely keeping his balance, pitching and tilting as the storm pushes everything around. Taggett whips his head to the right and a thick drop of blood hits the wall of the shack someone built around the wheel. "I told you, that's disrespectful," says One-Eye, breathing hard. He's lost the hat and the beard. His naked face, like a landscape made out of blood and pain, stares at Taggett in the flashes of lightning getting closer and happening more often.

Taggett takes a careful step back. "Sorry," he says. "You know I just can't help myself." He puts a hand on the wall of the shack to steady himself and risks a glance through the wax paper window the wind's making into nothing but a hole. When he looks back at One-Eye the ninja seems a little closer, so Taggett takes another step back. He spits another glob of blood out toward the ocean and says, casual as a diner asking about tonight's special, "So, uh, who's steering the boat?"

"NO ONE!" The ninja roars and leaps for Taggett's head. Taggett ducks under the leap, squatting on the wet deck, his forty-five under his right hand. He picks it up, rolls onto his back, shoots at the dark space where One-Eye should be. A fresh blast of lightning shows him the empty air he just shot into and the gap in the rail behind where the ninja should have been standing. Wide eyed, dripping with cold rain that might as well be fear sweat, the detective squats on the deck and covers a hundred and eighty degrees with the business end of his forty-five. The wind howls against his ears; thunder so loud it might as well be inside his head. The soles of his feet are feeling for any kind of vibration from the deck, any hint of a footstep.

From behind him he hears a voice say, "What the hell are you shooting at, Johnny?" He whirls around with his finger on the trigger and just barely stops himself at the sight of Chen, barefoot and blinking and coming out through the stairwell. Chen stops on a dime and puts up his hands. "Easy, Johnny," he says. "No one's gonna hurt you, you're just dreaming again."

Johnny says, "Did you see him?" Chen gives him a baffled look, so he keeps going. "One-Eye! The captain! Did he pass you as you were coming up?"

The storm's dying down enough for Chen to keep his voice low and calm, the kind of voice you use when you're trying not to excite the attack dog that's growling into your face. "No one passed me, Johnny," he says. "One-Eye's not even on this ship, and the captain's probably asleep. Everything's okay, right?"

"Not even close," says Johnny, coming up from his squat, gun still trained on Chen. "Tell me something that bastard wouldn't know."

Chen's eyes go wide and his hands go up a little higher. "Uh, the first time we met you almost shot me, remember? Thought I was one of the goons out to get you?"

The detective cracks a smile and lowers his forty-five. "I guess you're not him, then. He's been on the ship the whole time, playing captain, trying to get me to give up the Diamond." Looking over Chen's shoulder, Taggett can see the storm blowing away from the boat, the sky above him opening up to reveal a big bright moon. In that silver light he notices a blood stain where the ninja was standing in front of the broken stretch of rail. A dark chuckle pushes itself out through Taggett's thin lips. "I must have shot the son of a bitch overboard."

"Jesus," says Chen. "The captain was One-Eye? What a crazy setup." The younger man looks around at the deck, black stains of blood diluted by the rain and getting wider and less dark.

Taggett says, "Whatever. I'm just glad I'm done with it. I'll be happy if I never hear about the Violet Diamond again in my life." He holsters his forty-five and lets himself lean against the wall of the empty navigator's shack. "We better see about finding a radio and getting our asses back home."

CHAPTER FIFTY

So they drift around the Pacific for a while, smoking and eating up the rest of One-Eye's provisions. It turns out the ninja was the only crew on the boat, so the two partners move out of their little cell and spend their days lying on deck, Chen half naked as they drink the whiskey and soak up the heat of the sun that burns down from the center of the blank blue sky. Both men's beards start to grow out as Chen's skin gets dark and leathery. Taggett stays pretty much the same. With nothing to say, they stop talking to each other. Most of the sounds they hear come from faraway gulls and the slap of the waves on the boat's hull. Every now and then the radio in the empty navigator's shack coughs up a blast of static and then goes mute again. Time opens up around the two of them like a tunnel leading to an empty room.

Besides Chen and Taggett, the boat's carrying a secret load of opium, bricks of white powder wrapped up in brown paper with some Chinese writing on it. Taggett finds it one night shoved into a little cubby hidden by a loose board under what must have been the bunk One-Eye was using to pretend to be the captain of a smuggling ship. He shows it to Chen that afternoon and the younger man grunts. Taggett grunts right back and takes another swig from the bottle and lays package down next to the radio. The rest of the opium stays under One-Eye's bunk. The boat drifts around in the ocean. Time keeps spreading out.

Every now and then when he's awake and sober enough Taggett uses the Morse Code they taught him in the army to tap out an SOS.

The radio in that little shack, a black metal box with one set of wires connecting it to the switch and another set connecting it to the antenna pointing from the shack's roof to the empty sky, doesn't seem to have anything to say for a while except for the occasional belch of static. Then, after maybe two weeks, right around the time the provisions are starting to get scarce, a signal comes in from a steamer on its way to San Pedro. The steamer's captain isn't too happy about the idea of picking up a couple of extra mouths to feed, but they've still got enough of the whiskey Jie left them with to pay for the ride. "I'll just sell it off in the States," the steamer's captain says. That's pretty much all anyone says to either of them the whole way across.

By the time they're back on dry land they look and smell like a couple of hoboes. Lucky for them, Chen knows a guy who knows a guy, and they manage to trade the opium for bus fare back to San Francisco and enough left over for a shave and a meal for each of them. They stumble out of the station and along those twisted streets back to Lee Ming's. "May as well," says Taggett. "Way we smell, they probably wouldn't let us in anywhere else."

Ming's face lights up when he sees the tough detective. "Mr. Taggett!" he says. "You come back, so happy to see you. No gang man bother me since you beat up Fat Son." The little man's bustling around the place, dusting off the table by the window and pulling out a couple of chairs. "I give you good meal now you back home," he tells the two partners. "Free beer. I make it myself, you like."

Taggett takes a seat and pulls out a pack of smokes, offers one to Chen and lights one for himself, says to Ming, "Thought I was supposed to be some kind of villain picking on a poor cripple."

"No, no," says Ming. "Fat Son collect protection. Since you beat him up so bad we save lots of money, tell the new gang man you beat him up just as bad. So we keep your office for you like you never left." The little man hustles back into the kitchen and starts making noise with sticks and bowls and bottles. Chen shoots Taggett a questioning look and the tough detective just shrugs. A minute later the table between them gets crowded with steaming bowls of noodles and tall glasses of beer. Taggett and Chen eat and drink until they can't eat or drink any more.

"I haven't eaten this good in weeks," says Chen. "Guess it's a good thing I'm in business with the local White Knight." He pulls out a pack of smokes, offers his partner one, lights up. The flame of the match flickers a little from the breath of his chuckle.

Taggett snickers as he lights his own cigarette. "I'm pretty far from anyone's White Knight," he says, pushing his chair back. The two of them smoke for a moment as Ming clears the drained glasses and licked bowls off the table, then Taggett says, "What the hell, let's go see the old place. A man's gotta do something for a living."

As they amble up the street to the old grain warehouse, orange sun going down behind it so that it casts a big shadow for them to walk into, Chen just can't stop ribbing his partner. "So I guess this makes me your squire, right? Carry the lances, clean up after the horse?" He can barely keep his cigarette in his mouth from all the laughing. "I gotta tell you, it's just an honor to be in the presence of such a hero, such a great champion of the poor and downtrodden."

Taggett stops right in the middle of the street and says, "Enough." He puts a hand on Chen's shoulder to turn the smaller man around, looks down into his face, straight into his eyes. "I'm no one's hero. I've done too much killing for that. I'm just a sucker getting by like the rest of us, got that?"

"Sure," says Chen. His light voice is level as he stares right back up at the detective. "Like the rest of us." He flicks his butt into the street, and they both glance at the sparks dying on the shadowed asphalt. "You're just the one of us with some kind of magic gizmo that keeps you walking around when anyone else would be fertilizing some pasture in China by now. Just the one of us who saved my life, gave me something to live for." Chen blinks a couple of times and sucks a breath in through his nose. "We've both done plenty of things, Johnny. We'll both do plenty more. You just go ahead and be the hero and we'll see where that takes us, okay?" The younger man's eyes are shining a little as the sky gets darker.

City people push past them in two directions, day people heading back to their homes, night people headed out into their world. Taggett keeps looking at Chen as the crowd parts around them. Finally, he swallows and says, "Yeah. Okay." He puts an arm around his partner's shoulders and they make their way together into the old grain warehouse and up those creaky stairs and halfway down that uninhabited hallway to the office.

The door still has McBRIDE & TAGGETT INVESTIGATIONS painted on it, and the key Taggett somehow still has still fits. Chen snickers a little as the door swings open. "Guess I'm McBride now," he says.

Moving toward his desk, Taggett glances back to the younger man standing in the doorway and says, "We'll get that sign fixed soon as we make a few dollars."

"Don't bother," says Chen. "I like the idea."

"Then I guess that's your desk," says Taggett. He takes a seat as Chen steps into the office and finds a seat of his own behind the other desk. The tough detective lets out a sigh and takes out the last pack of smokes Jie gave them for the journey back, shakes one out, glances over at Chen, tosses the pack across the room to him. Both of them light up and lean back in their chairs, watching the room get slowly darker, not doing anything about it quite yet.

The ringing of the phone cuts through the soft sounds of the night starting up. Taggett twitches and straightens up. The phone's on Chen's desk, so Taggett gets up and walks across to where the smaller man is sitting there looking at the black pillar as the bell shakes it. He looks up at Taggett and says, "We expecting business so soon?"

Taggett snorts. "I gave up expecting things a while ago." He reaches down to the desk, picks up the phone and holds the earpiece to his ear.

A dark cloud of static pours out of the phone and into Taggett's ear. He stands there listening until a voice comes through, saying, "Johnny. I know you can hear me." The deep growl of it almost gets lost in the noise.

"Do I know you?" says Taggett. Chen's still looking up at him through the darkness in the little office. He reaches for the desk lamp but Taggett raises a hand to call him off. He covers the mouthpiece with his hand and says, "Might be across the street. We don't wanna be targets." Chen pulls back, sitting up straight.

"We have met many times, Johnny," the voice on the phone says, its deep tone betraying a hint of a laugh. "Our last meeting was at sea. You might remember, it ended quite badly for me, quite well for you. Did you make a good profit on the opium?"

Taggett's face goes slack and he can't help saying, "One-Eye." Chen's on his feet, chair sliding back as he leaps silently over the desk and crouches next to the door. Taggett steps around the corner of Chen's desk into the deeper shadows the moonlight can't get to through the window. "You're still alive," he says.

One-Eye says, "I am," and then there's some more of that buzzing silence. Taggett stands there breathing slow and steady, the tip of his tongue dragging along the back of his teeth. "So are you," says One-Eye. "We merely repeat the obvious. Ask the more interesting question, detective."

"Okay," says Taggett. "You're trying to get me to ask you how you're still alive. I'll play along. How does someone get shot off a boat in the middle of the ocean and live to tell the tale?"

One-Eye rumbles a definite chuckle. "Ask the Diamond, Johnny. Ask her what could turn a simple collector like Edgar Foulsworth into a walking ghost called One-Eye." The static on the line swells and swallows up the ninja's voice for a moment. Taggett sways a little on his feet.

He swallows and says, "You're Edgar Foulsworth?" Over by the door the shadowy shape of Chen seems to wobble a little. Taggett stands there blinking.

The faraway voice tells him, "I was. At times I still am. When we met on the train from New York to San Francisco I was very much Edgar Foulsworth. At the same time, when I removed those two men pursuing you, I was also very much One-Eye. I have many names in many places." The darkness fills the little office as Taggett keeps listening.

After another minute of that underwater hissing through the earpiece, Taggett says, "That's interesting news, One-Eye or Foulsworth or whoever. But why tell me? What's the point of your weird little story? Why tell me all this over the telephone?" His voice is getting tighter and louder. "Why can't you just leave me the hell alone?" He's starting to shout. "This game, this damn game you can't quit playing, why the hell don't you just leave me out of it?" The detective's knuckles are white around the phone in the darkness of the office.

"I do not play games, Johnny. I leave those to others." The ninja clears his throat. Taggett holds the earpiece away from his head and stares toward the door, invisible now in the dark, with Chen standing ready next to it. "I have telephoned you because I owe you a debt. For more years than I can count I have been entangled with Vivian Foulsworth. You have shown me the way to become my own man. I cannot kill her, but I can refuse her service. I can use my knowledge of her organization against her." Taggett lets out a breath. "Your enemy is my enemy, Johnny."

Taggett pulls out a pack of smokes, lights one up, winking in Chen's direction as the match flame lights his face. "So I guess that makes us friends," he says.

"Perhaps," says the ninja. "I may or may not forgive you for destroying the life I thought I had constructed for myself. We may meet again, Johnny Taggett."

Taggett reaches down and turns on the desk lamp. As he and Chen blink together in the sudden light, he says, "Do what you have to do. We'll be ready."